MW01484345

Praise for Yasmin Angoe

Not What She Seems

"Endless skeletons in the family closet . . ."

—*Kirkus Reviews*

"Angoe grounds the plot's surprising twists with lovable, fully realized characters. Lisa Unger fans, take note."

—*Publishers Weekly*

"Jac's return to her hometown reveals lie after shocking lie. You're going to want to help her dig up every dirty secret. *Not What She Seems* is a must-read for thriller lovers."

—Melinda Leigh, #1 *Wall Street Journal* bestselling author

"In a small town, secrets collide with the grief and guilt of our fierce, feisty heroine, Jac Brodie. As her world is falling apart, Jac pieces together a mystery that could change her life as she knows it. With an expertly drawn setting, pulse-pounding pacing, and an explosive climax, *Not What She Seems* is a magnificent read. This twisty, high-octane thriller instantly hooked me and never let go. I'm now a forever fan of Yasmin Angoe's stunning writing."

—Samantha M. Bailey, *USA Today* and #1 international bestselling author of *A Friend in the Dark*

"Anthony Award–nominated author Yasmin Angoe is an expert at blending fast-paced action, jaw-dropping plot twists, and flawed but likable characters. Her first stand-alone, *Not What She Seems,* is a must-read for domestic suspense fans. An excellent tale of cat and mouse, or should I say spider versus fly."

—Kellye Garrett, award-winning author of *Missing White Woman*

"Angoe not only creates believable characters, she crafts a layered mystery woven through with family secrets, sharp-edged revenge, and unexpected redemption. All that plus it has heart; the climactic scene brought tears to my eyes."

—Jess Lourey, Edgar-nominated author of *The Taken Ones*

"Yasmin Angoe's *Not What She Seems* is a powerful, electric novel that explores the deadly secrets we want to forget, and the lengths people will go to keep them buried. A story of painful homecomings and powerful reckonings, *Not What She Seems* builds upon Angoe's stellar library to present readers with her best novel yet."

—Alex Segura, bestselling author of *Secret Identity* and *Alter Ego*

"Jacinda Brodie, you have my sword. Never have I fallen deeper in love with characters than I did the Brodies of beautiful, troubled, small-town South Carolina. Yasmin Angoe's incredible blend of talents—her ability to deliver high-intensity blowups on par with the best action thrillers and her deep character work, which shines through her uniquely voicey prose—make *Not What She Seems* a total knockout. I laughed, I gasped, and—shockingly—I cried. In an astonishing feat, Angoe combines a dark-as-sin psychological suspense with a heartwarming tale of familial redemption, peppered with laugh-out-loud social commentary. Like me, readers will marvel at her virtuosity while eagerly awaiting her next."

—Ashley Winstead, critically acclaimed author of *Midnight Is the Darkest Hour*

It Ends with Knight

"Watch your back, Liam Neeson. This avenger is tough."

—*Kirkus Reviews*

"High-stakes action, intrigue, and a professional assassin . . . the thrilling conclusion to Yasmin Angoe's Nena Knight series has it all."

—*Woman's World*

"Nena Knight can cover Orphan X's six o'clock any day! Stolen from her village in Ghana, Knight reinvents herself as an elite assassin capable of all orders of badassery. One of thrillerdom's rising stars, Yasmin Angoe paints Knight with nuance, strength, and grace. These books burn hot and read fast."

—Gregg Hurwitz, *New York Times* bestselling author of the Orphan X series

"*It Ends with Knight* finishes this trilogy every bit as heart pounding, soul searching, and explosive as it started. Nena Knight now takes her place alongside crime fiction's most unforgettable heroines."

—Rachel Howzell Hall, *New York Times* bestselling author of *We Lie Here* and *These Toxic Things*

"Yasmin Angoe returns with both barrels blazing in *It Ends with Knight*. Nena Knight is such a well-crafted character, and Angoe's writing is an absolute joy. You need some pretty strong writer mojo to get readers to root for an assassin, and Angoe pulls it off. I truly hope *It Ends with Knight* is not the end of this wonderful series."

—Tracy Clark, bestselling author and winner of the Sue Grafton Memorial Award

They Come at Knight

An Amazon Best Book of the Month: Mystery, Thriller & Suspense

"There's nothing ho-hum about Nena Knight, the killer at the heart of Yasmin Angoe's *They Come at Knight* . . . In one blistering action scene after another, we get to see how good Nena is at what she does."

—*New York Times Book Review*

"A second round of action-packed, high-casualty intrigue for professional assassin Nena Knight. A lethal tale of an all-but-superhero whose author promises that 'in this story, there are no heroes.'"

—*Kirkus Reviews*

"This action-packed novel drives toward an explosive conclusion. Determined to survive devastating loss and mete out justice, Nena is a heroine readers will embrace."

—*Publishers Weekly*

Her Name Is Knight

"This stunning debut . . . deftly balances action, interpersonal relationships, issues of trauma, and profound human questions in an unforgettable novel."

—*Library Journal* (starred review)

"A parable of reclaiming personal and tribal identity by seizing power at all costs."

—*Kirkus Reviews*

"Angoe expertly builds tension by shifting between her lead's past and present lives. Thriller fans will cheer Aninyeh every step of the way."

—*Publishers Weekly*

"An action-packed thriller you can lose yourself in."

—PopSugar

"Memorable characters, drama, heart-pounding danger . . . This suspenseful novel has it all."

—*Woman's World*

"A crackerjack story with truly memorable characters. I can't wait to see what Yasmin Angoe comes up with next."

—David Baldacci, #1 *New York Times* bestselling author

"Yasmin Angoe's debut novel, *Her Name Is Knight*, is an amazing, action-packed international thriller full of suspense, danger, and even romance. It's like a John Wick prequel except John is a beautiful African woman with a particular set of skills."

—S. A. Cosby, *New York Times* bestselling author of *Razorblade Tears*

"It's hard to believe that *Her Name Is Knight* is Yasmin Angoe's debut novel. This dual-timeline story about a highly trained Miami-based assassin who learns to reclaim her power after having her entire life ripped from her as a teenager in Ghana is equal parts love story, social commentary, and action thriller. Nena Knight will stay with you long after you've read the last word, and this is a must-read for fans of Lee Child and S. A. Cosby. I found myself crying in one chapter and cheering in the next. I couldn't put it down!"

—Kellye Garrett, Anthony, Agatha, and Lefty Award–winning author

"This was a book I couldn't put down. Yasmin Angoe does a brilliant job of inviting you into a world of espionage and revenge while giving her characters depth and backstory that pull the reader in even more. This story has depth, excitement, and heartbreaking loss all intertwined into an awesome debut. The spy thriller genre has a new name to look out for!"

—Matthew Farrell, bestselling author of *Don't Ever Forget*

"This brave and profoundly gorgeous thriller takes readers to places they've never been, to challenges they've never faced, and to judgments that leave the strongest in tears. *Her Name Is Knight* is a stunning and important debut, and Yasmin Angoe is a fantastic new talent."

—Hank Phillippi Ryan, *USA Today* bestselling author of *Her Perfect Life*

"*Her Name Is Knight* is a roundhouse kick of a novel—intense, evocative, and loaded with character and international intrigue. Nena Knight is a protagonist for the ages and one readers will not soon forget. *Her Name Is Knight* isn't just thrills and action either—the book lingers with you long after you've finished. More, please."

—Alex Segura, acclaimed author of *Star Wars Poe Dameron: Free Fall*, *Secret Identity*, and *Blackout*

BEHIND THESE FOUR WALLS

OTHER TITLES BY YASMIN ANGOE

Not What She Seems

It Ends with Knight

They Come at Knight

Her Name Is Knight

BEHIND THESE FOUR WALLS

A Novel

YASMIN ANGOE

This is a work of fiction. Names, characters, organizations, places, events, and incidents are either products of the author's imagination or are used fictitiously. Otherwise, any resemblance to actual persons, living or dead, is purely coincidental.

Published by Thomas & Mercer, Seattle
www.apub.com

EU product safety contact:
Amazon Media EU S. à r.l.
38, avenue John F. Kennedy, L-1855 Luxembourg
amazonpublishing-gpsr@amazon.com

ISBN-13: 9781662529696 (hardcover)
ISBN-13: 9781662529672 (paperback)
ISBN-13: 9781662529689 (digital)

Cover design by Kimberly Glyder
Cover image: © Robert Lambert / ArcAngel Images

Printed in the United States of America
First edition

To my community of writers, mentors, and friends who help lift me up when I fall down.

All that glisters is not gold.
—William Shakespeare

PROLOGUE

He rolled down the window of his old Explorer, letting in the cool night air to help clear his muddled thoughts. Maia was at home, asleep with the baby, though his daughter would be up soon for another feeding. Maia would wonder where he'd gone. She wouldn't know just yet that he had been driven out of their home by shame.

He couldn't stand to look at her. No matter what, he was about to disappoint his wife, and he tried to figure out which disappointment would be the worst kind of hurt. That he had somehow allowed himself to be seduced by millions and sucked into their deal, agreeing to put his name on the offshore accounts, anticipating a cut that would set him and his family up for life? Or that he'd betrayed his wife, broken their vows, and had an affair with one of the company's receptionists, who, now that he thought about it, was way out of his league? But he'd been flattered, his ego stroked, by the attention of a beautiful, talented woman.

Which was the lesser of two evils—taking the fall for money he hadn't stolen or letting his wife learn that the man of her dreams was really a nightmare? He parked on the side and cut everything off. The only light illuminating the cabin was the bluish hue from his cell as he stared through blurry eyes at the images of him and Stephanie doing things that would make anyone blush.

He thought about the life he'd be able to give Maia now. He thought about how he'd never have to worry about the compounding medical bills for his little girl that fucking insurance continued to deny, deny, deny.

He thought about all this, oblivious to the back row, where his three dogs panted loudly, running from one window to another and fogging them up as the few cars on the freeway passed him.

The message given to him had been clear. Make a choice: Take the heat for those dummy accounts or let these pictures find their way to Maia and absolutely destroy her. He couldn't do that to her. He'd rather Maia think he was a thief than a cheater, though what he'd been was an idiot with no backbone when faced with adversity. He'd never be able to look her in the eye again if she knew how easily he'd betrayed their promises to each other at the time when Maia was at her most vulnerable, pregnant with their first child.

Screw it. He sent the text.

I'll do it. Destroy the photos, he typed.

He added NOW. As if he was tough and really had something to bargain with. He'd take the blame.

He waited as the dots pulsed until the response popped up.

Smart man.

Behind him, the dogs barked at the few cars that passed, since it was late and traffic was relatively light. He'd driven far out, heading east toward Riverside County. Which desert town he ended up in, he didn't care. LA was full of concrete problems, and he'd run from them, though those problems had still followed him.

His steps were heavy as he got out and opened the back passenger door, releasing the dogs from their confinement. They scampered off to frolic along the tree line while he watched, searing the memory of them into his mind. Just as he'd done with Maia and his baby girl before leaving their home. He hoped they wouldn't be out here for long. That they wouldn't come across any coyotes or cougars. He didn't want to leave Maia with the burden of them as well. Besides, they'd always been more his dogs than hers.

More tired than he'd ever felt before, he climbed back into his SUV and rolled the windows up. His next text was to Maia.

I'm sorry.

She was awake, and he read the stream of her frantic replies asking him what was wrong, where he was. He ignored the calls she began to make as he reached over the console and grabbed the barrel of the rifle that had been riding shotgun the entire trip there.

With him gone, there would be no need for the illicit photos. With him gone, they could say what they wanted, label him an embezzler, and look no further. He'd be on the news cycle for a day or two, if that, and then be old news. Maia would finally be left alone to grieve. But at least her grief wouldn't come with the knowledge that he'd betrayed her.

Pacing the length of the truck, no longer playing, the dogs whined from just outside the door, their instincts sensing something was amiss. He ignored them too. He removed his shoe, his sockless foot flexing from the freedom. He adjusted the muzzle, bracing the butt against the floor, and shifted his big toe to where he needed it to be.

Smart man.

The gunshot cracked, sending a flash of light. The enclosure muffled the sound. The dogs dropped immediately onto their haunches. They let out a singular howl as one into the night. They remained until daylight broke, when a motorist finally pulled over just ahead after noticing three Labs sitting in the grass as he passed by. When he got out of his car and approached them, the dogs did not move, their gazes fixated.

"Babe," he said into the AirPod nestled in his ear as he neared the animals, "you won't believe—"

He saw what kept them entranced: the jagged hole in the back window, the dark splatter on the interior of the windshield, the figure inside . . . the SUV that was now someone's tomb.

CHAPTER ONE

Isla

Six Months Later, Present Day

Isla Thorne had had a long day. She was still wearing her uniform of black slacks, a crisp white shirt now wrinkled from a full day of work, and a gold-plated name tag with **Isla** etched in black. She adjusted the strap of her cross-body tote over her shoulder. It held her wallet, a pair of black-and-white All Stars, and a clean black waist apron used when she was on back-of-the-house duty during one of the posh events the events planner booked her for. It really had been a long day, but the reward would be worth the effort.

Expensive cars filled the parking spots of the open-air shopping center she passed, a multicolor showcase of privilege on display as she trudged to the bus stop, intending to catch the incoming bus so she wouldn't be forced to wait another forty-five minutes for the next one.

Isla's stride slowed as she and a girl, late teens, crossed paths. The girl was dressed comfortably in sporty athleisure. Her thick, dark hair was pulled back with a headband and twisted into a messy braid that hung over her left shoulder, her natural beauty glowing even in the fading light. She looked as if she'd just stepped out of a commercial, which Isla wished she could be in as well instead of the stain-marked work clothes from the catering job she'd just left. The girl exuded an air of wealth none of them had. Maybe it was the sparkling green BMW M4—the latest model—that the girl was heading toward. Any other time, Isla would have passed by, continuing toward her bus stop.

Today was not one of those times.

The girl was moving at a pretty good clip but still unrushed, not paying attention to her surroundings, either, especially since she had parked so far out from the cluster of cars in the parking lot. The car chirped, unlocking.

"Hey," Isla called out impatiently.

The girl barely glanced up as she balanced her tan leather backpack on her shoulder and typed away on her iPhone with lightning-speed thumb action.

The girl slowed.

Isla said, "You can't drive on that."

The girl stopped, confusion clouding over. Her key hand dropped like deadweight to her side, but her phone hand remained steady.

"What do you mean?" She said it the way young people did these days, with an uptick into a whine at the end of their questions, which older people could find annoying.

"Your car has a flat," Isla said, pointing toward the sparkling car.

The girl's expression was still confused, as if she had no concept of car trouble. She stared at her car as if it had betrayed her.

Isla stepped off the sidewalk, and the girl shuffled slowly to meet her. She stared at the flattened rear tire on the passenger side.

"Are you serious right now?" she moaned. "My dad just got it for me, and it's my first time taking it out. How?"

She followed Isla toward the rear. She turned to Isla as if she expected Isla to pull a jack from behind and fix it. Her large brown eyes implored Isla to do something.

Isla waved her hands, warding off any expectation of physical labor. "Oh, I don't . . . do that. Can't you call someone? AAA? Your car insurance?"

"How long would it take for them to come and fix it? My mother will freak out if I'm late."

"Uber, then? Lyft?"

The girl shook her head. She hesitated. "I've never used one of those before."

Isla was truly surprised. *Who hasn't used . . .* she started to say but buried her judgment when she noticed how the girl's head dropped in shame at the revelation.

"We have drivers. Usually." The girl looked away like having drivers was taboo. A rich-people problem that Isla could not relate to.

"Drivers. What are you, the president's daughter or something?" If she had drivers, she'd never get behind the wheel or have to take public transportation ever again.

The girl fiddled with the thin chain around her neck. "More like the chairman," she mumbled.

Isla had heard her crystal clear but pretended she hadn't.

"I begged to drive myself to school and practice today. Now look. My mom will never let me drive again." She stretched *again* out to three syllables and ended it with an *ah.* Isla prayed for patience.

"A flat's not your fault, and you're not five."

"You don't know my mother," she retorted. "Consider yourself lucky."

Isla left that one alone. If she'd known her mother growing up, she might have been able to grumble to others about her.

Seeing it was going to be a while, she made their meeting formal, gesturing to herself. "I'm Isla Thorne."

"Holland Corrigan." Holland seemed to be waiting for a reaction. When there was none, she visibly relaxed.

Isla replied with an unimpressed *hmm.* "As in the Corrigan Group? I know the name." Isla's gaze slid toward the bus stop. "Your mom will probably have a heart attack if you come home on the bus, and since you're in a rush, I can use one of my rideshare accounts, but I'll need your address to order the car."

"Address?" Holland repeated hesitantly, suddenly on guard. Holland was maybe nineteen, stranded and with a complete stranger. Her sudden change gave Isla pause. Holland wasn't comfortable sharing her address with a stranger she'd met five minutes ago, even though Holland had been acting as if they were a step away from swearing eternal friendship and braiding each other's hair in sisterhood.

Instead, Holland was squirming as she tried to make a decision.

"If I was going to kidnap you, I'd have done it by now," Isla reminded Holland and put her phone away. "How about we use your phone, huh? We'll set you up so you don't have to tell me anything private. Sound good?"

Holland produced her phone quickly and waited expectantly. Isla could barely contain her disbelief. She thought people Holland's age came out of the womb tech savvy.

Isla asked, "Can I see?"

Holland held her phone in Isla's direction, and Isla went to reach for it. The phone slipped through her fingers when Holland released too early and Isla grabbed for it too late.

"No!" Holland screamed. The phone hit the ground hard with a sickening smack and immediately went black. Holland dove after it. Isla winced at the thick crack snaking the length of the screen.

Holland attempted every resuscitation effort she could. She groaned "No" over and over. She tapped hopelessly at her spiderwebbed screen in disbelief. Isla didn't point out the tiny specks of glass on the ground where the phone had landed. That would be rubbing salt on an open wound.

"I can't see anything. Nothing's coming up, and it's so hot," Holland said. "Maybe if we call my phone, it'll wake up from its coma? Right?"

"More like from the dead," Isla said dubiously. But she handed Holland her phone anyway. "*Don't* drop this one, or we're both screwed."

The call went straight to voicemail. Isla could hear Holland's teeny, bubbly voice telling them to leave a message.

"I'm gonna die," Holland moaned, her eyes watery again. This time the tears were well earned and very real. "What am I gonna do?"

Isla had no time for histrionics, already pulling up the rideshare app. She stopped, matching Holland's sorrowful gaze with a pragmatic one. "Address?" she said again.

This time, Holland gave it up without a fight.

CHAPTER TWO

They arrived at the guarded gate to the Corrigan estate, a fortified division between Holland's world and Isla's. Who didn't know about the outrageously wealthy family that lived on Bowen Mountain, best known for Monticello, where the famous Thomas Jefferson (or infamous, depending on which side of history one belonged to) had built the home for which another mountain was renamed? The Corrigans lived above Monticello, in an area where other gated communities and large mansions were hidden behind walls of dense forest. This was where wealthy business magnate, investor, and philanthropist Victor Corrigan, chairman and CEO of the Corrigan Group, had built his palatial estate, which rivaled most of the celebrity and wealthy homes Isla had seen in LA.

Hasaan, their Uber driver, and Holland had become fast friends and chatted nonstop the whole trip up the mountain. All the while, Isla had tried to figure out how she'd been roped into escorting Holland back home. Had it been the sad puppy dog eyes Holland had hit her with when Hasaan pulled up in his little silver Camry and Holland got shy again, acting as if she couldn't ride alone with a man she didn't know? It could have been when Holland had promised she would pay the entire fare, which meant Isla didn't have to take the bus, even though her ride time was now nearly tripled. Isla had always thought she was pretty good at getting what she wanted, but Holland seemed to have her own tricks up her sleeves, and Isla liked that.

She'd learned a lot about the two in the nearly hour-long ride and didn't mind the corny jokes passing between driver and passenger, or when Holland tried to tease her about her name.

"So Isla's . . . different."

Isla paused what she was doing. "And Holland isn't?"

Holland scoffed, "You're named after a body of land."

"So are you," Isla deadpanned, staring out her window into the darkening skies. "Though it's the Netherlands now. Maybe I'll call you that."

Holland acknowledged her defeat with grace.

Isla had been invested in Holland's explanation of the items she was pulling from the back seat of her coupe: a slender black canvas bag, a face shield, and a half-zipped duffel bag with a white pant leg sticking out. Hasaan helped her put them in the trunk of his car.

"Fencing gear. I'm on the team at my school," Holland had replied as Isla offered to hold her backpack so Holland could focus on moving her stuff. Isla fingered the school lanyard sticking from the outer pocket, reading "Mary Washington" etched on it.

Isla paused getting into the car, genuinely impressed, filing that information away for further thought. "A Black girl who fences. Who would have imagined?"

"Thanks," Holland said, with a pride that matched the sudden burst of feeling Isla had in her chest. "There aren't too many of us, but we're growing. Olympians, even. Lauren Scruggs won silver this year. Ruth White is a pioneer, Nikki Franke, all my idols."

Isla had never heard of those women and felt an immediate need to look them up, feeling as if she'd been missing out on some well-deserved Black Girl Magic. She was proud to see girls like her in all sorts of unexpected spaces. "That's cool as hell."

Isla and Hasaan even had a moment of older-sibling worry after he casually tossed back a pack of unopened almonds when Holland's stomach growled loudly in the confines of the car.

Holland moved to pick it up, took one look, and pushed it away quickly. Isla assumed Holland's actions were because as nice as Hasaan was, he was still a stranger offering food, forgetting rideshare etiquette and letting his good upbringing and care of others shine through.

"No big deal," Isla said under her breath, a little put off by Holland's dramatics. She didn't have to make the guy feel bad. "Just say thanks and throw it away later."

"I didn't think," Hasaan said, realizing his mistake.

"That's not it. I can't eat almonds," Holland said. "I'm allergic."

"Oh!" Isla said, grabbing the bag quickly and tossing it back up front like it was a hot potato as Hasaan apologized profusely. There'd been a girl at her group home who was allergic to nuts. Her reaction had been terrifying.

Holland assured them, attempting to calm them, "Not all nuts. Just almonds, weirdly enough. The last time I had a major allergic reaction was back when I was like nine. I ate some cookies without checking. No biggie. That's what EpiPens are for. It's okay."

Holland could try to appease them all she wanted, but the look Hasaan shared with Isla through his rearview mirror was clear. They could have killed a Corrigan, and they would have been next.

Two high, ornate wrought iron gates with majestic *C* emblems on each half marked the entry point and extended from there, a seemingly endless length of tall stone walling off the inner grounds of the house from the vast property, where much of the land remained natural and untouched.

Isla silently echoed Hasaan's low whistle. She imagined the opulence that was on the other side and already knew her imagination was not enough.

Any excitement they had was killed by Holland, who'd gone from relaxed and joking to nervous energy. She leaned forward in her seat, preparing to exit the moment the vehicle stopped, her anxiety ramped back up now that she was home. Holland's door was open before Hasaan could throw the gear in park, and a guard was already exiting the one-level building as floodlights illuminated the area. Isla grew uneasy when she noted two distinct objects, a Taser and gun, on either side of his waist. His hand rested lightly on the object that didn't have the bright-yellow grip. The gun.

The guard recognized Holland as she approached, his expression transforming from hostile to surprised. He called out something unintelligible, and the front gates began to open all the way, sliding away from each other on hidden tracks. He closed the distance between them.

Holland gestured to the Camry, and both Isla and Hasaan froze when the guard craned his neck to see into the darkened car. They hadn't done anything wrong, but Isla couldn't help feeling like these people would think they had.

The guard ran a hand over his face, his apprehension growing as Holland spoke. Isla didn't need to hear him to know what he was thinking. Heads were about to roll. Holland had come home in a strange car.

"Maybe we should go help the kid out," Hasaan suggested as he bit his fingernails and stared out the window. "You know. Help the kid out a little."

"I don't know," Isla answered. "They don't look like the welcoming committee."

But a tiny part of her felt like a coward. She should step out and explain her part before they really did call the cops for kidnapping or something outlandish. Not for the tenth time, Isla was second-guessing this entire thing, and the bus ride back home sounded better with each passing moment.

"I'll go." Her mouth said one thing; her body said another. It roiled with apprehension.

The guard was speaking when she reached them. "The whole estate on fire looking for you. Tracking the car, trying to call you. Searching the inner and outer grounds. Sending people out to search your last knowns," the guard was saying as Isla got near. "They found your car with a flat and no one around."

"Yeah, because I was on the way here!" Holland said, agitated. "I couldn't call. Remember my phone?" Holland held up a hand. "And before you ask, I only know my number."

Holland pulled her phone from her back pocket. She'd left her backpack with her wallet and all her valuables in the car with two people she'd known for barely an hour. However, the dead phone . . . she'd kept close.

"Totally dead. But I got home, thanks to Isla."

Isla waved at her name.

"Can we head in?" Holland asked, starting to head back to where Hasaan anxiously awaited them.

The guard shook his head. "They can't come in past the gate for security reasons, but"—he motioned toward the small building he'd come from—"Willis has already called up for a car to pick you up from here, since we can't leave post. Let's get you inside until they come down."

Holland had started to protest when the sound of approaching tires drew their attention. They watched as a dark-colored late-model sedan passed Hasaan and the Camry. It stopped near the entranceway. The driver exited, a serious-looking man giving off Secret Service vibes. He swept the area with his gaze, making his assessment, as he buttoned his suit jacket.

Noting the guard on the scene, he strode toward the car door Isla had left open when she'd rushed to join Holland. He peered in, sizing up Hasaan, who looked too afraid to move. Hasaan waved stiffly, but the driver didn't return the greeting, instead straightening himself and standing by as if awaiting orders. Isla wasn't sure what to make of his appearance, or the way he wouldn't leave the Camry, as if it—they—posed a threat, but she smartly kept her thoughts to herself. It was better to wait and see.

"That's Taylor. He's my brother Myles's driver-slash-everything," Holland remarked, practically glowing, excited at the new arrival.

CHAPTER THREE

The rear passenger door opened next, and Isla had to tell herself to stay cool when he got out. She recognized him instantly from TV and articles and the one time she'd seen him up close. None of those brief glimpses did Myles Corrigan a bit of justice. Isla had to force herself to not stare too long, to play it cool and focus on getting herself out of there. She'd done her part, brought Holland home safely.

Myles joined them, making his assessments as his driver had. Isla reminded herself to be quiet and look unbothered when she felt the opposite.

He stopped beside Isla. If he knew she was there, he didn't let on. Isla chuckled softly with a slight shake of her head. Of course. The rich were all the same. They saw no one they thought was beneath them. Holland was an anomaly, though Isla wondered if her kindness was genuine or because she needed help.

Myles waited expectantly, focusing on the guard. His silence was a directive that the guard understood. He ditched the bravado he'd had a few moments ago and began explaining away the grievous mistake, the loss of Holland, that he hadn't made.

"And Isla was a total lifesaver, got an Uber, Hasaan over there, to bring me home," Holland was in the middle of proclaiming, as if to avert impending disaster by assuring her brother that the two strangers were friendlies, not foes.

Up until then, the tall, sharp-featured man with serious eyes hadn't acknowledged Isla's existence, and it had pissed her off. But with his full attention on her, she started second-guessing if being nonexistent was a bad thing. Myles Corrigan had a way of making her feel everything.

His eyes raked over her in a way that made her feel lacking, insignificant, and weirdly attracted, if the way her stomach traitorously fluttered when she saw him was any indication. She straightened her clothes, hating how her mind went to her appearance. Did she smell like old food from the luncheon and cleanup earlier that afternoon? Luckily, it was dark, and any major stains were hidden. She'd never cared before about impressing anyone, believing that behind closed doors, everyone was the same, but being in proximity to him made her feel horribly inadequate and like she needed a redo on her first impression.

"Isla." The prompt came from Holland, and Isla realized they were looking at her, waiting for her.

She cleared her throat. "Right. I don't know about being a lifesaver, but I called an Uber, that's all. And we rode in the Uber together since it was her first time, and for her to be comfortable."

Myles made no comment. Instead, he considered Isla as if there was more to her story, and she looked right back, pretending that she didn't want to melt into the surrounding woods and away from his imposing stare, which made her feel like he knew all her secrets.

"Wasn't that nice of her?" Holland said pointedly, breaking their standoff. "Myles?" She shook her head, giving Isla an apologetic smile. "Sorry. My brother can be kinda intense."

Isla agreed, though not aloud, glad for Holland's intercession. The guard touched his ear, head inclined as he listened to his incoming message. "Miss Holland's car is coming up."

As if on cue, two dots of light appeared in the dark from the other side of the gates, growing larger as they got closer.

Myles finally spoke, his voice like deep velvet, decisive and authoritative. "Cancel it," he told the guard. "Cool with you, Holl, to ride up with your intense big bro? That way your mother won't get any more upset than she probably already is."

Holland muttered, "There's no 'probably' about it."

Holland agreed. She was thrilled to be riding with him. Isla could see that when he, who seemed so stiff and cold, looked down at Holland, warmth cracked through all that facade of impenetrable ice. Holland was his weak spot.

Myles instructed his driver, Taylor, to grab her gear.

Which reminded Holland, "Yes. The trunk too. Hasaan, could you please pop the trunk to get my gear?" She turned back to Myles. "At practice today, I got Stephen on three. Can you believe it?"

Myles half smiled. "You're killing it. Your coach back at school will love that."

Hasaan tried to be helpful, opening his door to assist.

"No need. You can stay in the car," Taylor said quickly from the back of the car.

Zykowski, the guard whose nameplate Isla could finally read clearly, handed Myles the phone. Myles sighed, showing it to his sister.

"Don't," Holland said before he could say anything else. She started to follow him back to his car before spinning on her heel. "I need to pay you back for the ride."

Isla waved her away. "Don't worry about it. I got it. I need to head back down now, though. Early day tomorrow. It was good meeting you." She threw Myles a sidelong glance. "And you, too, I guess."

If he heard her, he pretended not to, impatiently waiting for his sister to come with him. He didn't even look at her. Clearly Myles Corrigan was incapable of partaking of a bit of levity.

"Corrigans are never allowed to owe anyone. Not even each other," Holland said. "That's the one thing our dad hates the most. Owing people, and then cheats, thieves, and liars. Not necessarily in that order." It was Holland's attempt at a joke, but neither Isla nor Myles played along.

Isla nodded slowly, focusing on everything else so her thoughts wouldn't betray her.

Myles cleared his throat, cutting his sister off before she said too much. "How much do we owe you for your time and kindness . . . I guess?" His expression remained unchanged.

It wasn't that serious. They were acting as if they now owed her a blood debt. Definitely time to go. "Just pay it forward someday. It's not owing me." Isla started for the Uber.

"I insist," Myles said as Isla walked away.

She chose to ignore him, calling over her shoulder, "Holland, set up accounts for Lyft and Uber, okay? Next time I might not be around."

Isla wasn't fast enough, because Taylor was back at her opened door, blocking her hasty retreat with his body, his phone out with the camera pulled up, giving her no other option. Isla looked at him, dumbfounded. Could there be more to his and Myles's insistence on paying her? Could they be wanting her number so they could look her up? The thought chilled her, but she didn't let it show. Defeated, Isla got her phone and allowed Taylor to capture the QR code of her relatively new Cash App account. Within seconds, $1,000 was in her account.

Her eyes widened at the unexpected sum that had increased her balance, much more than the cost of the total ride. She mumbled her thanks, but Taylor was already heading back to the vehicle with Holland's belongings.

Holland was in the back seat, but Myles remained outside longer, concentrating on Isla as if she were a puzzle he was about to solve.

He must be great at parties. A real people's guy.

She offered him a little wave and the biggest smile she didn't mean. It was hard to see his actual reaction, but she knew whatever it was wasn't pleasant. That made her uneasy, like he could see right through her and knew her innermost, darkest thoughts. She had to get herself together. The night was almost done.

"Thank you, Isla," he said.

The way he said her name, deep and confident, made her stomach flutter with betrayal. With Myles waiting, she fumbled her way into Hasaan's back seat, troubled by her unsettled feelings. It wasn't until she shut the door, sealing herself off from him, that he finally followed his sister. Their car passed over the threshold, the taillights receding in the distance until the gates closed, separating the haves from the have-nots.

CHAPTER FOUR

Hasaan was already talking three miles a minute as he made a U-turn and began their long trek down.

"Do you think they're hiring? I'll even take the front guard position. Wow, that was unreal, am I right? Those people are intense! I think I nearly shit myself. But you're in luck, because I didn't!"

Isla rubbed her eyes, all the adrenaline oozing out of her. "If you give me your Cash App, I'll split the thousand dollars they sent me on top of the fare."

At the prospect of becoming $500 richer, Hasaan nearly swerved into the narrow shoulder with only the metal railing separating them from the perilous drop below. Isla's heart plummeted, and her thoughts ran wild. She tried not to read too much into signs or think that the dark abyss beyond that guardrail foreshadowed what was to come.

As Hasaan rambled on about his good fortune, Isla quietly removed a set of keys from where she had wedged them into a crevice between the passenger seat and door. A dorm key, car fob, and student ID jangled on the Mary Washington lanyard. She studied Holland's beaming image.

"Sorry, kid," she mumbled regretfully.

Hasaan asked, "Say something?"

"No." But she was about to do something.

She had been watching Holland Corrigan for days. The youngest Corrigan had a predictable routine when she was home on break from college. Practice with her trainer, then the coffee shop. Rinse and repeat. Usually she was driven, but when she was let off the leash and allowed to roam the city like a normal nineteen-year-old, her routine remained relatively the same, and it wasn't that hard to keep track of the unsuspecting girl.

At first, Isla hadn't been sure if Holland was the right way in. She was easygoing. Too sweet, too sheltered from the real world. Upon meeting the young Corrigan, Isla had found the girl to be very real. She had liked her immediately, though she hadn't wanted to. She'd even felt a twinge of protectiveness toward the naive Corrigan, who couldn't tell when someone was being insincere or had designs on her. And it had gone much better than Isla had planned.

Those same attributes were what made Holland the door Isla needed to get into their world. Someone who wouldn't easily suspect the friendliness of a stranger—one who happened by to offer assistance at the same moment her tire had obtained a mysterious flat—to be a setup. She wouldn't catch the purposeful hand miss that had rendered Holland's phone unusable. Or that her uniform-clad savior had chosen Uber because Lyft had a new algorithm that matched female riders with female drivers, and Isla knew that Holland Corrigan would balk at riding alone with a man not employed by her father.

Holland had fallen into the setup. She had trusted Isla emphatically, held out a branch of friendship. It tweaked at Isla's guilt. Holland was the path of least resistance, because once in, Isla would have enough suspicion directed her way.

Isla would have to atone for her deceit later, because if she wanted to expose the secrets the Corrigans thought they had buried, if she wanted to finally find out what had happened to Eden the night she'd disappeared without a trace, leaving Isla alone in this town they were just supposed to be in for a couple of days, then she'd have to set her conscience aside.

Still, Isla fought her conscience and trepidation all the way to her rented studio apartment.

She should, could, say something to Hasaan and end this crazy plan before it began, turn back and return the keys, go back home, to her real home in Los Angeles, letting guilt eat away at her and pretending once again that the Corrigans and that time of her life didn't exist. Even Eden.

But she didn't. Not when she was so close and could actually do something now, no matter the outcome.

Instead, she palmed the keys, feeling their weight and their significance, heavy in her hand. Holland was the first step to Isla's true objective.

"On to the next."

"What was that?" Hasaan asked over Kendrick Lamar. "Everything all right back there?"

As the car wound its way down the treacherous mountain road, Isla's grip on the door tightened. She imagined the steep drop-offs and shadowed valleys, all reminders of how precarious her situation was, of how she stood on the precipice. One wrong move, one misplaced word, and everything she had returned here to fight for could come crashing down.

CHAPTER FIVE

Six Months Ago

On Wilshire, Isla parked, turned off the car, and considered the high-rise office across the busy street, where she was to meet her contact at one of the PR firms she and her team worked with as their research and procurement—the ones who got the dirt to help the firm manage whatever crisis it needed to manage for its clients. She preferred the term *research and procurement*. It made her team sound moral, a step or two above *TMZ*, because at least they weren't selling salaciousness to gossip magazines to destroy someone's career. Isla, Rey, and Nat were there to help, not harm. Or so Isla liked to tell herself. In the passenger seat beside her was a manila envelope, innocuous in appearance, though its contents were contradictory and promised a world of hurt for someone.

She was reaching over to grab the envelope she was going to deliver when her phone buzzed from where it sat in its holder. She glanced at the screen, forgetting the envelope for a moment to answer the call, which connected through the car's Bluetooth.

She asked, "Everything all good?"

"Good as it's gonna get." Rey's voice filtered through the car speakers. "Are you there?"

"Yep," she said, her voice tight. She watched the traffic lights shift from red to green and the cars speed off. "This one, though . . ."

"Is no different from any of the others," Rey finished. "Our part's done as soon as you hand over the evidence."

Isla shuddered, the words having come across more ominously than Rey intended.

Rey tried to look on the brighter side. "His actions won't blow up happy families."

She sighed. "Except his."

"Well, maybe he should have thought about that before he started dipping and dabbling with coworkers. At any rate, the company is doing him a favor letting him go on his own."

"He doesn't seem like the type to start some illicit affair with a pregnant wife at home. Was Nat able to get any more from the receptionist?"

Rey groaned. "We pulled everything we could with the time we had, and there's nothing else. You know that, Isla. He's just some dude who could give the company a bad name and make shareholders uneasy with a guy like him handling their accounts."

Isla's mind churned, recalling the day two weeks ago when she, Nat, and Rey had been given the job. The sole directive was to find compromising information about the accountant, and quickly. But something didn't sit right with Isla. "People cheat. Why would a firm care what some lowly accountant does with the receptionist after hours?"

"And during, from what we got." Rey chuckled his appreciation.

"Still—"

"Doesn't matter why they'd care," Rey cut in. "He got caught with his pants down. If the company wants to get him out this way with no big drama, that's their business, not ours. Maybe he has company secrets they don't want him spilling once he's out."

"So they force his resignation through blackmail instead of just firing him for impropriety? They had just cause to do so."

"It's their business, and it's going to be however they want it to be. Let it go. It's already taken care of."

Let it go. For the past four years Rey, a technology savant; Natalie, their resident aspiring actress and usual decoy; and Isla had formed their own side hustle after a chance meeting at Rey's little coffee shop on Venice Beach's boardwalk. It was during their last year at UCLA, and Natalie and Isla needed more money than they were making at their menial jobs. Rey needed something to battle his boredom. He was a guy who was too smart, tapped young to work behind-the-scenes cybersecurity for huge tech companies that he'd never disclose. He was an employee they never spoke about but the kind you saw on TV who knew everything and could do anything with a keyboard and computer screen.

He needed something "fun," and in a town rife with scandal, celebrities, and Hollywood bigwigs who always wanted the skinny on the others, why not provide that service to the companies that needed the dirty secrets and hidden proof but didn't want to do all the hard work. That was the service they'd started a couple of years back and continued to this day, all because Rey wanted to have a little fun.

Some fun this had turned out to be. A man was about to have his career ruined for a personal mistake.

She'd been around long enough to know what "taken care of" meant. Nothing like mob hits, or so she thought. It usually meant one's indiscretions were laid bare for all to see and judge, and then one was canceled into oblivion. Or hushed up with money offered as balm so the high-profile person, or company, in this case, could save face, with everything kept under wraps.

Usually, they found information for clients of the PR firm they worked for, and they didn't get to pick the clients. They only took on the jobs assigned by the firm. They only found and delivered the information they were tasked with getting. What their employers, and the clients they represented, did with the information was not their business.

"Not our business," Rey reminded her, their mantra when sometimes the things they found were too difficult.

"Not my business," she repeated, tamping down the burgeoning guilt and unease. The guy had cheated during his wife's pregnancy and right after. His wife was his high school sweetheart. Moved here for his career. He was the lowest of the low.

She shook it off, killing any emotion, told Rey she'd see him later, and grabbed the folder. This was the job.

The inside of the PR firm was both bright and engaging and sleek and efficient, the usual makeup of LA businesses. It bustled. Everyone was moving so fast here and there that Isla wondered if they really had somewhere to go, or if they were just walking back and forth to look busy. She swallowed a laugh, imagining speed-walking around in four-inch Balenciagas, just 'cause.

Isla flashed her pass to security, who knew her well enough by now—she was the contact person with the clients. Her own heels marking her movement on the polished floor, she took the elevator to the top floor, the twenty-ninth, where the VIPs worked. Interesting, because usually she met her contact, Michelle, in her office. Never at the top. This client must be big.

Michelle, more jittery than usual from either too much caffeine or not enough, met Isla in the hallway.

The former model asked excitedly, "Do you have it?"

"We sound like a drug deal's going down," Isla joked to alleviate some of her own anxiety, which had renewed itself at Michelle's frantic appearance. "I'm joking, Michelle. What's up with you?"

"Ugh, you have no idea," Michelle whispered, on edge. Up close, Isla could see the bags beneath her eyes, which she'd hidden quite well with perfectly applied makeup. Still, her stress showed. "Gimme."

Isla gave.

And then retracted her hands as if she'd just handed off an actual bomb instead of a figurative one. Her body relaxed, her part in this venture complete.

"Whole package here. I think Rey already told you what we found, but Leonard was in hot and heavy with Stephanie, the receptionist. She's no longer at the company, but it's been a pretty lengthy affair, which made him less diligent with his job and opened the company up to discrepancies in the accounts. They could say he was negligent, because between her and the pregnant wife, he had his hands full. Things he should have caught likely slipped through the cracks."

"Good, good." Michelle nodded. She peeked in the folder at the photos that left nothing to the imagination, flipping through them with gusto. "This is perfect. This makes the guy look . . . desperate, sloppy. And cheating on a pregnant wife? I mean, what the actual fuck? We can run with this. He's so gone."

Isla debated. Should she mention her thoughts about how the whole affair seemed too convenient? That Stephanie, the receptionist—who was now gone, interestingly enough—seemed way out of Leonard's league? In a city full of centerfold-looking men and heads of companies worth millions who'd love a sidepiece like Stephanie, why boring Midwest-born-and-bred Matthew Leonard? He had a great-paying job, but still. He was mid in looks and wealth at best.

Michelle's freshly highlighted hair shimmered as she absorbed it all, smiling wider as Isla spoke. Every delicious detail seemed to imbue her with life, and she stared into the distance, already working out how they were going to use the information.

Michelle said, "Everything tracks. We can paint a picture of someone unreliable, entirely self-serving, a liar and a cheat. The head guy hates those the most. By the time we're done, no one will believe a word he says. Even if he tries to talk again, it won't matter. He's done for."

Done for, just as Rey had said earlier. The words made Isla even more uncomfortable now than before. It was like everyone was relishing the downfall of one dumb guy who'd let big tits and a small ass cloud his judgment. Why would this company care so much?

Isla took her shot. "Don't you think it's a little convenient that Stephanie and Leonard would have this affair? I mean, they were barely in each other's orbits. They worked in totally different departments. And not to say that beautiful people don't date regular ones, but Stephanie's history of lovers doesn't fit Matthew Leonard. Maybe she was put in his orbit."

Michelle froze mid paper flip. Her eyes rose to meet Isla's, blinking rapidly as if the information didn't compute. "How do you mean?" It sounded like a warning, not a real question wanting an answer.

Isla lost all bravado. *Not my business,* she reminded herself. She shouldn't have said anything. Now Michelle was looking at her weird, as if to ask, *Why are you thinking? You're not being paid to think. You're paid to produce.*

"Forget it." Isla waved it away, hoping she hadn't screwed up too badly with her overstep. She deferred in apology.

Finally, Michelle said, "Hey, I get it. This seems like small stuff in the grand scheme of things. Like, who the hell is Matthew Leonard, right? Why give a fuck if he's screwing some blonde or his bloated wife?"

Pregnant, Isla thought, keeping her face blank. *The woman was carrying a damn child.*

"Sometimes there is collateral damage. Sometimes there is the martyr. Whatever it'll be is not for you or me"—she tapped the folder to her chest—"to figure out. It's for the client to use as they choose. Your job is to investigate and find the goods." She smiled. "And mine is to control the narrative per the client's wishes. Leonard's going to be that narrative."

CHAPTER SIX

Isla took it all in, properly reminded of her place. "Roger that."

Michelle recentered herself, blowing out a long breath, eyes closed like she was in hot yoga class. "No worries. This has been stressful for all because of the fast turnaround, I know, and I appreciate you and the team for coming through like this." Relief was evident on her face, and Isla was happy about another completed job and satisfied client. "This is perfect. The chairman will be thrilled. He and his team are actually due for an update and strategy meeting in fifteen."

"Chairman of the accounting firm?" Isla asked, disappointed. "That doesn't seem like a big enough deal for the five-star, top-floor treatment."

Michelle laughed like Isla was an ignorant child, which Isla didn't appreciate, but she held her tongue.

"No, the chairman of the Corrigan Group, which owns the accounting firm."

The Corrigan Group was worldwide. Explained all the bells and whistles.

"For some reason, Leonard rubbed the company the wrong way. He's pissed them off enough that the big man over everything is paying us a visit to get his update firsthand. Whatever Leonard did, they'll make an example of him. Quietly, of course. Pushing him out with some pictures is light work, in my opinion."

Isla remained stone faced, averting her gaze so Michelle wouldn't see anything more than an agreeable contractor. This guy wasn't going to just be discredited. How was he going to explain why he'd resigned to his wife? He'd lose everything. But Isla said nothing more.

"Fantastic," Isla said with finality. She readied to leave, securing her bag over her shoulder. "Invoice has been sent electronically, I'm sure."

Michelle beamed, hugging the file to her chest. "And already paid, with a bonus for such expedient work. You all are godsends."

Or doing the devil's work.

Michelle's phone beeped. She was instantly nervous and fidgety again, and Isla had to wonder who these people were who made the too-cool-to-be-unnerved Michelle Jell-O on legs. "God, they're coming up. You might want to head out now so you don't interact with them."

"Muddies the waters," Isla replied, appreciating that Michelle remembered how Isla never wanted to be seen by the clients. What she did was in the dark. Not that Michelle was listening. She was already click-clacking down the hall to the large glass-encased conference room ahead, where other employees hustled to make last-minute preparations for the colossal meet. Michelle waved a hand up in the air as she retreated, calling over her shoulder that she'd be in touch soon.

"Insane," Isla murmured, glad to be done with it all. She pivoted toward the four elevators for a quick getaway.

An elevator pinged an arrival. Isla stepped closer to the opposite side, attempting to make herself small and insignificant. She busied herself with the contents of her bag when the elevator door slid open and an entourage of suits disembarked from the car. She couldn't help sneaking a peek at this "big man" chairman who had made Michelle's knees tremble with fear and awe.

Isla nearly dropped her bag, because none other than Victor Corrigan stepped out first from the middle of the group, and at sixty-nine, the older man looked decades younger.

Talk about "Black don't crack." Isla forgot herself, openly gaping at the distinguished chairman of the Corrigan Group conglomerate, who'd retained the looks of his youth. Victor carried a level of command that was otherworldly, never losing a step. That same air of importance and power emanated from him, stretching from him like tentacles, wrapping her in them in the small space they were in. It was equal parts suffocating and astounding, seeing him in person, being so close that if she wanted, she could touch him. Well, right before his group of men and guards ground her into dust.

Victor was every bit as large in person as he'd been in the photos and interviews she'd seen throughout the years, yet there was something else about him that she couldn't put her finger on, even though she knew he was cutthroat.

He was flanked by several others. The ones she recognized from the time she'd spent performing cursory searches of the family were his trusted right-hand manager and everything man Dixon, who never left his side; Bennett, the younger of Victor's two sons, from his current marriage, who looked like a model in a tailored designer suit, with a touch of haughtiness that said he knew how good he looked; and Myles, the oldest, from Victor's first marriage, who was the spitting image of his father in both looks and demeanor. His hard-set, reserved demeanor contrasted Bennett's softer and more conciliatory one. Another man, who was tall, stocky, and sporting a well-cut beard, had an eternally tanned look, even in winter, and spent most of his time in the gym, kept a step behind Bennett. The other men who stepped out last, she guessed, were lawyers, accountants, or security. It was difficult to tell the difference among all the suits and grim expressions.

"You'd better have answers," Victor was saying. His tone was fierce, and though his words weren't directed toward her, Isla still shuddered. Isla inched closer to her side of the elevators, praying one would open before any of them noticed her. She kept most of her back to them, but the urge to get a good, long eyeful of the man and the myth she'd heard about ten years ago and basically cyberstalked since then was too great, and she sneaked sidelong glances while also trying to pretend as if she wasn't looking and definitely wasn't listening.

He paused to continue talking, the group stopping short of bumping into each other to prevent themselves from touching him. "I want to know how this was overlooked and how he was able to pull it off. This was on your watch, Bennett, Danny."

"Yes, sir," Bennett and the stocky tanned one said in deference.

None of them acknowledged her. She thought they didn't realize there was another person lurking in their bubble, listening to him grouse, or else they'd surely have shut him down, though she doubted anyone could. Victor Corrigan started walking again, and then his posse, as she inched around the rear of them to slip into the elevator they'd just vacated. She breathed a sigh, dodging that bullet, but her curiosity wouldn't let her be.

She popped her head out through the doors as she held them open for one last peek. The group had taken a right at the corner, heading toward the conference room, but the older son, Myles, slowed a half step, his attention caught by the elevator's ping from being left open against its will. He took a step back, and his gaze shifted in her direction. A second too late, Isla threw herself back inside, pressing against the wall and praying he hadn't caught her watching them or, worse, wouldn't come looking. She struggled to find the same circular *L* button she'd pressed a hundred times before. The doors began sliding shut, and when she gathered the courage to look back up, no one was staring back at her.

Isla leaned against the handrail in the elevator as it zoomed down twenty-nine floors. Now everything came crashing down on her. They didn't recognize her. But why would they? It wasn't her they knew. It was Eden. Still, the sight of Victor Corrigan was a gut punch back to the past, forcing all of it to rush back with nauseating clarity and memory.

She'd never met Victor Corrigan in person. She'd never known he existed until her best friend at the time, Eden Galloway, had spoken of him. That was over ten years ago, back in Daytona, where she and Eden had met.

The few times Eden had referred to this family, she'd said they were powerful, that her mother had once worked as Victor's personal assistant and was accused of something and abruptly fired. She said her mother was driven out of Charlottesville and was never the same afterward. Eden had made them sound ominous and threatening. This family had destroyed her mother's life and Eden's as a result. The few times Eden had mentioned him, it had been with contempt, bitterness, and rage.

Then, after Eden's mother Elise died and Eden and Isla decided to run away to LA, they took a Greyhound cross-country, making a stop in Virginia. When Isla asked why they were there, Eden only said she had unfinished business with the Corrigans. She left Isla alone in their motel room one night, saying everything would be over after then. That was all Isla knew.

That was the last time Isla saw Eden.

CHAPTER SEVEN

Six Months Ago

A week later Isla was at her three-days-a-week part-time job as an eldercare companion, halving one of the Tuscan turkey sandwiches for Miss Lydia so they could sit for lunch as they always did. She was half listening to one of Lydia's daytime talk shows when the local station interrupted with breaking news.

"I'm standing on the side of the 91 East, where early this morning, a vehicle was found with one deceased individual inside."

"Goodness," Miss Lydia said from her spot on the pale-blue couch. She leaned toward the TV to get a better look and listen. "How awful."

"Passersby noticed three tagged dogs several yards away from the SUV and checked it when the dogs continued to linger near it. There they found the body deceased from an apparent self-inflicted gunshot wound," the anchor continued somberly. "The employee, just identified as Matthew Leonard, worked in the accounting department for an LA-based shopping mall, a subsidiary of the Corrigan Group."

The steady slicing of the green apple set to be part of today's lunch slowed to a stop. Isla stood in the kitchen, the knife hovering in the air, the apple a distant memory. Like Miss Lydia, Isla leaned in the direction of the TV to get a better look and listen.

"Mr. Leonard had just recently left the company after coming under increasing scrutiny for alleged misappropriation of funds and was facing mounting legal and financial troubles. He leaves behind a wife and a baby less than a year old."

Isla moved so she could see the screen in the living room. It flashed a smiling photo of Matthew Leonard, his arm over his wife and the baby cradled in her arms, with their faces blurred. Then the screen switched to the company doors as entering employees shied away from the cameras while reporters threw questions at them, asking if Leonard's alleged dealings and his sudden resignation had played a part in his death.

Of course they did. Isla leaned against the doorframe as she watched Bennett Corrigan and that Danny fellow wave off the throng of reporters with no comment and enter the building.

"They move fast," she mumbled.

"What was that, honey?" Miss Lydia asked from the couch. "This is the first in a while I've heard bad things about the Corrigan Group. They do so much humanitarian work. Even I know them from before I retired."

She went on, but Isla was in her own head. Leonard had died last night, but the news already had so much information about a misappropriation of funds. Nothing about an affair. Isla didn't know anything about missing money. How had her team missed this?

The anchor continued, "This incident has left his family and the company shaken and taken by surprise. Chairman Victor Corrigan, through a company spokesperson, said, 'The Corrigan Group and all its subsidiaries are a family here and worldwide. One of our family was lost. The allegations don't matter. What matters is that Mr. Leonard's life is honored and his beautiful family is taken care of. And if you or anyone in need of help is thinking about self-harm, please dial 988 or contact any of the appropriate local numbers listed below. Please reach out to someone. We are so sorry for Matthew and his family. It is a deeply tragic loss, and we at the Corrigan Group hope you will respect the Leonards' and our grief during this devastating time.'"

Isla's mind started working. If Leonard had been embezzling from the company, why blackmail him with photos of an affair? What was there to blackmail? They had enough to get him and send him to prison. What's more, why hadn't Rey gotten wind of any of it, even with the time they'd had to pull up dirt on him? And what had driven him to make the choice he did when either choice, the affair or embezzlement, would have hurt his family? No word about his affair either.

Maybe to him, being labeled a thief was better than being labeled an adulterer. Was this what the Corrigans considered "taken care of"?

His death left a mark on her, like the deaths of others who had been in her life.

Her father. Here one minute. Gone the next.

Eden. Here one minute. Gone the next.

Now Matthew Leonard too.

She was hit with an even scarier thought. What if what had happened to Matthew Leonard had happened to Eden too? At least what had happened to Isla's father and Leonard was clear. They were dead through different circumstances, with their bodies found. They had had and would have funerals, where their loved ones could grieve. But what had happened with Eden was left unresolved. No one even knew she'd gone missing except Isla, because the only two people who would have cared were Elise, who was dead, and Isla, who was just a kid on the run back then, one of the unseens in this country because she didn't fit the mold of a normal kid with a home and parents.

It was the knowledge, trauma, and guilt that had haunted her every day for the past ten years, and finally apathy, which had driven her to tolerate Charli's ridiculous get-rich-quick schemes, which sometimes did or did not involve her against her will. They'd met on the train at Peachtree Station in Atlanta before a long train ride across the country to LA. By the time they'd arrived at Union Station nearly four days later, Charli was offering a place to stay and a helping hand.

People feel more comfortable with you when a kid's around, Charli had said, with Texas as their scenic backdrop. *I know a guy who knows a guy who can help you get an ID so you can make a clean break. Start a new life. I won't ask and don't give a damn.*

Thus, Isla Thomas became Isla Thorne.

Because it's better to keep some parts of you true, Charli continued, happy to have some sort of apprentice by now. *Then all you gotta do is sign your initials, and no one can say it's a forgery.*

She was just selfish and an opportunist. Isla couldn't call the brash and overbearing woman an adoptive mother because Charli was anything but. But she had helped Isla out when she'd needed it the most.

Isla worked multiple jobs, earned her GED, went to college, and got her degree. Met Rey and Nat and was here now, still living with Charli but enjoying life, hanging out with Miss Lydia and not putting her degree to its best use as one-third of their discovery team. That's what they considered themselves, because they discovered the needle in all that hay and let their clients decide whether to stick it.

The Corrigans were untouchable. Though they were considered philanthropes, made humanitarian efforts globally, it seemed that when someone crossed or offended them, this family erased them entirely and came up smelling like roses.

Isla hated the smell of roses. She hated bullies with unlimited money and power more.

A fire she had long resigned would never be extinguished had been reignited by Leonard's frozen face of despair and confusion. A memory had resurfaced. One long hidden away.

Eden, in Daytona, drunk after a night of partying, grabbing Isla's hands and in a moment of fevered clarity saying from nowhere, "They'd have made me like them, or worse, if I'd stayed. They are a nest of vipers."

Back then, Isla had smiled and nodded, attributing Eden's words to the ramblings of a drunk girl taking care of a dying mother.

But there was the other time, when the two of them had stopped in Virginia, in their double-queen room on the second floor of the Red Roof. They could have afforded a better place, but Eden had been on edge, had been weird the moment they'd arrived. Isla didn't know why they'd stopped here when they were going to be the Black-girl version of Thelma and Louise, only live in the end, and bus to Los Angeles. They'd live on all the money Isla had saved from working at McDonald's and a backpack of money Isla hadn't known Eden had been carrying around.

Eden had been her first and only true friend until Rey and Nat. She had been a big sister. Eden's mother had been the mom Isla never had until the moment Elise couldn't fight her illness anymore. Isla had been there. She and Eden had sworn to always have each other's backs, but Eden had always been guarded and quirky, which was why Isla hadn't asked any questions when they'd arrived in this town. She'd let Eden go in and out without asking where she was going, why, and to see whom.

Eden's final words to her, before she left the motel room to meet some old friends: "This is the last thing I have to do with them. I might be late, so don't wait up."

Old emotions assailed Isla one after the other. She was no lightweight. In their line of business Isla had uncovered the worst of the worst about people. Secrets and scandals they'd probably have killed to keep hidden. Leonard was the first time a job had felt personal, because it had made her feel again.

Pieces of the past began to click together in her mind, one by one. The way Eden had vanished without a trace. The silence afterward, with no one to turn to. And now, seeing the might of the Corrigans and particularly their might against those who'd crossed them. Had Eden done that? Crossed the Corrigans?

Isla handed Miss Lydia her sandwich and chips and opened her laptop after promising to eat her own lunch in a minute. She typed in the search bar, pulling up what always came up. Very little information about the actual family: Victor, Bennett, Myles, Brooke, and Holland. All upstanding citizens. A beautiful family. It was as if their digital footprints had been sanitized to the most generic details. The majority of the information was about the Corrigan Group and all the companies and subsidiaries under it, like the intricate network of a family tree. No scandals. No disgruntled workers. The final picture was of the family smiling together at a charity function for their foundation. Eden's words echoed.

A nest of vipers.

"Isla, you need to eat. You look so serious. All that frowning will give you wrinkles, and you're too young for them," Miss Lydia said. "So am I, as a matter of fact!"

Isla grinned. "That's right, Miss Lydia—you look better than me."

"Damn right I do." Miss Lydia touched up her hair, posing because she knew she still looked good at eighty.

Isla closed her laptop, appreciating the sweet older lady who favored the late, great Ruby Dee. The idea churning in her head wasn't about guilt over Matthew Leonard or unfinished business over Eden. Well, maybe a little. But mostly it was about truth.

Victor Corrigan and his crew had entered her world, stoked buried feelings, and reminded her of a debt that she had yet to pay. So it was high time Isla entered his.

CHAPTER EIGHT

Six Months Ago

Isla slid into the back corner table of Rey's semibustling shop, It's Just Coffee, Okay?! The aroma of freshly ground coffee beans and sound from the whirring milk frother filled the air. Rey was behind the counter with two of his employees, concentrating intently on the foam art he was applying to a latte. His dark, curly hair was slightly disheveled, and a curl fell onto his forehead when he looked up briefly to grin at Isla before resuming his duties. He finished with a flourish, sliding the mug across the countertop to a customer and smiling brightly when another satisfied patron squealed her glee at his artistry. Outside, the beach was brimming with its usual constructive chaos—patrons at the muscle gym lifting and bench-pressing in the open air, skateboarders and in-line skaters weaving precariously though clusters of tourists and locals meandering along the walk, street performers drawing curious and awestruck crowds, and the line of merchants, temporary or stationary, hawking their brightly colored wares.

Whenever she visited, Isla was begrudgingly impressed at how Rey managed to juggle providing contracted security analysis for his clients, working with her and Natalie on their "discovery" side gig, and managing his coffee shop.

When they asked why coffee when it barely brought in money and he never advertised, he'd laugh and say, "If people wander into my shop, then it's fate. Plus, I own the whole building, and it's not about making money. Some people like making pottery or surfing. I like coffee."

Today was different. She glared at the coffee scene before her, wondering how Rey was standing there happily plying customers with caffeine addictions like a drug dealer when they had just screwed up royally with this whole Leonard situation.

Natalie Wang, the final member of their trio, strolled into the café, the bell dinging her arrival. Rey and Isla zeroed in on Nat, and the three of them had silent communion. Nat had just finished up an improv session and was still radiating from that high as she casually made her way through the café to the back. Isla picked up her belongings, and the frappé forced upon her, and followed her friend, and Rey finished up and gave last instructions to his staff before joining the ladies on the back stairs leading up to where the real action took place.

As they ascended the stairs in the back of the store to a door marked MANAGEMENT ONLY, the ambience shifted from cozy café to high-tech command center, which was exactly what it was, where they did all their major work. No one but them was allowed up there, and even Isla and Nat didn't go there unless Rey knew first. The loft was a sprawling room filled with computer screens, servers, and an array of advanced tech equipment. The walls were lined with monitors displaying streams of data, surveillance footage, and complex algorithms Isla didn't bother trying to decipher. It reminded her of *The Matrix*.

During their senior year, when Rey first allowed Nat and Isla to enter his domain, Nat had asked how he afforded all this, and his response was "Let's just say I've done well in tech investments and a few other ventures. This first-gen son of Venezuelan immigrants knows how to work and make his money multiply!"

As a first-gen Chinese and Ghanaian, respectively, Nat and Isla understood fully.

They took their usual spots, Rey behind his nearly complete circle of side-by-side computer screens along with one massive gaming computer screen, sometimes used for its original purpose, most of the time for cracking secrets and codes. Isla dropped onto the couch opposite Rey's workstation, a small table separating them, while Nat slid elegantly onto the opposite side of the couch.

Setting her hobo bag next to her sandaled feet, Nat asked, "God, who died?"

Nat had a penchant for being spot on yet so blessedly oblivious of situations sometimes that Isla found it endearing. She almost wished they wouldn't have to burst Nat's innocence.

Isla didn't answer, allowing Rey to have the honors. She wasn't surprised that Nat didn't know what had been splashed all over the news the entire day. When Nat was in improv, she was fully devoted to her craft, which worked perfectly when they needed up-close information gathering. She just considered those moments practice for the breakout role she knew was coming. Isla hoped that happened for her. Nat deserved to be on billboards and accepting awards in a dazzling dress. Then maybe Isla could be her plus-one and be a real guest instead of hanging around as backup while Nat played whatever roles to get the intel they needed.

"We've got a situation," Rey replied.

Nat pursed her lips, waiting for him to continue. When the drama king did not, she finally said, "Explain like I'm five." Isla sighed, waiting for the show to begin.

"Leonard." Rey's voice tightened. Gone were the bright smile and pleasant demeanor of an easygoing coffee shop owner. Now they were about the business. "You haven't seen the news at all today?"

Nat reached for her phone, because when someone said "Haven't you seen the news?" it meant you should absolutely check out whatever disaster was currently happening.

"Let me spare you the finger strain," Rey offered. Around him, the screens were waking up from their slumber and began to illuminate him from all sides, casting him in a bluish-white hue. The reflections bounced off his thick Marc Jacobs glasses. "Leonard, the guy whose intel we gave to Crabtree and Elliott PR, offed himself last night."

"Get the fuck out!" Rey's announcement didn't spare Nat's fingers one bit. It only prompted rapid-fire finger flying across her screen as she keyed in search words and the results popped up. Her mouth dropped open.

Rey pointed a remote at the fifty-inch mounted on the wall across from Nat and Isla, and the screen lit up, showing the same smiling face Isla had seen plastered over the news all day.

"But how? It was just an affair and resignation."

"An affair and resignation could mean everything to some people," Isla answered.

"Doesn't he have, like, a wife and kid?"

Isla nodded, her chest feeling heavy with guilt. They had supplied the proverbial bullets for the gun that killed Matthew Leonard.

"Shit on wheels," Nat said, done with her phone and leaning over to place it on the table.

Rey rubbed the side of his face distractedly. Isla didn't like the way he looked, uneasy, as if there was something he knew that they did not.

"What is it?" Isla asked, wondering if she really wanted to know.

Rey let out a huge breath, his expression looking exactly like what Isla was feeling. Like shit. "The information we gave them about him wasn't complete. It seems."

Isla's eyes narrowed. She touched her fingers to her chest because it felt like something had gripped her heart and squeezed. "What do you mean 'wasn't complete'? The affair was real. The times, locations, all verified by that Stephanie person. But the other stuff the news is saying—misappropriating funds—is that true? Where did that come from?"

They should have asked for more time to work this. Better yet, they should have said no. Corporate dealings were never clean cut. They all knew this, and yet.

"Could it be a setup?" Nat asked, in the beginning stages of a panic that was amplified by her ability to become highly emotional at the drop of a hat, even when she was being genuine, like she was now. "I knew something was fishy."

Rey ran his hands through his freshly cut dark hair. Today, his shaved sides had waves cut into them that resembled the Pacific's waves, which he loved to surf in. Isla preferred land, which was odd, since she, too, had grown up near the beach, except hers was on the Atlantic.

"That's the thing—it checked out *too* well, you know?"

Isla didn't like the crack in his usually calm demeanor. He was the unflappable one of their group. Nat was very flappable—unless she was in character. And Isla was the . . . well, she varied. Maybe the angry one. Maybe the one who had faith in no one. Always waiting for the other shoe to drop.

CHAPTER NINE

Rey said, "Before, when we got the job and I started looking, the affair popped up pretty quickly. There was nothing in his accounts that seemed off. We talked to the woman; she confirmed and showed pictures and receipts."

Nat nodded. She had been the contact with Stephanie. Isla motioned for Rey to continue what she already knew he would say.

"But after we dropped off the info, Isla was saying how something didn't feel right, and when Victor Corrigan showed up, I started wondering too. Why did a company care if two of their employees were banging? He wasn't her superior. And I thought maybe it was because the company is big on image. An affair when one of them is married with a baby on the way is a bad look, but it still wouldn't damage the company because that's personal shit."

"Truth," Nat seconded.

Isla said, "So you looked again."

Rey nodded gravely. "So I looked again. Deeper this time."

Isla waited. "And?"

"And this time, there was something. A big something. Like Nat just said—like we *all* said," he corrected when Isla was about to protest. "This job was a quick turnaround. Urgent, right? What usually takes us weeks to find and verify and verify again, we found in days. Like it was just waiting for us to find it."

"A present wrapped in a perfect bow," Isla added.

Rey pointed at her, a silent *bingo*. "We found what they wanted us to find. The affair is true. The embezzling . . . I'm not sure, because why wasn't it there when I initially ran it through my cursory systems? Why pop up all of a sudden? How'd the media get ahold of info that I, who am way better than Chinese hackers, mind you—no offense, Nat—"

"Wait." Nat startled. "What?"

"—could not find?" Rey finished, dodging a projectile Nat threw at him. "Hey, watch my shit."

Isla said, "Because someone planted it."

Rey pointed. *Bingo* again.

Nat groaned and leaned over with her knees on her elbows and her forehead dropped into her hands. Her long, dark hair fell over her like a curtain.

"Like someone had the affair ready for us to find. Yeah," Rey confirmed. "I went back in now that Michelle and her management weren't up my ass to get this info in."

Isla asked, "Do you think the firm was in on this?" She hated to think that Michelle would have anything to do with a setup that had led to someone's death.

Rey shook his head. "Nah. They don't make the bombs. They just light the match to the fuse. We were the ones who filled it with the components so it could go boom."

Nat dismissed his extended analogy. "Forget all that analogy shit, Rey. What's the bottom line?"

He checked himself. "So I find all this evidence of embezzlement, right? Looks like he did the shit. He's up a creek, okay? But when I looked deeper, the info has inconsistencies."

Isla prompted, "Like?"

Rey faced one of his keyboards and began typing. The screen showed one of Leonard's bank statements that they'd delivered to the PR firm and the Corrigans. "Well, for one, the bank account Leonard supposedly established and funneled the money into was in his own name. Smart people who are embezzling and setting up accounts wouldn't use their names and have such an easy path to link them. That account wasn't his. It was established by someone else under his name, and the money was just transferred to accounts he owned, not long before we got the case."

Nat asked, "How would you know that? If they did it under his name, where's the proof?"

Rey looked at Nat like she was some poor, unfortunate soul. "For one thing, the IP address of the computer that created the account didn't originate from either his work or his personal computer."

"And how would you know that?" Nat asked, making Rey work for it.

"Girl, come on. Who am I and what do I do? Don't try to play me," Rey said. When Nat rolled her eyes at him, he returned the act, then continued unfazed. "The IP address originates from Virginia. Leonard hasn't been to Virginia in years, if ever."

Virginia. The word struck at Isla like a bad violin cord, plunging her into a basin of anxiety she thought she had long overcome.

"I cross-checked the witnesses too. The woman who had the affair with Leonard, Stephanie? Ghost. As in she no longer exists. At least, not her name, Social, address, phone number, or anything else she gave me. The company ID we found for her was a fake name for a temp employee who was interestingly hired in those same two weeks the fake account was established. She was there just long enough to strike an interest in poor Leonard, get him hemmed up in her love so they could hold it over him."

Isla said, "So that he'd be the fall guy if the embezzling was ever found out." She was boiling. The unease and guilt she'd once felt? Gone. She was pissed now. This was supposed to be child's play to a person like Rey. He found the tech stuff. She planned and set the scenes. She was the POC with Michelle and their other clients. Nat was the decoy or the prop, with Isla as backup. Rey's tech support was never problematic. It had always been ironclad and never failed them. Until now.

Rey shook his head regretfully. Then he tried to appeal to the both of them. "But this was really convincing, high-level stuff. Like I said, if we'd had more time to vet and vet again . . . you know we like to rinse and repeat before we give the info up. If we'd had more time."

"More time?" Isla seethed. "A man is dead, Rey. A family is ruined because of 'more time.' That can't be our excuse."

Rey shrugged. "It's all I got. But all my preliminary checks were solid. Nat met with the fake temp receptionist, and she was convincing, right?" He was half standing, leaning over his screens, imploring Nat for a save.

Nat nodded vigorously, twisting her long tendrils of hair in her hand. "If she was acting, she could teach me a few things. I can admit when I've been outperformed." She almost looked like she was impressed by the fake temp receptionist.

The room was getting too hot, and Isla slipped out of the light jacket she'd been wearing. She stood up and paced the floor while Rey and Nat continued discussing how majorly fucked up this was. Isla stopped moving, and their conversation stopped as well. They waited for her to speak.

Isla asked, "What do you think, Nat? You're the storyteller here."

"I just perform stories. I don't make them," Nat corrected. "But I think he was given the choice of which was the greater evil to him."

"But he wasn't embezzling," Rey said. "What was the blackmail?"

Isla picked up the thread Nat had begun to unravel. "The greater evil, Rey, is whether he wanted his wife to learn he was unfaithful or for her to think he stole money. He could always say he'd tried to steal the money for their family. He couldn't explain screwing around while she was having his baby. So he agreed to take the heat for the embezzling. But the damage was done."

Rey finally got it. "He realized Stephanie was a honey trap. He was going to be named as the embezzler anyway. He'd betrayed his wife. He couldn't face it. In his mind, there was only one way out for him."

CHAPTER TEN

"A man is dead." Heat built behind Isla's eyes. She put a fist to them to cool them and calm herself. "Please tell me it wasn't murder." That would be too much to handle.

"I got into the LAPD's system. The autopsy is still being done, and that will take a while, but it is definitely suicide. They said he rigged the shotgun in the car to go off using his—"

"Spare us the details." Nat looked green and tried to center herself. "I don't think whoever did this expected him to do that. I think they assumed he would go away quietly. They may have even offered him money."

"Then he should have taken it and gone off into the sunset to be forgotten tomorrow when the next scandal hits. This is LA. Where embezzlers and cheats are aplenty," Rey wisecracked.

Isla didn't buy it. "Not to some small-time accountant from the Midwest whose job was his identity and his pride, especially working for the Corrigan Group. He was humiliated. Probably thought he could never look his wife in her face again."

Nat slouched back against the pillows of the couch, her usually animated, glowing face pale and drawn. "So we set up an innocent man?"

"Looks that way," Rey said grimly.

Isla wasn't going to claim that. "No. No, *we* didn't set up anyone. *We* were duped just like he was."

Rey clicked back to the photo of Leonard, smiling, fresh faced, excited. No more. Isla went to the fridge and got herself a water. Then one for Nat when she indicated she needed one too. Rey opted for the bottle of tequila he pulled from under his desk. He sank back into his tailor-made ergonomic swivel chair built for endless hours of sitting. His frustration was clear. He looked defeated, perplexed, and a little bit angry. The same as Isla felt, only hers was more.

Isla said, "He was an innocent."

Her words hung heavily in the air. She looked at Matthew Leonard on the big screen, his face looming so that it seemed to fill the whole room. He was smiling in this picture, yes, but she began to imagine his eyes staring at her accusingly. She'd delivered the information they had used to destroy him. She was the sword someone had used to cut him down to hide themselves.

Nat rubbed her temples. "What do we do now? Go back to Crabtree and Elliott and demand an explanation? Cut ties with them?"

"Demand an explanation about the information that *we* provided to *them*?" Rey scoffed. Nat shifted so her back was half to him, clearly embarrassed by her suggestion. Isla shot him a warning glance. Now was not the time to get weird with one another.

"My bad, Nat," he apologized. "We can't go to the firm because it was our intel, even if it was a rush job. I'm nearly positive that they didn't know a frame-up was happening. They were used like we were, and we don't want the Corrigans coming after us."

"But someone out there is definitely behind this," Nat said. "Someone inside that corporation."

"They're in the wind now. No one's going to look any further now that the main 'culprit' is dead," Rey admitted, finally turning the screen off.

Leonard's photo was gone, but his image was seared into Isla's mind. She hated being used. She hated making mistakes. What ate at her the most was that Leonard was dead and her team had been an unknowing accomplice to the act that they couldn't speak out against.

"But they'll want their money," Isla said, venom filling her. "No way they're leaving millions sitting in the account of a dead guy. They knew how to get it in; they'll want to get it out. You said the IP address originated from Virginia? The East Coast is headquarters for the Corrigan Group. Matter of fact, the family has their main estate in Charlottesville."

Nat asked, "You know that how?"

"Research," Isla said quickly. For now, she kept to herself that the Corrigan name was deeply ingrained in her mind and that she had some history with them, sort of.

Rey said, "So someone, maybe someone in the family, set Leonard up using the PR firm and us, and even brought in the top guy to give the theft more clout?"

That's right, Isla thought. Victor Corrigan was here in the flesh. And his sons. Nearly ten years. The ten-year anniversary of the day Eden vanished was approaching near the end of the year. Now the Corrigans had reappeared. It was like the heavens were telling Isla it was time for her to finally do something. Something she could possibly do now that Leonard was dead too.

Nat asked, "What now? We just leave it alone? Go on with our lives and pretend we didn't have a hand in this? Even if we didn't know? We let ourselves get pressured, and Rey always says pressure leads to fuckups."

"I love when you remember what I tell you."

"Shut up."

Isla wasn't listening to their banter. Two people gone. The Corrigans. "We go to the source." Her voice steeled as resolve took over.

Rey said, "Say what now?" Like he hadn't heard clearly.

"I may not know a lot about how their businesses are run, but I know they are more impenetrable than the Pentagon," Nat added, sharing a concerned look with Rey.

Isla's mind rewound ten years, twelve. Back to when she was fourteen and her father was suddenly not there. Her mind fast-forwarded two years to the morning she awoke and realized Eden had never made it back to the motel room. She looked at her partners with a cold clarity that made them visibly shiver. "We owe it to Leonard. And I owe it to someone else."

Again they shared a look. Nat rose and asked if Isla was okay. They knew nothing about Eden. It was a part of her life she had been too ashamed to tell them about. How she had run away scared when Eden never returned. How Isla had taken the money in Eden's backpack even when she wasn't 100 percent sure where Eden was, only had the feeling that Eden was gone for good. How Isla had saved money from every check, every payout she'd received ever since, intending to pay back what she had used, as if it could ever be recompensed. It couldn't. Recompense was going back and handling business.

Determination infused her. "It's time I did something I should have done long ago." She took in a centering breath, preparing herself for whatever reaction Rey and Nat would have once she told them. She wouldn't fault them. "You should pour more tequila, and some for me and Nat too."

She took a seat at the table. Rey joined her with the tequila and three shot glasses. Nat pulled herself from the couch, following suit. They sat around the table in tense silence, waiting for Isla to speak, while Rey's central command whirred softly in the background against the hum from the air conditioner kicking on to combat the heat from the electronics. The sounds from the bustling pier below faded into the background as Isla began the story of her and Eden and her plan for what came next.

When she finished, neither of them said anything, too shocked by what Isla now wanted to do.

Isla's resolve was unwavering. They'd never seen this side of the usually easygoing, unbothered Isla Thorne. The weight of what Isla was about to do was oppressive. She was forging into uncharted territory, stepping into shark-infested waters.

Going up against Goliath.

With no telling who—or what—would be waiting for her when she went back to where it had started.

CHAPTER ELEVEN

Present Day

The following evening, the Lyft pulled to a slow stop in front of the same gates where Isla had been a little over twenty-four hours ago. The pink-velour-suit-clad driver adjusted her rearview mirror to appraise her customer. Dubiousness furrowed Kim's brow. "Want me to wait until they send you packing?"

The question drew Isla away from the thoughts that had been consuming her, ones of how she'd manage to find a way in, because Kim was definitely right. If the guards in the station were anything like the ones last night, they weren't letting Kim's car cross their line, much less Isla. Even if they did, what if they made her walk the half mile to the estate? Isla's wedge sandals weren't made for walking.

Isla was also thinking about her conversation with Rey the night before and how they'd run through contingency plans should Holland not feel appreciative enough to personally get her keys back.

Kim continued. "These are the kind of people who won't let anything other than limos and private cars in."

"Your car is private," Isla pointed out.

Kim sucked her teeth. "You know what I mean. This is King's Valley. The Corrigan property is in the richest section off the Main Line. I'm surprised we made it up this far, to tell the truth."

Isla was thinking the exact same thing but didn't want to admit her concern out loud.

You're really doing this? Last chance to back out and come home.

It had been Rey's question to her after Hasaan had dropped her off at the Home Stays short-term-lease hotel last night, just in case the Corrigans had followed her, before she went on to the Red Roof. It was what Isla asked herself right now as Kim stopped before the gate and they both watched, mesmerized, as the gigantic gates slid open and a guard stepped out of the building to greet them. Was she really doing this?

"You don't have to do this, you know," Rey had said over FaceTime. "You can just come on back."

He was in his usual spot, surrounded by his computer screens. His face was illuminated in the multitude of colors from the screens as he watched them all one by one in the setup secretly housed in the loft of the small storefront café he owned. A cover for what really paid the bills, cybersecurity work for Fortune 500 companies, and the little side hustle that Isla was in on but was currently taking a sabbatical from. Or maybe this trip was their latest job. A personal one for her. An unprofitable one for him.

"Cut your losses—hey, hear me out," Rey said when Isla began to protest. How could he say that when they were talking about a missing girl? Her friend? How could he not understand that even though it'd been so long, Isla had never forgotten Eden and had always felt guilty for leaving her. For taking the money when she hadn't shown and running. Isla owed Eden, and this was the way she'd pay her back. By finding out what this family had to do with Eden's disappearance.

"I said I'm going at this on my own, so if anything goes down, there's no blowback on you or Nat. Our clients won't know. It'll all be on me."

"That's not what I mean, and you know it. Don't do that thing you do," Rey said, in the initial throes of agitation.

She studied the wall. "My thing?"

"Yeah, purposely misinterpret everything anyone says to cause a fight and create a way for them to be pissed at you so you can be on your own."

"Oh."

He rolled his eyes. "Yeah. *That* thing." He snorted, sitting back in his seat. "Where's Nat when I fucking need her? She's better at talking you down off cliffs and shit that's going to definitely be self-destructive. Does Miss Lydia know what you're doing? And we're not even going to start on Charli, who'll blow her lid when she finds out where you've gone and who you've gone to. The dollar signs will be cha-chinging all through LA."

"She won't know if you and Nat stay off her radar. Don't be around when she comes looking for me."

"No matter what you see or whatever happens, don't break cover. Don't ever let them onto you until you're ready to drop the bomb and expose them."

"Yes, teacher, I know this already. We've covered just about every possible scenario. Plus, I've done stuff like this with Nat for jobs."

"Those were all jobs for clients. This is real life, and you're going into their territory. Me and Nat aren't right outside or on the street waiting in a van. We're thousands of miles away. You're going to be embedded. You're gonna be at their mercy."

"Or they're going to be at mine because they don't know I'm coming for them."

Rey couldn't settle down in his seat any farther, but his face showed a truth bomb was coming. "You don't know what you know, and you'll need them to tell you what you don't know so you can uncover the truth. It won't be so easy to escape if they get onto you. This family . . ."

He didn't need to finish. She knew it all. This family was powerful. Too powerful. Not Hollywood-celebrity-and-elites power but real power that could blip a person into nonexistence. Isla had seen that happen firsthand. That was what she was back to rectify. What had happened to Eden?

"Whatever happens, you need to act as if it doesn't faze you." He paused. "No matter what you see, you do not break cover."

Break cover. She cracked a smile, like she was some secret agent or something. Some kind of awkward 007. She wasn't a spy. She was there for truth.

"Are you laughing? Because this is serious." Though he had relaxed and was unable to mask his own humor and relief that she wasn't slipping back into the depths of depression. If it hadn't been for his idea to work with him on his "search-and-find team" . . .

For his benefit she repeated, "Nothing fazes me. I don't give a damn."

He eyed her. "No matter what."

She said it again, mimicking his tone: "No matter what." She almost held up a Girl Scout honor sign but, since she'd never been one, wasn't sure quite what it looked like.

"Don't get angry. And remember, they're all like sharks. Even the most innocent-looking ones. Assume someone's always watching. No matter who it is, their family comes first. Even if they seem to personally like you. You're the outsider."

"Got it." She knew all this. She studied the photos of the family members stuck to the back wall in the closet and the network of associates, employees, and staff she'd gathered information on so far.

"Honey, he's talking to you."

Kim's voice cut into Isla's thoughts. She needed to get it together. She was on as of this moment.

"Sorry," Isla said, and she gave a quick rundown of the night before. "I've been trying to call Holland all day to tell her I have her ID and keys but haven't been able to get through. I just figured I'd come and drop them off now after work. I'm sure she's looking for her keys." She didn't dare ask to go in and raise suspicion.

"A girl needs her keys, you know," Kim chimed in.

The guard at the gate glanced back into the little control room, saying that the family was not to be disturbed unless there was an emergency.

"I would just hate for them to get lost waiting to get into her hands, you know? School ID, dorm keys or something . . ." Isla let him think about the consequences. "Are you sure you want to be responsible for not calling about something like this?"

Kim tutted under her breath, then said, "I mean, buddy, do you know who you work for?"

He mumbled into the tiny communications unit on his shoulder.

She held the lanyard out the window. "Or I can leave it with you? Do you have one of those big yellow envelopes or something? She can come get it later when she has a moment, but I gotta get back to town, and these rideshares only have a five-minute wait before they have to go."

"Oh, don't mind me," Kim said. "I'm here to see this little drama to the end."

Isla waved the lanyard at the guard, beseeching him to take it from her and relieve her of this responsibility. He backed away even farther, as if the lanyard was the president's football with all the codes to send nukes.

"Just give us a moment to get the word, ma'am."

Isla balked. *Ma'am.* She touched her face, displeased with his choice of label.

"Ma'am," she whispered. "Do I look like a ma'am?"

Kim chuckled. "Honey, they have to call everyone that. I think they even call kids 'little miss' or 'young such and such.' They're super proper here, I heard. I have a cousin who used to work in the kitchen for them."

The guard watched them warily as Kim and Isla switched to discussing the pros and cons of both rideshares.

A second guard jogged over to them. Beyond the gates, Isla spotted tiny headlights heading toward them.

"Barnwell, what are you doing? They're waiting at the house, and a car will be here soon to take her." The second guard was an older man in his forties and clearly the senior guard.

Isla asked, "Take who?"

Barnwell tried explaining, but his words were nothing more than hand gestures toward the locked door and at the two women, one glaring from the driver's seat and the other looking as if she wanted to run.

"I just wanted to return the keys. I said I'd leave them at the gate," Isla offered.

"Get back to the station and monitor the screens," the older guard said to Barnwell before redirecting his attention to her. "Yes, my apologies, Miss Thorne."

How he knew her last name was lost on her, and hearing him say it so easily threw Isla off.

"Miss Corrigan asked that you bring her belongings to the house. She'll meet you there."

Holland. That's right, Isla thought with relief. They had introduced themselves when they first met.

Kim whistled, restarting the car's ignition with gusto. "I should play numbers in the lotto, because what?" Exactly. Which was why Isla needed to play it cool and like getting inside was never in her plans.

Kim continued, "But we are in there. Hell, I just knew they were gonna turn us away faster than a hot flash at the country club's garden party."

The guard's face colored. "Not you, ma'am, just her."

Isla asked, "We can't just drive in and out, then? I'm already in this car."

He shook his head, his expression conveying his familiarity with doling out rejection and disappointment. "No, ma'am. No unapproved and unregistered cars on the premises." He flicked his gaze at Kim, then back to Isla. "Ma'am." His hand inched toward the door handle, prompting her.

A dark-silver sedan arrived and came to a stop inside the gate. Guard number two was much nicer. He offered Isla a smile as Kim unlocked the doors, clearly disappointed that she wouldn't get to see the famed estate up close and personal.

Isla gathered her things and stepped from the air-conditioning into the mugginess. "Look, I'm just dropping this off. Can't I just leave it with the person in the other car? Because how am I going to get back home, Mr. Groyer?" She sounded out the name written on his tag.

He stood straighter, and the smile he gave her went from polite respect to genuine kindness. Isla had learned from her father long ago that names were important. Referring to people, even those who served you, by their names let them know you saw them, because it was too easy for many to be unseen.

"They'll find accommodations for your return."

"I don't feel right about leaving her like this when that wasn't the plan." Kim spoke up, in a true mama-bear move that Isla found touching.

"We'll get her home safely, ma'am. You can turn around right here and have a safe drive back down and a good night, ma'am."

With that, Isla and the ever-protective Lyft driver, Kim, said their goodbyes and went their separate ways, with Isla heading to the waiting sedan, where the driver had already opened the door for her.

The other side of the gates was like entering a new world. They followed the road deeper onto the property, the guard gate and the rest of the world becoming faint behind her. The tree-lined road to the main house led a half a mile toward the actual property.

Lights from the inner grounds and sprawling $15 million mansion loomed ahead just behind the crest of the hill like sunrise, and even though Isla was not there just to return the keys she'd taken, she couldn't deny how beautiful the estate was. It wasn't like being on the tour buses in LA. Isla reminded herself that behind all this beauty was something bad at its core. That she was there to infiltrate the family. To insinuate herself into their good graces using whatever means necessary.

She didn't ask questions as she took in the scenery, committing even the most minor thing to memory. The driver didn't point out any landmarks as they drove past the staff quarters and maintenance buildings, then guest quarters—the buildings becoming more ornate and regal the closer they got to the main house, though all of it looked fancy to Isla—the small lake and personal golf course designed by Victor himself, perfectly manicured acres of lush green lawn and shaped bushes, trails where staff would transport any guests, staff, and family members in golf carts without making conversation as they drove, remaining as serious and wordless as Secret Service. But that was okay. Because Isla Thorne had gone further and quicker than she'd anticipated. What a stroke of luck. But her work wasn't nearly done.

She'd only made it inside.

CHAPTER TWELVE

Isla adjusted the strap of her bag again and rubbed her damp palms over her knees as the sleek sedan slowed while it wound along the long driveway and through another set of inner gates to the main house. She'd prepared herself for what she'd see if she made it in, but she still couldn't help the feeling of entering a whole other world. Her stomach churned with a mix of anxiety, curiosity, and anticipation. The beauty of the Corrigan property was undeniable. She looked out the window like a kid on her way to Disney World. Her eyes traced the gates that loomed in front of the car and began to open automatically, but Isla saw no guard station.

"How?" she marveled to herself because they hadn't spoken throughout the entire drive.

"Each registered vehicle has coded access that scans automatically when the car is in range," the driver explained, his eyes never leaving the road in front of them. "Similar to a gated community."

Unlike the new guards back at the perimeter gates, Isla's driver did not wear a name badge, so unless he volunteered his name, she would know him only as Mr. Driver. The car rumbled forward between more lines of trees that cast long, wavering shadows in the dimming light. Isla held her bag tighter. It was her thread to reality in this very unreal place.

As they approached, the estate's true scale came into view, and Isla couldn't pretend any chill. Better to get it out before she saw Holland or any of the other Corrigans, especially Myles. Isla wondered if he'd be there too.

The actual property sat on thirteen acres. The rest of the twenty-seven stretched in a circular radius around them, most of those areas remaining untouched.

The main house was illuminated with landscape lighting and surrounded by meticulous gardens. The cobblestone drive split into a circular driveway, and in its middle was a fountain with statues she couldn't make out just yet. The driveway was large enough to park dozens of vehicles but only had a few at the moment. Isla guessed these luxury cars were the private cars of family members, with a spare or two for drop-ins like her. She already spied Holland's BMW gleaming as the lights bounced off it.

The car slowed, and Isla's face was nearly pressed against the window as she caught her first real close-up glimpse of the King's Vinings stucco-and-stone mansion. According to Google, the design was a blend of French Normandy architecture and modern luxury. Its front was grand, and it extended out in symmetrical wings on either side, which she knew wrapped around to make a square with an inner courtyard and other amenities. That was just for the family. Outside the main home, there were a building for staff housing, guesthouses with their own pool, a golf course, and a lake on the farther regions of the property that fed into a creek in the outer community. But none of that cursory research had prepared Isla for seeing it up close and personal. She couldn't wait to tell Nat and maybe Miss Lydia all about this home of the ridiculously rich and pretty damn famous.

Before she knew it, the car door had opened, and the driver was waiting patiently for Isla to gather herself and get out. He didn't rush her, even looked ahead of him like he didn't notice how dumbstruck she was. He was used to this reaction and allowed her time to have it. Isla appreciated that. And this was only the outside. She didn't know how she was going to act when she saw the inside. If she was allowed past the front door. Who knew?

"Unbelievable," Isla muttered to herself, one foot firmly planted on the ground. She shook herself out of her stupor and got out, noticing the faint scent of flowers from the manicured hedges framing the driveway and along the mansion. The smell reminded her of the days in Daytona with Eden and Elise. And then again during a much sadder time, when only the two of them remained. Eden and Isla had sat on Eden's mother's lanai with glasses of lemonade in front of both, just like Elise would have served them, trying to enjoy the scent of Elise's meticulously tended garden, which in her absence was becoming less and less cared for.

Your mom has a real thing for gardens had been Isla's obvious observation one day.

Eden had replied, *You think? It's one of her most precious, beautiful things.*

But Eden was letting it go to waste. She had been changing since the death of her mother weeks ago. She was hardening, and the garden under the harsh Florida sun and heat was suffering for it.

Did I ever tell you where my name came from? After the Garden of Eden? Eden said after a long silence. *Yeah, my mom always said that when she found out about me it was the happiest moment of her life. And when I was born, I was the most beautiful thing she and my father had ever created. She wasn't very religious, but she remembered reading about this garden God created for the first man and woman. It was the most perfect place on earth. And she said I was the most perfect creation she'd ever made and would ever make. So she named me Eden. She said I was her Garden of Eden.* Eden half laughed, half cried, fingering the delicate locket chain her mother had never taken off until her last day. It matched the delicate bracelet with the tiny key that Eden also never took off. *Corny, huh?*

It wasn't corny at all. It was the most beautiful thing she had ever heard.

The memory took her up the steps, and the double doors flung open before she had a chance to register she'd walked up herself. She had been right. The outside was one thing; the inside, entirely another.

This was where traditional met modern, she thought as she was led in by one of the house staff.

Isla didn't have a chance to admire the high ceilings and extraordinary chandelier, or the impressive curved double staircases leading up to the family's living quarters. Expensive rugs with intricate designs softened the glass walls and reflective glass panels that gave a more sleek, edgier look. And the array of African and Black American artwork gave the home culture. This was unexpected, and Isla felt an immediate kinship, the African art reminding her of her father and his culture, which he'd tried hard to instill in her. But she couldn't afford to think of him, or what had happened to him, now.

She had come tonight for a clear reason, because returning Holland's keys served two purposes. The first was to connect with more of the family and find an opportunity to gain access to them. The second reason was to upload the Trojan horse malware so Rey could hitchhike into their computer system.

CHAPTER THIRTEEN

"Isla!" Holland squealed as she thundered down one of the long staircases. She launched herself at Isla as if she was five and not taller than Isla, younger, and full of more energy. Plus, she fenced, right? So the girl had power under her couture athleisure. She nearly knocked Isla over.

Isla froze, temporarily forgetting herself and nearly shoving the girl off in reflex. Isla wasn't a hugger. Or much of a toucher. But she let Holland do just that, and she awkwardly wrapped her arms around the young Corrigan.

"Hey there, Holland," she said hesitantly. She was muffled by Holland's shoulder. She gave her three pats to signal time to tap out and get off. Holland didn't seem to get the signal, so Isla gently wiggled some space for herself and pushed Holland off with as soft a touch as she could.

"You don't know how glad I am that you're here." Holland's words tumbled out in her usual rush, no different from the night before. "I didn't even realize I lost my ID. I was so focused on not getting in trouble for the car and with getting a new phone."

Holland had priorities, and losing something as important as her school ID and keys was apparently not one of them.

"I tried calling all day so I wouldn't just pop up unannounced and uninvited," Isla explained. "I'm sorry for the intrusion."

"Oh geez, don't apologize." Holland rolled her eyes. "You just don't understand how boring it can be here with all these adults. Everyone is always so uptight and serious looking. Like, drop a deuce and relax already."

Isla coughed to mask her shock and amusement. She hadn't thought prep school girls spoke like that, but she should have known better. What did Holland think Isla was? She reminded Holland that she was in fact an adult.

Holland giggled, covering her mouth with her hands. "Oh, I know you are. I mean the boring adults."

Isla only responded with an unsure smile. Well, that was good, at least. She wasn't boring.

Holland looped her arm through Isla's like they'd known each other for years instead of less than a day, and the act was equal parts sad and guilt-ridden for Isla. Not just because Isla wasn't there to be friends, but also because Holland seemed desperate for a friend and Isla couldn't be that, not under these pretenses.

With her free hand, Isla pulled out the lanyard with the keys and handed it over. Holland barely looked at it before tucking it in her jacket pocket.

"You're not going to check that everything is there?" Isla asked, frowning, as she let herself be led away.

Holland was confused, her ponytail swinging. "For what?"

Isla left it alone. Maybe then the pang of remorse at her deceit toward someone who'd taken a liking to her would subside. Isla used her awe as an excuse to stare and get the lay of the land. She'd already started clocking valuable information about how everything ran. How only the security guards and staff wore name tags, but the drivers, personal guards, and employees who worked with members of the house did not.

The staff member who'd let Isla in wore a navy blue uniform that looked freshly laundered and ironed, along with a black Apple Watch. The driver who'd brought Isla to the house had worn one, and Taylor,

Myles's person from the night before, had worn one too. This must be how they communicated around the estate.

An older, distinguished woman met them in the middle of the grand foyer. Isla stopped, staring at the floor. In the center of the foyer, beneath twelve large, thick square glass panels, was a scaled-down model of what had to be the expansive estate property.

The floor mosaic was a terrarium in the shape of the Corrigan property, covered in lush green sphagnum and vibrant plants, with ponds and streams. It was the breathtaking focal point of the home. Only when Holland giggled did Isla realize that she'd knelt down on the floor for a closer look.

Blushing, Isla quickly got to her feet, apologizing for her lack of decorum in front of this woman who wasn't Holland's mother. Isla knew well what Brooke Corrigan looked like.

"Don't worry," the woman said, "it happens to everyone. Even heads of state." She radiated an air of authority that told Isla she was someone important—not family, because she was dressed in a long, dark conservative skirt with a cream-colored blouse, but not regular staff either.

The woman Isla guessed to be in her late fifties studied Isla with TSA-level scrutiny, not averting her gaze like the other employees who scurried about like they had to constantly be on the go. Isla pretended not to notice the curious peeks at the new friend that Holland had brought home.

"That's Alice," Holland said of the younger woman who'd let them in. "And this is Mae. She's been working for my dad since before I was born. She's the real boss of the estate, but don't tell my mother."

Mae offered a hand to Isla. "The official title is *house manager*," she clarified. "I've heard plenty about you in the less than twenty-four hours this child has known you. You're all she's been able to talk about."

Isla dismissed the praise, swallowing the prick of guilt. When the truth came out, it was Holland Isla would feel most sorry toward. The first part of their plan, the infiltration of the Corrigan home, had worked. Now, Isla needed to make herself indispensable, figure out a reason to get them to allow her access to their home and them.

Holland dragged Isla through a maze of halls and rooms, naming the rooms as they passed: sitting rooms, plural; the kitchen the size of one in a hotel and just as equipped; the formal dining area large enough to seat twenty; an office—one of several, apparently—and on and on. Isla wasn't sure if she was in a family's home or a stadium.

They used one of the back stairwells to the second floor, which deposited them at the end of a hall Holland announced was basically hers. The first room they passed had a set of closed double doors that Holland said nothing about, instead pointing out the few guest rooms and common areas they passed after it.

Isla hadn't noticed until they came across another room, its double doors identical to the ones at the end of the hall. But one of its doors was open wide enough for Isla to glimpse that what Holland called a bedroom was more like a penthouse suite with plush pale-blue carpeting and white furniture. The room was a sky with clouds, and Isla wondered what it was like growing up in a place as luxurious as this.

The first room had to be a bedroom, like this one, but Holland had said nothing about it. As a matter of fact, Holland had pretended the room didn't exist, rushing them past. Isla glanced back at the room at the end of the hall, preparing to ask who owned that room, but Holland was already nearing the front of the hall, unaware Isla had fallen behind. Isla rushed to catch up.

Up until then, Holland had happily played tour guide, answering every question Isla had, and Isla had committed everything to memory as best she could. The home, of course, looked different from the blueprint Rey had been able to find in ways only he knew. They stopped at the beginning of Holland's hall. There Isla saw how it was one hall of several, each expanding out from the circular center like spokes on a wheel.

"My brothers are down that hall. Mother usually takes up residence there. Dad over there," Holland pointed out, leading them down one side toward the start of one of the main staircases. "They like their space."

They were at the double staircases Isla had barely noticed when she'd entered because she'd been distracted by the mosaic down below. She looked over the railing, taking the artwork in from above, appreciating it as it was supposed to be appreciated. She reluctantly pulled herself away when they were at the landing in between the two staircases and came face-to-face with the largest family portrait she had ever seen. For the second time, Isla stopped for a better look. She backed up, amazed at the power a mere portrait could exude.

The Corrigans immortalized. Victor seated front and center, with his usual look of dominance and arrogance as he leaned forward just a little in his chair, one hand planted on a knee and the other at his hip, as if preparing to make a deal, the slightest squint of one of his dark eyes, arrogance and dominance emanating from just a picture. Directly behind him stood his wife, Brooke. She had one hand placed on his shoulder and wore an assured smile like she knew all this was hers. Her elegant features were more pronounced with her poised demeanor, and the deep red of her lipstick exuded confidence and fight. She was adorned in diamonds. To her left and somewhat apart was the brother Isla had met the night before. He looked the same, detached and mildly hostile even in the portrait. His sharp, deep-brown eyes were observant and unreadable, just as they'd been the other night. His body language was odd, as he was facing the family but at a distance from them too. Isla bit her bottom lip, wondering what this family portrait was telling her about the relationships of its members.

On the other side of Brooke, the only Corrigan daughter stood close to her mother. Holland was a perfect blend of both of her parents. She was what Brooke and Victor would look like if they ever smiled like they meant it. Holland had already surpassed Brooke in height. Her hair was down to her shoulders, and she was the only one to look like she was trying to either scare or impress or inspire awe in whoever was looking at them. Last, Bennett stood right behind Holland, his runway-model features haughty and mischievous. He was certainly gorgeous, favoring his mother more than his father. Isla would have thought him an angel, but his arrogant smirk killed all that.

Isla had seen this portrait before in a past magazine spread about Brooke and her love of the exotic plants in her well-maintained greenhouse on the premises and her dedication to the Bennett & Corrigan Foundation, the philanthropic arm of the Corrigan Group.

"It's something, huh?" Holland asked, appearing beside Isla. "It was not fun posing for that. I think only my mother and brother enjoyed it."

"Myles?"

Holland snorted. "Hell no, Bennett. He likes the limelight."

"How old were you?"

Holland shrugged, thinking. "I think it was maybe nearly two years ago? I was turning sixteen."

That checked out. The magazine spread had come out late the previous year.

"It took my mother forever to get Dad to agree to it."

Isla finally tore her eyes away, refocusing on her surroundings and the way she also felt on top of the world from her perch at the top of the stairs, overlooking everything else. She laid her hands on the top of the banister, leaning over it to peer down before her. So this was what a little bit of power felt like.

"Why wouldn't he?"

Holland didn't answer, shrugging instead, and stepped away quickly. Isla noted Holland's sudden attitude shift. She was closing herself off. Seemed there were some things Holland wasn't willing to open up to her new bestie about.

"Come on," Holland said suddenly, her voice going higher and her spirits brightening back up. "Let's go." Isla was nearly pulled off her feet as Holland snatched her hand and pulled her away.

"Dad!"

Isla nearly suffered whiplash from jumping from the house tour to meeting the man himself. He was more imposing in person than on TV and in the photos. He was in deep conversation with another man, and the two of them stopped when interrupted. Holland introduced Isla to Victor Corrigan and Brian Dixon, his right-hand man and manager of operations.

All the months of preparation and waiting for the right moment had come to this. It would be her only shot. Her make or break, and she would have no other opportunity to make a lasting impression, good enough to get in, than this moment. A flash caught Isla's eyes when Dixon buttoned his suit jacket as he was acknowledging her. Victor's right-hand man was carrying, making Isla wonder what Victor Corrigan could be into that made his seemingly mild-mannered employee who gave off accountant vibes carry a concealed weapon. Even in the Corrigan home.

CHAPTER FOURTEEN

Holland took a few big steps toward her father. Isla followed behind with more measure. He glanced at Isla, his dark eyes assessing her in a single sweep, then moving back up to her face to study more intently. She tensed, wondering if she'd seen a glimmer of recognition in his appraisal. She readied herself for him to call her out and kick her out on her ass. But when his eyes cooled to the detached expectation of someone waiting to be told why this new person mattered, she relaxed.

Holland made the introductions. "This is my friend Isla. Isla, this is my dad, Victor Corrigan, and his right hand and go-to, Dixon."

"Good to meet you," Victor said politely enough, watching his daughter and her new friend with curiosity.

Dixon leaned toward his ear. "Miss Thorne is the young lady who assisted Holland last night when her car caught a flat. She helped Holland get home in a rideshare."

Victor's thick and commanding eyebrows rose nearly to his perfectly cut hairline. "Rideshare? When we have a fleet of cars and drivers?"

Holland rolled her eyes. "We've been over all this already, Dad. Earlier today when you went on and on about keeping one of the guys around and having my car checked out and not breaking phones and—"

Isla jumped in, not wanting an argument rehashed with her present. "It's my honor to meet you, Mr. Corrigan." She pretended not to see the way Victor and Dixon looked at each other in amusement. Had she laid it on too thick?

"What I mean is that you're very well known around here, and I guess all over. I mean, the Corrigan Group and all its subsidiaries and interests? Your company portfolio is massive and varied. You don't just stick to a certain type. Your asset management company. Commercial real estate like the shopping center in Los Angeles. You have a shipping company that coincides with the trucking company. Your research and development arm vets the ventures you're interested in taking over." She'd only named a few, though that already seemed like too much. Listing his whole portfolio too early would look too obvious, and she had to play this just right. "And the Bennett & Corrigan Foundation as well. Can't forget that. It's done phenomenal work."

Victor said, "You've done your homework. If only some of my employees did the same."

"I minored in international business and public relations, so the Corrigan Group business model is something the professors referenced often."

Victor looked to Dixon again with a raised eyebrow and a hint of amusement Isla wasn't sure was a good thing or bad. She wasn't easily moved, but Victor Corrigan was intimidating, and she could tell that when he wanted to be, he could even be terrifying.

"Did you know we are taught and referenced often at schools, Dixon?"

"I did not, sir."

Isla said, "You're making fun of me."

Victor was surprised, and for a split second, his guard dropped. Something softer and nostalgic slipped in when he looked at her. "You sound like . . ." He stopped himself, shaking off whatever had just come upon him. "No one's called me to come speak at one of their classes. Not even UVA. You'd think they'd ask a local."

Dixon asked, "Do you want me to tell them to extend you an invitation to speak?" There was a hint of a tease.

Holland rolled her eyes. "Like you'd ever agree to chatting up a bunch of college kids. You're not the most chatty outside the boardroom, and the students would probably annoy you."

Isla was surprised at Holland's frankness in front of company. She watched Victor for his reaction, expecting him to have a volcanic-size eruption because of the short fuse and no-nonsense attitude people said he had. He didn't meet her expectations, laughing as if Holland had delivered the funniest line. It caught Isla off guard because she hadn't found one photo of him where he was anything but serious. It must be Holland who brought out his softer side, something Isla hadn't thought he had, not if he was the unfair ogre Eden had made him out to be. Maybe he was different with his employees than with family. Maybe that was why the image Eden had created and the man Isla observed now with his daughter were starkly different.

Holland said, "Well, it's true. You don't have the patience to sit around and answer a bunch of college kids' questions, so you'd be intolerable. Dixon, back me up."

The three of them looked as Victor's second weighed his words.

"Dixon," Victor warned teasingly.

Dixon replied, "I would say Holland is accurate in her analysis of your behavior if asked to speak with students. And you have received many offers to speak, be interviewed, or be the subject of a thesis and so forth. We just don't push them up to you."

Victor grunted like he was unsure if he liked that. "How do you know I wouldn't do it if you didn't ask?"

Dixon, with all the seriousness in the world, replied, "Because I know you, sir."

"At any rate, still let me know. I value education. Even if I say no a hundred times, I want to know what's coming in. One day I may say yes."

Dixon nodded, instruction received, but his expression said he had no intention of following through with that. Dixon probably knew Victor way better than he knew himself.

Victor's attention was back on Holland, who was catching him up about the wallet and Isla bringing it. Isla only added a few responses to his questions, feeling the weight of his judgment even in his brief moments of levity.

"Good Samaritan times two," he said, his tone back to cursory politeness. It wasn't his daughter he was speaking to but a stranger who'd appeared in his relative orbit twice. "Sorry for your trouble."

Isla brushed it off. "Wasn't any," she lied. It was plenty. All day waiting until the right time. The nearly hour-long drive back up the big-ass hill. The even longer ride it would take to get back down and to her temporary housing, just to hope there would be another opportunity for her to get in and stay in. The only person who seemed to want Isla around was Holland, and she wasn't sure that was enough.

They were interrupted by the faint jingle of jewelry approaching as Brooke Corrigan entered. The quick click of her designer heels on the marble floor spoke of impatience and annoyance. She was deep in conversation with a tall man with dark hair and piercing blue eyes that looked like they didn't miss a thing. Isla didn't need to search her memory too deeply to connect a name with the face. The guy was Jackson Russell, maybe mid-fifties and the lawyer for the Bennett & Corrigan Foundation, which Brooke had founded twenty years ago.

From what Isla remembered, Jackson had started working for Brooke's father's company right after college, until she married Victor at twenty-three and joined the Corrigan Group. Then he worked under the Corrigan Group, quickly rising up the ranks and eventually becoming the lawyer for the Bennett & Corrigan Foundation, which Brooke had established as a new arm beneath the corporation. Jackson pulled out a pack of gum, slid out a foiled piece, and popped it in after he'd unwrapped it.

"Darling," Brooke said to Victor. She moved close to him but not enough to touch. "Donna and I were trying to plan for the Man of the Year award you're getting soon. If I could have some time to go over the details with you?"

Victor said, "Check my schedule with Dixon and Mae to see if something's open. I don't want a big event. They really can just mail the plaque, or whatever they're giving me, and we can avoid wasting money on a party to show it off."

Brooke let out a deep sigh, and in it, Isla could sense there was a lot going on. Even his wife had to make an appointment just to talk. Isla nearly felt bad for her until Brooke's attention landed on her, her eyes narrowing in a way Isla didn't particularly like.

"You're the one who assisted Holland," she stated through a polite smile that didn't reach her eyes. Her tone dripped with skepticism. "How'd you come to be here?"

Isla kept her expression neutral, but registered the rude question as well. She was about to answer when Victor spoke up for her, informing his wife that Holland had left her keys and Isla had been gracious enough to return them. They should be thankful. It was a clear warning from him to her to be nice.

Brooke swallowed down whatever comment she wanted to make, her gaze flickering to Holland, then back to Isla. She managed another thin smile. "Very kind of you to return her keys." She turned back to Holland. "Did you check that you have everything?"

Holland blinked back her surprise, stammering, "Mother?"

"Nothing's missing, right? Donna, maybe we should have the locks changed, just in case. You understand, of course," Brooke said, like she wasn't making implications toward Isla.

Isla reined in her irritation, refusing to show she'd been affected by the slight in any way. She wouldn't give Brooke Corrigan the satisfaction.

"It would be pretty dumb of me to make a copy of someone's keys, hand deliver them to the owner in her heavily guarded home where everyone can identify me, and then break into her dorm afterward," Isla said.

Brooke's manicured fingers curled, and Isla believed that if she could, the woman would kick her out on her ass. She looked like she wanted to rip Isla's face off. She was about to say something back when one of the kitchen staff called for dinner.

"Holland, honey, why don't you call for a car to take Isla home? It's getting late, and I'm sure she has things to do."

Isla shook her head. "No, not really." The way Isla had timed it, she'd hoped to arrive around this time, and most appreciative people would offer a meal to a stranger who had gone out of her way for one of theirs.

Holland was back at her side, arm looping through Isla's. She announced that Isla would stay for dinner. "That's fine with you, right, Dad? You'll stay right, Isla?"

Isla agreed quickly, much to Brooke's chagrin. She wasn't sure how she'd offended Brooke so quickly or why Brooke was acting so territorial.

"Whatever you want, Holl," Victor said, already down the hall with Dixon a step behind. Myles had appeared and quietly watched the scene play out, taking in all the players. Not the players—one. Isla. She'd have to be careful with him.

Again, Brooke looked like she was about to say more and override Victor, now that he was out of earshot, but Jackson coughed. When she glanced at him, he gave the slightest headshake, and she retreated.

"Guess I'll have someone set the table," Brooke said curtly, though Isla was sure there were always extra settings for moments like this. Surely Donna, Dixon, and Jackson were going to join, since they'd made no moves to dismiss themselves when dinner was called.

Still, Isla didn't miss the undercurrent of anger in Brooke's voice as she instructed another staff member to ensure there were enough settings.

Brooke watched each movement her child made with hawkish eyes. Then those eyes slid over to Jackson, and he shook his head ever so slightly. Isla kept her thoughts to herself, processing it all. Had anyone else noticed how Brooke looked to Jackson for assistance or backup instead of her husband? Or how distracted and detached Victor was as they all moved to the dining room?

A bigger person would read the room and bow out of dinner. However, Isla was not a bigger person. Despite Brooke's obvious and odd hostility, and the ease with which Victor had suddenly lost interest in all of them, and the small comforting smile that Jackson offered Isla as a way of easing his employer's behavior.

He mouthed, *Sorry.*

Isla tensed. It felt like an odd action for Jackson. He was probably trying to be helpful, but it came across as throwing shade at the person he was supposed to be loyal to. It was as if he were trying to get into Isla's good graces and hedge his bets for some game Isla wasn't yet aware of.

Or maybe, Isla, the man was just trying to make you feel better.

It could just be that too.

Dinner would be awkward but a gold mine of information. It was an opportunity to ingratiate herself while piecing together the family dynamics during a time when they should be enjoying each other's company. A chance to observe them up close and determine what her next steps would be. Isla would play her role well—polite, graceful, appreciative, awestruck as if she were at Disney World, with occasional flickers of curiosity at the brooding oldest brother across from her.

Myles remained at his perch against the wall, watching everything go down, hands in the pockets of his tailored charcoal slacks. His matching vest hinted that beneath was evidence of fastidious workouts and bench presses.

Not the time, Isla.

But it might have to be. She might have to play up a crush on one of the brothers to keep them off her scent, to cozy up and dig around for any proof of Eden.

Jackson couldn't apologize away Brooke's unprovoked hostility toward Isla. For some reason she didn't want Isla there, sharing space with them. Clearly she thought Isla wasn't worthy. Maybe she felt Isla was some kind of threat gunning for Victor or one of his sons. Isla absolutely had ulterior motives, but it wasn't for the reasons Brooke Corrigan thought.

CHAPTER FIFTEEN

The Corrigan mansion had settled into quiet, but Isla sat cross-legged in the middle of a king-size bed, fully clothed, wide awake, and trying to unravel the Rubik's Cube of emotions and thoughts she was having. She should have been elated at the fact that her plan to get in among the Corrigans had worked so well and so quickly. She should have been bursting with the possibilities of where and with whom to begin her search for any clues about Eden's disappearance, or how to go about getting the family one-on-one to press them about any knowledge they might have about her or her mother.

Instead, Isla was watching every shadow crossing overhead in the beautiful guest room, letting her imagination run childishly wild. She couldn't help it. Being in new homes and in unfamiliar beds had always been an issue for her since the age of fourteen from living in different group homes before she'd met Eden and they'd decided to leave Daytona.

For one thing, Isla never knew how long she'd have a particular bed, so she never let herself get too comfortable with it. Second, the room and home always had new sounds and smells, creaks and groans that made her imagination spiral out to the point she was often still huddling under her blankets the next morning because she thought she'd seen something in the shadows.

When Isla had made it to LA after the long cross-country bus ride, she'd connected with Charli, grabbing a room in Charli's halfway house. Eventually, Isla got used to being there and in that space. The scary shadows became familiar and like family. But Isla's disconcertion with new spaces and places always remained, creeping up at the most inopportune times. The Slip 'N Slide feeling in her stomach that she could only attribute to homesickness or just feeling displaced and out of place . . . that feeling had never gone away.

She tried to take her mind off her unease. Isla was actually surprised she was in the main house. Brooke, once she'd begrudgingly agreed to Holland's suggestion that it was too late for Isla to be trekking back to her apartment, had originally intended to have Isla stay in one of the guesthouses on the property. But Holland once again came through like a champ, reminding her mother that it was just one night. Why take Isla all the way out there when they had plenty of free rooms right here in the house? Isla chimed in, first to decline the offer, of course. Because she had no intention of intruding, and she'd already horned in on their family dinner, and that was enough, and, well, she didn't have a change of clothes or toiletries, so she really should be heading back home, but thanks for dinner.

But upon Holland's insistence, and with no protest from Victor, Brooke gave in. Isla promised she wouldn't be a bother and would leave first thing. She wouldn't even need breakfast. She might have been laying it on a little too thick, but it was intentional if Isla was going to come across as an unaware, awestruck new friend.

Isla made sure to avoid Myles's indifferent and oddly irritating gaze as he tried to figure out this new person who had been sprung on them, and by Holland, no less. Isla worried that Myles might have recognized her from the two-second run-in at the elevators of Crabtree and Elliott six months ago. But she'd kept out of full sight, and he couldn't have remembered seeing someone so insignificant for two seconds.

That dinner show had ended two hours ago. Now Isla waited in her room. One of a few empty ones in Holland's section of the gigantic home, with its nineteen bedrooms alone. She had a good understanding of the house's layout. There were no cameras in the house because Victor valued privacy in his home and didn't want to feel Big Brother was watching, even if Big Brother was paid by him. She was in the clear there, but there were locked rooms and a very good security system, with silent alarms for areas like his office and other rooms she assumed were offices of the main family if they worked out of the house.

"The outside property," Rey had said, "has eyes everywhere, so remember that. Anywhere you walk, eyes are watching. I'll be able to get a better feel for it once you put in the drive and get me the Wi-Fi. They'll have the one they use and a guest one. They may have a third Wi-Fi for business—I won't know until you're there to pull up the available networks."

In her hurry to get here, she hadn't thought to bring her laptop—dumb move—because she hadn't thought she'd get in far enough to have dinner and spend the night. She'd told Rey so on the burner phone she used for communication with him on job so that the Corrigans' security wouldn't have a way to access her phone and her contacts when she signed in to their system.

"Do you have guest Wi-Fi?" Isla asked before Holland unwillingly left her room for the night after Isla had feigned exhaustion.

Holland considered the question. "Yeah, but I don't know what it is. I'll just share our main one with you." Holland pulled out her new phone, and in seconds, Isla had a "Holland wants to share a password" notification pop up on her screen. Main Wi-Fi.

The mansion, as beautiful and picturesque as it was, felt like a gilded cage to Isla—a place anyone would feel lucky to live in, let alone be invited to stay for the night. Isla seemed to be the only person who noticed that while they were the epitome of sophistication and high class, of an idyllic conglomerate family, beautiful and chic, they were more than a little cold to each other. It wasn't like Isla was an expert on family dynamics, though, since it had always been just her and her dad until he died.

She was an expert at nonnuclear families, making connections and family with found members rather than blood, and she knew family dinners were important, but in this family, the connectivity was absent. She observed them as she ate. The pockets of various conversation that Holland weaved in and out of. The hostile glares from Brooke, as if Isla were intruding upon her territory—and in a way, Isla supposed she was. The way Victor batted away any conversation either Brooke or Jackson attempted to strike, forcing them to give up. Isla pretended not to notice the cool appraisals from Myles and wondered whether it meant he shared the same feelings as Brooke, disliking her and thinking she was beneath him because she wasn't their kind or if there were other thoughts Myles had swirling around in that mind of his. The only person missing on this chessboard was Bennett.

"You know how hard Bennett works for the company around the clock. But I'm relieved to at least have Myles join us for dinner." Brooke's voice was saccharine, though she was being anything but. The conversations dimmed as her voice rose above the rest. "It's good that at least one of you can be with the family while the other continues to be so dedicated to keeping the company up and running. We're lucky you have so much time to spend with us."

Isla shivered at the drop in temperature. She was confused because Brooke came across like she didn't like her oldest son. For the first time, she felt bad for Myles as she watched him concentrate on the wine he sipped. The sibling rivalry had to be intense. The temperature dropped. The only person who didn't seem to care was Victor, who continued to enjoy his rib eye and speak quietly to Brian Dixon beside him, though Victor was listening to every word being said at the table.

Each moment that passed before Myles attempted to acknowledge Brooke was agony, until Isla could no longer stand the deafening silence. "I for one am grateful that your son was able to hang out tonight with the family. Better to be a loyal son to the family than out there running the streets doing . . . whatever." Isla gave them a conspiratorial look.

"Son?" Brooke wasn't sure what she wanted to respond to first.

Holland leaned in, whispering, "Myles is my mother's stepson from Dad's first wife."

Isla's mouth dropped dramatically. Her hand flew to cover it, tapping it lightly in faux admonishment of her mix-up. "Whoops." She didn't miss Victor looking away in amusement or Dixon's uncomfortable cough. Or the way both Jackson and Myles considered her—one with intrigue, the other like she hadn't done him any favors.

CHAPTER SIXTEEN

Myles waited a beat and shifted to Brooke, locking in on her. If Brooke hadn't been trying to provoke her stepson and tear him down in front of Victor while building her own son up, Isla might have felt sorry for her being the subject of Myles's withering glare, cold enough to make Isla uncomfortable.

The corners of Myles's dark eyes crinkled as if his private thoughts amused him. "I mean, Bennett has a lot to clean up right now at the Foundation, what with the loss of an employee at the LA office under Bennett's leadership and all. I truly aspire to be more like my overachieving little brother when I grow up." Then Myles raised his wineglass in mock salute before downing its contents, his expression remaining the same all the while.

Isla choked on the sip of water she'd drunk from the crystal goblet to keep from laughing and immediately wished she'd had more control of herself, because Brooke's attention snapped to her with such ferocity—she was the easiest mark to pick on.

"It's not like Bennett's the only one missing from dinner," Holland began, her voice suddenly shaky as staff swept in to switch out dinner for dessert, a raspberry torte that looked delicious. Isla couldn't wait to dig into it, but Holland wasn't finished.

"I don't know why all of a sudden, but I wish Edie were here." She peeked over at Isla, whose spoon stopped midway to her torte when she heard her name. "Maybe it's because Isla's here like Edie used to be." Holland sounded so wistful, so sad.

There was an audible gasp from Brooke and a clatter as Jackson's fork hit his plate. The mood at the table shifted from an impending duel between gladiators to a chilling frost.

Even Victor set the glass of water he was drinking on the table with a hard thud. Emotions filtered over his face as he breathed, and everyone waited for his next move.

Holland's hand slammed over her mouth like she was stanching the flow of any more errant words. Her eyes were wide and instantly apologetic. The name, this Edie, had the power to send the room to subzero degrees. Holland attempted to apologize, but the words died on her lips as she looked helplessly from him to her mother and then to Myles, who could only offer a wry smile in an attempt to make his sister feel a little better.

What if? Isla sat back in her seat, observing the group with keen attention, registering every stiff gesture and every tense expression they wore.

This Edie . . . the name sounded coincidentally, strangely, too much like Eden. What were the chances?

Victor stood, his chair scraping hard against the floor. He tossed his linen napkin on the table. Isla chanced a look. He was unreadable, a stony mask replacing all the unrestrained emotion from a second ago. He rumbled out something about needing to make some overseas calls, an obvious excuse to leave early, and no one stopped him. He left without another word, with Dixon close in step. He regarded his daughter as if she had wounded him. The air was thicker than the torte Isla wasn't allowed to finish because the staff swooped in to take her plate too quickly, sensing correctly that dinner was over.

In the aftermath Isla felt like she was somehow to blame. Even though Holland had uttered a name that seemed to be stricken from the Corrigan annals and could stop their world on its axis. Was this Edie her Eden? Had she been Holland's friend, a playmate, driven away because her mother had been fired by Victor Corrigan? Was the reason Victor didn't want her name mentioned that something bad had happened and everyone knew the answers except the outsider who wasn't even supposed to be there?

CHAPTER SEVENTEEN

Holland's insistence that after dinner Isla might as well stay the night, and Isla's too-quick agreement, was now a decision she regretted. The idea that she was already steps closer to finding out something had been too enticing. When reality had begun to hit as she sat in an unfamiliar room, surrounded by unfamiliar people, some of whom didn't care for her, it had been unnerving. But she'd asked for this, hadn't she? So did she have the right to feel as freaked out as she was? Nat and Rey had warned her about this. Nat had said that what Isla was stepping into wasn't improv and she wasn't on a stage.

"This is real life," Nat had said. "And Rey and I won't be around to jump in if things go left. Be careful."

Maybe staying the night on her first night wasn't being careful.

The mansion had settled into an uneasy quiet, with everyone in their respective places.

Even if she wanted to, she didn't know how to leave, and she couldn't just leave, and that realization set off waves of panic that forced her off the bed. She downed the bottle of water that had been sitting on a tray on the nightstand next to her, but she needed more than that. She needed air, too, and maybe if she got a feel for her surroundings on her own terms, she'd feel more in control. Holland was one thing, but Victor was the key. He was her whole reason for coming back to this damn town.

She was out of her room and heading toward the front of the hall, trying to recall the home's schematics she'd committed to memory. She passed Holland's room, hearing low music coming from the other side of the doors. She crossed into another hall, not remembering whose hall it might be. Isla seemed to walk for ages, hoping she'd be able to get back to hers without getting lost.

She rounded another corner, passing artwork and decor she knew cost more than she'd ever make in her lifetime. She was now in another area of the expansive home that faced the back, she guessed, from the number of corners she'd turned. This hall was designed differently, like all the others. Each branch, or wing, was different according to the resident's preference. This section was familiar, furnished in more traditional, simplistic, understated decor, but Isla had no doubt everything she was seeing cost thousands at least.

Isla was doing what came naturally to her, a survival instinct kicking in as it did whenever she had to know where she was and how to get around. She'd done the same thing after she had arrived at Union Station, riding around LA by bus until she knew the city and its surroundings like the back of her hand.

Isla recalled how the mere mention of this Edie had ended dinner, driving Victor out and causing Brooke to shoot daggers at her as if she had been the one to speak this infamous name.

Edie. It pressed heavily on her chest. The next question followed. Could she really be Eden, or was it wishful thinking and too much of a coincidence?

Isla determined she had entered Victor's hall. It was only nine, and she was surprised at how quiet the mansion was. She wondered where the staff was. Surely everyone hadn't already retired for the night. She was intending to not push her luck and to head back to her room when familiar voices stopped her. The hall was empty, so she pressed herself against the wall, edging closer to the cracked door with a beam of light spilling through.

"I'm sorry I brought her up again, Dad," Holland was saying. "It's just sometimes I really miss her, and I wish you'd find her and tell her you're sorry. Let her come back. I don't think it's right, us erasing her like this. Not speaking of her, like she doesn't exist."

"I'm not erasing her, Holland." Victor's tone was sharp. He paused, then readjusted. "It's better for all of us, less confusing for you, if we go on as if without her. Edie's decided she doesn't want to be here with us. Let's let her stay gone."

Isla's chest tightened.

Holland insisted. "But she's not gone, Dad. You said she went abroad and doesn't want all the Corrigan hype. I get it. But if you promise her you'll keep her out of the limelight, maybe she'll come back. Whatever you did, just say sorry and bring her back."

"Stop it," Victor barked, his voice reverberating down the hall. "You don't think I want to? You don't think I've tried? She doesn't want to be found, and I have to respect her wishes. This life . . . is not what she wanted for herself. Shouldn't we respect that and wait until she's ready to return?"

"If Edie's mother was alive, she'd want you to find Edie no matter what. If I hadn't gotten sick and my mother hadn't freaked out, Edie wouldn't have left in the first place. You shouldn't have let her leave." Holland's voice hitched. Isla felt intrusive, listening to their private conversation about personal matters. Their pain locked her up. She considered leaving. It felt wrong to listen in on such a personal conversation, but something kept Isla rooted to her spot.

There was a long stretch of silence and then a couple of sniffles. When Victor resumed speaking, his tone was softer. "One day she'll come home, okay, Holl? But for now keep up your practice and your classes. I expect perfect scores from your matches. And let's talk less about Edie and her mother. It makes your mother uneasy."

Isla wasn't sure what she was hearing. Why would anything about this Edie or her mother make Brooke Corrigan uneasy? What had really happened with these people? Isla's own unease continued to grow.

"We don't speak of them because my mother can't tolerate even the memory of them? It's been years, Dad. Who cares?" Holland was angry now.

"I care that we have peace in this house, Holl. You said I know how your mother can be? So should you. I don't want to fight with her. There is too much going on with the companies, things I'm looking into. Not to mention you have school. Your fall break is about over. You'll head back, giving your studies and fencing your full attention."

"Whatever, Dad. You just want me out of your hair so you don't have to worry about me. Just like with my mother, the only people you care about are the ones who will take over when you step down. Me, I already know you hope I get a husband with another company you can have. I get it. If it was me who'd left the family, you wouldn't bother looking for me either."

"Holl, that's not true," Victor argued, sounding shocked and hurt. "That's not what I—"

He was cut off by a rush of noise. Isla barely had time to hide herself around a corner before Holland rushed past, sniffling angrily. Isla waited until Holland's footsteps faded and the silence returned.

CHAPTER EIGHTEEN

Isla remained in her hiding area in case Victor decided to follow his daughter to console her and explain what he *had* meant to say. When he didn't, she chanced a look, the need to see what was going on too strong for her to stay tucked away in a corner. She edged to the doorway, where Holland had left the door wide open when she stormed off.

He was seated at his desk, head in his hands. Isla crouched low to the ground, watching him from outside, hesitant to move on, feeling that there was something more she was supposed to see. She found Victor Corrigan impossible to turn away from. His normally composed demeanor was gone, replaced by the same rawness and vulnerability she had seen in his daughter.

Victor sighed deeply, picking up a small key. He knelt out of sight, and the next thing Isla heard was a drawer opening. When he stood again, he was holding a small wooden box. He placed it on his desk and stood there unmoving, deciding whether to open it. He opened it after one last push. When he did, he stared down at its contents without moving or taking anything from it. He just looked.

"Edie," he sighed, his voice growing thick with emotion, "how'd it all come to this? Why didn't you just come to me? Why didn't you tell me about your mother?"

Despite her purpose coming here, she felt intrusive and confused. The heartless tycoon he displayed in public was not the man she was witnessing now. This man was very much the opposite. Isla felt like a voyeur watching Victor at his most vulnerable, but whatever that was in the box making him so emotional had piqued her interest. He gathered himself quickly, snapped the lid of the box shut, put it back where he'd gotten it from, and began moving toward the door. Isla rushed back to her hiding place. If she tried to make a break down the hall, he'd see her, and she'd have no excuse for being there. She squeezed in just as Victor emerged from his study.

Victor closed the door behind him, lingering in front of it, deep in thought. Isla pressed back farther against the wall, willing her heart to stop beating so loudly she swore he'd be able to hear it. She held her breath, hoping the shadows held her in their cloak of invisibility. Isla didn't breathe again until his footsteps faded away and the hall was clear.

She straightened, her knees unreliable from her previous position. She turned to go back the way she came before her luck ran out and someone caught her where she wasn't supposed to be. But the secret box encouraged her to push her luck a little bit more.

She expected the door of a mogul to be locked, but it wasn't. Maybe he thought no one would dare trespass in his own home. Or maybe he'd forgotten after the blowup he'd had with Holland. Isla didn't ponder it long. She turned the knob and entered the study, lit only by the moonlight shining in and the one desk lamp he'd left on. She closed the door behind her just in case someone passed by. Time was short, and she hoofed it across the large study to the desk he'd just vacated.

Luck was with Isla again, because in Victor's haste to leave, he'd pushed the drawer closed, but he hadn't ensured it had closed all the way, which meant the lock hadn't engaged, leaving the drawer open a crack. The contents of that drawer called to her like a siren.

She opened it, doing just as Victor had done and pulling the box from it. She didn't sit in the chair. She stayed there on the floor, tracing the intricately carved lines on the box. The edges of the box were worn from too much handling. She opened the box.

Her two worlds collided.

She saw the photograph first and picked it up as if it were made of glass and might shatter upon touch. She recognized a younger version of the girl she knew as Eden. Eden—Edie, as Holland had called her—smiled back at her. Her arm was slung happily around Victor's neck. They were outside, amid an oasis of bright flowers and lush greenery. They both looked younger, and happier than Isla had ever seen either of them be.

Isla blinked away tears. She clamped a hand over her mouth to stifle the grief and pain from spilling out. Eden was a Corrigan? Isla set the photo aside, a glint of metal catching her eye. Her breath caught at the bracelet, the one with a tiny key to the locket chain Eden's mother owned and had given to Eden before she died. Eden had worn her bracelet and her mother's chain ever since.

In the time Isla had known Eden, the bracelet had never left her wrist. But here it was, in a box in Victor's study. She took out the last item: a letter-size envelope addressed to Victor, with Eden's name and a return address that was Eden and Elise's home.

Carefully, she opened the letter.

> Dad,
> Mom's dead and I blame you. She died because you broke her heart, and for that, I'll never forgive you. You never really cared about us, but I get it. My mom wasn't prestigious like Myles's mom, or some perfectly cultured beauty like Bennett and Hol's. My mom was just a lowly assistant who you were too ashamed to be with in the open. You pretended it was for her own good, made her leave, and then you forced me out too. We were your dirty little secret—never good enough for your world or your Corrigan name. You bulldoze over everything and anyone, using them up until you don't need them anymore. But I won't let you do that to me. The most important thing to you is your name, your money, your power. And I don't want any of it.

> Not your money or your name or your indifference. Mom is gone and I may be alone, but I'm not coming back. Not ever. I'm going to live my life as I want. Away from all of you. If there is nothing else you do for me, do this . . . Leave me alone. Consider me dead because that is what you are to me. Dead.
>
> Edie

Isla's hands trembled as she read and then reread the letter, trying to understand the words that made no sense. She stared at the photos, her mind numb. Eden was *Edie Corrigan.* These people were Eden's family. No wonder Eden had always been so evasive about her past. The stories she'd told about her mom being fired by some horrible rich family who treated her mother like shit had been half truths at best. Eden hadn't been some powerless, nameless nobody to the Corrigans. Eden was one of them.

The weight of the discovery was too much, and her limbs felt heavy. Her best friend, who was like a sister to her and whom Isla had trusted implicitly—had trusted with her life—had been lying to her the entire time. But why? Why go to such lengths to hide her true identity? Why couldn't Isla know who Eden really was? Did Eden think Isla would only want to be friends with her because she was rich? Or was Isla nothing but a joke to Eden, someone to yank around while she played rich-girl games with her billionaire father? To make promises that they'd be sisters against the world only to up and disappear without so much as an explanation or goodbye?

Where was Eden's letter to her?

She was angry. Was hurt and betrayed by the person she'd trusted the most. Her mind screamed with questions, but through all the tornado of emotions expanding like a hot-air balloon, a thought pinpricked, releasing her rage in a thin stream of air.

Isla picked up the bracelet and held it against her fingers so it caught in the dim light. Eden had been wearing this bracelet the night she disappeared. Isla was sure of it.

Eden would have never separated it from the matching chain her mother had given her.

The letter. Isla picked up the envelope and flipped it over to look at the postmark, which said "Daytona" with a date stamped weeks after she and Eden had left Daytona together. Weeks after they'd arrived in Charlottesville and Isla had been forced to leave alone.

Could Eden had doubled back after they'd separated? But why? There was nothing left in Daytona for Eden—that was the reason why she'd wanted to start fresh in LA. The house was being sold. No other family. None of it matched the Eden Isla knew. Eden had never let on that she was an heiress. She and her mother had lived in a little home, and Eden had never sounded like the Corrigans were her family. Or maybe Isla had just misunderstood what Eden had been saying. Nothing was adding up.

The realization crept over her like the cold dead. Someone had sent this letter. Someone had sent Victor Eden's bracelet, which meant that *that* someone had to know where Eden was. And whether she was alive or . . . Isla couldn't finish the thought.

Isla put everything back as she had found it. She even left the drawer cracked open, as Victor had by accident. She left the study and somehow found her way back to her room without incident. If she fell asleep that night, Isla couldn't say. But one thing was certain, the story she'd thought she knew about Eden—now Eden Corrigan, heiress to the Corrigan empire—and her disappearance was even more twisted than she had thought. Because if the Corrigans did have something to do with her disappearance, they hadn't gotten rid of some random girl—they'd gotten rid of one of their own.

Which begged the question: What was a secret big enough for them to go to those lengths?

There was a reason why Eden had hidden such a significant part of her identity. Isla was even more determined than ever to uncover it and blow up the world that Victor Corrigan had built.

And now that she was here, she wouldn't leave until she had answers. No matter what it cost her.

CHAPTER NINETEEN

Ten Years Ago

"I am so sorry about the way things turned out. I should have stayed there. I knew what I was getting into, and I shouldn't have hoped for any more than he could give. It was me who changed and messed everything up."

"That's ridiculous," Eden mumbled. Then, but in the brighter, more chipper voice that both she and Isla had conditioned themselves to speak in because they wanted Elise to only have happiness and light in her life, what was left of it, she said, "Oh, Mom, don't worry. We don't need my father. I'll make it well enough on my own and get a beautiful house where you can have your own room that lets out onto the patio and backyard, where you will keep your garden just like you do here."

They both knew that Elise wouldn't make it long enough to see the end of the month, much less years down the road, with enough money to buy a home they could live in.

"And Isla too," Elise wheezed through labored breaths, a wave of pain coming up on her. Isla's throat closed up. Elise was thinking about her. At this time.

Elise flopped a hand to wave away the attempt of the hospice care nurse to give her morphine. She wanted to be lucid in this moment. She had something to say, and maybe Isla shouldn't be here for it. After all, she was only a friend. Not family, though Elise and Eden had never made her feel anything but—Isla a parentless ward of the state about to age out of the system with nothing but a couple thousand saved from her job at McDonald's.

Isla's throat hurt from the emotion she tried to stifle. She tried to do as she'd always done, detach herself from anything that felt like emotion. Keep a poker face. Show that nothing and no one could faze her. Because that was the only way to survive the heartaches of child services—the hope of adoption or fostering in a system that was overworked, understaffed, and criminally underpaid. It was the only way to survive the initial moments of hope that maybe a family would take you in and see your worth and want you to be a part of theirs, only for them to choose a younger, cuter kid or send you back to the group homes. Group homes that could be bad or good or bearable. One had been pretty bad. Two too good to be true. The rest of them bearable once she came to the realization that no one there was bad, or out to get her. Everyone—staff and kids alike—was just trying to survive. They were all in it together.

She had been hardened for so long, resigning herself to a life alone. She'd made herself okay with that. In a couple of years, she'd age out of the system, and Florida's child services would give her a couple of bucks and well-wishes on a productive life. They'd mean well, but they wouldn't be able to do much for her. So yeah, she was set to be on her own, but Eden and her mother had managed to crack through and wiggle their way in enough for her to care about someone else again. They had given her hope that maybe being alone in life wasn't going to be her fate.

But they all had secrets. She had her own regrets. Her own guilt from inaction and fear, which had eaten away at her since she was eleven.

"We can be the Three Musketeers. Or Amigas. She doesn't have anyone, and when I go, you need someone in your corner, because this world . . . that family . . ."

Isla finally allowed herself to admit that she liked being part of a family and never wanted them to go, even though Elise's illness was the first thing Eden had told her about two years ago when they'd first met.

~

"My mom's sick and is probably going to die from it."

Isla had been sweeping the dining area, part of her job as cashier when they were in between afternoon and dinner rushes. Weekends were all-day work. Anything was better than counting minutes at the home or fussing with one of the girls about who had used whose makeup, transactions of which she was never a part. She used her own and expected no one to touch hers. Again, the point was to not make relationships too deep when one of them could be adopted, reunified with their parents, transferred for space, or aged out, a.k.a. just gone. So why bother?

Anyway, when Eden said that about her mother, Isla slowly stopped sweeping. What did she want Isla to say? Did she want one of those lines people said that didn't really mean shit? *Condolences for your loss* and *prayers for your family*, which Isla supposed people meant even if they couldn't really empathize. What did the grieving really want in that moment when they'd said their loved one was gone?

Isla pushed the broom head back and forth. "My dad ended up in the river because he was too nice to say no and caught the heat for something he didn't know about. And as for my mom, well, a baby wasn't a good look for her, so . . ." She shrugged. "Who knows where she is now or even *if* she is now, you know what I mean?"

That sparked life in Eden, and she watched Isla like she was alive and not the zombie she'd just been.

"Death sucks." Isla swept again, this time with a little shrug as she did it. "You know?"

"Thank you," Eden said, shaking her head like she couldn't believe Isla's audacity. She'd been expecting those true but empty lines of sympathy. She hadn't been expecting the truth. Isla had taken a chance with a surprise attack, and she wasn't sure why. She didn't know Eden from a hole in the wall. She'd seen her around, sure, at the counter or in the drive-through. They'd never talked. And Eden had never dined in until today. Isla had shocked her into forgetting temporarily about impending death with a death that had already happened, as if she were saying, "See, I got nothing and am still sweeping."

They say *the rest was history*. But for Isla and Eden, it was also a beginning.

~

Hearing Elise struggle opened up a wound Isla had barely begun to heal—the death of her dad and her life as a ward of the state. She was pissed at the world, at God, at fate for letting someone as good as Elise die sad and still thinking about someone from her past. It was one thing to see someone you cared about leave and never come back. It was worse to actually watch them die. Isla couldn't take the room, or how warm it was in there because Elise was always cold. She couldn't take the smell of impending death, both sour and sweet, anymore. She had to step out, abandoning Eden for the first time ever. She'd have done anything for Eden. But this thing, watching Elise die, was one thing she couldn't do. She couldn't be the strength for either of them, for all her tough talk. All she could do was run away.

She didn't go far, though. Just right outside the door, where at least a wall could be between them. Where she could still be there without being *in* there.

Elise said, "You are the best gift he could have given me. You know that? My Garden of Eden."

Eden sniffed. "Some gift. I can't even help you."

"But you can. And you were my perfect baby girl. The best thing. You are loved, Eden. By me. By him. Go back, okay? That thing that happened. Forget it all. Sell this house. Use the money I've left you.

Do all you want to do, but let the past go, okay? Forgive yourself. Take this." There was movement, and Eden protesting, "I can't take that."

"Please. So I'll always be with you. My chain to your bracelet, a matching pair. It shows he loves you. Please talk to him."

"Sure, Mama" was Eden's reply. She sounded light and chipper on the outside. But Isla could tell it was all bullshit. Whoever Eden was supposed to forgive and talk to, she wouldn't. Whoever had caused her and her mother to be here, she'd never let go. Isla knew that because Eden had told her over and over. But she'd tell her mother anything she wanted to hear. Elise had lived a life of hurt and regret. And Eden would take on her mother's pain in the deepest grudge, which Isla would never understand.

"All right, then," Elise said. Isla took the cue to peek in on them, watching as Eden gripped her mother's hands.

Elise's sigh was deep and tired. "You should go now. I want to rest. Just put my pills on the stand in case the pain comes, but I have the IV to help too."

The machine would only dispense pain medication every few hours so that Elise could never administer too much.

The thought made Isla cold inside and out.

Eden hesitated before finally coming out of her mother's room. She gingerly touched the gold chain that was now around her neck. Her mother had always worn it, just as Eden had always worn the bracelet on her wrist. Neither of them had ever been without these pieces until now.

Eden and Isla stayed up in the living room with the TV on, though Isla couldn't have told you what was on. They fell asleep to the methodic beeping from the machines in Elise's room. Then, at 2 a.m., something woke Isla. A light breeze moved across them where they sat with *Murder, She Wrote*, one of Elise's favorite old shows, playing in the background. The breeze was light as a feather, grazing the tips of the hairs on Isla's skin, making them rise. And just as it had come in, it was gone, like the scent of perfume lingering behind. She and Eden looked at each other, not needing to say what they both knew because the machines had started beeping.

Elise found a way to administer too much.

CHAPTER TWENTY

Present Day

Panic was what chased Isla awake the following morning in an unfamiliar room with all its piped-in hotel-fragrance scents. She'd slept a fitful sleep full of memories she hadn't wanted to think about.

It took a moment for her mind to get itself in order and begin to recognize where she was. The Corrigan estate. She nodded, confirming this was correct. The next thought was why she was there. To infiltrate this family in order to find Eden.

Eden.

The revelation slammed into her as if she'd been punched in the chest. She even placed her hand over her rib cage to help steady the heart that was rapidly beating harder and faster. Their Edie Corrigan—the elusive sister who was supposedly living abroad, practically banned from being mentioned by the family—was her Eden Galloway. Her best friend. The friend she'd mourned all these years. The one who'd vanished into the dark that night after telling her to hang tight and that she'd be back. Only, she never did come back.

All Isla wanted to do was get away from this place and regroup. Go back to the tiny motel where life wasn't like living under a microscope. A place she controlled. She had to go now. She'd think of another way in when she was in her space, but for now, she needed out. She lurched out of bed and searched for her clothes. She found them on the bench at the end of the bed, folded and placed beside a white retail bag from a high-end store. In the bag was a fresh set of clothes.

Isla shot up on full alert, searching for danger and where the person still lurked. She stepped away from the bench as if there was an improvised explosive device in it about to go off. When it didn't, she paced the floor, nibbling on a nail, deep in thought. When exactly had the bag materialized and the clothes, which she'd thrown carelessly all over the floor as she'd rushed into the room after Eden's true identity blew up her world, been folded nice and neat? Alarmed, she looked at the door. Someone had been in her room while she slept. She put her hand over her mouth at the realization that she hadn't even realized when she was not alone.

She went to the door and turned the handle. It was locked. Then how? She couldn't remember locking it when she'd returned and apparently slept the sleep of the dead. Despite her unease, Isla manage to shower and dress in the new clothes that happened to be her size. After placing her old clothes in the bag, she left the guest room. She checked Holland's room and found it empty, so she went ahead downstairs, nodding at the various staff who passed her along the way. She reached where the double stairs connected and was once again in the presence of that majestic family portrait that had a whole new meaning for her now. Before, it had held intrigue and allure. Now Isla felt it held terrible secrets and maybe monsters behind the glamour of the perfect family. The secret of why one of the members wasn't in the portrait, glaring down at her like the others. Erased as if she didn't exist anywhere except Victor's study.

One of the house staff happened to be passing as Isla took the last step, and Isla asked where she could find a ride back to town. When the young woman gave Isla an annoyed look for being interrupted, Isla nearly called her on it but checked herself. The regular Isla would have given the girl a taste of her own medicine, but she was not supposed to be regular Isla. She was a guest and had better stay in character at all times, like Rey had repeatedly drilled into her.

"I apologize for interrupting whatever you were on your way to do. It was my first night here, and I'm feeling a little out of place and not sure how to get back home, Mandy." She read the gold-plated name badge. "I'm hoping you could help me?" she asked, hoping friendliness would encourage their helpfulness.

Mandy or any one of them could come in handy. Besides, one of Isla's past jobs had been a brief stint in hotel housekeeping, a thankless job that overworked and underpaid. Working here was probably a better gig if you learned the ways of the family quickly. Isla wagered Mandy and the rest of the house staff knew more about the individual Corrigans than the actual family knew. She'd become their friends if she could.

The house staff would know everything if they could be made to talk.

A blush spread across the sprinkle of freckles on the young woman's face. She was dressed in fitted navy slacks and a matching top. Dark attire similar to that of waitstaff, to blend into the background, not seen, not heard. She looked around nervously, as if checking to see if anyone was around to catch her blatant frustration toward a guest. Then she dropped her eyes demurely in apology for her initial reaction. Isla could understand. Mandy was probably on a directive, and Isla was unknowingly delaying her progress. She nodded, answering Isla's question.

"Is anyone up yet? Holland, maybe?" Isla didn't care to run into anyone else if she could avoid it.

"Yes, ma'am—"

That word again. She was only twenty-six. She wasn't nearly a ma'am yet. But Isla couldn't fault the staff for doing what they were trained to do.

"—Miss Holland is in the breakfast veranda with her brothers."

"Oh." Isla's hope for a quick getaway fizzled. The way she was feeling, she didn't think she could put up a front for much longer, not after last night. Rey had warned that pretending would be hard. She'd thought she could handle it. It was all to find out what had happened to Eden, but learning Eden's true identity had been too much.

"They're waiting for you there. Just go down this hall halfway and make a left. Would you like me to . . ." She looked at Isla expectantly.

Isla shook her head quickly. "No, I can find my way. Thanks."

But Mandy was already gone after another quick nod, on her way without insisting she take Isla there. Anyone else might have been offended at Mandy's hasty getaway. Not Isla.

Holland was waiting near the kitchen in the breakfast veranda, where delicious smells of cooked sausage, bacon, and eggs wafted to Isla's nose. Her stomach growled aggressively, and she slammed a hand over it to stifle its noise. Luckily, the kitchen sounds and various other chatter ensured that no one but Isla heard her stomach betray her.

Holland looked distracted from the usual lighthearted self that she'd shown Isla so far. She was probably still upset over her late-night argument with her father, Isla thought. Remembering the conversation herself and the connection she now shared with the Corrigans twisted the screw already lodged firmly in her chest. Holland wore her fencing training gear, with the suspenders of her fencing pants hanging down at her sides, the corners of her mouth turned down. She was fidgeting with her foil mask.

"Morning," Isla greeted her, forcing cheeriness when she felt anything but. "I was hoping to get a ride back to town. Can I call a rideshare or taxi? I've got some things I need to take care of."

Holland asked, "Why so soon? Did something happen? Or someone?" She sent a suspicious glare at her brother Bennett, the one Isla hadn't officially met yet. He was too busy taking Isla in to notice his sister's accusatory gaze right away and did a double take when he caught Holland's eye.

"Why are you looking at me?"

"Because I know you," Holland said accusingly.

He held his hands up to proclaim his innocence. "This is the first time I've seen her. I just got in this morning."

Holland said, "What's wrong?"

Isla wavered. "I woke up to a message this morning saying I was let go from my job. It was probationary, and I missed a job last night, so they don't need my services anymore." Just the way she and Rey had intended. "I wasn't even scheduled to work last night, but oh well. I need to figure out what I'm going to do."

"Oh no." Holland was genuinely upset. She'd never have to know the joy and pain of getting and losing a job.

"Care for breakfast, Miss Isla?" one of the kitchen staff asked. Isla jumped. She'd materialized from nowhere at Isla's side. This lady was older and didn't bother calling her *ma'am*, which Isla was happy about. She gave Isla a reassuring smile, which made Isla hate herself more for her lie.

CHAPTER TWENTY-ONE

Isla struggled to think of a way out now that she'd laid the trap. Another freaking meal. This family seemed to find importance in eating together, but if it was going to be anything like last night's dinner, she wasn't sure she could sit through another. "I should really get back, and I don't want to impose more than I have already."

They looked at her as if she were speaking another language.

"More like the imposition was put on you." Bennett spoke up with a trace of sincerity. "Since you got fired trying to do a good deed for my little sis. But everybody's got to eat, right? And there's no rush for you anymore, seeing as how you're unemployed." An easy smile spread across his face as he took her in.

Myles hadn't looked up from his reading when she'd entered, hadn't acknowledged her or anyone else's existence until now, when he glanced up at his brother with disdain while Holland called Bennett an asshole.

"Am I lying?" Bennett shrugged, making no attempt to hide how his eyes blatantly moved over Isla from head to toe. "Have a seat."

Bennett was different, more relaxed than the stiff and straitlaced older brother who sat across from him, engrossed in the papers nestled within the leatherbound portfolio he held. While Myles came across like she irritated him and had regarded her both times they'd interacted like an annoying little gnat buzzing around unwanted, Bennett, on the other hand, studied her audaciously, and Isla, while far from a prude or shy about her curves and her beauty, still felt overly exposed beneath Bennett's perusal of her person.

There was a spark in Holland. She said, "You should eat first."

Bennett nodded at his sister's suggestion, urging Isla along with a hand. "So, new friend, *who* are you?"

The way he said *who* was a vibe Isla recognized instantly. He probably used this on all the women just before he got them in his bed. He looked the part, too, and if Isla had to admit it, his suaveness nearly got her as she eased into her seat between Holland and Myles.

She matched him, refusing to let him think he'd make her like another of his toys he'd play with and toss. Because Isla could recognize Bennett Corrigan. His boyish features, sharp and striking, which made him look innocent enough and like you'd want to bask in his sunshine all day long. The twinkle in his eyes presented him as jovial and flirty enough, but there was something hidden behind the grin as he waited for her next move.

"Isla Thorne," she finally answered.

He watched her with appreciation.

"Isla, did you sleep well? Nice outfit," Holland said, offering Isla a glass and pouring pinkish juice into it. "Guava juice," she replied to Isla's raised eyebrows.

Isla glanced down at the new clothes she'd found waiting for her in her room. White formfitting capris with a strapped, white, fitted crop top dotted with yellow flowers and tiny green leaves, along with an oversize off-the-shoulder sweater.

"Thanks, Holland. You have great taste. But you didn't need to lend me your stuff. I could have changed when I got back."

"That's not from me," Holland answered breezily, taking a bite of her buttered toast.

"Your mom, then." Though Isla couldn't believe someone who showed such disdain for her would be that considerate.

Bennett snorted into his cup of coffee. Even the young lady replenishing their table, though the food there was barely touched, fought to keep her face blank.

"Myles had all of it ordered and delivered early this morning. One of the staff put it in your room. I think it was all supposed to be discreet, but . . ." Holland shrugged.

Myles. A totally unexpected move from the guy who remained in the same position she'd found him in, one leg crossed over the other, reading intently. He didn't twitch an eyebrow when Holland outed him.

"My big brother is so thoughtful, isn't he?" Bennett teased, his light-brown eyes dancing. "Always thinking of all the minor details no one else ever thinks of. He's got you country-club chic."

Isla frowned at the dig disguised as a compliment; she was unsure who it was meant for. Myles didn't bother replying; instead, he flipped the page in his portfolio, but Isla could see the red flush beneath his nails from his fingers digging into the leather.

Two could play this game.

"He's very thoughtful. A great host." Isla beamed at Myles, who still wouldn't acknowledge any of them. "Thank you for the clothes, Myles. You have *spectacular* taste, and are very thoughtful. A girl could get used to that kind of consideration."

She gushed more than necessary just to knock Bennett down a peg or two from whatever trip he was on.

The glacier finally dislodged, and Myles cast a quick look at her from the corner of his eye, appraising her quickly. She thought she caught a trickle of amusement until a succession of approaching footsteps with accompanying voices drifted from the hall; the loudest Isla recognized as being Brooke. Whatever warmth had been there snapped back shut inside his vault.

"No big deal," Myles said flatly, his ice settling back in, frustrating the hell out of her.

Isla ignored the twinge of disappointment that followed his dismissive words, but she bottled that for later and forced herself to remain smiling as Brooke, Victor, and Dixon entered. Myles placed his reading material on the table, waiting for what would come next, as it always did.

CHAPTER TWENTY-TWO

Brooke's voice filled the kitchen. "I don't know why you're so against this, Victor. You have been the perfect candidate for Man of the Year for years. Now you're finally getting recognition for all your work. You should be enjoying this," Brooke said, her tone insistent, with threads of frustration woven in. "All they want is to do an in-depth profile of you—an entire spread, Victor! They don't dedicate so much space to someone often. It'll be great—your life, your accomplishments, your family. Back me up on this, Jackson, Dixon," she said as Jackson entered the house through the kitchen door.

Jackson poured himself coffee, glancing over his shoulder at the trio. "What are we talking about?"

"The Man of the Year profile they want to do on him," Brooke said, looking over each of the people at the table. "But he won't let the reporter in to write the article." Her eyes landed on Isla, narrowing. "Still here," Brooke said in a low voice that everyone heard. Two words that said many things.

"I think it's a great idea," Bennett interjected. "Let them have an inside peek at the man behind the enterprise."

Jackson joined in. "He's right. The board would love it. Great publicity."

Dixon said nothing because his face said it all. He was with Victor on this.

Victor accepted a cup of coffee from a staff member. "Thank you," he said, acknowledging her, and she melted back into obscurity while the conversation resumed.

"I've already told you—I am too busy." His response was curt, as if they'd been down this road before. "*Invasive* doesn't begin to cover what you're describing. My life isn't fodder for some glossy puff piece for an award I never asked for."

"People don't usually ask for awards, Dad," Holland said cheekily. "They just earn them."

Victor shot her a look that said she'd betrayed him, but his annoyance with her wasn't genuine. "You know what I mean."

"It's not just about you. It's about the family," Brooke snapped, standing next to Jackson as if they were about to have a face-off in the breakfast veranda. "This isn't just your legacy, you know. It's all of ours. Our philanthropic branch. Our outreach programs. The companies and subsidiaries. The millions in endowments and charitable offerings we've given. Your kids." She motioned in their general direction. "If you won't do it for yourself." Her voice dipped into sweet and pleasing as she sidled up to her husband and touched the lapel of his suit with her glossy red polished fingernail, smoothing it intimately as if they were the only two people in the room.

The room quieted. Bennett looked down at his pristine shoes and grinned, knowing his mother well, and Jackson regarded the scene from his perch against a far wall with cool blue eyes. He set his cup of coffee aside and pulled out a green pack of gum, then slipped a piece out and popped the stick in his mouth.

Victor watched her as if she were a specimen and he was wondering what she would do next to get what she wanted. His lips held a hint of a smile Isla couldn't discern. Nat could learn something here, because these people were the epitome of performance at its finest.

"For you?" Victor asked, his head bowed low toward her to make up for the difference of his six feet in height to her five-four. Victor sighed. "My dear," he began. Then he stepped back so that her hand hung in the air and the trance was broken. "Your priorities are showing again. This isn't about the family, or me. It's about you wanting the spotlight again. Have at it. But leave me out of it."

Brooke retracted her hand, but before she could retort, before Isla could even think about what she was saying or doing, Isla was out of her seat and saying, "I think Mrs. Corrigan is right about you doing this spread."

Eyes were on Isla and her plastered-on smile. She hoped none of them could hear the thundering of the rapid heartbeats that pounded in her ears. When opportunity arose, you had to jump on it. She balled her hands into fists at her sides so no one would see her fingers trembling. The air was charged with tension.

Brooke faced her, astounded at Isla's audacity. The whole room was, but where everyone else was rendered speechless, Brooke Corrigan had plenty to say.

"This is none of your concern, young lady. I think by now you've been well thanked for helping Holland out, but that doesn't mean you can insert yourself into business that's not yours." Brooke said it calmly, with an undercurrent of malice. "I think it's time for you to head back to your world now." She raised an eyebrow high. She looked like a goddess. The evil kind that ripped and shredded people to pieces.

Your world.

Because Isla's world was less than Brooke's. Brooke believed everyone who wasn't as rich and polished as she was, who didn't live in an oversize mansion near the top of a mountain where they could rule like gods over this small town, who didn't lunch at the country club, play pickleball, and screw their tennis trainers, was beneath her. Isla's world indeed.

"You're absolutely right," Isla said brightly, effervescent charm spewing forth to mask her true emotions, contempt and anger at

Brooke's line of delineation between the worlds of the haves and have-nots. Isla's nails dug so deeply into her palms they'd leave crescent shapes for the rest of the day to serve as a reminder. "I have probably overstayed my welcome."

"No, Isla, that's not it," Holland tried to intercede. She addressed her mother. "Mother, I made Isla stay for breakfast. She was trying to leave because she just got word she was let go from her job."

Isla waved her away. This fight was not Holland's to make. She'd used Holland enough, and it was time to sink or swim on her own.

"It's okay, Holland. Your mother's right. You have been gracious enough to have me here, Mrs. Corrigan. Really. Truly. Thank you from the bottom of my heart." If Brooke took her sentiment as disingenuous, that was exactly how Isla meant all of them to take it.

Isla ignored Bennett's snicker and Jackson's smirk as the room waited for Brooke to take Isla's head off, or for Dixon to whisper to Victor that they really needed to get on the road.

She sensed Holland's anxiety growing—and, on Isla's right, Myles's feigned indifference giving way to tension emanating from him. He was just as interested in the end result of her play as everyone else in the room.

Isla turned her attention to Victor, because he was who mattered, not the shrew about to erupt next to him. "It'll be a win-win for you, Mr. Corrigan, if you get the right person to talk to. That's all I was trying to say. I'm sorry for overstepping."

Brooke said, "And yet you continue to do it."

Victor was interested. "How so?"

"You are all Corrigans and Corrigan adjacent." She gestured at Jackson and Dixon. "But I'm from the rest of the world, and I can tell you without a doubt that the world would love to know about the man behind all of this. You can control what they know about you in a way that you'll be comfortable with, and I'm sure this transparency will go over well with your board members and possible business ventures. When I was on the UCLA newspaper staff, telling a story the right way was imperative. And trust, you know? There's got to be trust between the subject and the interviewer. I'm saying Mrs. Corrigan has a point, and not many people know about the man behind the empire. People want to know the secret of how you became so successful. For what it's worth." She took a breath because it was now or never, and if he said no, she'd have to figure out the truth from the outside in. "I'm not a big-time reporter for a huge magazine. I've only ever written for my school newspaper and am trying to build up my writing credits enough so that reputable organizations will give me a chance. I could write about you. If you'd let me."

Brooke scoffed. "Oh please." She looked away, shaking her head, moving to stand beside Jackson, who laid a placating hand on her arm.

Victor ignored his wife, his consideration of Isla unwavering. "You?"

She shrugged. "Like Holland said, I'm out of a job, so I'm available, don't have an agenda to make you look bad, and will have a solid writing sample to use during interviews."

He continued to watch her, his expression unreadable, demeanor stern and intimidating. She saw him in Myles and knew where Myles had learned it from. The seconds stretched, and she hoped she hadn't overplayed her hand by jumping in. Even though she continued to stand her ground, Isla's mind whirred, trying to recall plan B, or C, or even D if this failed. She second-guessed herself. Waited for him to say something.

The corner of his mouth twitched in spite of himself, and he let out a wry laugh of disbelief. He looked at Dixon as if asking for input, but Dixon had none to give, only pointing at his watch.

"We need to go. We have to helicopter to DC and are already behind schedule."

Victor looked around the room, finally taking in who else was there. "Holl, you have practice today?"

Isla backed up a few steps to give the man space to take stock of the room. He seemed to be closing the book on her and her offer, his interest in her depleted.

Holland waved her face mask in the air with a wide already-on-it smile.

He pointed at her. "No slacking when you head back to school and the team, right? I want wins from you." Holland agreed.

Bennett plucked an apple from the center plate and was about to leave with a suave wave, straightening his tailored suit, when his father stopped him in his tracks. "We'll need to discuss the LA office, Bennett," Victor said curtly. "All that business in LA? I need to know what's being done. I need to know how that happened."

Isla held her breath, tension mounting in the air. Matthew Leonard.

CHAPTER TWENTY-THREE

Bennett's winning grin crumbled. He looked like a deer caught in headlights as he looked at Jackson and his mother, then focused on his father. He straightened to his full height, two inches taller than his father.

"It's under control," he replied. "I've got it handled."

Victor inclined his head as he considered his son. "Do you? Well, I'd like to know how you're handling it that won't be another massive screwup like it was six months ago. Find out how it happened. Understand?"

Bennett's face tightened, and his complexion flushed red. Isla wouldn't have believed someone as cocky as Bennett had been earlier was capable of shame, but there it was for all of them to see.

"Yes, sir." He looked away, burning a hole in their imported flooring with his glare.

If Victor noticed that he'd embarrassed his younger son, he didn't show it, or didn't care. He moved to the next item on his internal list, leaving Isla still standing with her question unanswered.

"Myles, I'll need you with me for those DC meetings," Victor said.

Myles finally came to life by looking up from the table or floor, wherever he'd been directing his attention, to meet his father's expectant gaze. Myles's eyes flickered to his brother, whose displeasure and embarrassment were palpable, filling the room with their noxiousness. His full, dark brows knit together as he navigated a minefield, before he said, "I don't mind hanging back today. Maybe Bennett could join you in DC? I have a couple of calls and meetings with Special Projects that really need my attention today."

Now, *that* was interesting. When everyone else—save Holland—was vying so hard for Victor's time and attention, Myles was not. Isla thought the two brothers were in competition to be the next in line, and that meant never saying no to their father and always being accessible when he called for them. A glance around the room reflected Isla's exact thoughts. They all looked at Myles, taken aback. Except Victor and Bennett.

Bennett's nostrils flared, and Isla half expected smoke to come out. The muscles in Bennett's mouth flexed, his lips pinched, and his body grew taut as if he were barely restraining himself. Victor let out a deep sigh, glancing briefly at the ceiling as if asking why him.

Bennett spun toward Myles, about to speak, but their mother, sensing things were about to get worse, artfully stepped in front of him, breaking their line of vision.

"I actually need Bennett's advisement on some things with the Foundation." She offered a defeated smile to Victor and a tolerant one to Myles. "So he'll be too busy as well. But thank you, Myles. You're always so kind," she finished placatingly, her large jewelry glittering around her neck.

Myles considered her with his head inclined. Then his brother. Finally, he dipped his head, accepting Brooke's save of her son instead of addressing Bennett directly.

"Let's get you a car home," Jackson offered to Isla. He was the only one to remember that she was still there.

Isla barely acknowledged what he'd said. Was competition all this family knew? Which son would be the next ruler of the empire? Would they have to duel it out to determine the winner, and was that really what Victor wanted? She'd assumed he would be more traditional, choosing his firstborn per the traditional rule that magnate families typically believed in—primogeniture, with the firstborn heir (initially male but now modernized) inheriting everything, whether they had earned it or not.

However, Victor hadn't automatically made Myles his successor, which gave Bennett as much chance as Myles to assume the position. It could be because Myles had gone into the air force right after graduating high school and served for eight years before returning to the family business. His absence had cleared the way for Bennett to take the spotlight and become the golden child who was being groomed for the position. If Eden had been here, what part would she have played in the succession struggle? Or had she been taken out before she even got started? Isla would ask Holland about Edie the next chance she had, away from all of them, where Holland might feel more comfortable talking about the sister she clearly missed. But the question Isla couldn't stop asking was why Eden hadn't said these people were her family. Or had Isla just misinterpreted what Eden had been saying? She was losing confidence in her memory.

There was a reason why Myles had opted to go into the military after graduating, disrupting his father's plans. There was a reason Myles didn't fight Bennett when it came to company matters, opting to let his younger brother have his way. Myles preferred to remain the silent observer in the background. Isla didn't buy it. There was more to Myles's silence than just being apathetic about the family business.

And Eden had left, too, and was bitter and angry because of it. What had been the difference? Isla thought about a famous line in Eden's favorite play, *Hamlet*.

"Something is rotten in the state of Denmark."

Something most definitely was.

Only this wasn't Denmark in the 1600s. It was the Corrigan estate in the twenty-first century.

Victor turned to leave, with Dixon a step behind. Myles was already up and following behind them, his portfolio tucked under his arm as he slipped his hands in the pockets of his charcoal slacks. He accepted his matching jacket from one of the staff, who anticipated his needs before he even spoke them.

Isla's shoulders sagged in defeat. Victor hadn't outright rejected her, but he hadn't agreed either. Instead, he'd changed the subject, which was the end of that conversation and the end of the sliver of hope she'd had for getting in easy. She didn't know how else she could get access to the family now, especially with Holland returning to school soon. Maybe she could work at the country club they frequented. She hadn't even been able to get to a computer to put in Rey's malware. The whole thing had been unsuccessful—she'd learned a lot but achieved nothing. Now what?

She didn't have long to wallow in self-pity, because the mischievous Bennett had turned into something else. When he thought no one was watching, Bennett glared at Victor and Myles as they left together. Anger and jealousy were a dangerous combination, and they simmered just below his surface. His fists balled at his sides so tightly, the veins bulged. He looked as if he were about to blow. His eyes were hard and directed so much hate at them it was toxic, and Isla wanted to get as far away from it as she could. He took a firm step to follow them, rage rippling over his face.

CHAPTER TWENTY-FOUR

Isla closed the door behind her and leaned against it for a moment to catch her breath. Since she'd arrived at the Corrigan estate the evening before, everything had been a whirlwind. She was glad to leave them, even if her earlier play had failed. Having one of the estate's drivers return her to the rented studio apartment she'd been staying at for the past six weeks was like coming back to the real world. When she thought the car wasn't lurking around with instructions to watch her, Isla walked the couple of blocks to the Red Roof Inn, where it had all begun for her.

The apartment was what they could know about her. However, this motel room was what she had to keep hidden. It was where she'd come to reconnect with the past, the memories of the time she'd spent in this very room serving as a reminder of why she'd returned to this town. Now, she needed to regroup and think of a contingency plan since shooting her shot with Victor Corrigan and failing miserably. Her phone buzzed.

Pack your bags and see you soon!!!

Isla was confused and read the words again, which did not compute. She was still trying to figure it out when a call interrupted, the number unknown. She answered, preparing to hang up if it was spam.

The voice boomed from the line as loudly as if he were in the room. "Isla, I'll give you a shot with this article my wife wants me to do," Victor said.

"But Mrs. Corrigan doesn't seem to like me at all or want me around."

"Is she the subject of this damnable piece, or am I? You let me worry about my wife. She'll see it my way." Isla didn't believe anyone could see anything Victor wanted any other way than his.

She was stunned. "Why me? Like I said, I don't have much experience."

"Experience starts from somewhere, right? You said this could be what you need to get in the door. Plus, you got balls, and even though my wife has not welcomed you with open arms, that doesn't deter you." He sighed, the humor leaving his tone. "Plus, you remind me of someone I haven't seen in a while."

Isla's heartbeat doubled. "Who might that be?"

There was a long pause, and without the rush of air in the background, she'd have thought he had hung up. "Just don't get in my way. My schedule is tight, and I don't know when I'll be available for you, but I expect the piece to be done prior to the awards. Just be available when Dixon calls. Sound good?"

He didn't wait for her response, disconnecting the call instead.

She gave Victor the reply he hadn't waited to hear. "Sounds great."

She went over to the tiny nightstand and pulled it away from the wall, turning it as she ran the tips of her fingers on the back of it. Her fingers stopped when they glided over the grooves in the wood. She turned it some more until she saw them. She traced the letters scratched roughly into the cheap wood with the tip of the metal emery board from her nail clippers.

EG & IT

WERE HERE

She let out a deep breath, refusing to allow the tears that wanted to spill to have their way. She couldn't believe it had worked. She'd gone off plan, by gut, and it was such a sloppy scheme—built on a lot of chance, luck, and the goodwill of people—it shouldn't have worked. But she'd done it.

CHAPTER TWENTY-FIVE

She surveyed the room, images of where Eden had been and where she had been weaving in and out of her memory as they had for the past six weeks Isla had been in town. The room smelled faintly of old fabric and stale cigarette smoke, though the **No Smoking** sign was very conspicuous on the door. The thin curtains barely kept the sunlight from creeping in and would be of little help if one needed the cocoon of darkness to sleep. There were two double beds with matching bedding that was an upgrade from ten years ago. A small desk set up for someone to work at, but it was lit with not-so-great light, next to a decent-sized flat-screen TV (another upgrade).

She twisted the lock above the doorknob, then flipped the top lock over the latch. She made sure to catch housekeeping every couple of days before they came in to change the towels and tidy the room. And the **Do Not Disturb** sign was always swinging from the doorknob on the other side because no one needed to walk in and see what she had inside.

The sliding glass doors leading to the balcony were across the room, to her right. The closet was to her left, and the tiny bathroom was as well. Isla went to the closet and slid its door open, revealing weeks of hard work—a sprawling collage of photos, sticky notes, and taped printouts covering most of the good-sized wall, with room to grow.

She sat on the floor, propped against the bed, as she looked at the back wall of the closet, where photos of the Corrigan family were strategically positioned, their closest associates extending from the Corrigan they were connected with. She looked at Eden's photo—her best friend's wide smile, from years ago, before her mother's death, when she was happier—away from all the others while Isla had tried to figure out Eden's connection to the family. Now Isla knew, and it left her with more questions than she'd had before.

Before, Isla had always wondered what Eden's connection to this family was. What had drawn her to Charlottesville when it was not their final destination? Then, Isla had believed Eden wanted to speak with the Corrigans about her mother's dismissal from her job as Mr. Corrigan's assistant. Isla had wrongly assumed Eden was angry at the family for firing Elise and was looking to blame them for how Eden and her mother had ended up, even her mother getting cancer. But it wasn't a wrongful dismissal. It was a freaking love triangle. Elise had a child with Victor who would have been about Bennett's age. An affair, getting both women pregnant at the same time? Very messy and definitely a reason why Brooke and Victor would have wanted this dirty secret gone.

That couldn't be it. Eden had told Isla she'd come to live with her mother after living with her father up until then. But she'd left it at that. Eden had always been vague, and Isla had respected her privacy. In Isla's world, every kid had had stories they weren't ready to share. Then, what had made Eden suddenly leave the estate after living there all her life—her mother's illness? And what had angered Eden so much that after two years she still wanted to confront the Corrigans? Had it been bad enough for them to get rid of her?

Isla inched closer to the closet. She took Eden's photo from its location and repositioned it with the rest of the Corrigan offspring in chronological order from youngest to oldest. Holland. Eden. Bennett. Myles. She considered them all for a long time, along with the small stickies, color-coded and assigned to specific family members, and her careful notes on each.

A Post-it beside Brooke's photo read, *Runs B&C Foundation, philanthropic, PR and marketing savvy.* She took that sticky and added, *Manipulative, nasty piece of work, classist & obsessed with the image of wealth and perfection. No fan of Myles.*

Isla didn't have to guess why. Brooke suffered from the classic and fabled evil-stepmother syndrome. She wanted her own children prioritized above any previous or other children her husband had. She'd do anything for Bennett because he was cultivated in her image. He was a son and was a perfect candidate for succession. He was also just as hungry as Brooke was. Holland was something different, Isla mused. More like Eden—sensitive, genuine.

Victor: *CEO—larger than life. How far will he go to protect TCG?*

Myles and Bennett had their own sections with the areas of the family business they oversaw, photos, and notes like *Left for military—why? Won't fight Bennett. Why?* These were for Myles. And for Bennett: *Set up Leonard? Erratic. Resentful. Jealous. Charming.* All that after knowing him ten minutes. Bennett thought he wasn't, but he was an open book. A separate corner of the map held Leonard's obituary and a question mark connecting Bennett to it.

She'd nearly forgotten. She went back to Myles and scribbled, *Jackass, rude AF.* But then she remembered: *Bought me clothes in right size. Very observant.*

That was kind of nice of him, she hated to admit. He was always watching. She'd have to be careful with him. She trailed her fingers over the stickies with their corresponding photos.

Jackson: *Foundation lawyer, but with whom does his allegiance lie? Brooke or Victor?*

Eden: *A Corrigan. How does she fit in? What made her leave? Why did she lie to me?*

The thoughts were coming back in a rush faster than Isla could write them down.

How does V have E's bracelet? Date of postmark. She drew three bold lines beneath the words.

Isla marked the day they'd left Daytona on a Greyhound, the day they'd arrived at the Charlottesville bus depot, and the day Eden had disappeared. Now she wrote the date marked on the postmark. Two weeks after their arrival in Charlottesville.

Did Eden go back to Daytona?

Isla doubted that. Unless she'd thought she'd be tracked and wanted to confuse them. There were too many questions. Too many unknowns.

Before she left for the estate, she needed to make sure all her notes were put away. She'd be gone for longer now, and if housekeeping did decide to enter the room, she doubted they'd go in the closet, but just in case they peeked, she'd make sure to prop the foldable luggage rack against the wall to cover her handiwork.

It was time to check in. She pulled out the burner phone and dialed Rey. He picked up on the second ring.

Rey started in, "What the hell, girl? Hold on, let me dial Nat in. She was about to call the cops, no lie. You know how she goes zero to a hundred in a second."

Isla couldn't tell if he was talking about the epitome of calm Nat or himself. When Nat was connected, Rey continued. "We've only been blowing you up all night long. No calls, no messages since you left to return the keys." The frantic tone of his voice made her smile. It felt good to speak with a friend and to turn *off*.

"I know. Sorry." She hadn't considered that her friends could be freaking out until this moment. "But I have an update you're not going to believe. I'd barely believe it if I hadn't seen it myself. Also, these Corrigans are intense. I can't even explain how much." She backed up against the bed and leaned against it as she sat on the floor, refusing to think about the last time the carpet was cleaned.

"I can't believe it fucking worked," Rey said while Nat cheered in the background. "The cover held?" he asked incredulously.

"Me coming down here to work some big events with the East Coast branch of Elite Events Services. Great hookup you had with your brother. Oh, and thank him for firing me this morning."

Rey laughed. "It'll be the first time he's ever been thanked for firing someone. Now I owe Manny big-time. I was able to get access easier because he heads the West Coast branch, which enabled me to create a personnel file for you and get you on the roster over there. So that means you owe me big-time for this big-ass job we will not be getting paid for," Rey reminded her. He waited a beat. "You sure we can't blackmail these people when you find out whatever huge secret they're hiding? They're good for the money. I checked today for the hell of it, and the man is worth $114.7 billion."

"Rey, this is for justice and to fix our screwup with Leonard," Nat chastised. "We've been through this. Get over it."

Rey whined, "But so much money."

Isla didn't want to ask, but had to. "Charli?"

"Still off with a boyfriend at the casinos or wherever she makes them take her to spend their money on her. She's not thinking about you," Nat said. "Yet."

"Well, when she does, you know what to say. And you stay away, Nat. You can't take her interrogation. She should have been a cop."

Rey laughed. "And give up the good life of being a kept woman while having a sucker—I mean, intelligent young lady—manage the retirement facility that she's supposed to be managing?"

Nat cut in before Isla had a chance to retort. "What's the next move?"

Isla let the dig slide, instead focusing on the wall. She told them everything she'd learned and her major discovery.

Rey breathed, "You're shitting me." Isla heard him typing at his keyboard. "Nothing. We've already searched under her mother's last name, Parker. There's nothing on Eden Corrigan. Not now. Not ten years ago. Not before then. It's like any information on her was scrubbed. Wiped clean."

"Like off the face of the earth," Isla muttered.

Nat asked, "You had no idea? You spent so much time with her and her mother."

"She never said who her father was. But that's not unusual, because I don't talk about my mother. I've never met her." Isla shared the earlier questions she'd had about Eden with them.

"She's younger than Bennett? She'd be, what, pushing twenty-nine now? He's thirty, with Myles four years older. So Victor cheated on his wife, Brooke, when Bennett was a baby?" Nat asked.

At the same time, Rey said, "What a stud," totally impressed.

"Look deeper into the background on the family. Business associations. Rey, could you hurry with finding the origin of the accounts in Leonard's name? Who knows how long we have before someone tries to take the money out?"

"Working on it," he said tersely.

"I'll try to figure out Eden's trail the day she disappeared and how it traces back to the Corrigans. There was likely a secret Eden knew. Maybe she confronted one of them and ended up . . ." She stopped herself short, unable to bring herself to say the word *dead*. The fact that there was no body meant there was a chance, though Isla didn't know if she really believed that. Not like Victor and Holland seemed to believe.

"They really think she could be alive, living somewhere off the grid?" Nat asked. "I mean, it's rare but possible. People go missing and end up found years later, living their best lives. Some of them just walk away because they've had enough of the lives they were living."

Isla would hang on to any glimmer of hope, even if it meant Eden had left her behind. But if that was the case, why send a letter from a city they had already left? And what about the bracelet that never left Eden's wrist?

"There's something about Bennett that rubs me the wrong way," Isla said. "On the outside he's fun and can be charming as hell, but he's hiding something dark and ugly that's itching to come out. He's like a loose cannon."

"Keep an eye on him, but be careful," Rey said.

"What about Myles?" Nat said dreamily. "He's delicious looking. This family has great genes. He's—"

"A wild card," Isla finished. "With no personality." She left out the part where he'd gotten her a change of clothes.

"Watch out for him too," Rey warned.

"I know," Isla said, her chest tightening. She changed the subject. "About this article. I have some clips from when we were at UCLA, but could we doctor up a couple more in case I need to prove it? Get a portfolio together? It needs to look legit. Nat?"

"I'm on it," Nat said before Isla could finish. "I can have it by the end of the day."

"Only work on the laptop I gave you," Rey said, back to business. "And don't connect to their Wi-Fi. Use the hot spot I gave you too. Everything will be encrypted, so if they have someone trying to backdoor you, it'll block them. But you do need to put my USB drive into one of their computers. A home and a work, so I can get in easy. This is just another job, okay? Think of it that way. Leave the emotions out."

"I know," Isla said, looking once again at the board.

Someone in that house knows the whole truth, but each of them holds pieces to the puzzle.

"At least I'm in. Right?"

Nat replied, "Sure, but this won't be easy. You'll have to be 'on' twenty-four seven. Even actors stop filming at the end of the day. You can't break character. Ever. If they ever suspect you . . ." Nat whistled. "Just don't end up like your friend, okay?"

"Kinda harsh, Nat."

While they argued over who was the more insensitive one, Isla fought against the burn behind her eyelids as the weight of her reality began to press down on her. She didn't want to speak, afraid she'd betray her feelings.

Isla zeroed in on Eden's smiling photo. *Eden, what did you know? And why did you have to disappear to find it?*

No matter how terrified she was, she couldn't let Rey and Nat ever know.

CHAPTER TWENTY-SIX

There was a little time before the estate car came for her, and it was as good a time as any to begin retracing where she and Eden had been. Her first stop was where they'd eaten a couple of times. She pushed open the door to Mabel's Country Kitchen, the same one she'd entered a decade ago. Only this time she wasn't sixteen, terrified, and confused, with no one to turn to. She was older, with over a decade's more experience and a whole lot more nerve and sense that she belonged. This time, she had people, even if they were thousands of miles away. Still, she couldn't help the slight trickle of déjà vu and a triggering recall of having felt deserted and confused that morning long ago.

The smell of bacon and coffee, the ting of metal to porcelain, and the happy chatter of people filling their bellies greeted her. She scanned the room until her eyes landed on a woman wiping down the counter, where luckily one seat was vacant. She slipped onto the stool after getting the okay that she could seat herself and plucked the plastic-covered menu from the napkin dispenser that kept it upright.

"Good morning," Isla said, offering a warm smile to the woman behind the counter. "Hot tea please?"

The woman's name tag informed Isla that she was not the famous Mabel from the restaurant's moniker.

Isla looked around. "So where's Mabel?"

Becca looked Isla over with curiosity as she flipped over the mug and pushed toward her a steel container of an assortment of teas—of which Isla picked Earl Grey—and poured the hot water. She snorted. "You must not be from around here, hmm?"

Isla shook her head. "That obvious, huh?"

"Not really. Plenty of people visit Charlottesville and the nearby towns. But you asking about Mabel is the giveaway. She's my grandmother. Passed on many years." Becca looked to be about in her fifties, strands of blondish-gray hair escaping the bun she'd swooped to the top of her head. "What brings you by? You here to visit the Blue Ridge Mountains or Monticello? That's a huge draw." Becca pursed her lips as she considered Isla. "You don't look like the mountain-trekking type, though."

Isla dunked her tea bag in and out of the steaming water by its string. "May I have creamer?"

Becca raised an eyebrow. "Creamer? That's . . . unusual."

"I learned it from my dad. He was from the west coast of Africa, and most will drink their tea with cream—or evaporated milk, rather—and sugar." Isla shrugged. "You know, colonization and all that. It's a British thing that stuck." One of many things that stuck.

"You don't say?" Becca appeared unaffected by the colonization part or the implications beyond it. What did she care?

Isla ordered bacon and eggs, scrambled hard with cheese. She thought about ordering the home-fried potatoes, but she just couldn't get into that. Fried potatoes had been her father's specialty, and she still couldn't eat any without thinking of him and feeling the sadness that came with some of those memories.

The morning rush was clearing out, leaving Becca free to engage without much distraction. There were other servers to bus the tables. One seat over was a man in a police uniform, his radio set to low as he plowed through his big breakfast platter. Isla had seen that item on the menu and known it was way out of her league.

"I was actually working some temp jobs around town and recently began some contract work for the Corrigans."

Isla swore the noise, even the sizzle from the griddle in the back, died down when she mentioned the name.

Becca came closer. "That so?"

Isla nodded, finishing the food in her mouth before continuing. "Yep. He's receiving the Man of the Year award in September, and so I am doing a profile on him. His life and career. I'm talking to pretty much everyone to get a good sense of who and how he is. Local perspectives, you know?"

Becca twisted her lips in mild distaste. "Victor Corrigan, huh? You probably won't get much dirt on him in town—people either adore him or fear retribution if they say anything untoward. You know what I'm saying? The Corrigans don't take too kindly to a bad public image."

Isla pretended nonchalance, taking a sip of her slightly cooled tea. Perfect. Just the way she liked it. "I figured as much, and that's fine. The profile is supposed to make him look good, you know?" She paused, pretending to think. "What about his family? Any stories there? I've met his three kids, Holland, Bennett, and Myles. Met his wife too."

Becca's look of aversion sparked Isla's curiosity even more. How much about the family dynamics did Becca know?

"I know there is another daughter, but she's not around, apparently hasn't been for a while now. Eva—Edith—"

"I wouldn't be around either if I was her. You're talking about Edie, or I guess Eden if you want to be proper when you cite it. But when she was around, everyone knew her as Edie. She was Elise's daughter."

So they knew. Isla tried to hide her surprise, but she wasn't fast enough.

Becca smirked. "Oh, you thought an illegitimate child popping out at the same time a legitimate one did wouldn't be news among the common folk? Please. Rich people aren't as subtle as they like to believe they are, and we aren't as stupid as they'd like to think we are," she said. She continued when Isla had nothing to add. "Nice girl. Sweet. Didn't want anything to do with that family of hers, I suppose, which is why we haven't seen her around. Have we, Bowen?" Becca addressed the officer to Isla's right.

He looked up, looked at Becca with raised eyebrows, then finally at Isla. Isla was bringing her mug to her lips at that exact moment and stopped when she came face-to-face with him. He was the cop she'd run into back then. He and another older man who was an asshole. He was the one who had pulled her back from walking into traffic without looking because she'd been so distracted after Eden's disappearance. Her eyes widened as they connected with his. Did he recognize her from the brief snatches he'd seen of her back then? Did she look different enough? Her hair was pressed into long waves, not curly and in its natural state like it was before. She was older. Changed. But cops were trained to remember faces, weren't they? Or specific details that stood out to them. At least that was what some of her connections in law enforcement had told her back home.

Did Officer Bowen remember her as she clearly remembered him? And what's more, where was the asshole partner of his? Hopefully retired.

She sipped to keep herself from staring too hard, and he glanced at her without any sign of recognition. He actually looked a little annoyed at having his big breakfast platter interrupted for idle chatter.

"I guess so" was all he said before nodding to Isla and going back to his plate.

Becca said, "She's probably living in the lap of luxury, like all young heiresses of a billion-dollar empire. She's not thinking about this little town anymore."

Or maybe not at all, Isla thought grimly.

"Edie wasn't that type of person," Officer Bowen remarked. He wiped his mouth with a paper napkin and balled it up. "She wasn't what you'd expect an heiress to be."

His comments surprised Isla, and she chanced another look at him. He was maybe mid-thirties, just a little older than Myles. His remarks put Isla off. She hadn't expected him to have that kind of opinion.

One like he knew Eden personally. She'd have to think about that and Officer Bowen further. But she couldn't risk him eventually recognizing her if she said or did too much around him.

Becca nodded in agreement. "You're right, you're right. That's why it was a big ole surprise when she attended the local schools here. Not the private one her siblings went to." Becca leaned against the counter, settling in, while Isla nibbled on a perfectly cooked piece of bacon. Not too crunchy, not too limp. Just right.

"To be honest, she was something special. I think because her mama was more common like us than them, meaning not from money, Edie could get along with everyone well, without coming across pretentious. You know what I mean? If you don't, you will when you hang around that family long enough. Pretentious and privileged and thinking everyone works for them. Huh, Tolson Bowen?"

Bowen sighed. "I don't know what you mean, Becca. I'm just trying to enjoy my breakfast before my shift."

Becca motioned for Isla to lean closer to her, and Isla obeyed. "Bowen's one of the good ones," she whispered in a nonwhisper that Bowen could clearly hear. His ears reddened. "Don't get me wrong, the police here are great and do their job well. Even if sometimes they look the other way for certain people. Just saying."

Bowen pushed his plate away, downed the rest of his coffee, and slid off his seat. "And that's my cue. Don't mind her, ma'am. Everyone's treated the same around here. At least by me," he said breezily. He nodded at the both of them. Had his eye lingered a hair too long on Isla? She couldn't be sure, but she brushed it off as nerves. He hadn't recognized her. If he had, he would have said something for sure. Right?

"I think you offended him," Isla pointed out innocently.

Becca dismissed him with a wave in his recently vacated direction. "I didn't mean him anyway," she said.

"So she went to the local high school," Isla redirected to get them back on track. "That's pretty cool that they let her."

"Yeah, she was special. Loved the theater. She was in the theater club with my niece, Sara."

Isla silently said, *Of course Eden would have been.*

"But about six or so months into the school year, she left to go live with her mother in Florida. At least that's what Sara told me."

That tracked. Eden had shown up in the middle of a school year, though they hadn't attended the same school. Different districts. "Why do you think she left so suddenly during a school year, especially since she seemed to love the theater club here so much? This would have been her junior year maybe?"

Shit. Becca had never mentioned what grade they were in, or Edie's age. Isla might have messed up. Thank goodness Becca had chased the cop away, because he surely would have picked up on that. Hopefully Becca wouldn't notice. Isla held her breath.

Becca's eyes darted around the relatively empty diner, and she lowered her voice. "I couldn't tell you. But Sara might know, since they were close. She lives a few blocks from here—on Third, fourth house on the left. Little blue number. Really cute. I'll text her and let her know you might be stopping by?" Becca raised an expectant eyebrow.

Isla affirmed. "Thank you. You were a huge help."

Becca gave a satisfied nod. "Good luck on your profile. And kudos to you for getting in that ivory tower."

CHAPTER TWENTY-SEVEN

Isla packed the last of her belongings and glanced around the small motel room. It was nothing spectacular by far, but in these past several weeks it had become her refuge and grounding place, a small squarish room that was the only place where she could be her truest self. She wasn't sure when she could come here next without sparking curiosity or suspicion. She'd committed her wall to memory, and from here on, anything new would have to be worked out in another way.

"By the time I come back here," Isla began, pausing at the doorway with a duffel and a large hard-shell rolling suitcase at her feet, with her laptop backpack secured on her back, "I'll know what happened to her." She promised this to the empty room that had once been her and Eden's three-day sanctuary on their way to living life on their own terms.

She kept the motel room. Her complete privacy wasn't guaranteed at the estate, and she wouldn't be able to explain the case board of Corrigan facts and notes she'd accumulated.

Now comes the real work, she thought. *No turning back now.*

She'd already paid through another month, but still stopped at the front desk to explain that she was leaving for a work trip and wouldn't need any services to her room while gone.

She'd just made it back to her apartment when her phone alerted her to the arrival of her car, courtesy of her new temporary employers.

The trademark Corrigan car waited at the curb, and Pete, the driver, was already out of the car and approaching to take her bags before she had cleared the entrance.

As they wound up the mountain, the steady flow of traffic tapered as they neared the estate's property lines until theirs was the only vehicle on the road. She would never get used to how close they were, right on the other side of the railing, to the drop-off edge, no matter how many times she'd been on this road or the winding ones in California. The thought of one wrong move plunging a person to their death rankled her.

"Has that ever happened before?" Isla voiced her thoughts. "A car going over?" It was one of those questions she really didn't want the answer to, but she had to know, like the glutton for punishment she seemed to be.

"Oh yeah, sure." Pete's answer was casual with no VIP in the back seat. "Only once that I really heard of, but that was, like, over a decade ago."

Isla's imagination took her places no one should go.

Pete continued, unaware there was a struggle behind him. "But I don't know much about it 'cept that it was a family from out of town or something. Really sad."

"Were they visiting someone here?"

The car pulled up around the impressive spouting water sculpture situated in the middle of the circular driveway and stopped in front of the stone staircase leading to the estate's front doors. The scene in the bright of day was even more amazing than at night.

"Not on this mountain. It was around where the old Abbott farm is, another one nearby. A lot of people hike trails, go hunting and off-roading around here. Visitors come here to do the same. But their story, I'm not sure. Wasn't as much talk about it as you'd think, it being an entire family and all. There wasn't a lot in the media about it either. Some people around town say it's a cover-up, because who wants to vacation where an entire family died like that?"

CHAPTER TWENTY-EIGHT

Ten Years Ago

The day they decided to leave Daytona, Isla was sixteen and worried about what she would do once she aged out of the system, and Eden was eighteen, grieving the death of her mother. She was now just as alone as Isla was. They had been like sisters ever since the day they met. Eden's mom was like a mom to Isla; their home was her pseudo foster home. Theirs was a place she could get away to when her days at the group home were too much. They'd planned their getaway while sitting in the back booth while Isla was on break during one of her shifts.

After Elise's funeral, Isla hadn't seen or spoken to Eden for a long while. She'd wanted to give her space, but she was terrified she'd lost the only real friend she had. After nearly two months of barely any communication, Eden showed up at Isla's job like nothing had changed, ordered her usual, and told Isla she'd be leaving. "I can't be here anymore, Isla. Not with my mom gone. I need to get far away."

Isla tried to keep her composure, because she was at work and her manager was watching her with hawk eyes from behind the counter. Eden had said she was leaving. But she'd said nothing about where Isla fit in. Isla asked her where she planned to go.

"To LA to become a theater actress." She grinned dreamily, dunking her fry in her milkshake. "Just like a cliché. But I don't care. I'll try to make it big and also start a new garden like my mom used to keep."

The idea of Eden leaving left Isla in a panic. She couldn't imagine staying back in Daytona alone again. Knowing her had made life interesting, given Isla hope of a decent future once she left the home. Knowing there would be one person who really cared about her. Who knew she existed.

She swallowed her disappointment like she'd trained herself to do years ago. After her dad had been killed, her life had been one disappointment and rejection after another. She guessed this would be another, but this one hurt the most. This one she had truly wanted.

"Well," she started, praying her voice would hold steady. "Good luck with all that." She got up to get back to work even though she had fifteen minutes left.

"What do you mean?" Eden asked. "You don't want to come with me?"

Isla's heart and breath froze. She didn't dare hope Eden was being for real.

She asked, "Seriously?"

Eden nodded, looking quite pleased with herself.

Isla dropped back onto the bench because her knees had gone wobbly. "Okay."

Eden raised an eyebrow, fry in midair. "Really? Because I'm deadass serious. What about Westin House?"

Isla thought about it. There were so many kids coming in and out and too few staff—who were overworked, underpaid, and with limited resources—to pay close attention to all their caseloads.

"I can figure out a way. No big deal, as long as you're really serious. If you say you're leaving, we really gotta leave. You're eighteen and I'm not. It would be illegal and shit. Question is, are you cool with that?"

Eden snorted. "That's the least of my worries."

"Then what's the biggest?" Isla expected her to talk about the loss of her mother, but Eden was taking the death in stride. Better than Isla had or could.

"Unfinished business I have to take care of in Virginia with those people. Things I wish I had done differently and now have to set right. Then I'm free and clear."

Isla got it. There were plenty of things she wished she had done differently. Like telling her dad not to go when she felt in her gut that something bad was going to happen. Like waiting too long, until the cops came for her. Maybe if she had called the cops when he'd left in that car, they'd have found him in time.

"Then it's a plan. We go to Virginia so you can do whatever, and then we get far away to LA. You'll become a big-time star, and I mooch off you like a proper little sister." That got a laugh out of her, first Isla had heard in a very long time. Isla wished she'd known that it would be the last time she would hear her laugh like that. She wished she'd known a lot of things, like that when they arrived in Charlottesville, and then Eden left Isla at the motel to handle her unfinished business, that would be the last Isla would see of her.

CHAPTER TWENTY-NINE

Isla remembered to wait until Pete opened her door for her. Brooke sauntered by casually, with Jackson not far behind. He was always observing, and from Isla's short experience, he was one of the few who could keep Brooke at bay. They were walking out the front doors, watching them, and Isla glanced away, not wanting to give the woman any excuse to resent her more than she seemed to already, or to punish Pete, who Isla promised would not see the wrath of anyone. She rather hoped he'd be her assigned driver if she were to have one.

Isla saw Holland waiting, waving and practically bouncing on the balls of her feet like a giddy little kid, still in her practice gear, with her fencing jacket open, revealing her white T-shirt underneath. Isla was touched that someone was happy to see her. The warm feeling turned cold when Brooke stepped up to join her daughter, her expression anything but welcoming.

Brooke stood erect, folding her arms across her chest. Her sharp eyes looked down on Isla from her perch above, every bit the madam of the house . . . in control and very displeased. Her bloodred lips were set in a firm line as her perfectly manicured nails tap-tap-tapped impatiently against her elbow, like a ticking bomb counting down to boom. She raked her eyes over Isla, not bothering to hide her disdain and suspicion.

When Holland realized it was her mother beside her, probably when she felt the frigid gust of wind suck the joy from her soul, Holland's arm came down, and she wiped her face smooth. She couldn't play it cool entirely, because her body was still fidgeting nervously beside her mother, her eyes widening and darting between Isla and her mother when Isla joined them on the top step, her smile bright and polite, though her pulse quickened as she readied herself for whatever came next.

Brooke appraised her and found her subject sorely lacking. "Ah, the illustrious and lucky brand-spanking-new documentarian." Her voice dripped with such condescension and contempt that Isla wondered exactly what she had done to warrant this type of behavior. "Welcome back to our humble home."

Isla couldn't restrain herself, scoffing at the understatement of the year. If this place was humble . . .

"You find me funny?" Brooke asked sharply.

Isla shook her head, clearing her throat and tapping the base of her neck as if something was caught in her throat. "Never, Mrs. Corrigan." She offered Holland a reassuring smile before the girl had a stroke. "Thank you for the greeting. It's a pleasure to be here." Isla refused to let the iciness get to her, at least on the surface, painting on such a wide smile, her cheeks strained from the effort.

"Let's get you back to your room," Holland cut in, reaching to grab Isla's wrist and tugging at her to follow. Isla hesitated, sensing more was coming.

Brooke's mouth twitched, and her light-hazel eyes held no warmth at all. "Not so fast, honey." She never broke eye contact with Isla, gearing herself up. "Since my daughter seems to have a penchant for charity cases and my unpredictable and sometimes irrational husband has given you permission to create this absurd profile or whatever the hell you claim you're going to do for this extremely important award that you better not screw up"—she took a quick breath, preparing herself for the rest of her delivery while Isla braced herself—"you'll be well compensated for this work you actually volunteered to do. And so those who are in our employ and will be on the premises reside in staff quarters."

Isla didn't show the slight deflation of her body or the sigh of relief she eased out slowly. Was that all? Isla had seen the building where the staff lived when they were on duty rotation. Not even guest housing, though. Staff. This woman was a real nasty piece of work.

Holland gasped, her mouth dropping to her chin. She was appalled and embarrassed. "Mother, Isla's a guest. What do you mean she's staying in staff housing? You can't put her there—she's a guest."

Brooke barely batted an eye. "She is not." She finally looked at her daughter, her gaze softening slightly as she took her daughter in. She shook her head as if she felt bad for her child, as if she weren't the one causing the issue. Then she returned to Isla, everything about her rehardening. "We can't make exceptions, even if what she does falls under Special Projects, and even if she helped you in a pinch. And I hope, Isla, that mentioning how you helped out my daughter will be the last drop you will milk of that whole situation. That cow has dried up," she said.

"Oh, but, Mrs. Corrigan," Isla said, her voice sweet, innocent, and seemingly deferential, "I haven't mentioned that at all. It's *you* who keeps bringing it up, and frankly I'm a little embarrassed by all your attention. Oh, hey there! Are you part of the welcoming committee too? Geez, you guys are really too much. I'm overwhelmed by the hospitality."

Brooke had been revving herself up, incensed by Isla's audacity. She pointed a finger at Isla, ready to fire back. Maybe even kick Isla out and ban her for life, damn what Victor had instructed, but her retort was quickly swallowed when she realized there was now an audience of two, and Isla had addressed them. Bennett and Myles were standing off in the corner and observing the exchange.

Bennett leaned casually against the stone railing, clearly entertained, as if he were watching a live performance. Meanwhile, Myles was in what Isla deemed his own uniform of dress slacks, shirt, and vest, since it was the only way he seemed to wear his suits. She wondered what he wore when he relaxed . . . *if* he even knew the word *relax*. He watched them inscrutably, unreadable—she couldn't tell whether he was enjoying the confrontation, like his younger, carefree brother, or if he, too, couldn't tolerate her, like his stepmother.

Isla kept her composure, channeling the fake charm she'd perfected, if only to needle the woman. Perhaps this was the best way to get Brooke to crack and find out how she might have played a part in Eden's departure. Because Isla had a feeling that Brooke had definitely had something to do with it. Brooke was too nasty not to have wanted anyone who didn't come from her out to clear the competition. That was why Isla was in staff housing instead of in the main house. To shame her. Put her in her place. To drive Isla out. Of course this woman would think this an insult. The staff housing looked better than many of the homes Isla had lived in.

But Brooke didn't know who she was dealing with. Isla was ready for whatever this woman had to offer. Still, she toned down her enthusiasm to a manageable level. She wanted to come across carefree and awestruck.

Isla addressed Holland, who was stressed beyond words, making Isla feel immediately sorry for her behavior. She'd have to make sure not to needle Brooke when Holland was around. Holland couldn't handle it. Holland reminded Isla very much of Eden, highly sensitive, and that drove Isla to squeeze her hand into a fist at her side from the guilt. Holland and Eden would have been the best of sisters.

Isla said, "It makes perfect sense for me to be in staff housing." She was interrupted when Bennett cursed in surprise. The brothers had missed the part of the exchange that had gotten them all to this point. Myles straightened, his hands still in his pockets. But he was clearly upset and struggling with whether to say anything.

"I *am* here to work. I shouldn't forget that." She dropped her eyes, sneaking a tiny look through her lashes to gauge the room. Brooke seethed but held her tongue. Holland looked like she wanted to wrap Isla in a huge hug. Isla couldn't see the brothers, but they were still watching.

"The accommodations you've put together for me will be more than enough while I do this. And it's farther out on the grounds, so I get to enjoy the property more as I walk around conducting my interviews." *And launching my investigation,* Isla thought. "I even get to check out your solarium, Mrs. Corrigan. I hear it houses some of the most beautiful, exotic plants around."

"And deadly." Myles spoke up, surprising them all.

Isla agreed wholeheartedly. "Oh, definitely. Beautiful and deadly. I'm sure that's why they're flourishing so well under your care."

Isla couldn't help it. It just slipped out. It was like Myles served, whether he meant to or not, and she volleyed. She'd do better. Next time.

Holland gasped, eyes going wide again. The girl was going to need eye drops with all that eye widening she kept doing. If Brooke's expressions were any indication, she'd be shoving some of her deadly plants down Isla's throat. But she didn't matter. Bennett emitted a low whistle and stifled a laugh, his face reading as impressed. That could work for her. He signaled his approval, and, satisfied Isla could manage Brooke, he left as quickly as he'd materialized.

They were left with uncomfortable silence hanging over them like a rain cloud about to burst. Tense air crackled between them as Isla waited for Brooke to continue her pissing match.

Finally, Brooke plastered on a tight smile. It looked like it pained her to have to do it, and Isla wondered why she even bothered pretending politeness with Isla. Maybe it was a rich-lady thing.

"Well, I'm glad you're . . . enthusiastic about the arrangements."

Isla dipped her head graciously. "Absolutely, whatever makes it easiest for everyone. And I am very grateful, for what it's worth." Isla realized she meant that. Not because of Brooke but because it was really Holland's kindness and Victor wanting to shake things up on his own terms.

Brooke nodded curtly before turning on her four-inch heel with the red sole. Even though she was shorter than Isla, Brooke still managed to look down her nose at her. Isla decided being this nasty was a talent. "Holland, please show Miss Thorne to staff housing. Make sure she gets settled, hmm?"

"I look forward to speaking with you more in depth later!" Isla called out as Brooke left them, reentering the house with Jackson in tow.

Holland threw Isla an apologetic glance before heading back down the steps with her to the waiting golf cart that would whisk them away to Isla's new neck of the woods.

CHAPTER THIRTY

At the bottom of the steps, Mae waited in the driver's seat of a golf cart with Isla's luggage already in the back seat. The people here were efficient at their jobs.

She begged off Holland's offer to accompany her to her quarters and help her unpack and get settled, and deflected Holland's apologies for her mother's behavior.

"She just needs some time to get to know you," Holland offered, trying hard to be sincere.

Holland and Isla burst out laughing when Mae sighed, mumbling something inaudible—something about hell freezing over—and started up the cart, cuing Isla that they needed to go.

"I can go, really." Holland couldn't stifle her big yawn. "I'm sorry. I had practice earlier."

"Get some rest," Isla urged, turning Holland around and gently pushing her toward the steps. "I'll be fine on my own. And—" Isla made sure Holland was focused on her. "Thank you for helping me get here. For everything. You don't even know me."

"When'd you get so sentimental? Geez," Holland said, blushing and dismissing her. "I might seem like I'm not into everything that's going on around here, but I know good people when I see them. And you, Isla, are good people, which we are in desperate need of around here."

With that Holland started back up the steps while Isla watched her leave, thinking how disappointed Holland would be when she proved Holland wrong. Isla was not good people. At least, not while she was here.

Mae pulled away from the curb with practiced ease, then rounded the drive and branched off onto one of the paved paths. As they bumped along the winding path leading to their quarters, Mae began her rundown of the estate's inner workings, her tone brisk but friendly, like she'd done this many times before.

"As you already know, the Corrigans are demanding and"—she searched for the right word—"unique. But they take really good care of the house staff and the company's employees. Mr. Corrigan is very firm on ensuring his people are well treated, so you won't find high turnover here. When people come on board here, they tend to stay."

Eden's mother hadn't.

"We provide around-the-clock care and availability for the family and their guests." She side-eyed Isla.

Isla jumped in. "Which I'm not."

Mae scoffed. "We'll see about that. But for now, no, you're not a guest."

They passed the elaborate guest housing, equipped with its own pool and other amenities. Guests were living nearly as well as the Corrigans, Isla thought, gazing at the buildings as they passed. Mae mistook her awe for disappointment or wistfulness.

"I think you'll be pleasantly surprised at your accommodations," Mae told her. "Mr. Corrigan believes that if his people are happy, then they will do their best. They'll be loyal. Grab that box right there."

Isla did as told, leaning over to pick up a black box. Isla looked at her inquisitively, then opened the box to reveal a sleek black Apple Watch. She looked back at Mae askance.

"All staff wear a watch when they're on shift. When the Corrigans need them, they send messages, or they'll ask me to send messages to whichever staff member they need. Staff are to be reachable at all times when on duty."

Isla nodded, staring at the watch inside. She wondered whose idea the watches were, and three guesses led to Brooke. Having people at her beck and call sounded right up her entitled and pretentious alley. The lid of the box closed with a light pop. "Thanks, but I think I'll pass on this." She didn't even bother with the excuse of being a contract employee. She just refused to be on a leash, which these watches were. It was also a way to track her whereabouts. "Mrs. Corrigan can come see me if she takes issue with it."

Mae raised a brow but didn't press the issue. "She will notice. She doesn't miss much."

"I'm counting on it," Isla muttered under her breath.

The cart rounded a bend, and Isla's new three-story home came into view. The building was large and looked newly built. It was open and airy, plainer than the guest quarters and the main house but matching the rest of the estate. There was even an elevator, which Isla appreciated. Isla spotted some staff entering and leaving the building, some on and some off duty. Mae parked the cart next to several other carts and led Isla inside.

"Pretty fancy for staff housing," Isla said, taking everything in. The inside was equally impressive, with polished hardwood floors and light-gray walls.

There was a communal lounge on the ground floor furnished with comfortable-looking couches, bookshelves, and a huge wide-screen TV built into the wall. Mae walked Isla through the common areas, showing her the gym, the laundry facilities, and the café-style kitchen with a large restaurant-grade refrigerator, freezer, and dishwasher. Through the large windows showing the back, Isla could see outdoor seating areas and a large firepit, where some of the staff were lounging after a long day's work. Dorms—the place reminded Isla of upscale college dorms; it was all-inclusive, with everything the staff might need when they were away from the main house and their own homes.

Isla's apartment was on the third floor, a fully furnished one-bedroom suite with a small kitchenette, a plush queen-size bed, and a balcony overlooking the grounds. She nodded approvingly, her thoughts going. Impressive.

"Thought I'd be stuck in a dungeon," Isla muttered, forgetting she wasn't alone.

Mae laughed. "I doubt Mrs. Corrigan could get away with that. Even if you are temporary, you were specifically chosen by Mr. Corrigan himself. And your position falls under Special Projects, which is run by Myles Corrigan."

Isla ignored the little zing at Myles's name. Jackass.

Mae continued, "Everyone knows how you got here, and so that's why you can get away with not wearing the watch." Mae looked at Isla mischievously. "And be kept out of the dungeon."

Isla froze. "Because there really is one?"

Mae broke out laughing, and Isla joined tepidly, unsure what to make of it all. The woman didn't say there wasn't one. Isla sat on the bed, taking it all in.

"You'll meet the others soon enough as they pass by. They're a good group. Everyone does what they're supposed to, and they keep Corrigan business to the Corrigans. We ask no questions here."

Isla raised a hand. "But that's what I'm here for. To ask questions. For the profile."

Mae nodded. "They will accommodate. To an extent. And I hope you'll have discretion. Contrary to what you've encountered from Mrs. Corrigan, the majority of the family are good people."

Better to start now. Isla asked, "Then you know of their daughter . . . the one who is gone or something? Edie, I think?"

At the mention, Mae stiffened, her face becoming stony and her door shutting. She was too far in to talk so easily, Isla chastised herself. Mae would take work. She'd have to see Isla's sincerity. "At any rate, everyone will try to help you out as best as they can."

As if on cue, two young women in staff uniforms passed by the open door. When they noticed there was an occupant, they stopped to introduce themselves. A bubbly brunette named Lisa leaned against the doorframe, wearing a grin.

"Fresh meat," she said. "Mae, you haven't scared her off yet, have you? Crack a smile, will you?"

Mae rolled her eyes, pushing past Lisa at the door. She turned to Isla. "I'll leave you to it. Let me know if you need anything or anyone gives you trouble. I have your cell should I need to reach you, so could you at least keep that on you?"

Isla grinned. "Since you asked so nicely. Of course I will."

When Mae was gone, Lisa and the other one sauntered in, taking in the room. "Corner room with the best view. Nice." Lisa plopped herself in one of the chairs, studying Isla. "I've been off and only heard about the newbie who got Mr. Corrigan to hire her as a writer or something."

The other one, a redhead with pale-green eyes and a tag that read **Doris**, said, "I hear there's already some kind of battle over you. The mister loves you. The missus wants to throw you in the lake and kick you out on your ass. What did you do?"

"You know she didn't do anything. Mrs. Corrigan hates anyone Mr. Corrigan likes. She probably thinks you're vying to be the third Mrs. Corrigan."

Isla made a face. "The man is old enough to be my father or more. He's pushing seventy."

"Right, twenty years older than his wife, so maybe he's looking for a newer, fresher model."

Isla shuddered. That was not the vibe she got from Mr. Corrigan. "You're way off base."

Lisa said, "Agreed. If Mr. Corrigan plays around, it's not where he eats, you know what I mean? Anyway, you met the Playboy and the Ice Prince yet?"

Isla tilted her head. "Who?"

"The sons," Doris said dreamily, like she was about to swoon.

"I bet you can guess who is who."

Isla said, "Bennett is the Playboy and Myles the Ice Prince?" She found the titles very fitting.

"Ding, ding," Lisa chimed, using her fingers to mime a tiny bell. She moved to the edge of her seat conspiratorially, and Isla drew in closer, captured by the allure of a good secret. "Bennett will flirt with and bed anything that breathes. Though not really the staff. His entourage too. He doesn't shit where he eats either, if you know what I mean. I think that comes from Mr. Corrigan. Their father is a big stickler about messing around with staff. Not that he took his own advice." She gave a look that suggested otherwise, and Isla took note.

"Okay, Lisa, come on." Doris looked uncomfortable, as if one of the Corrigans might suddenly pop out from behind the bushes and catch their staff talking dirt about them.

Isla waved away Doris's sensitivities, not wanting Lisa to lose her momentum. "Go on."

"But you'll meet the rest of Bennett's friends soon enough, I guess. They are unavoidable and more inclined to flirt with staff," Lisa continued, undeterred. "And Myles . . . well, he is the cold, brooding type. Just like you'd see in a movie? The gorgeous dark character you just can't quite figure out. He's neither nice or mean. He just *is*? He mainly just watches from the background, but when he gets involved in something, you'll definitely know it. He's a tough nut to crack, and believe me, I've tried."

Doris said, "No, Lisa's not saying it right. Myles is low key, is what it is. He'd rather stay in the background. Bennett is the complete opposite."

Isla said, "Yeah, I've already had a dose or two of the brothers. I'll keep everything you said in mind."

Lisa stood up to leave, with Doris following suit. "Then you just might make it around here."

CHAPTER THIRTY-ONE

Isla was too wired to be in her room. Unpacking could wait. She was walking along the row of remaining carts, trying to match the number on the cart with what was written on the key tag in her palm, when she literally bumped into someone, and a clump of fresh mulch was dumped on her feet.

"Well, damn," she mused, looking at her feet.

"I'm sorry," a voice said, "I didn't expect anyone to be standing there."

Isla looked up to see a pair of jeans-clad legs, heavy tan work boots, and the tail of a flannel shirt. The rest of the person was obscured by a very large bag of mulch. He set the mulch down with a grunt and a thump, revealing the rest of him to be a man in his forties with a weathered face and a dismayed expression as he studied the mess he'd caused. He made a move, preparing to dust Isla's shoes clean.

"Oh no, I got it." She waved away his hand and kicked her feet as clean as they were going to get.

He got a better look at her. "Are you lost, Miss . . ."

"Isla. I'm new, and staff, so forgo the formalities." They straightened. He was striking, with salt-and-pepper stubble and what she thought were kind dark-brown eyes. "I'm here to document Mr. Corrigan for the award he's getting next month."

Recognition hit. His eyebrows rose, and his look turned inquisitive. "So you're the one." He cracked a smile. "The guest Mrs. Corrigan relegated to staff. Ouch." He finished, chuckling.

Isla looked away in embarrassment. The last thing she wanted to be was the talk of the estate. "News gets around quick. Geez."

"This place may be huge, but people talk, and anything that disturbs any of the Corrigans spreads like an epidemic."

It was an interesting choice of words. Negative and hinting that man wasn't a fan of gossip, like Lisa and Doris, and that the talk was negative.

She stuck out her hand.

He hesitated initially, conscious of his dirt-smudged hands, but overcame his consideration and took hers in his calloused hand. She matched his firm shake and offered him a smile. She didn't know why, but she felt at immediate ease with this guy, whose name he still had not revealed.

"I'm Lawrence. Head groundskeeper on the property, and apparently a newly ordained shoe dirtier. Welcome to the circus that is King's Vinings Estate."

Had a sense of humor too. She appreciated that.

She agreed. "It's definitely quite the place from what I've seen and experienced already."

Lawrence nodded, glancing in the direction of the main house. "Yes, I've heard that too. Mrs. Corrigan, right? You should be careful around here and with the Corrigans. They can be nice one moment and turn the next. Even on each other."

Lawrence was solemn as he spoke, his words nothing like Doris and Lisa's lighthearted banter earlier. She didn't get the sense that he was gossiping, more that he was warning. Or preparing her for what was to come.

Isla nodded. "Got it. Any exceptions to that warning?"

"Not a warning." Lawrence thought about it. "Consider it advice. Advice from an old hat to the new."

"Advice," she reiterated.

He scratched at his stubble, taking her question into deep consideration. This was a person who didn't speak without thinking. One who held his cards close and kept his head down. She noted that too.

He said, "Maybe the youngest not so much. But she's rarely around now that she'll be going back to school soon."

"What about Myles?"

"What about him?"

"Any insight?"

Lawrence shook his head, amused. "That's all you're going to get out of me, Miss Lucky Lady." He moved the mulch against the trunk of an oak, propping it so it wouldn't fall over, and dusted his hands on his jeans.

"Why do you call me that?"

Lawrence gave her a look that said she should get serious. "Let's just say you should play the lotto, as lucky as you are to get this gig the way you did. We've all heard about it."

"Could I interview you about Victor to get some insight on him from your perspective? It would be invaluable."

He scoffed. "How would you know it's invaluable? We just met two minutes ago."

She tapped near the bottom of one of her eyes, grinning mischievously. "I have a good eye for these things."

Lawrence made a face like he didn't believe her but was just humoring her. Isla bet Lawrence did this often with the people he worked with and for.

"I'll think about it while you go around a bit. I'll be interested to hear what your good eye uncovers."

Isla paused. Another interesting choice of words. Very deliberate from someone who spoke very purposefully. She looked at the key again and did a sweep for the matching cart.

"I was going to go around and get the lay of the land, but I'm having an issue with finding the right cart."

"I think walking gives you more perspective and appreciation for the grounds. I can show you around to some key places you probably haven't seen yet."

Isla nodded, slipping the key in her back pocket and hoping no one would come looking for it anytime soon.

Lawrence led Isla down a gravel path while pointing out where the maze of curved pathways would lead her. "I have a map of the property that I've drawn up that I can make a copy of for you if you like. It's nothing official. Just helped me when I got here and throughout the years as the estate has expanded out. What I mean is that you have the main property that's been developed, and then we have what's beyond the gates and back fencing of land that belongs to the Corrigans but has yet to be built upon. You likely won't need anything out there. Can be dangerous."

Isla nodded and walked, taking everything in, glad Lawrence felt comfortable enough to chat with her, let alone be her tour guide. Ahead of them loomed a large glass structure nestled among the thatch of live oaks, pines, and cedar trees. Its steepled glass roof stood higher than anything around, and Isla couldn't help, for the second time since being at the estate, staring in awe. As they neared and she was able to see through the large panes of glass inside, she glimpsed how vibrant plants and flowers bloomed and loomed and gave off a heady mix of sweet and spiced fragrances. Breathtaking, just from out here.

"The current Mrs. Corrigan likes to take credit for it, but it was the first Mrs. Corrigan's brainchild. But when she became ill and eventually passed, a former employee named Elise worked on it and made it what you see today. Before my time, though. I heard about it, since I often need to tend to it. Mrs. Corrigan likes to bring guests around to admire it."

Isla mumbled, "Like another piece of her jewelry."

Lawrence coughed, and she realized she'd spoken out loud. She had to watch out for that.

Isla redirected from her embarrassment. "Former employee? Elise?"

Lawrence glanced at her as they slowed to a stop at the solarium. "Mm-hmm. But like I said. Before my time."

"And how long have you been working for the Corrigans?"

Lawrence studied her, taking time to answer. He was doing the same thing she was doing. Figuring her out. Her angle. "Little over ten years. Maybe eleven. Elise had already been gone for a long time prior to that, but her daughter Edie was here when I started."

Isla ignored the tightness in her chest and forced herself to keep her tone light and casually curious. "Edie. I heard brief mention of her, but I don't see anything about her anywhere. And it seems like the family doesn't want to discuss her. Was she some kind of black sheep or something?" Isla held her breath, hoping she didn't look too eager for just a little bit of information that might hold the key.

Again Lawrence scrutinized her. "Edie left to live with her mother about a year after I got here. That's all I know."

Isla made a *Gotcha* gesture. "You said gossip spreads like an epidemic. You should know all the details."

Lawrence mimicked her, breaking into a grin. "Touché. But unfortunately I was too new to the grounds and determined to keep my job to pay much mind to gossip and rumors."

Isla looked at the solarium, now with even more respect. Things she knew of the mother and daughter connecting little by little. Of course Elise would have something to do with this greenhouse. It explained the care she had taken tending the small garden she'd had in her modest backyard. And it explained Eden's name. Isla wondered if anyone knew the meaning of Eden's name. She wondered if Victor knew. She'd have to find out.

"Sounds like she was very talented," Isla said.

"She was. I didn't have to do much when I got in there, it was that well kept. She cared about this place the most."

Isla believed it. She'd witnessed the type of care Elise was capable of herself.

Lawrence started walking farther down the pathway while Isla lingered for a moment, taking in the building's beauty and its significance. She finally made herself move, walking fast to catch up to him and half listen while he pointed out some other landmarks and the quickest way to get to the main house from staff housing. Isla tried to remember it all, but she would be glad to get that copy of the map when Lawrence had the chance.

They parted ways where they'd started, having made a large loop. Lawrence hefted up his bag of mulch and adjusted it to a comfortable position while Isla watched him.

"Thanks again for taking me around and speaking with me."

He smiled. It was genuine, warm, even protective. "Of course. Staff look out for each other here. There's staff, the company employees, and them."

"Them?" Isla frowned, trying to keep up.

"The Corrigans. Each faction always looks out for themselves first, especially the Corrigans. Remember that, and you should be okay."

It was the best piece of advice that Isla could have received.

CHAPTER THIRTY-TWO

Victor Corrigan's rich mahogany shelves were filled with neatly arranged books of every kind, many of them well worn. He sat introspectively in his high-backed leather chair as she set down her bag and equipment and made no pretenses about looking around his room. She remembered herself, pausing momentarily.

"Do you mind?" She glanced over at him, asking sincerely.

He steepled his hands under his chin and nodded that it was okay, his eyes kind before he returned his attention to the several wall-mounted TV screens around the room, each on a national news channel, Bloomberg displaying the fluctuating Nasdaq stock prices. He watched them like they were football games, commenting when it seemed a particular stock was going to go down or maybe up by the end of the day. He instructed Dixon to check in with Myles in Special Projects and Research, see if it was a good company to buy into, or entirely.

Meanwhile, Isla finished taking in his study. She was surprised to find classics mixed in with his mounds of books about business and large binders labeled with the names of the various branches under the Corrigan Group, the departments and subsidiaries beneath. Similar to the family tree Isla had hidden in the motel closet, but where branches of family members would be, businesses were instead. The entire map of the Corrigan empire in its full glory. Isla couldn't hide how impressed she was at what this family had amassed and all it was into.

She crossed the Persian rug on the gleaming wood floor, took in the scent of leather from his furniture and the reek of stale cigar smoke. A sleek liquor cabinet stood in the corner with several decanters of various brown- and amber-colored liquids in them, untouched.

What stuck out to Isla, like a beacon of light shining brightly against all the other books lining the wall, was the Shakespearean play *Hamlet.* Isla paused in front of it, reaching out as if to touch it but stopping short, memory coming upon her. Eden's favorite. She'd mentioned a time when she used to be in theater in high school and found it the best thing about high school, if there was such a thing as the best part of high school.

What is it about Hamlet? Isla had asked. *Everyone dies.*

It's about revenge and redemption, Eden had said solemnly with awe mixed in. *It's about revealing everyone's dirty secrets and their betrayals by holding a mirror in front of them and cutting out the rot that was the ruin of that family.*

Isla had shivered listening to her. *Like I said, depressing and everyone dies.*

Yet here it was. Eden's favorite play. She pulled out the well-worn book and showed it to Victor.

His eyes squinted as he read the title, a wry smile spreading on his lips. "It was the favorite play of someone special to me. She loved Shakespeare and the British classics. But this one really spoke to her. I brought it here because it was something she loved. Makes me feel close to her, wherever she is. Careful—that particular edition was extremely expensive to obtain." Isla put it back.

Victor offered, "Sit." He gestured to the chair in front of his massive desk, the imposing piece of dark wood polished to a mirrorlike sheen.

Isla sat in the chair he'd indicated, trying not to fidget under Victor's steady gaze. He leaned back in his chair, fingers again steepled under his chin as he studied her, his expression unreadable. Isla sat up straight, determined not to falter in front of him or make him feel she was being anything but authentic and innocent of any ulterior motives.

"You'll forgive me," he finally said, low and measured. "I'm not accustomed to being interviewed by my employees. I'm usually the one doing the asking."

"Thanks again for letting me do this. I know it's not your norm. Everyone practically fights gladiator-style to work for you."

"Yet you got in so easily and quickly," he said, narrowing his eyes, still looking at her intently. "That's not our normal protocol, and believe me, I've heard about it from my wife, sons, Dixon, security. Why do you think that is, Isla?"

Isla smiled brightly, though her heart was pounding. She shrugged. "My winning smile?"

He huffed out a laugh. It rang through his office and likely could be heard outside. Dixon popped his head in inquisitively, but Victor waved him out.

Isla let herself relax a little. So far, so good. She had to tread carefully. This was the start of her investigation into Eden's disappearance, and she couldn't afford any mistakes. Not with a man like him.

"I'm glad you find me amusing. I think there are still some of the family who haven't taken to me quite yet."

He smirked, raising an eyebrow. "You must be referring to my wife." A statement rather than a question. "I heard she has you in staff housing rather than a guesthouse. I can get it changed if it's a problem for you. I've already heard about it from Holland. Her mother can be a bit . . ." He looked to the ceiling for the right words.

"Petty?" Isla muttered. Rey and Nat would get a kick out of this. Charli would ask who this alien being was.

Victor controlled himself. "Yes," he breathed out truthfully. "Don't let her get under your skin, okay? She can be overly protective of—" He broke off.

Isla kept a straight face. "Her territory?"

Victor frowned, but it wasn't serious. "Isla, that's my wife. My family." Like he felt the need to offer a flimsy attempt at showing respect for his wife. "That's a less than diplomatic way of putting it. My wife, in particular, has a talent for making her opinions known."

Isla nodded sagely. "Yes. Yes she does." But she offered no apologies, and he didn't push for one. "The staff housing is better than some of the places I've lived. And the scenery is to die for. I don't need much. I'm adaptable." That was the truth.

He looked as if she were feeding him a load of bull. "Are you now." A statement, not a question.

But she knew it was really a test. Everything with Victor would be a test to see what kind of person he was dealing with and what it was they wanted from him, how far they'd go to get it. Isla would try her hardest not to fall into that trap.

"Really. I'm just appreciative and honored you gave me this shot, since you don't know me so well."

"Speaking of." Victor opened up a manila folder in front of him and read through its contents. "Isla Thorne, graduate of UCLA, major in journalism, double minor in film and TV and business, as you already told us. You live near Venice Beach and work as one of the caregivers at a retirement facility, Brighton Springs Retirement. You've been working there for eight years. Before then, McDonald's." He considered her. "Why McDonald's?"

"I liked the Big Macs," she quipped.

She prayed Rey's technical genius held. She'd kept a pretty low profile anyway since moving to LA, but she hoped there wasn't anything left to link her to Daytona and Eden. It was odd having parts of her life read back to her—the scrubbed and sanitized parts, thanks to Rey and even Charli, who'd come through long ago with a fake ID that put her at two years older than she was. There would be no information about Daytona and her being a ward of the state.

Victor chuckled. "They have great fries."

Isla snorted. As if any of these people would ever step foot in a McDonald's. She doubted *fast food* was in their vocabulary.

He was amused. "You think McDonald's is beneath me?"

"Mr. Corrigan, you're one of the richest men in the US alone," Isla said. "You have five-star chefs at your beck and call. You're not going through the drive-through ordering a number one with a chocolate milkshake."

"I prefer the Hi-C Orange, young lady."

Isla gave him side-eye because he kept playing with her. "You don't even know what a number one is."

"Who doesn't like a Big Mac, Isla?"

And here she'd thought Victor was only eating Wagyu steak and freshly caught New England lobster.

He settled comfortably in his chair and looked at her expectantly after glancing at his watch. She was unsure of what he was waiting for her to do.

"Seriously, Mr. Corrigan, I honestly didn't expect you to know anything about McDonald's, let alone have a favorite meal there."

He almost looked insulted. "My father may have started our business, but he taught me hard work."

"You worked at one of his textile mills from the bottom up to prove you'd be able to run it when he stepped down. You grew your empire from the trucking and textile companies your father started into a global conglomerate with your first wife, Gayle Corrigan, rest in peace"—Victor raised an eyebrow—"and now you have interests in nearly every facet of business, technology, and industry. People say you take over failing businesses and restructure them, either selling them off at a huge financial profit or folding them under one of the Corrigan Group's many branches. You have several foundations, the largest being B&C, the one managed by your wife."

"You've done some homework." He gestured because Dixon had entered the office.

"She did." Dixon piped up, taking the cue. He laid a few folders on Victor's broad desk and took a seat in the vacant chair next to her. "A knack for adequate research is a good attribute for a journalist to have, I think."

Victor agreed. "That and keeping an open mind. Not believing everything you think you know about someone. Letting them show you who they really are." His words were pointed; Isla wasn't sure if the message was a warning about something she'd done or advice on how to proceed with him.

She said, "You probably know everything there is to know about me." Everything Rey had made sure was available, minus their investigative side hustle work. "I'm sure Dixon even gave you my credit score and student loan amounts."

Victor didn't deny it. He didn't agree either. He just gave a wry expression that said they were laying their cards out. It was better to come at him straightforwardly, no chaser. That was the interaction he valued over flattery and putting up pretenses.

He said, "I did build on what my father started. I was always underestimated until they couldn't afford to underestimate me anymore. You know being Black in business—in any field, to be honest—means always having to be better than the basic of white people or anyone else. It's a privilege we don't have, mediocrity—which is unfair. We have to work harder. Be spectacular. Be innovative all the time. We have to constantly wow everyone to make them take us seriously. It's exhausting, don't you think? White people don't have that baggage. This makes us have to be more callous and vicious than we'd prefer because they'll never make it easy for us. And then when we do all of that, are callous and vicious because they made us that way, they call us angry, aggressive, say they don't feel safe around us. I'm how I am, my work ethic is how it is, because I never again want to feel like I have to dance a jig to be accepted. I'm the one who accepts, or rejects."

His words hung heavily, ringing true. Their connectedness caused her to temporarily forget her reason for being there—that she was there not to understand Victor but to uncover what they had done to Eden. "Can I quote you on that?" she asked when she remembered her purpose.

He smirked. "Has the interview begun?"

She blessed him with a winning smile. "The moment I pulled up with my bags."

Myles entered with the leatherbound portfolio that Isla had decided was a part of his uniform, along with the dark suit slacks, matching vest, and crisp button-down shirt. "Dad, we really need to discuss the LA issue—" He broke off, noticing Isla and Dixon hanging in the background. The comfortable atmosphere between his father and this new addition took a moment for him to rationalize.

Isla waved him in as if the office were hers, not Victor's. She offered a disarming smile, even threw in a little flirtatious look to make it seem like he'd momentarily distracted her. Myles cleared his throat, looking unsure of what he was walking into. She wasn't sure what he was thinking, but he sat down next to Dixon anyway. She swallowed her small win. Whether he wanted to admit it or not, she intrigued Myles Corrigan. She could practically see the block of ice melting. Victor noticed her fluster at his son, and Myles's feigned uninterest, with keen eyes, not missing a beat.

Isla had committed the narrative Nat had taught her to memory and was ready to sell it to the man who'd mastered the art of a deal. The hard part was already done. She was in. Now, she just needed to stay in.

CHAPTER THIRTY-THREE

Isla slipped out the USB drive that Rey had instructed her to insert into their computer system to let his backdoor phishing program in, the Trojan horse that would piggyback off whatever file or email Victor opened and should permit the highest levels of access to the Corrigan Group system. "May I? I'd like to show you previous work I've done so you can see I'm for real. I don't have hard copies on hand."

She offered to have them run her drive through a check for viruses or anything else, but Victor waved it off, uninterested. "If there's something, our security systems will find it right away."

She hoped that wasn't the case and that Rey's expertise exceeded that of all the techs Victor paid. She inserted the drive and let Rey's program do the rest unseen as she pulled up her past work, some real, some embellished.

"Of course yours will be more in depth. Think *The Atlantic* or *The New York Times*, *Forbes*. Stories that combine human interest, business, and a theme. In your case a man who would rather show his accomplishments than talk about them, as many in your position often do."

Dixon glanced at the screen and the past articles she, Rey, and Nat had worked together to assemble in an electronic portfolio for her. "These are mainly school articles, no major publication outlets."

"Not yet," she said. "That's why I'm here, hoping to shoot my shot with Mr. Corrigan. Imagine, a nobody who gets an exclusive interview with the most elusive billionaire around."

Myles said, "A nobody, hmm?"

Isla nodded vigorously.

Victor stood and leaned over his desk, his sharp eyes scanning the layout. "This is . . ."

She held her breath, while Dixon and Myles looked as if they were waiting for the other shoe to drop.

"Ambitious," he finished, to her big expelling of breath.

"Ambition is the only way to do justice to a legacy like yours, Mr. Corrigan," she said seriously. "Think about what you said earlier about having to be practically perfect as a Black person to get acceptance and be taken seriously, like a real contender. This isn't just about a Man of the Year award in my book. It's about telling a story that will resonate long after the event—not just for the business world, but for those who have a dream, are up and coming, and look like you. Now they have a model to follow."

"Laying it on extra thick," Myles said under his breath. This time what she gave him wasn't a smile. She wished it could be her middle finger.

Victor seemed to agree, his lips twitching with the faintest semblance of amusement. "I'm not one for flattery, Isla Thorne. Let me hear your plan."

Not to be deterred by either one of them, she began to lay it out, telling them how the story would follow the typical three-act structure. The first would focus on his upbringing—his drive and determination to use what his father had started and build on it to create his empire.

Victor made a noise she took as approval.

"Second," she continued, "I'll highlight how you built the Corrigan Group, the Foundation, and their overall global influence, especially your outreach in Africa. That's really significant. I love how you're big on finding roots and going home to them. Even if there are those who say their roots begin here in America with their enslaved ancestors, your outreach gives credence and value to knowing where you're from, wherever you're from."

Victor looked at his right-hand man. "She's good, right? We could use her in marketing. Maybe in Special Projects and Research, hmm, Myles?"

"All right, Dad," Myles said, like he'd had enough.

Victor was unaffected. "Well, if you don't want her, I'm sure Bennett would be more than happy to have Isla working in one of the areas he heads up." Victor was enjoying himself a little too much, and Isla didn't like feeling like she was being passed around or about to be betrothed to anyone.

She demurred. "Let's not get carried away. Okay?" Victor shrugged as if it were her loss. "And we'll end by focusing on your role as family patriarch and your ongoing contributions to philanthropy and support of research and the Virginia and national libraries, among other philanthropic ventures."

Victor watched the screen. His silence encouraged Isla to continue.

"To keep it authentic, I'd like to include some of your challenges along the way. For example, the market crash of '08 and how you navigated the company through it. How you deal with issues then versus now." She hesitated, feigning a pause of deliberation. "Like the recent trouble in LA with your employee who passed away unexpectedly after being involved in some scandal."

Victor's sharp eyes bored into her, trying to read her intent. His expression didn't betray much except that she shouldn't mistake his politeness for trust. The frost in the room was so real, she almost lost her courage.

He asked coolly, "And how exactly do you plan to fit *that* into a story meant to showcase my accomplishments?"

Isla acknowledged his concern, adjusting her stance. She kept her tone even, ensuring the sudden case of nerves she felt didn't come through when she spoke. "You know I've already done some preliminary research. It's how I came up with all this overnight. What happened in LA is public knowledge, and since I live there, it was big news. A huge company. Death of an employee. Including something like that—acknowledging that there are pitfalls to go along with your successes and not everything is perfect—humanizes you. It kind of makes you relatable, especially to many who view you as larger than life. Like me, right? I was blown away when you said you like Big Macs and Hi-C Orange."

"Really, Dad?" Myles said, sneaking a look at Dixon, who feigned ignorance.

Isla chimed in, "No, but that's great. That's relatable. People respect honesty and resilience, and the Man of the Year is one who will give them all that."

Victor's attention had gone elsewhere, and he said softly, "You'll find there are parts of my life that don't fit neatly into any narrative. Some things are better left out entirely."

Isla's pulse quickened, but she kept her tone steady. "Sure, Mr. Corrigan. I only want to tell your story the way you want it told—the way it needs to be told," she added pointedly. "But sometimes the things we leave out are just as important as the things we include. They shape the context, if you know what I mean."

He settled back in his chair, looking thoughtful, as she began gathering the storyboard. When he gave permission, she removed the USB drive, sure that it had done its job and gotten Rey's worm in.

He asked, "For example?"

It was now or never. Who knew when she'd get this chance again, and even though they weren't alone, she felt Dixon and Myles wouldn't be a hindrance.

"Well." The room felt smaller, warmer, because though Myles had been there the entire time, his presence had become hard to ignore, and she was finding it harder to stay on track with the way he trained his attention on her.

She purposely swept her eyes over the wall behind Victor's seat until they landed on a photo she'd noted when she came in. She'd waited until the right moment to bring it up. All the kids were displayed in their own separate five-by-seven picture frames, smiling—or sort of smiling, in Myles's case—including Eden.

"I see all the Corrigan kids, but she is? A cousin?" Isla prompted.

She was pointing to a picture of Eden sitting on the edge of one of the fountains on the property, her dark hair wild in the wind, her expression bright and carefree. It was so at odds with the memories Isla had in her mind of the super-serious girl who was filled with so much sadness and contempt. Very rarely had Isla gotten to see Eden like this, and never again after her mother died.

Victor didn't have to look. He knew exactly who Isla was referring to. His lips pressed into a thin line as he contemplated how to reply. Then, his expression softened slightly, the edges of his hard demeanor cracking to reveal deep hurt and sadness inside. "My daughter Edie."

Isla feigned surprise, looking first at Myles, who stared intently at the Persian rug on the floor, and then at Dixon, whose expression remained stoic. She returned to Victor.

"I didn't realize . . . I thought . . . but the portrait downstairs . . ."

"Was commissioned recently, so she was unable to be in it," Victor said simply. "Edie has been away for many years now. She opts to live away from the home—abroad. It's complicated."

You have no idea, Isla thought. Or maybe he did and he was just playing with her. But that wasn't the sense Isla was getting from him.

"How old is she?" Isla said, as if trying to figure out where Eden fell in the birth line of his offspring.

"She's a little younger than Bennett," Victor replied, looking at Isla when he delivered that. "She'd be about your age. And before you ask further, yes, she was born after my marriage to my second wife, Brooke, and the birth of our son Bennett."

There was heavy silence in the room as his words settled on Isla to make her conclusions and judgments. She kept her thoughts and her surprise at how open Victor was being to herself, lest he change his mind.

Before she could probe any more, Victor said, "I think we've started with some good material for you. I have business to take care of, so we can talk more some other time. Just let Dixon or my admin assistant know when you'd like to meet." He looked past her. "Myles, will you walk her out? Help her with her things? Come back later, and we can talk about what's on your agenda."

As she headed toward the door, following Myles while Dixon joined Victor at his desk, Isla stopped as if remembering. "I'll be heading to town soon to gather outside perspectives on you and the family, along with speaking with house staff and employees I come across. It'll help round out the whole piece."

Victor broke out in a smile, his sadness temporarily wiped away. "I'm not sure I want to know what they all think of me." He winced. "Even I have feelings, contrary to popular belief."

"You might be pleasantly surprised, Mr. Corrigan," she said, back to her bubbly self. "I promise the finished product will be unforgettable."

She was at the door, about to walk through, when he called out, "You've got tenacity, Isla Thorne. I'll give you that. Just be careful when you go around—this family has a way of testing people. And not everyone is up for the challenge."

"Oh, don't worry about me. I'm up for any challenge you throw at me."

He laughed. "Now that, I believe."

CHAPTER THIRTY-FOUR

The following day, Isla was glad she was used to walking as she headed toward the guard station at the front gates. She needed to get to town, and knowing no rideshare would be allowed beyond the gates, she would meet them there. She was walking down the tree-lined road that she'd ridden up on the day before when suddenly she wasn't alone anymore. A car slowed beside her and stopped when she did.

"Myles," she said with surprise, ignoring the annoying little flutter in her stomach when the window rolled down and she saw him behind the wheel this time. No driver, his own personal car.

He asked casually, "What are you doing?"

She told him her plan, and then she heard the door unlock. She looked at him questioningly.

"The walk to the gate is over half a mile. You should have just asked for a driver. Dad instructed everyone to help you with what you need."

She wished she had known that before she'd started this trek.

"I can take you into town," Myles offered. She couldn't tell if the offer was genuine or because of the directive from his father. Plus, she was planning to visit Eden's high school friend Sara. She didn't need Myles knowing what she was up to.

"Or not," he said when her reply was taking too long.

She got in, saying, "I'll take the ride to the guard station. I'll order an Uber from there so I don't take up your time. I know you're busy."

"Did I say I was busy?" he said through clenched teeth. She'd annoyed him again. She didn't know how to be around him.

"Sorry," she mumbled, deciding silence was her best bet. They remained that way until they got to the gates and pulled up behind an idling car, one from their fleet.

"You can use that car to get around since riding with me must be unbearable," Myles said gruffly, his eyes ahead of him.

"That's not what I meant!"

It didn't matter. "The guards have the keys." When shock and confusion kept her in her seat, he prompted, "If you don't mind"—the doors unlocked, and he still looked ahead—"I'm rather busy."

~

Eden's high school friend was next on Isla's list of interviewees. Sara's house was blue, like Becca had said, very cute and modest, with a neatly trimmed yard and a welcome sign featuring a mini wooden replica of the larger house hanging on the door. A small red Mazda was parked in the driveway. Isla knocked, and after a moment, a woman with eyes similar to Becca's and auburn hair pulled back in a low ponytail answered. She was wearing an oversize UVA sweatshirt, leggings, and a pair of thick furry socks.

"Can I help you?" she asked cautiously, looking Isla over.

Isla was presentable and hoped she looked pleasant looking and approachable in dark denim jeans and a light, airy white shirt to stave off the summerlike heat. She had a tan messenger bag slung over her shoulder, and it held the equipment she'd picked up from her post office box at the local USPS office. She had a mic; a small video camera in case she couldn't use her phone; her laptop, which was also connected to Rey and which he could access at any time so they could transfer information virtually undetected; notebooks and pens; and a pair of

Ray-Ban Meta smart glasses (compliments of Rey, of course) that looked like dark, oversize sunglasses but had two tiny cameras embedded on either side of the lenses.

"The GlimpZi glasses are better, in my opinion," Rey had said the other night when she'd checked in. "But the camera is right in the middle and really obvious at first glance. They're also chunky looking, so I think you're better off with the next step down, especially if you're using them in a crowd. Less noticeable."

"Okay," Isla had replied, not really caring either way. She did what she was told. She only planned to use them in public settings and not during one-on-ones. That would make the interviewee uncomfortable.

She introduced herself. "Your aunt Becca at Mabel's may have called you about my coming over to chat?"

Sara was biting her upper lip as Isla spoke. "She did. Said you're interviewing about the Corrigans."

"That's right. It's a project about Mr. Corrigan, actually, for an award he's receiving. I'm trying to get various perspectives about him so I can portray him accurately and thoroughly. I heard you knew one of his daughters, Edie, pretty well in high school?"

Sara's face softened at the mention of her old friend, and she stepped back, pulling the door open with her, and gestured for Isla to enter. They sat opposite each other in two armchairs in Sara's cozy living room, in front of her large bay windows with sunlight streaming through, bathing the room in a warm glow.

Sara self-consciously patted her hair when she settled into her seat after accepting Isla's refusal of any hot or cold beverages. "Will you be recording? Is it video or audio? I don't think I'm camera ready."

Isla laid her bag on the carpeted floor next to her feet. "I don't think that's necessary. I don't have time to watch interviews for the article I'm writing on Mr. Corrigan, so notes will suffice. If you don't mind."

Sara didn't mind. Still, she straightened her sweatshirt and pulled her ponytail through a hand to tame any strays. Isla noticed a stack of papers on the center table, a teacher's planner notebook, and another notebook with **Gradebook** printed on it. She pointed, brightening.

"You're a teacher."

"Yes, seventh grade. Middle school, I know," Sara added when Isla grimaced. Isla remembered how middle school had seemed especially hard when she'd had to endure it. She imagined it was ten times worse when you were a teacher and had to combat a hundred emotional teens on a daily basis.

Isla continued to make the nervous woman comfortable by discussing what Sara did best. "I thought grades were done electronically now?"

Sara followed where Isla was pointing. "They are, but my mentor teacher—she was an older lady—taught me to always have a backup. On the news the other day, I heard the grading system in an entire state was hacked and the state superintendent had to announce it to everyone. I don't think grades were compromised, but if it ever happened in my district, or throughout Virginia, I have a hard copy right there. I'm trying not to regrade a hundred twenty argumentative essays."

"Smart," Isla said. "You're a true hero, being a teacher. No, really, you are. It's not easy at all, and more people on the outside looking in should realize and respect what you do for how little you get."

Sara smiled, looking away bashfully, letting Isla pile on the compliments.

"But off my soapbox. As I was doing a preliminary walk-through of the Corrigan estate—massive, by the way—I realized there was one Corrigan unaccounted for, their eldest daughter, Edie."

"Not *their*. *His*. Mrs. Corrigan isn't Edie's mother by a long shot, thank God." She rolled her eyes as if Edie had dodged a bullet on that one, and Isla couldn't have agreed more. "Her mother is Elise and lives in Daytona."

Isla swallowed. Clearly Sara didn't know that Elise was dead. Isla wanted to tell her, but that would mean blowing the little bit of cover she had. She wasn't supposed to know anything. This was supposed to be fact-finding before she decided what to do with it all.

"Right. Mr. Corrigan's daughter. Your aunt mentioned the two of you were pretty close?"

A tiny smile played on Sara's lips as if she were remembering something pleasant. Isla hoped she was. Nothing but pleasant thoughts of Eden.

"Yeah, Edie and I were really close," Sara began, her voice coated with a nostalgia that Isla could relate to. Her own throat started to thicken and hurt from trying to keep her emotions at bay. This woman had known Eden when she was a totally different person and lived a whole life Isla had known nothing about. The two worlds clashing in this moment was proving to be more difficult than Isla had thought it would be. How much worse would it get?

Sara continued, and Isla pulled herself out of her own feelings to listen. "She had this light about her that drew everyone to her. Like, she was a really good person. Innocent and kind of naive, which was saying a lot for a Corrigan. They aren't known for being innocent, kind, or naive."

Isla could attest to that too.

"We were in theater club together, which was where she really shone. Before that, she was really quiet and low key. She was aware of her status and her name and didn't want any fanfare, since she was at a regular public school and not at the private school all the country-club people on the hill send their kids to. She just wanted to blend in and be regular."

Isla could see that too.

"But when she joined theater club, that's where she couldn't hide who she really was. She shone, and I'm not just blowing smoke, you know? She was really good. We also had English together the year and a half she attended—"

"Year and a half?"

"Well, she began attending our sophomore year. I guess she tried the private school for a year, hated it, and made her dad let her attend public. So she attended Jefferson High all of sophomore and half of junior year until she left in the middle. I remember British literature was her favorite, Shakespeare especially. She loved all his works. She even got me into theater and convinced our director, Mrs. Hall, to let us put on a production of *Hamlet.*" Sara shook her head. "She was really into tragedies. That's . . . depressing. Right?" she said as if realizing it now for the first time, then laughed ruefully at her friend.

"You mentioned she left Jefferson High midway through her junior year. Did she tell you why she was leaving?"

Sara shook her head glumly. "I wish she had. Maybe I could have helped. All I know is she started becoming withdrawn after Labor Day junior year. She wouldn't say why. And the weeks after that, she would say less and less, and then she was gone."

Isla asked, "But was there something that happened around Labor Day that made her change suddenly and become more withdrawn afterward? Any event that stands out to you now that you think about it?"

Sara pressed her lips together, trying to recall something. "Nothing I can think of that was a big deal." She quieted, thinking more. "Wait. I think there was some bad car accident that weekend and people died. Yeah, when we came back to school, that's what everyone was talking about. Crashes down mountains don't happen as often as people who don't live around mountain roads think. Everyone knows how to navigate them here. But I didn't really believe there was anything major because there was nothing on the news or anything. No one except a few students was talking about it. I chalked it up to rumor and forgot about it. But yeah, that's about the time Edie started changing." Sara looked at Isla beneath raised eyebrows. "Don't you need to write or record any of this? How will you remember?"

"I guess you're such a great teacher and former theater participant that you tell such a great story, there's no way I'll forget it," Isla admitted, chuckling. An understatement. Sara had Isla's mind reeling, and the questions kept piling one on top of another, but she'd better jot down something to keep up pretenses. "Did Edie's family support her interests? I would think so, since her father let her attend your school."

Sara hesitated. "I remember her saying how much her mom did. And she wished her mom could come and see her perform. But of course she was all the way in Florida. But the rest . . . they were complicated. I think her oldest brother came to pick her up after practice sometimes, and he seemed interested enough. He and her father even came to a performance. Just the two of them. She got really emotional then."

Myles . . . so he wasn't as hard and icy as Isla thought. He might have had a soft spot, and that might have been Eden. Isla made a note to dig in deeper later, when she spoke with him.

"But the rest . . . her brother Bennett—who was a total ass back then—and his friends Danny, Roger, and James. They always came around causing trouble. I hear Bennett's grown up some now, matured some, though he's the typical rich playboy. Thinks he's God's gift to women. All the women around, especially the 'elite' ones"—she used air quotes—"are vying to be the next-generation Mrs. Corrigan for both brothers. And I bet their little sister, Holland, has a bunch of wannabes who are itching to be the next son-in-law."

Isla needed to redirect and wrap this up; she felt she'd gotten just about all the information she needed from Sara for now. There was just one final thing Sara had said that had struck a chord. "Bennett and his friends?" she prompted.

"She couldn't stand them. They'd get off school and come around ours, trying to make trouble. They were bullies and assholes and played too many lame, childish tricks on everyone who wasn't in their upper circle. That meant all of us little people down here."

"Tricks like . . . ?"

"I don't know because I never saw them doing it. But like the ones you might see in some of those really old eighties movies about wild teens wreaking havoc on their town? Edie hated their constant mean tricks and hated that she had to go back with them because her father had told Bennett he needed to get his sister." Sara paused, thinking. "Except James."

"James?"

"Yeah, he wasn't like the others. Danny and Roger were all bravado and clowning, getting into all sorts of mayhem. They were a complete menace. But James was different. Quieter. Sensitive. His downside was he was a follower. Maybe it was because his dad owned one of the biggest law firms here and also worked as counsel for some Corrigan interests. I don't know, but I never understood why he hung around those guys. I think maybe he followed them around because he liked Edie and she liked him, though she never admitted it out loud. If they had, Bennett would have figured out a way to kill it, I'm sure. Bennett wasn't fond of his sister—or at least that's what it seemed—but he didn't want his friends dating her either, especially James."

In Daytona, Eden had never shown any romantic interest in anyone. Now Isla was hearing there was a boy she'd left back home. What could have been that serious to make her leave him?

"Do you know where I can find James? Is he still around?"

"Of course. Most people are born and raised and stay here. Especially if their family holds a lot of sway around town, as all those guys' families did. Except Edie. I guess she escaped the weight of the Corrigans and all that. James is around, though. He lives off Birch. You sometimes see him around Bennett and the others, but not like when Edie was here. Something broke him too."

CHAPTER THIRTY-FIVE

James Mitchell's home on Birch was more understated than she expected it to be, considering his connection to one of the most prestigious law firms in town. It was simplistic in design and looked as forlorn and lonely as its owner. The paint could have used an update, and the lawn was overdue for a mow. The place looked ignored, to be honest, and Isla bet the only people who paid any attention to it were probably his parents if they had to visit. To keep up appearances, probably. Who wanted a recluse of a son? It had been years since he'd last seen Edie, and he was just out of high school by that time. Would Eden's leaving have made that much of an impact on a guy whose friends were as Sara described them?

Isla got her answer a moment later when he opened the door, a tired-looking man with listless eyes that barely acknowledged her beneath a mop of unruly hair. Isla was taken aback by how disheveled James looked, and she found it hard to believe he was one of Bennett's close friends.

"James?" Isla asked, just to make sure she had the right guy, and this wasn't his hapless brother.

"Who else?" His voice sounded bland, but his eyes suddenly held a hint of life. "And I already know who you are," he continued before she could begin her intro. "Word gets around fast here, especially when it has to do with the Corrigans and is coming straight from Bennett. Didn't think you'd be stopping by here. Not much I can tell you about the big man that you can't get from everyone else."

Isla could only imagine what Bennett had to say about her. "Maybe so. But can you tell me about his daughter Edie?"

His expression darkened at the mention. She prepared for the door to slam in her face and was mildly surprised when, after a slight hesitation, he stepped aside to let her in.

The inside looked much better than out, homier if relatively sparsely decorated. The furnishings that were there definitely had a mother's touch. James didn't look like he could be bothered with anything relatively decorative.

"Why do you want to know about Edie?" James asked when they'd settled in his kitchen. Unlike Sara, James didn't offer any refreshments, though Isla didn't expect him to be that kind of thoughtful host, not because he felt animosity toward Isla—at least not yet—but just because he probably thought he wouldn't have anything in his fridge that an unexpected female visitor would want.

Isla started the spiel she'd put together to get herself in the door, but James stopped her midway through. She was kind of put out. She'd worked hard rehearsing with Nat and Rey, making sure her bit sounded realistic and enthusiastic enough to believe.

"Let's skip to the good part, okay?" James said. He looked tired, like he hadn't been getting a lot of sleep.

As they walked through the halls to the kitchen, Isla checked out the array of photos that chronicled his life thus far: his graduation from their private school and then Virginia Tech, and then Georgetown for his law degree. All of them with James standing in between a pair of proud parents. His proud mother with her energetic smile reminded Isla of Sheryl Lee Ralph, which made her age indeterminable, and James's father was the lighter mirror image of his son, sharing the same clear blue eyes, prominent nose, and lanky build.

He repeated himself when Isla looked confused. "What does Edie have to do with a spread on her father? She's been gone"—he swallowed—"years. From what I hear, she doesn't keep in touch."

Well, all right, Isla thought, sitting back in her chair. No need to butter him up. He liked things straight. She could respect that.

Isla had taken out a notebook for her talk with James, and she looked at the page with various notes she'd jotted down thus far to show she was keeping track, as if trying to decide where to begin. She asked, "Do you know why that is? You're one of Bennett's friends. I hear from Sara that you, Bennett, Danny Crawford, and Roger Monroe have been very close friends since school. You all were tight. You should know why she left and why she hasn't returned, shouldn't you?"

She watched his reaction to the last question, and she got a ding, because the man most definitely flinched as if he'd been zapped. And then his shoulders slumped, and sadness came over him. Isla didn't know whether to be suspicious or comforting, because the guy sitting across from her was definitely conflicted. Isla didn't know what James knew, but he knew something.

She said softly, "She deserves the truth, don't you think? Sara said the two of you really cared for each other, and from what I'm seeing now, I think you really did. You probably know more than anyone what happened to her. Maybe she confided in you?"

She was going in hard, she knew. But since there was something between them, maybe Eden had reached out to him when she and Isla had come to town back then.

James stared at the table—any harder and he would have burned a hole in it. His hands were clasped tightly in front of him. "Edie and I were . . . she trusted me. And I . . . I didn't stand up like I should have."

Isla leaned forward, feeling the answer was right on the cusp of her knowledge. "What do you mean you didn't stand up? What happened?"

He shook his head like she wouldn't understand. "So much happened. Too much. But you gotta understand we were all young. Me and Bennett, Rog and Danny, we were on break from college, and Edie was in high school, always trying to be accepted by Bennett. She really wanted him to like her. And I did too," he admitted in a small voice. "I mean, I'm not a jock like Danny, or funny like Rog, or someone who has everything come easy to me like Bennett."

"Your dad owns one of the most prestigious law firms in this region, which you work for and will become partner in and take over. The firm does business with the Corrigan Group too. That seems like a privileged life to me," Isla retorted.

She couldn't help it, but when those who *had* whined about what they *didn't* have when there were so many people with so much less, it got on her nerves. If James struggled, it was because of his own doing, Isla wagered. Not because his family couldn't provide.

James let out a shaky breath, not seeming to notice Isla's snark.

"What was the deal between Bennett and Edie?"

"He just couldn't stand her. He called her a Goody Two-shoes. He and the other guys could be cruel and play around too much. And me and Edie, we weren't like that, and we started talking, yeah. But I was older, and she was a Corrigan, and Bennett's little sister."

"But he couldn't stand her."

"That didn't mean he'd want me or any of his friends to get with her. Allowing that would mean she might be happy, and for some reason only Bennett can understand, he didn't like any of his siblings being happy. Not Myles. Not Edie. He made their lives miserable. At least Holland was young enough that she wasn't in his orbit. And after Edie left and Myles was gone to the air force, Mr. and Mrs. Corrigan kept a closer eye on Holland. Plus, Holland wasn't competition. So he left her alone."

That all tracked. Bennett pretty much acted like Holland didn't exist, and his contempt for Myles radiated from him.

"I thought I could protect her. I could talk everyone down. But I wasn't strong enough."

Isla's heart pounded. "Protect her from what, James?" she asked. "Do you know why she disappeared?"

James shook his head. "Probably because I couldn't protect her. If only we hadn't gone riding that night. If only we hadn't been drinking at the old Abbott farm . . ." He swallowed hard, like it hurt him to do so. "She probably believes I betrayed her, and I probably did. Twice I didn't stand up for the person I cared about the most. She wouldn't let that happen a third time."

Isla could taste it. The truth was right there. A huge piece of the puzzle—maybe the biggest piece. If only he would just say it.

"This sounds like a huge weight on you for years," she gently prodded. "You'd probably feel a lot better if you explained it all. I'm sure Eden would forgive you."

He sat up. "Why do you call her that?" he asked sharply.

Isla was confused. "Call who what?"

"Eden," James said suspiciously. "No one would call her that around here." He eyed her sharply, his voice gaining strength. "When you got here, you called her Edie. It's how we've been referring to her. But just now, you called her Eden."

Isla was at a loss for words. She could have kicked herself for her slipup. "But that's her name." The first excuse she could think of.

He said warily, "Why are you really asking about her? What is it you want?"

She lifted her hands as if innocent. "I just want to learn about Victor Corrigan."

"And yet you haven't asked me one question about him."

He was right. She was too eager to find out about Eden. She was forgetting her own story. Isla attempted to pacify him, trying to look innocent and save their moment. James was the most important person in this story. He was the one she could get closest to out of all of them because he had something none of the others had. He had guilt, and it'd been weighing on him to the point he'd almost spilled. But in her eagerness—her hunger—she might have ruined her chance. She was coming in too hot. Rey and Nat would have told her so if they could hear what was going on.

She decided to pivot. "Asking questions about an estranged child is about Victor, James," Isla said lightly. "It lets me know what kind of kids he's raising. It helps me mold the types of questions I'll ask Mr. Corrigan when I sit down with him soon," she explained as patiently as she could. She hoped she looked earnest enough and not desperate. She couldn't afford to scare him off. But the skepticism with which he looked at her made her feel her chances were lessening by the moment and she needed to back off.

"Also, it seems like you had a lot of things on your mind. Like you had no one to talk to, and here I am. An objective ear to help you figure out what to do next to relieve some of these feelings you're going through. I think Eden . . . and I say that because I don't know your Edie and the way she was presented to me was as Eden. So I'll likely switch back and forth between names as I'm figuring out how she fits into Mr. Corrigan's story." That was the most truthful thing Isla had said about herself since she'd been here.

James stared at her dully, the fight going out of him, leaving only residue. "She doesn't fit into his story. It's why she left. Her family was too much for her. They broke her. That's what they do. Even to their own."

CHAPTER THIRTY-SIX

Isla thought about James her entire ride back to the Corrigan estate. His haunted demeanor troubled her as she returned the car she had borrowed and walked back to her room. When she was alone, she sat on her bed and typed up everything she remembered and the multitude of questions she had on the laptop Rey had given her. She called him and Nat on three-way.

"Sounds to me like he and his buddies were involved in whatever happened to her," Rey said.

"Two things," Isla mused. "First, what happened that changed Eden so much over Labor Day weekend? I think if you run some checks around that year and time and cross-reference a car accident, that could help me ask the right questions. And then there's what happened when Eden and I got here two years later. She had to meet someone. She told me she was doing that, setting things right."

"Whatever James the coward and his goon-squad friends did, Eden was involved, and James didn't stop it," Nat continued over the noise on her end. "What if she came back to settle the score before she came to LA with you?"

"And what? It went sideways?" Isla asked before she could think about what she was saying. She was talking about her friend, not a third-party job with no ties. *Sideways* meant someone who didn't like the score Eden was settling could have hurt her. Isla whispered, a crack showing through her businesslike demeanor, "Do you really think they would have hurt her over some high school thing? Really?"

Isla didn't want to believe it. She couldn't. The Corrigans were a lot of things: ruthless in the business world, fiercely protective of their members, private. But were they capable of more than that? Were they deadly?

Rey cut through. "I'll do some searching here and let you know."

"Got it," she said.

Nat said, "And promise me one more thing?"

"What's that?" Isla asked.

"To be careful."

CHAPTER THIRTY-SEVEN

Isla was back at the row of parked golf carts, determined to get the right one this time and go for a spin around this place. She was looking for number 8 when she noticed someone familiar strolling down one of the maze of pathways coming from the estate, his hands in his pockets, in a suit with the vest but minus the jacket. This wasn't his stomping ground, and if he needed one of the staff, he'd message them on their watch.

She found number 8 and was slipping in the driver's seat as he passed her. He looked deep in thought. She wasn't sure he'd seen her.

"Myles," she loudly whispered.

He stopped short. Startled, he looked around until he followed where the voice had come from and spotted her sitting in the cart. She flipped on the light, and he threw an arm up to shield his eyes. She laughed, turning it off.

He strained as his eyes adjusted. "Isla? There you are." The sound of his deep baritone after so much quiet sounded like a foghorn. It was the best sound she'd heard all day. "What are you doing sitting in a cart in the dark?"

"What are you doing walking through this neck of the woods? This here is for staff and workers. Main-house people don't come past the guesthouses unless you're going to play golf. I doubt you're doing that this late."

"Looking for you, actually." He paused. "And then literally looking for you when you weren't at the main house or staff quarters. They said to check the cart lot because you've been itching to get in one since you got here."

That was right, because Lawrence wanted her traipsing around on foot, something entirely unnecessary.

He was here for her. She pointed at herself.

He made a face. "Don't act so surprised."

But she couldn't leave it alone. She'd always figured she'd be the one going to Myles Corrigan, not him coming to her. "You've barely said two words to me since we met that fateful night. And you've been scarce since."

"It's only been two or so days, right? I didn't know I made such an impression on you, Miss Thorne. I apologize for not being at your disposal." She half expected him to bow, as his voice dripped with sarcasm. Isla considered running him over with the idling cart.

She ignored his jab, instead motioning for him to join her. He could sit in the passenger seat. He hesitated before doing so, likely considering insisting on doing the driving, but Isla patted the passenger seat and turned on the lights.

When they were on their way, following a path that looked as good as any, Myles asked, "Where are we going?"

She shrugged. "Beats the hell out of me." She cast him a sidelong glance, noting how he gripped the sides of the golf cart like he was holding on for dear life. She pressed the gas to give him a little more excitement. He bared his teeth, and that satisfied her. That was for the times he'd acted like she didn't exist.

She asked, "Why were you looking for me?"

"Because Holl asked me to. She said you were probably avoiding the house because of her mother and maybe me." He mumbled the last part. "She said I haven't been hospitable."

"Well, they don't call you the Ice Prince for nothing," Isla told him.

His brow arched, but he didn't respond. Isla paid attention to their every turn, determined to learn the ins and outs of this place so she could move easily. How well did he know the layout of his own home? If she got them lost, would he be able to find their way back? They were about to see.

"Why's that?" she pressed. "I don't think you're trying to hide how uninterested you are in being here. You even went into the military right after high school to get away."

"I wanted to experience life outside all of this."

"But you came back."

"Because this is my family and they needed me." His tone made Isla take her eyes off the road because he sounded so resolute and determined.

"But you act as if you can't be bothered with what goes on around here. Dixon is more invested than you are, and he's not even related. And you let your brother get away with a lot too. He struts around the place like he's the eldest and like he's going to be the next CEO."

"He probably is," Myles said simply.

She slowed the cart to a stop right in the middle of the path. Ahead of them was a large lake mirroring the moon. It rippled from the insects and fish in it.

"You all even have a lake," she mused, shaking her head in wonder. She got back to business. Understanding the dynamics of these people was critical to figuring out how Eden fit or didn't fit, according to James.

"Why not fight for it yourself? Why are you content being where you are, running Special Projects and Research and Asset Management?"

He was silent for so long she thought he wouldn't answer. Finally, he said, "Because Bennett wants it. And some things aren't worth the fight. I think we've lost enough because of sibling rivalry and competition."

His words were calm but carried a weight that pulled at her. There was so much more in those few lines he'd spoken. Deeper, more hurtful things.

"That's vague. And depressing." His only reply was to continue looking out at the rippling lake. "It seems to me only one sibling is competing. Now your sister has been estranged for years."

The mention of Eden lit a fire under him, and he spun on her, making her jump back and get ready to run from the golf cart. Had she said something offensive? Was he going to get as weird as James had?

"That's exactly why I'm not going to enlist in some epic battle for my father's position. We already lost one sister. I don't want us to lose anyone else."

"Lost her," Isla repeated slowly. "Lost her how? Like she's-off-grid-and-damning-the-whole-family-to-hell kind of lost? Or dead-and-gone kind of lost?"

The sadness in Myles's face made Isla want to reach out and touch him, but she held herself back. She didn't trust herself around him.

"The last time I saw Edie, she was in school and loving her theater club. Then, when I was in the service, she disappeared. My father found out her mother had died. Edie left this letter denouncing the family and saying that we'd never see her again. We haven't. For my father's sake I hope she is out there in the Bahamas or Montenegro or the Maldives, living life as freely as she wants. But the reality is we'd have heard something by now. Her trusts haven't been touched. There is no financial trail for her. No pings on ID, nothing. If she has any money, it's money her mother saved for her that my father isn't in control of. But we can't share those thoughts with my father. The only thing he has to hold on to is the belief that she's just too angry to deal with him. That's why her room remains the same as it was the day she left for Daytona. It's the room of a high school girl."

Eden's room. She had to get inside it.

"But why would she be angry? What made her leave here in the first place?"

"I'll leave that question for the old man to answer when you interview him." He looked at his watch, which had lit up, an Apple like those of the staff.

"Are you being summoned like one of the staff?" she said incredulously.

He scoffed. "One of us has to be, right? Since you refused yours. I need to get back to the house, so let me drive? You're like a little old lady, except that time you tried to scare me earlier."

He got them back in record time. In Isla's opinion the ride was too quick. There was much more she wanted to know about Myles Corrigan beyond Victor or Eden. He had spent all his time wrapping himself up in a nearly impenetrable cocoon. Why?

As they neared her stop, Isla ventured, "Now that we've had a nice conversation, could you be a little nicer to me? Maybe melt some of that ice so they call you Slushy instead of Ice Prince?"

He gave her a pitiful look. "That wasn't funny."

She shamefully agreed, wondering when her joke-telling ability had become so corny.

The cart stopped, and she hopped out as he said, "I'll think about becoming more of a slushy. Tell them I've taken the golf cart so they don't freak out thinking it's missing."

She nodded, stepping back so he could be on his way.

Myles grew serious. "Remember to watch yourself around here. This place—the people—may come off perfect, beautiful, elegant. But that's all a facade. Life here is not that simple."

She thanked him for the warning, trying to tally the number of times Myles had helped her out and figure out what his help meant.

She stepped inside the building and glanced back. He was still there, watching her with an expression she couldn't read. Then, in a blink, he was gone, and her most pressing thought was how she could get into Eden's room.

CHAPTER THIRTY-EIGHT

She wasn't able to get into Eden's room until a few days later. During that time, Isla utilized her access to the estate and the people on it under the pretext of her profile of Victor Corrigan. She'd gained more insight about who Eden had been pre-Daytona from the people who knew her. Eden was loved, and no one, except maybe her stepmother, had anything negative to say about her, and it seemed like they missed her.

It was as good a time as any for Isla to be in Eden's space from when she had been Edie. Maybe that would give her a clue about what had forced her to leave. It was for the greater good, Isla told herself. With Holland now back at school, Isla felt free to do what she needed without guilt hanging over her head. And gradually, the staff, Mae, and Lawrence were warming to her. Even Myles treated her with less frost. She'd take it.

The lock on Eden's bedroom door gave a soft click, and Isla slid the master key that she'd borrowed from Mae's key ring back into her pocket. She hoped Mae wouldn't realize it was missing, and even more, she hoped Mae wouldn't be too upset with her for lifting it if she did.

Isla hesitated, feeling intrusive, but she pushed past her doubts. This was the room no one entered. It had been frozen in time on Victor's command, and no one dared—save Mae every so often to dust—to enter it. Not even Victor. The door creaked open from being underused, revealing a room set thirteen years in the past.

There was even a lingering scent of lavender in the air from the last time the room had been dusted. The decor was eclectic and simple, the room bathed in soft pastels that offset the array of bold theatrical posters that hung from her walls—the infamous *Hamlet, A Streetcar Named Desire, The Phantom of the Opera, Rent, Grease, West Side Story, Chicago.* Isla bet Eden had seen them all on Broadway when they first came out. She would have loved *Hamilton* and the latest versions of *Wicked* if she'd been around. Also up were posters of the River Thames and the Globe Theatre, where many of Shakespeare's plays had been performed.

Her furniture was expensive yet reflective of her character—understated elegance, light and dainty. Stacks of playbills littered the top of her desk. Eden's room in Daytona had been fairly bare, minimalist, with one or two reprinted posters. Nothing like what Isla was seeing now. It was Isla's first true glimpse into Edie Corrigan, and she was awestruck. There was even a half-burned candle on the dresser. She sniffed it. Lavender. Maybe that was where the lingering scent had come from.

Isla moved quickly but cautiously, scanning the room for anything she thought would give her more information. Where would a girl like Edie hide her most precious things? Eden had never kept a journal or diary back home, but here maybe she had. Isla checked under the bed, pushing herself all the way to the other end in case it was against the wall. She slid her hands beneath the extra-fluffy pillows, checked in her desk drawers and between the few books there. Nothing. It was surreal. Everything here reminded Isla of her friend and also taught Isla about her friend. She wanted to sit in the middle of the floor and soak it up. She could see why Victor kept the room locked. It was too hard to look at on a daily basis. Isla rubbed her aching chest.

A narrow bookshelf caught her eye. Among the rows of classic novels and poetry collections topped with Hello Kitty stuffed characters and cute, furry bears was a small dusty stack of DVDs and VHS tapes. Isla raised her brows, trying to think back a decade—had people still used VHS tapes back then? DVDs, maybe. Now both were considered ancient, and if you admitted to knowing what they were, much less how to use them, you were deemed old, historical.

She pulled them out, examining the titles. *Breakfast at Tiffany's*, *Casablanca*, *The Wiz*, *Fences*, *Othello*, featuring Denzel Washington—a masterpiece, in Isla's proud opinion—and *The Merchant of Venice* with Al Pacino. One tape in particular stood out among the rest, its case misaligned. *Mommie Dearest*. Well now.

Isla let out a low chuckle at the irony, forgetting she was not supposed to be here and pulling the black, plastic, rectangular tape from its case. If Edie was anything, it was the queen of subtle shade, and Isla suspected this movie was in honor of Edie's very own live version of Joan Crawford's horrible character. As she pulled the tape free, a square piece of yellow paper fell out. She knelt to pick it up, heart beating as she saw the embossed *E* in script at the top of the paper.

> I'd never hurt Holl. How could he ever think that? But I'd rather leave since they want me gone so bad than let Dad look at me like I'm some monster. I already am one after how we left them. If I stay any longer, either I'll become like him, or I won't be at all.

Isla's hands trembled as she read the neat but rushed handwriting again. It was as if Edie had written this in a moment of desperation. This was more than just a clue. This was a window into Eden's state of mind before she'd left here. This was the explanation for why she'd always seemed to be holding a piece of herself back when she was in Daytona. Her words carried the weight of betrayal and the pain of being blamed for something she hadn't done. And what was it that Edie had supposedly done to make Victor look at her like she was a monster?

She was so deep in her thoughts that she didn't hear the door creak as it widened or feel that the doorway was now filled with an imposing figure that cast an ominous shadow in the room.

"Why the hell are you in here? What do you think you're doing?" Victor roared. He was so angry his eyes were reddened and his face was covered in a sheen of sweat.

Quickly she got to her feet, shoving the note and the DVD case behind her back, caught right in the act. She worked to put the video into its case and the note in her back pocket as she thought of an explanation that would wipe the complete anger off Victor's face.

"I was . . ." Normally she was so quick, but words were failing her now. "I was looking for stuff that might help me with the project. Edie was—is," she corrected when he reacted, "such a significant person in your life that I thought being in here would give me better perspective." She was blathering. She'd never been so scared in her life. Not even when that rowdy gang of gambling thugs had chased her and Rey all the way down Alameda Street until they lost them.

"This room," he began, his voice low and violent. He was still in the doorway, hadn't stepped a foot inside. "Is off limits. No one comes in except Mae to clean. This is Edie's private space, and she wouldn't want some stranger in it."

She was caught. She had made a misstep.

"I thought—"

"You thought wrong," he growled. His eyes swept the room, looking for anything displaced, and landed on the shelf of videos she had disturbed.

Silently, slowly, she replaced *Mommie Dearest* where she had found it.

"You come out of there right now. Now, Isla, now!" He pointed at her. He refused to step over the threshold, like some invisible barrier kept him from entering. She realized it was because he couldn't step in. Stepping in meant giving in to an acceptance of something he did not believe. He wouldn't step in until Edie was there with him.

He motioned for her to come out, and Isla obliged. Showing him that nothing else was disturbed. Opening her palms to show there was nothing in them. All she had was Mae's master key. She neared him, and he moved back into the hall, as if he couldn't get away from the room fast enough. He was the most powerful man around, coming undone.

"Close it," he thundered, his voice reverberating through the hall.

She looked at the crowd that had gathered, feeling shame and indignation washing over her in equal parts. Yes, she'd broken into a private room, but it was to help the very daughter Victor clearly missed and had regrets about. Only Isla couldn't say that. She had to wallow in Brooke's glee and Bennett's jubilee. She had to shoulder Mae's disappointment and violation, because it was her Isla had stolen from. Brooke smirked a crooked, satisfied smile. She finally had something on Isla Thorne. Bennett chuckled softly, shaking his head as if the guillotine was coming for her right now, and a smattering of staff gawked at her in disbelief at her audacity.

"What is going on?" Brooke said as she glided up to them and stopped beside her husband. She slipped a hand into the crook of his arm, and when he didn't pull her off, she relished it, squeezing in a little tighter in solidarity against Isla.

Isla turned her back on them and saw Jackson hanging way back, watching with an unreadable expression. She reinserted the key and locked Edie's door and braced herself for what would come next. It took all Isla's courage to face them.

"Were you in there?" Brooke asked, eyes wide with genuine shock. She'd tried for days to make Isla the enemy, and Isla had handed the opportunity to her on a silver platter.

Isla didn't answer, seeing another familiar face through the growing crowd of staff: Dixon.

Brooke continued to Victor, "Oh, darling, I know how much you cherish that room."

From somewhere in the group, Jackson said, "Brooke, maybe we should head to the Foundation. Things seem taken care of here." His face was beet red, and his blue eyes flashed with urgency. Meanwhile, Dixon did what Jackson didn't: He began dispersing the crowd that had gathered.

Brooke ignored him. "Our Edie would never want someone like you touching her things."

Isla balked at Brooke's use of *our*, taking ownership of a girl she despised. Despised enough to kill? The question slipped into Isla's thoughts like venom, and her anger blossomed. As if Brooke had ever considered Edie anything more than a thorn that had to be removed.

"'Our Edie'?" Isla repeated in disbelief, not caring if she was about to expose herself. "Interesting you claim her as yours now that she's been gone for years. Gone so long you've kept her out of your family portrait."

"Excuse me?" Brooke asked incredulously.

The hall was icy, and any remaining staff had slunk away, sensing an explosion was about to occur.

"I found something interesting in Edie's movie collection. She has a well-worn movie that she must have watched many, many times, about a horrid adoptive mother who abused and terrorized her innocent kids. Ever seen it? 'No wire hangers' and such."

Brooke inhaled deeply, understanding Isla's words even if no one else did. But if they thought hard enough, they'd understand Isla's implication about what Edie thought of her stepmother.

Victor didn't care. "I've given you pretty much full run of my home, property, and even offices should you choose." His already sizable body seemed to grow even larger as he became angrier. "The one place that was off limits was that room, and you couldn't respect that."

It was the first Isla had heard him raise his voice, the first time he'd ever shown his true feelings. And these went beyond anger. There was the pain of a reopened wound, and Isla was the one who had opened it.

She dropped her head, regret replacing her anger toward Brooke. She was sorry for hurting him. She did not regret going in.

Brooke rebounded, attempting to ingratiate herself by pretending to plead Isla's case. "Honey, maybe she just wanted to understand Edie better. Maybe she's heard so many great stories about her, and they'd be around the same age. Maybe she was trying to emulate Edie for you since she knows how much you care for her. Isla was curious."

"Curiosity killed the cat," Bennett said, leaning casually against the wall with a leg propped up behind him. "You screwed up big this time. The old man doesn't forgive easily and never forgets."

Heat rose up Isla's face and through her body.

"I would never try to be like your daughter," she said defiantly, glaring at Brooke to back off. "I'm sorry for upsetting you. I'll understand if you'd like me to leave. I can go pack my bags." She walked to Mae and returned the master key. "I'm sorry for taking this. I didn't use it for anything else. I won't do it again." She looked at Mae, searching for belief but finding disappointment instead.

Isla weaved through the onlookers as she heard Brooke say, loud and condescending, "I'm sure she meant well, honey. Don't be too upset. People from where she comes from usually don't know how to stay in their lane."

Isla didn't look back. She hooked her finger in her back pocket to ensure the note was securely tucked away. Her mind raced, not just about the contents of Eden's letter but also about what the letter was referring to.

CHAPTER THIRTY-NINE

"I'm sure you're trying to get to the bottom of Eden's disappearance, but you can't afford to alienate yourself from them now," Nat told her when Isla called her right after hightailing it to her room. She was beyond embarrassed and thinking about the judgmental eyes and gossip that would run rampant throughout the estate.

"Like a disease," she said, voicing her thoughts.

"What?" Nat asked. "What disease?"

Isla shook her head, though Nat couldn't see. "Nothing." Isla sighed. "So what do I do now? I've lost all face with him. Back to square one. I wouldn't be surprised if Victor was sending his people down to kick me out."

"Doubt it," Nat said. "I've never met the man, but it seems like he likes you. I mean, he didn't let a complete stranger into his home for no reason. He may be mad now, but he'll calm down, and then you can give him a reason to trust you again. Say it's part of your research and you can't know him without knowing about Eden—Edie—you know who I mean. Are you ready to tell him the real truth about your connection to Eden?"

"If I do that now, they'll think I'm nothing but an opportunist trying to get a payday. I need to first find out what happened to her, and then I can lay it all out for him. Victor is someone who needs cold, hard facts. This award ceremony will come up faster than I'm making headway. I need to push harder on the person I know can give me something I can use."

"And that would be?"

"James, the guy Eden was into before she left."

"Good. Do that. And go back up to the house. Swallow your pride. Go to Victor first."

The last thing Isla wanted to do was go back to the house and face them.

"One thing . . . Charli." Nat trailed off like she didn't want to continue.

Isla groaned. Charli wasn't a person to be ignored, but she was such a wild card that Isla was hesitant to reach out and get on Charli's radar, not when she was closer than she'd ever been to learning what had happened to Eden.

Isla's fingers tapped her lips nervously. "What about her? Tell her I'll be back soon and it's hard to reach me."

"Isla, she's not an idiot. You haven't left for longer than two weeks since I've known you. Now you've been gone a lot longer, with no word where you went. She swears you're on some big moneymaking gig and are trying to cut her out of it. You might need to call her to calm her down, because I don't need her coming to my job or my home or Rey's café causing trouble. You know how spiteful she can be."

"She's just in between boyfriends and has too much time on her hands is all. She'll find one soon at the casinos or wherever and be out of your hair."

Nat grumbled. "Well, just call her, okay? Tell her whatever you need to to get her off my back."

~

The kitchen was bustling when Isla returned to the main house. All talk died down when they realized she was there, and she had several pairs of eyes on her in various states of emotion, from curiosity to irritation to awe to disappointment. The disappointment was from Mae, the one person Isla didn't want to be on the outs with. She went immediately to her.

"I just want to apologize again, Mae." Isla watched all the hands preparing the family's meal so she wouldn't have to look at the people. "I hope you didn't get in trouble because of me. You've been good to me."

She finally looked up to see Mae watching her curiously. "What did you think you were going to get from it?"

"A little bit more of the truth," Isla replied.

Mae shook her head. "Sometimes the truth can be worse."

They were interrupted by approaching heels clicking on the floor. The kitchen quieted down as Brooke entered the room.

"Still here?" Brooke asked, gleefully surprised. "Upstairs was quite something, hmm? I'm sorry for Victor's behavior. He can be very emotional when it comes to Edie's belongings. You couldn't have known how serious it would be, even if the door was locked."

She just couldn't help slipping one in.

Isla tried to concentrate on what everyone else was doing in the kitchen. She wanted to be of help somewhere so she wouldn't have to be currently engaging with Brooke.

"We're too close to the award to find another person to write a spread on him, not that he'd agree to it, so I'd say you need to make amends, Isla dear," Brooke suggested. She looked around the room for anything that could serve as a peace offering. And while she moved, the others quickly scurried out of her path.

"You know, he's been having a rough week. Today especially, and nothing calms him down better than one of his favorite drinks, hmm?" She gave Isla a conspiratorial smile. "Why don't you bring him a drink? It'll show you're trying to make amends and start the conversation going again."

Isla caught Mae's eye and saw caution there, which reflected her own feeling. Why would Brooke all of a sudden help her now? Brooke had wanted her out from the beginning. Finally, Mae nodded that Brooke was right.

"He probably doesn't want to see me right now," Isla said.

"Nonsense," Brooke interrupted. "Follow me."

Isla hesitated until Mae nodded encouragingly. The worst part was over. This could help salve open wounds. Brooke clicked into a side sitting room, and Isla cautiously followed. Brooke went to the wet bar there, where an array of decanters of brown liquids of various shades, along with clear ones, were displayed. She looked over the assortment, picking up this bottle and that, setting them back down where they were, or close enough. When she was done checking the options, she addressed Isla.

"He loves a classic scotch. Just a splash of something sweet and aromatic, a little smoky. You should find everything you need here. I'd do it myself, but you're the one in the hot seat right now, and you need a win so I can have my peace and award night can be a success. I can't have an unsuccessful event, you understand." Her bloodred lips stretched into a wide smile.

Isla tried to figure out her angle. The suggestion felt innocent enough, and the reason made total sense. At this point, with weeks left to go, Brooke needed Isla to stay around and finish what she'd started. So it wasn't that Brooke was trying to help her out. It was that Brooke was trying to help herself out.

She studied the bottles neatly arranged at the bar. Among them was a small bottle that she picked up and sniffed. Almond liqueur—unlabeled but distinctly shaped and placed next to common mixers like honey, simple syrup, grenadine, and some bitters.

Isla looked around, thinking. Brooke had said sweet, aromatic, and smoky. The only thing close to smoky was the almond liqueur. Going with that, she added a small splash of it to Victor's scotch.

She passed the kitchen like a prisoner heading for lockup. They had perfected the art of busying themselves while also being very watchful. Mae and Brooke trailed behind—for moral support, Brooke said. Victor was in his study, in his chair, looking less aggrieved. And there was a woman with them. They introduced the statuesque beauty as Claudia, a family friend. She and Bennett were seated and chatting with him. Dixon was nearby, as usual, watching but saying little.

"Forget about Myles. I'm right here," Bennett was saying to Claudia. "We can go out. Have a good time. I'm a lot more fun."

Claudia laughed, and it immediately annoyed Isla. Even the woman's laugh sounded wealthy and pretentious. Which brother was Claudia there for? Because she clearly had an agenda and was going fishing in the Corrigan pool.

Their conversation stopped with Isla's tepid knock on the door. She stepped in, feeling like the most out-of-place person. Victor looked at her warily.

"I come with a peace offering," Isla said, producing the drink. He had his own bar in his study and could have made a drink if he'd wanted. Yet here she was, giving him something he hadn't asked for. Too late now.

She said, "I heard your favorite drink to relax is scotch with something a little sweet." His brow wrinkled in confusion but cleared when she continued. "So I fixed you a glass. I hope you know how sorry I am for upsetting you, and I hope it doesn't mess up the good thing we got going." She grinned, hoping he'd found his humor again.

He considered her, first appearing as if she wouldn't get another inch with him. He gradually began to relax, easing back into his seat. The fire in his eyes extinguishing, he gestured that she could give him the drink.

She watched apprehensively as Victor took a sip of the drink she'd prepared, since she didn't know how well it had turned out. His brow furrowed as he licked his lips, trying to place the extra touch she'd put in. He cleared his throat.

"Is it too strong? Should I have put in more of the sweet?" she asked, unsure of her bartending skills. She should have used simple syrup.

His clearing of his throat became louder. He loosened his tie knot, setting the glass down hard on the desk, making Isla jump. It splashed its contents on the desk.

"What—what—" He couldn't finish. His breathing became labored, and his face flushed a deeper shade. He grabbed at his throat, looking frantically at Dixon. "Can't. Breathe." He slumped in his chair.

CHAPTER FORTY

At first, the room was silent as they watched Victor writhing in his chair. Then realization hit, and the room erupted into chaos. Isla could only watch, transfixed by the scene before her. Brooke and Mae shoved past her. Bennett was out of his seat and by his father's side almost as quickly as Dixon was. In Dixon's hand was a prepped EpiPen, its needle gleaming.

"Victor? What's wrong?" Brooke's look of genuine concern made Isla even more terrified, and she didn't know whether to step forward or back. What was going on? What was the pen for? Why was Dixon slamming it into Victor's upper thigh while Victor wheezed and everyone around him called his name? Called for 911. Called for Jesus—that was Mae.

What was happening? Isla stared at the drink, rooted to her spot. Her fists balled at her sides.

"What did you use?" Brooke demanded. Her voice was sharp and urgent.

Isla pointed to the ground. "The almond liqueur, because you said something smoky, and I thought that was it."

Brooke's eyes widened. Her hand went to her mouth. "Almond? Victor is severely allergic to almonds."

"I—I didn't know he was allergic to nuts. I've seen him eat—I didn't know!" Isla was horrified, her mind unable to comprehend how close she'd come to killing Victor Corrigan. She had to hold on to the corner of a bureau to keep from falling.

Brooke said, "It must have been left out by mistake, or someone forgot to get rid of it when restocking. We've had new staff in. Oh no. Mae, we need to ensure there's not a speck of almond in the house."

Sweat poured down Victor's face. His breaths were labored, but his coloring had started to return. He continued to cough in attempts to clear his throat. Why the tumbler of scotch was not whisked away and the table wiped clean, Isla found perplexing, but she didn't question anything. He was handed a bottle of water. Myles had appeared at the door, having heard the commotion, and he ran to his father's aid, not even glancing her way.

"I am so, so very sorry," Isla said, tears welling against her wishes. She couldn't believe what was happening. First being caught in Eden's room. Now this. They were going to think she had done this on purpose.

Victor was waving almost everyone away from him to get space. He was disheveled and jittery, allowing Dixon and Myles to aid him. Brooke stood with Bennett and Claudia, watching as Dixon and Myles tended to Victor and Mae ensured they were doing it right. Brooke turned to Isla.

She said, "I only meant for you to give an olive branch, not to poison him!" Brooke took a calming breath. "I should have clarified . . ." Brooke addressed Mae, looking for where to lay blame. "Mae, what was the bottle doing there in the first place? You know Mr. Corrigan and Holland are allergic to almonds. There should be no almonds in the house!"

Mae nodded slightly. "Yes, Mrs. Corrigan. I'll get on it right away."

Mae backed away from the desk, ending up beside Isla, who stood trembling like a leaf. Isla looked at her. "I didn't know," she whispered, barely able to see anything but wavy shapes for the tears clouding her vision.

"How could you not know?" Bennett demanded, rounding on Isla. "This is basic information, and you're the one who's supposed to be learning all about my father. How do you miss what he's allergic to?"

"But I don't feed him" was all Isla could think to say. In all her prep work, should she have known about Victor's very specific allergy?

Brooke said, "Now, Bennett, it's possible for her not to know. She sees nuts around the house. It's rare for people to be allergic to one type of nut and not the others. Don't be too hard on her. She tried."

If Isla was thinking clearly, she would have guessed what Brooke was doing. How she was planting seeds of doubt and sowing discord, adding to Victor's distrust of her after Eden's room. There was nothing she could have said that would have sounded right in this moment.

"I'm so sorry you had to see this, Claudia dear," Brooke continued. "Myles, why don't you walk her to the car?"

"I'm not going anywhere," Myles said firmly. "I'm not leaving my dad."

Isla wanted to do the same. She needed to make sure Victor was okay, because it was her fault he had been hurt. But what she wanted didn't matter because someone else made the decision for her.

CHAPTER FORTY-ONE

A pair of strong hands grasped Isla by her arms and pulled her back to the door and out of the room. It was Mae, holding on firmly as she guided Isla away from the scene.

She'd poisoned Victor Corrigan. It was all over for her. Not only would she be kicked out, but she'd also be sent to prison.

"Mr. Russell," Mae greeted Jackson as they passed him right outside the room, as he had yet to enter. While he didn't reply, she could see how tense he was. How he radiated anger as he stared into the room like he was trying to restrain himself, his mouth in a tight line. Whoever he was looking at like that, Isla was just glad it wasn't directed at her.

The staff in the house were silent as Mae led Isla downstairs and outside to an awaiting golf cart. There was no salacious gossip or dirty looks. If there had been, Isla must have missed them. That was how out of it she was. It was when they finally made it to the staff building that the shock wore off and was replaced by anger and guilt.

Mae sat her down on the sofa, the others milling around. The word had gotten out. Isla was a hot commodity today, and all she wanted was for it to end so she could regroup. She wished she could run to the Red Roof and really be alone, but she was stuck here. They had gotten her today. They had made her look bad and put Victor's life in danger. Not they. She.

With Mae, Lisa, and Doris around her, Isla recalled what had happened from the point she and Brooke had left the kitchen for the parlor. As she was finishing, the back sliding door opened, and Lawrence came in after removing his dirt-crusted boots at the door.

"I've never been so terrified in all my life," Isla admitted, her hands still shaking. She felt outside herself. As if this wasn't real life, her life, but a movie. "I gave someone something that could have killed him. I nearly put a man in the hospital. How I'm not outside the gate and walking down the mountain, I don't know."

Doris said, "Well, they say Brooke interceded on your behalf. She said it was an honest mistake."

Lawrence and Mae shared a long, solemn look worth a thousand words. It was too long for the three of them not to notice.

"What is it, Mae?" Lisa asked. "You've been here the longest. With Mr. Corrigan the longest. You know all the skeletons."

Mae shook her head slowly. "No, I don't know about all the skeletons because the Corrigans are a different kind of people. Ones you don't cross even if you come from them."

"But what was the look you two shared? What is it?"

Mae seemed to debate with herself. She was the house manager. She was supposed to be above the fray and gossip. She was the liaison between the Corrigans and the staff. But she was also the one who needed to look out for the staff, especially when she knew how this family could be.

Lawrence said in his low, gravelly voice, "Mae, you aren't betraying anything by telling her what just happened. It's happening again, and Isla seems to be walking a similar path as Edie. She needs to know what she might be dealing with."

Isla looked from Lawrence, and the way he squeezed his hat between his hands, to Mae, who sat prim and proper, like the grand auntie she was to them all. Hard and soft all at once.

"What does he mean it happened before?" Isla asked.

Mae looked around. "What I say here stays between us. Lisa, Doris, don't go around saying anything to anyone unless you want to stir up a hornet's nest and be cast on your rears." They shook their heads, appropriately scared into silence.

"There was no way you would have known about the almond allergy. Mr. Corrigan doesn't let anyone know about that. Holland shares the same allergy as he does."

That was right, Isla thought, remembering when Hasaan, the Uber driver, had thrown the bag of almonds to Holland. She'd mentioned being allergic. She hadn't said her father shared the same allergy.

Mae continued, "What happened tonight, the 'suggestion' that you make him an apology drink and the almond liqueur suddenly being available for use, is too much of a coincidence. I can assure you there was no bottle of almond anything at that bar—or in the house, period. She put it there and manipulated you into using it."

Isla dropped into the cushions, totally blown away. Replaying the whole thing in her mind. How Brooke had stood at the stand. How she had touched the decanters and bottles, moved them around. Like one of those con people who said to watch the ball as they shuffled boxes around only to reveal there wasn't a ball under any of the boxes. She had done a bait and switch. And Isla, normally shrewd and not so believing, had walked right on into it because she'd felt bad about the room situation.

"No one can be that evil," Lisa whispered. "Can they? That could have killed her husband."

Mae shook her head. "It wouldn't, because she knew Dixon would be right there with the EpiPen. And if he wasn't, Victor has another in his desk. And if we checked her, I'd bet you she had a pen on her too, just in case A and B were unavailable."

Isla scoffed. It was the only thing she could trust herself to do.

"You asked why Eden left in the middle of the school year and so quickly."

The note! Isla remembered the item she'd taken from Eden's room and pulled it out, telling them where she'd gotten it. The other four leaned in to read it. Mae sat back in her chair, her face grim and angry.

"That proves it," Lawrence said. "In Edie's own words."

Doris asked, "You found it where?"

Isla told them.

Lawrence clapped his hands proudly. "That's a smart girl. Smart girl."

Mae said, "When Holland was young, Brooke suggested Edie make her a snack. They should have sister time because she was tired and needed rest. Mind you, there was a nanny, and Brooke isn't the mommy-duty type of wife. But Edie was happy to do it. She was told where to find the snack. Cookies from the local bakery that were okay to eat, no almonds. It wasn't until after Edie and Holland started eating them that Brooke came running down, frantic. The cookies had almond paste in them. Eden would have never known. But Brooke sprang into action. Holland started to react, but Brooke was there, ready with the EpiPen before it got bad. When Victor came home, she made up some story like she'd asked Edie to help her out with Holland and that Edie was upset because she wanted to do other things. Brooke made it seem as if Edie took her anger out on Holland, as crazy as that sounds. She put her own child in jeopardy to get rid of Edie."

"Why, though? What did Edie do that made Brooke treat her that way?" Isla asked.

"Edie was the reminder of the wife that should have been, you see," Mae said. "Mr. Corrigan loved Myles's mother, his first wife, but she passed not long after Myles was born, leaving him independently wealthy. Edie's mother Elise took care of Mrs. Corrigan while she was ill and stayed on to be Mr. Corrigan's assistant and caretaker for Myles. The two of them fell in love. Real, deep love. With the first Mrs. Corrigan there was an equal partnership and respect. He loved her. But with Elise . . . he was in love with Elise and she with him. I think she would have been the next wife if Brooke hadn't slid in with her eyes on Mr. Corrigan. She made her daddy pressure him with a huge business merger. She acted sweet as pie to Myles to kiss up. In the end, Victor chose business and married Brooke, who immediately got pregnant. I'm sure Elise was hurt, but she still stayed. They were still together. Mr. Corrigan was going to make it work somehow. Then Elise also got pregnant about a year and a half after Brooke. There was no way Brooke was going to stand for having Elise and her child in the house. One of them had to go, and Elise decided to leave so Eden could be raised according to her birthright. She cut herself off entirely from Mr. Corrigan. She gave him up, knowing she would never have all of him."

Lisa and Doris both had tears in their eyes. "This is like a drama I watched the other day. Oh my gosh. Why didn't he leave Mrs. Corrigan and go with the nice lady?"

"Because Brooke came with an opportunity to grow his wealth and resources. Brooke was high class, her family Virginia nobility, and he could move within their circles without any thought. Everyone would see Elise as low class, a caregiver, gold digger—whatever you can think of, she would have been that. And now Brooke's doing it again. Back to her old ways. She doesn't change her colors. Anyone who's a hint of a threat, she gets them out. Anyone who Victor Corrigan slightly likes, even if it's wholesome, she removes one way or the other. Even though he only tolerates her for the kids, she can be the only woman in his life, and her kids can be the only apples of his eye. That's why Myles went into the military for a while. And that's why Eden left. She was driven out, and her dad let it happen."

"Maybe he didn't know?" Lisa asked.

Isla shook her head, angrier than ever before. "Willful ignorance doesn't excuse his responsibility," Isla muttered. "At the center of everything is Victor Corrigan, whether he knows it or not. He is the big catch that everyone is fighting over."

Now it all made sense. Now Isla understood Eden's animosity toward the Corrigans for how they had treated her mother and then her. Eden had come back to settle some scores, and the person who'd had most to lose was Brooke. She wasn't above putting her own child and husband in harm's way to clear her path. If Eden had returned to blow up the world Brooke had carefully crafted, she wouldn't have been above taking care of Eden.

Permanently.

CHAPTER FORTY-TWO

Isla had barely closed her eyes before it was time for her to wake and the events of the night before rushed back. Somehow she'd made it back to her room, and security hadn't come kicking down her door to drag her out. Or, worse, the police to arrest her for attempted murder.

She prepared herself mentally for the hammer to come down, but she wouldn't sit here and wait for it. Even if she couldn't be at the estate, Isla still needed to find out what had happened with Eden. The ordeal with Victor would have to wait. Though she wanted to see if he was okay, she was probably the last person he wanted to see, so she'd keep a low profile.

It was midday, so the town was busy enough to pay no attention to the woman on a mission. Libraries today weren't old, with air smelling like aged paper and varnished wood. They were brightly lit, colorful, and engaging. The librarians greeted you with a smile, not a hush, encouraging respectable noise. There were groups of people meeting, another holding a cooking class, and clusters of small children converging for reading time on primary-colored foam mats that were put together like a huge puzzle.

In response to her quick question, a librarian busily restacking the latest rack of returned books informed Isla that if she wanted to look up any old newspaper articles from before 2019—she needed earlier, about 2012 by her calculations, because Eden had appeared at Isla's McDonald's counter early the following year—she would have to go elsewhere.

She was directed to Central Library, where older archives were held on microfilm, and she'd need a library card. She'd even need a card to use one of their public computers to do an internet search. She had known that. She could have asked Rey to get her a false card or into the library system, but that took more time, and time was running out. Rey continued digging up information about Bennett and his pals Danny, Roger, and even the pitiful James.

Isla didn't know how Victor played into everything. She wasn't sure how much he really knew about Matthew Leonard and if he was in cleanup mode or genuinely trying to root out the true villains. No matter how much it pained her to consider it, she didn't know if he knew things and had covered them up or if he was totally in the dark. Not yet. She'd made herself scarce this morning after the fiasco in Eden's room.

Isla had experienced firsthand the depths to which Brooke would go, and she understood how Eden had felt, being driven out of the house with no one to back her up. She now understood how that anger over being wrongly accused could have festered and forced Eden to return and confront the person behind everything, Brooke—or maybe the person who had to have known what was going on in his home and had opted to look the other way for peace and appearances, Victor. That betrayal, Isla surmised, could have been enough to make Eden go farther than LA, to go entirely off grid, even if it meant leaving Isla behind. After what Isla had gone through last night, she didn't blame Eden.

She was back at Mabel's, thinking over a cup of hot tea and the same breakfast she'd ordered the other day. She was deep in trying to decide if she was going to chance getting a library card, if she could with an LA driver's license and no real address. Could staff quarters count for a home? Not really. Everyone who lived there had actual homes to go to, and hers was across the country. It took her a second to realize that she was no longer alone at the corner table where she sat. She looked up and into the eyes of Officer Bowen.

She stared at him as he looked back, ten years her senior, if that, but still as boyish as he'd been when she'd seen him back then. And there was no denying the expression on his face. He remembered her—not from a few days ago but from years ago, when he'd saved her from being hit by a car and then chased her when she ran from him and his partner.

He started with "I wasn't sure it was really you at first. You disappeared off the face of the earth."

She didn't speak, taking time to think carefully. This was the law. He was someone who could identify her and totally blow her flimsy-enough cover. He could place her with Eden the night she went missing. But Isla was tired. Tired of running around. She wanted answers, and she wanted to be away from people who poisoned their kids and husbands to eliminate fake threats.

"From the other day? You're Officer Big Breakfast or something," she replied and sipped her tea. She wouldn't break cover. She'd let him lay his cards out first. Then she had a thought. What if he was here to arrest her, not for back then, but for last night? What if the Corrigans had pressed charges for attempted murder!

He scoffed, shaking his head ruefully. "Why'd you run like that? Where'd you go?" Bowen said, his gray eyes searching hers. "I looked for you everywhere, and no one knew who you were. It was like you were a ghost."

"I could be."

He chuckled. "Funny." Then he grew serious. "What are you doing back?"

"Is it against the law?"

He scratched his stubbly cheek. His face was a little more filled out than it had been before. She wondered if he had a wife and kids like true adults were supposed to have, not living in the past chasing ghosts.

"Is this how it's going to be with you? Vague answers and responding to questions with questions? I could take you in."

She inclined her head. "For?"

"Not sure yet, but I can come up with something." Those were triggering words to a Black person coming from a white one. But Bowen's teasing smile showed he wasn't serious. He was just a bad joker.

She decided she didn't have time. She had to be frank. "Are you on duty yet?"

He shook his head. "Not till later. I just like coming here for breakfast."

She waited expectantly for him to say something further. When he didn't, she did. "Why are you bothering me?"

He almost looked hurt. "Because I lost you back then, and I don't intend for that to happen again."

Isla wasn't expecting how sincere he looked. She didn't know how to respond or what he meant. She only knew her stomach did somersaults, like it did when she was around Myles. God, was she about to be one of those women who couldn't decide between two guys? The cop and the billionaire? Bowen could also be trying to do his cop thing, luring her in with niceties, and then bam! Hauling her in for questioning on her attempted murder. But looking into his gray eyes, which showed nothing but genuine curiosity and a touch of caution, she decided something had to give.

"Then can I borrow your library card?"

She said she'd follow his car, not wanting to draw attention. She wouldn't put it past anyone on the estate to have her followed, especially after the incidents with Eden's room and Victor's drink. And riding in a cop car was not anything any girl aspired to do, unless she was trying to be a cop, which Isla was not. Plus, she didn't want to be at Bowen's mercy—stranger danger and all, even if he was a cop. He could be a Corrigan cop. She was sure the town was filled with them.

They parked at Central Library, and it turned out Bowen's face, or badge, was enough, and they were directed to the area where the microfilm was located. She hadn't answered Bowen's initial questions, and he was definitely intrigued by her lack of sharing and her search contents. She didn't know why she let him tag along, probably because he was the only one around who had known her back then, even if it was for a few brief, highly charged and terrifying moments.

"No offense, but hush for a minute," she said at the computer, the program for the microfilm pulled up. Bowen was amused but complied.

Then she found it—a slim article buried in the back pages of a *Gazette* issue, its headline unassuming and easily missed:

> Tragic Accident Claims Family of Four on High View Drive.

CHAPTER FORTY-THREE

Through the rush of adrenaline, she read the short article of vague details. The crash had occurred thirteen years ago on a narrow road on the same mountain where the Corrigan estate was located. The victims were a vacationing family whose car careened off the road and rolled downhill. Witness accounts were even vaguer. The coroner ruled that the victims had died on impact. The police report offered little clarity, citing "driving too fast for conditions" and "driver error due to unfamiliarity with the area" as possible factors. It was the only article about the accident, written by a Nathan Collins. The family's name had been withheld pending notification.

Bowen tapped the screen as he sat next to her, practically breathing in her ear as he leaned in. "I think I remember this," he mused. "Happened a couple of years before you showed up."

"Looks like it." She studied the contents on the screen.

"Are you family or something?" Half joking, half serious. She was entirely something else.

"Did this turn into an interrogation, Officer Bowen?" she asked, turning to him.

He pulled a face. "That's *Detective* Bowen," he said, mildly offended. "Put some respect on that."

She apologized, motioning he should continue.

"I don't think they ever followed up and said anything more about it. It was a tragedy. Whole family."

"I see," she said as he pointed out the obvious.

Something didn't add up. The road described was one leading directly to the Corrigan gates. Why would a family from out of town go there at that time of night instead of nearby, to Jefferson's Monticello? That was the tourist attraction, not the Corrigans. Isla pieced together what she knew.

Thirteen years ago, Eden would have been a junior in high school—around the same time her demeanor suddenly changed, according to Sara, and she eventually left for Daytona. And the lack of information in a town this size for an accident so tragic was odd. It was as if Isla's team had swooped in and sanitized all the identifying information and the PR firm had pushed this story, or lack thereof. Who had called in the accident? Who else had been there? And why wasn't there more? And the most glaring question . . .

What was it about this accident that had had Eden so shaken?

Isla was deep in her thoughts, barely hearing Bowen speaking to her.

"Back then, you mentioned something bad had happened. You looked scared as hell, but you wouldn't talk. You ran before I could get more out of you."

"You'd run too if cops were chasing you in some strange town."

Detective Bowen continued, "It was more than cops chasing you, Isla. You were worried before we got there. You wanted to tell us something."

Isla debated if she could trust Bowen. She didn't know him. But she needed someone closer who could help if she needed it. She needed an ally, and if he was still anything like the kindhearted officer from ten years ago, he could be trusted now, with limitations. She couldn't decide where to begin. "My best friend disappeared, and I was a runaway who could have been sent back if I was caught. I'm back to find out what happened to her."

"Care to share a name? I can run it through the missing persons database."

She gave him a quick smile. "Not yet. There are things I need to figure out first."

Bowen's expression was grim. "I won't press," he said. "But I advise you to be careful. Whatever you're digging up, whoever you're trying to find, I don't know how that relates to the Corrigans. But when you're dealing with that family, if you're not careful, they'll chew you up and spit you out, just like they've done to everyone else."

CHAPTER FORTY-FOUR

Isla and Bowen left the library, and she knew she owed him something now. He had behaved, kept quiet while she looked, asked very few questions for a cop. He was definitely very different from his partner back then.

He asked, "My turn now?" They stood between their parked cars, one cop, one civilian.

She clutched her bag, holding the printed copies of the article to her side, and nodded for him to continue. She braced herself for what she would tell and what she wouldn't. He studied her.

"Why the rush to leave back then?"

When she and Bowen had crossed paths back then, she hadn't known him and had said nothing. Today, she knew him a little more and still said little because she still didn't know enough. "I had a bus to catch?"

He narrowed his eyes, not buying it. "Now you're at the Corrigans'. Word like that goes around fast. Plus, you've been talking to people in town."

She nodded, shifting and making it obvious their time was running out.

"Now you're back," he said. "And running up against an extremely powerful family with unlimited resources. You're playing with real fire here, you know? Are you sure you need to continue down this path?"

She was too far on it to get off. The only way was to see it through to the end.

He straightened, his gray eyes concerned. He handed her a card with his contact information.

"I hear you, Detective Bowen." He, like Myles, was warning her off. "I appreciate your concern."

He waved her off, breaking their eye contact. "Yeah, well, I wasn't able to help you back then, and the way you ran off has always bugged me. This is the least I can do. I can help if you need me, but you have to be careful."

~

She planned to return to the estate and spread everything she had accumulated in her research across the bed in her room. The timeline was falling into place, and the picture was clearer now but far from complete. She went back to her talk with James—his cryptic words and profound guilt—and reread the note in Eden's scrawl that had been tucked into *Mommie Dearest*, alluding to an incident that had happened before. The old Abbott farm. Something had happened there on Eden's last night. But before that, something else had happened that had changed Eden, Sara had said. Was it a stretch of the imagination to think someone had made sure to keep silent about the accident, worried about the fallout?

The fact was this: Something horrible had happened afterward that had changed both James and Eden, something that James could never forgive himself for and that had to do with Eden's eventual departure. Truth just beyond Isla's reach pressed on her as she stared at the scattered evidence. She wasn't sure what was scarier—the secrets she was uncovering or the realization that she was now a part of them. Isla was tugging on a loose thread of a tightly bound ball begging to be unraveled.

CHAPTER FORTY-FIVE

When Isla received the text from Jackson that said he had finally cleared time to meet with her but wasn't at the estate or Foundation but working from home, it was the last text she wanted. The tone of the message indicated that if she didn't take this opportunity, there wouldn't be another. The last thing she wanted to do now was talk with Jackson when she was worried about whether Victor would finally hand down her marching orders over that drink. But talking to Jackson could get her closer to finding out what had happened to Eden, so she gritted her teeth and reversed course for Jackson's home.

Jackson was already at the door when Isla arrived, and she followed him inside, where he gestured toward the couch in his living room. His home was like an art gallery of paintings she couldn't decipher and sculptures too fragile to touch. With expensively glossy wooden floors, recessed lighting, and abstract art hanging on the walls, the place felt more like a gallery than someone's home. There were large potted plants with wide, spiked leaves fanned out and exotic flowers she bet came from his employer's greenhouse. The sterile, cold house suited Jackson's personality perfectly. She couldn't put her finger on what it was about the house or Jackson that felt less than hospitable.

She chose one of the chairs over the couch.

"There aren't many people who find a reason to visit me outside the estate."

She didn't like the way he said "find a reason" as if she had an ulterior motive for wanting to be around him. She forced a smile and declined when he offered her a drink. "Maybe you don't give off welcoming-kind-of-guy vibes."

He chuckled, sitting on his sleek leather couch, making himself comfortable. "You just have to get to know me."

"You've been with the Corrigans for a really long time. Thirty years," Isla began, notepad in hand. "You could retire if you wanted to."

Jackson chuckled softly. "Are you saying I look old?"

"Not at all. I'm saying that kind of loyalty is rare these days."

"Loyalty is a dying art. Most people only look out for themselves. I look at the bigger picture."

"Must be exhausting," Isla pressed. "Always looking at the bigger picture. Always cleaning up other people's messes. Being at their beck and call and at the mercy of their whims."

His smile didn't falter, but there was a flicker in his eyes. He looked away to disguise it. "I do what's needed. But it's not about glory, right? It's about stability. The Corrigans have a way of . . . attracting chaos. You should know all about that, right? You were the cause of it last night."

Isla told herself not to react, because it was what he wanted. She was done playing into people's hands, and she was damn sure he knew Brooke had set her up.

"Stability," Isla repeated, getting back to the point. She let the word hang in the air. "What about you, Jackson? What do *you* get out of all this? Really? No matter what they do, how they act, you and Dixon remain by their sides. What do you do if they ask you to do something that goes against your beliefs?"

His eyes sharpened as he leveled them at her. "You gotta check your beliefs at the door, or you won't survive in *this* world. I know when to speak, when to act, when to move. I protect myself always. Everyone does. You should too. You're too green."

Isla tilted her head. “Survive? That sounds more like a soldier than a lawyer.”

Jackson leaned back, swirling the amber liquid in his glass. “The world needs soldiers. Not everyone can be a general.”

Midway through the interview, Jackson’s phone buzzed. He glanced at the screen and stood abruptly. “Excuse me. I need to take this. International call from Japan I’ve been waiting for.” His disarming expression begged forgiveness, and Isla bet many a woman fell for his unflappable *GQ* demeanor.

“Do your thing,” she said, standing up. “I’ll use the restroom while you’re on the phone.”

He motioned in the general direction of three closed doors without indicating which was which, distracted by the call he wanted to take, and stepped out onto his back patio, closing the door behind him. She guessed he didn’t want her to hear what he was saying, but she could still hear him, even if she couldn’t pick out actual words. Any other time, she’d have tried to listen in, but this was a prime opportunity.

Isla seized the moment. Her heart pounded as she rose from her seat, moving quickly but quietly. She wandered down the hallway, peeking into each room, passing his bedroom with its immaculately made bed, which made her shudder. She didn’t want to think about what went down on it.

Kitty-corner to the bedroom was a room with a slightly ajar door. She peeked in. His office. Before going in, she strained her ears to ensure he was still on his call. When searching for information, with limited time, she had one guess where the big-ticket find might be. The desk. She immediately went over and did a quick scan over the several neat stacks of paperwork. Her heart was thundering, and she calmed herself down. How many other times had she secretly sneaked into spaces to get dirt her clients could use on whoever was threatening their interests? She couldn’t be greedy. *See what you can find, and think about it later.*

As she quickly moved from stack to stack, one misaligned piece of paper stood out from the other contracts, memos, plans, and so forth stacked on the desk. She went in for a closer look. It was an invoice for a storage unit. It shouldn't have meant anything, but the invoice was for a storage company in Ruckersville. What stood out the most was the size of the unit. It was huge at ten feet by thirty feet. She wondered what he could have in storage outside town. She wasn't sure how far out it was, but that was a question to figure out later. She pulled out her phone and took a picture. She left quickly, closing the door to the point she'd found it. He was still on the phone, his voice raised, and the conversation sounded heated. She tried her luck, because directly across from her, three steps away, was the bedroom, with the bathroom in between the bedroom and office. She flipped on the light in the bathroom, flushed the toilet, and ran the water in the sink, dipping in a hand and drying it with one of the paper towels, which she tossed in the trash. She hesitated at the doorway of the bedroom.

The bedroom was immaculate, with dark furniture and a bed that looked barely slept in. Her eyes were immediately drawn to a recessed wall beside the closet and a black safe tucked discreetly into the wall niche. It looked expensive—had an electronic locking system, she could tell from her cursory glance. She quickly whipped her phone back out to take a photo of its face and brand.

People locked up valuables and things they didn't want others to get or know of. The safe called to her. What could Jackson be hiding in there? Isla was so engrossed in her thoughts of what was in the safe and how she could get in that she forgot to keep a listen out. She forgot she was on borrowed minutes.

Footsteps echoed down the hallway, and Isla didn't realize Jackson's call had ended. Not until she felt the heat of a presence behind her. She spun around, bumping into him, her nose smashing into his chest. His arms immediately wrapped around her back, pulling the rest of her closer to his body before slipping down to her waist. She looked up and he looked down, his eyes crinkling at the corners as he smirked, taking in her flushed face and nervous smile.

"This isn't the bathroom," he said, his tone both amused and getting husky with desire.

"Yes," Isla said quickly, hopping out of his embrace like he was an atomic bomb. Her whole body was on fire from a tumult of feelings—shock, horror, discomfort, revulsion. She gestured vaguely. "I, um, thought I heard an alarm or something going off in here after I was done. False alarm." She let out a high giggle; she had no idea where it came from. Usually so cool under fire, she was not this time. "Get it?"

His eyebrow lifted, a knowing smile playing on his lips. "Hmm."

She absolutely didn't like the way his eyes raked over her from his vantage point, like he was Superman and could see right through her jeans and V-necked T-shirt, which she now wished wasn't so tight and low cut. She tried to turn away in a vain attempt to shield herself from him.

"If you wanted to tour my bedroom as part of this interview, you only had to ask. You do that for the others too? Or is it only me who gets the pleasure?"

Isla forced another, more controlled laugh, brushing past him so she was no longer cornered with him blocking the path to the door. "You're funny, Jackson. No beeping, but then I saw this minibar setup you had and got distracted. My apologies."

His hands were balled on either side of him, his fingers rubbing together as his stare did not waver. He was seeing right into the depths of her soul. She was a caught rabbit, unable to move or think, or come up with one of the witty Isla-isms that usually disarmed weird moments. Never before had she felt this vulnerable in this way.

Finally, finally, he broke, smiling widely. His body and the vibe that he was on the edge, about to dive into his deepest, most unrestrained desires, began to retract.

"The interview," he started.

She was already backing out of the room. Turning fully to head back to the sitting room, she tried to think of ways to end things now and also how she might return later when he was gone. "Yes, well, um . . ."

He said, "Can you give me a rain check?"

What? She did an about-face, genuinely surprised and confused. "What? Why?"

He frowned. "I need to get back to the office. That call from Japan? There are some things there at the office I need to follow up on because of it."

She readily agreed, hustling to the couch and grabbing her bag and blazer, feeling off kilter and relieved and a host of other things. Like she'd dodged a Jackson-size bullet.

At the door, he stopped, and she crossed the threshold. "Isla," he called, casting a spell that made her feet involuntarily rotate to face him again when her mind said to keep walking. He was looking at her again, his head inclined like he knew things about her she didn't know.

"Let's do this again. Yeah? I think our time would be well spent." His eyes lingered where they shouldn't have, his thoughts practically playing like a movie reel.

She shuddered, not even caring if he saw her do so. She gave him a tight smile with no answer and left like the devil was chasing at her back.

CHAPTER FORTY-SIX

Incoming docs. What do you want to do?

Isla sat in her room, her laptop glowing faintly as she read. The documents Rey had sent filled her screen—financial records, emails, and damning evidence of the accounts Bennett and Danny had opened to put the Corrigan Group's siphoned funds in. The more she looked, the clearer it became that Matthew Leonard's death wasn't just a tragic accident—it was the result of a carefully orchestrated cover-up.

Her fingers hovered over the keyboard as she debated the best recourse for the evidence Rey had sent her. Should she take this immediately to Victor and Myles and let them rectify what Bennett and Danny had done, knowing that whatever Victor did, if anything, would be internal and that it wouldn't see the light of day because he would protect Bennett and the company's image? Matthew Leonard hadn't had that luxury of protection. He'd been thrust out in the open, his name destroyed for something he didn't do. His wife and baby left alone to shoulder everything else. What was the fairness in that between the haves and have-nots?

As much as she was beginning to like Victor and see him in a different light, for once, the have-nots needed a win. Her fingers pressed the button to send.

Isla slipped her off-network laptop into the far corner of her closet, behind a laundry bag, just in case Brooke or even Bennett had someone enter her room. She couldn't be too sure that everyone who worked here could be trusted.

The phone rang, and it was Mae on the other end, summoning Isla to Victor's office in the main house. She didn't want to admit that she was apprehensive about meeting Victor. She'd given him and the main house distance since the incident, but it seemed there was no more avoiding it, and Isla would meet her fate. Victor would either send her packing or have the cops waiting.

She ran through any possible scenarios and how she might keep herself on the estate if Victor did decide to get rid of her. It was a beautiful day, and the trees and flowers in their autumn colors made for a beautiful view that Isla hadn't enjoyed since she'd been here. She took a deep breath. It was going to be what it was going to be.

Isla turned right on one of the now-familiar pathways to the house, her thoughts on her visit to Jackson's home and how he played into everything. She had a pretty good handle on everyone else. But Jackson was a mystery. He didn't work with Brooke like Dixon did with Victor. His role on the estate seemed more like that of an observer with a gum addiction, and the Brooke whisperer.

Victor was considerably older, and his impatience toward his wife was evident. But Jackson . . . a tall, clean-cut, Midwestern-looking dude might be more Brooke's cup of tea. A good-looking, available man who was at Brooke's beck and call and happy to be that. Outwardly. When Isla was with him, she had a sense that Jackson held something deep inside, and it might not be a good thing.

CHAPTER FORTY-SEVEN

She entered the house through one of the side entrances and found Brooke at a table in one of the attached lanais, arranging a vase of vibrant bluish-purple hydrangeas. Isla had kept a distance from Brooke ever since the almond incident, unsure of how to best deal with someone who would go to such lengths to force her out. She tried to pass by unnoticed.

"I wouldn't get too comfortable if I were you," Brooke's voice rang out, stopping Isla just as she was passing. "Your time is growing short."

Isla stopped just in the doorway. "I wonder if you also said that to Eden after you framed her for setting off Holland's allergy to almonds," Isla chanced. "Who will you use those on?" She motioned to the poisonous flowers whose errant leaves Brooke had snipped.

Brooke gripped her gardening shears, her head snapping up. She would likely use them on Isla if she had the chance, but Isla left before anything more could be said or happen.

Dixon was waiting for Isla outside Victor's office. She tried to read him and failed, which was maddening. He could have given master classes on the art of maintaining a poker face.

She motioned for him to bend closer to her height. He hesitated, casting her a curious look before he obliged.

"Am I fired?" she asked, trying to get ahead of the problem and come up with a quick solution.

She might be able to come up with something to save herself if she had a little heads-up.

"Just let me know so I'm prepared. I didn't purposely poison him. Honest."

For a split second, there was a crack in Dixon's facade, and humor shone through, shocking Isla. She'd thought the man was devoid of all human emotion. "Only way to know is to go in, Miss Thorne," he said, his polite refusal to give anything away annoying her even more. He was too damn loyal. "Let's not keep him waiting any longer."

Victor was standing at his desk. Papers were spread out before him as he studied one he was holding in his hand. He didn't move as she approached. Usually, she was cool under fire, but the night before had done a number on her.

"Are you going to stand there staring, or are you going to have a seat?" He put the paper he was holding down and moved around the side to his chair. She took a seat, but not before her eyes swept the documents; she recognized ledgers and printouts of what looked like account transactions.

"I can explain about the drink," she began, wanting to get ahead of everything.

He waved her off dismissively, taking a quick look at her. "You seem nervous. Aren't you supposed to be some intrepid journalist? What happened to *her*?"

Isla's mouth opened and closed; she was at a loss for words.

He shook his head disappointedly, removing his black-framed glasses. "Are you nervous? Because the Isla Thorne I know doesn't look like she's about to jump out of her skin. You stood in my kitchen and told me to hire you."

"I almost killed you."

He smirked. "Takes more than a few drops of almond extract."

"How can you be so cavalier about a severe allergic reaction?"

"Because sometimes you have to choose your battles, and this isn't one you were waging."

She was confused.

"There hasn't been almond in this house ever since Holl had a reaction. Suddenly it makes an appearance and is used by someone who had absolutely no idea about it. The only people who know are staff, some employees, and family. Maybe there's someone who doesn't like me. Have you noticed that during your interviews? Who have you spoken with, and do they hate me?"

"I've asked around here. Also at your offices downtown and around town with locals. I've even visited the Foundation's headquarters on Fifth. But I'd like to shadow you one day. See you in real action."

He asked, "Really?" He laughed. "That's the Isla Thorne I hired. Who does that come from, your mother or your father?"

"My father is dead, and my mother isn't in my life," Isla said quickly, wanting to stay as far away from her history as she could.

Victor said, "Can I be frank?"

"Please," Isla encouraged.

"You're good with words, Isla. You can talk your way into and out of just about anything. I know that from dinner. A family like mine doesn't intimidate you. And like I said, Holl likes you, and she's rarely gotten close with anyone ever since Edie left. You managed to finagle your way into my home, spend the night, and ask for a job. Did you really think I needed someone to interview me for an award that means nothing to me?"

"Mr. Corrigan," Isla stammered, caught off guard by his bluntness.

"Whatever your reasons, you shake things up. You shake this family up, and I'm curious to see who falls and who rises to the top."

She had no words. She was confused about who had been playing whom all this time. "You're—you're using me as your sword?"

He smirked. "Ask me your questions."

CHAPTER FORTY-EIGHT

Before she could begin, Victor interrupted, giving a series of instructions to Dixon about business Isla couldn't keep up with.

Victor returned to her. "Impress me with your accumulated knowledge so far."

She filed through the information she had, picking out what she thought he'd like to hear. "The emblem of the Corrigan Group is inspired by the *abe dua* West African adinkra symbol for wealth, resourcefulness, and self-sufficiency. Its palm tree is a symbol of resourcefulness because many different products are made from that single tree. And in the same light, many companies and products can be and have been made through your company, like with the palm tree. A nod to your African ancestry."

"Absolutely that. Thank you. Now if only my children would understand the importance of being resourceful and self-sufficient . . . in the right way," he said dourly. He pulled himself out of whatever hole he was about to fall into and gestured at her. "Continue."

"You grew up working at your father's textile mill to learn the business from the bottom up. He wasn't just going to hand it to you, very much like what you're doing with your sons. The mill trucked the products up and down the East Coast, and you drove those trucks. Later, you restructured your companies and began buying and restructuring others, diversifying and building the Corrigan Group to where it is now, with its many subsidiaries and endowments and hundreds of thousands of employees worldwide. You shed sweat, blood, and tears along the way to build what is now one of the largest corporations in the US, not to mention internationally.

"You're driven, not only because you're a businessman but also to grow multigenerational wealth, and additionally because for a Black family in America, the bar is set higher, and you unfortunately have to prove more, just for the simple fact that you're Black. You've gone against the odds when everyone said you weren't qualified enough, which means, if we're honest, you weren't the right race to have this level of success and status. You want to make sure that whoever your successor is, it isn't about power, money, or self. You want someone who will care about the company, the people who keep it running, and what the company stands for."

Victor had a small smile playing on his lips as he observed Isla. He shared a look with Dixon, who tried to busy himself with his own black portfolio of paper and things. She wasn't sure if he appreciated her analysis or was about to have her proverbially executed and booted off the premises. But she continued on. There was a point to everything, yet she still hesitated. "I know about your history with your wives." She took a breath. "I even know about your history with the love of your life, Elise, Edie's mom."

This earned his scorn. "Your point, Isla? I know my history and don't need a rundown of it from my guest."

"Thought I was the interviewer here."

"Whatever it is that you are today. Point is, I don't need to rehash about me. Let's wait until I'm dead and they write a huge, sweeping eulogy and biography about me. Then you can sit at my grave and read it to me, where I'll have no choice but to listen then, won't I?" It was a joke, but he was dead serious.

"Fair enough."

"You broke in, Isla. You went against instructions, overstepped, and invaded her privacy."

"I am very sorry about upsetting you." She didn't want to, but Victor needed a little push. She had to know why, if he believed Edie was still out there, she was basically erased in the house save for her room and a couple of pictures he hid in his office. Why hadn't he brought her home? But no one would talk about Edie, who'd been gone ten years. No word, no sign. "Don't you care?"

Dixon tensed from where he sat. His head shot up, and he looked at Isla with utter surprise and horror, about to intercede on his boss's behalf and whisk her out of Victor's sight.

Victor thundered, "How dare you! You're not even thirty and telling me about me and my children? You are lecturing me?"

She waved her hands. "I wouldn't dare, sir. No. I'm just asking why you have a shrine to Edie. Where is she?"

"Out there being angry with me," he said after a long time, his emotions—sadness, rejection, fear, hope—taking over every part of him. Isla didn't see the multibillion-dollar business mogul with the Midas touch. She didn't see a cutthroat and ruthless man, even though she knew he'd allowed illegal things to be done on his or the Corrigan Group's behalf.

"Why did Edie leave?" Isla pressed, trying to sound casually curious.

Victor leaned back in his chair, his gaze distant. "Edie . . . wasn't suited for life here. She inherited her mother's . . . temperament. Some of us aren't built for the weight that comes from being a Corrigan."

Isla wasn't sure what to make of what he said or how Victor could be so cold and callous about his daughter. Holland had said as much about herself, that the family didn't take her seriously and her parents would rather she marry well, as Brooke had, than work as her brothers did. Isla didn't know what Holland wanted for her future, but to be like her mother was not one of them.

Isla asked, taking a gamble that there was more to Victor's feelings for Eden than that she couldn't hack being a Corrigan, "Do you miss her?"

"Of course I do!" Victor's eyes became razor sharp, fixing her with a piercing look. For a moment, she thought she'd overstepped, but then he sighed. "I've been searching for her," he admitted quietly. "For years. No one knows—not even my wife. Only Dixon. It wouldn't do for the family to see me . . . weakened like this."

Isla blinked, stunned, confused at why searching for his daughter would make him look weak, but then again, this was the same man who didn't want anyone to know he was allergic to almonds.

"So you've been looking for her." Isla was surprised. "Even though you tell everyone here not to talk about her?"

"How could a father ever stop looking for his child?" he said, heaviness in his voice. Victor's gaze drifted to the photo of Eden. "Edie wrote me a letter. Said she wanted nothing more to do with this family. Said she hated what we were. But . . . sometimes people write things they don't mean. Or they mean them at the time but feel differently later. I thought if I could just find her, talk to her . . . maybe things could be different."

Isla was seeing a part of Victor she wished Eden had been able to see. But she could understand Eden too. If Victor had believed Eden was capable of hurting her sister, that might have been unforgivable. If it had been Isla, she wouldn't have been able to live under the same roof with them either.

Eden had had a tumultuous relationship with her stepmother. It was a classic story. Eden had been a constant reminder of Victor's relationship with Elise. Knowing your husband not only didn't love you but also had cheated on you, gotten the other woman pregnant the same time you were expecting, would have angered and embarrassed anyone. Enough to make her mistreat the kid.

But Brooke's hostility wasn't the only issue. Something else had happened that had changed Eden, according to her friends Sara and James. It was only a guess, but what if Eden had somehow been involved in that accident that had been swept under the rug? What if their parents had covered it up and that was the unfinished business

Eden was so determined to take care of? But this was all conjecture. Isla had nothing concrete. Just old articles and even older feelings that no one wanted to elaborate on.

But what if Victor had given up wanting to raise her as a Corrigan and made her leave on purpose, knowing life away from his ruthless and possessive wife was safer for everyone?

"One day, Isla," he said, "I'm going to bring my girl home."

Isla only hoped Victor would bring Eden home.

"Unfortunately, some of us have to work," Victor said, putting an end to their conversation. "It's something I do in the downtime when Isla Thorne isn't sticking her nose in my business."

She held up a finger to stop him. "You hired me to stick my nose in your business and write it up fancy."

"You sweet-talked your way into the opportunity to stick your nose in my business. Are you trying to rewrite history? Should I have Dixon remind you? His memory is as sharp as a tack. Dixon!"

Dixon was on his feet, prepared to lead Isla out of the office. "She offered to write—"

"Don't worry about what she offered to write," Isla cut in, glaring at Brian Dixon like the traitor he was. "We employees have to stick together. Us against them."

Dixon's expression was that of an enlightenment.

Victor chuckled, shuffling the papers on his desk until they formed small stacks. "Dixon's been with me for decades. You? You basically just got here."

"I think I like you better as silent and brooding, like your son Myles."

Victor didn't respond, and Isla took it as her cue to leave, but on her way out, he said, "Oh, and the job shadowing you suggested? Why not."

Isla was glad he couldn't see her reaction. The tycoon was more agreeable than she'd been prepared for. And she didn't know if that was a good thing, or bad.

CHAPTER FORTY-NINE

Isla entered the Corrigan Group office building and was led to Victor's office by Victor's executive assistant, who was already aware of the visit and was waiting at the security station when Isla arrived at the downtown office. Isla thought it would be "a day in the life of." What she got was a war room.

"How the hell did she get company information?" Victor bellowed.

Isla hesitated in the doorway, a flash of fear running through her, afraid that Victor was speaking about her. She'd been exposed, and this would be it for her, and the cops weren't far behind.

Dixon looked up from his phone. It was the first time she'd ever seen his eternally businesslike demeanor replaced by one that was flustered and nervous. He ignored Victor's rapid-fire questions and his commands.

"Get those boys in here. And Myles. Now!" Victor seemingly said into the air, or to Dixon, until she saw the steady red light of his phone indicating he was on a call. Victor mashed his finger on a button, ending the call.

Dixon held a remote, pointing it to one of the two large-screen monitors mounted on the wall across from Victor's massive desk. The screen flickered on to a special news report that then cut back to the anchor desk of a national news network. Isla didn't wait to be kicked out or invited in; she made the decision herself as she read the breaking news scrawling across the screen and relaxed. She'd showed up at the right time after all.

Isla was rapt with attention as she watched Matthew Leonard's widow, Maia, clutching their infant daughter. Her tear-streaked face was raw with anguish. Her eyes flashed with fire.

"I received an email with proof," Maia Leonard choked out, bouncing her daughter. "Proof that my husband was framed for stealing from his company. Matthew didn't steal a cent. Do you understand? My husband's gone because someone else let him take the fall. As soon as I saw the documents, I had to speak out."

The reporter asked, "Why did you reach out to the station instead of the authorities?"

"Because," she railed, "we're talking about the Corrigan Group. There's no telling who's in their pocket, and the world needs to know about their underhanded dealings."

Good for her, Isla thought, crossing her arms over her chest. She wiped the satisfaction from her face that she had made the right decision in sending the documents to Maia and leaving her with the decision of what to do about them. Isla was even impressed that the national station had picked up the story, but then she remembered everything Corrigan-related was national news.

The image shifted back to the news desk, where the anchor picked up the story. "Matthew Leonard, former accountant for the LA branch of the Corrigan Group, took his life six months ago after being terminated from the company amid allegations of a misappropriation of funds. At the time, the evidence against him showed funds from company accounts tracing back to Leonard, but today's revelation is a challenge to that conclusion. Mrs. Leonard claims that the documents she received via an anonymous source are proof that Leonard's name falsely appeared on the financial records. The question that CEO and CFO Victor Corrigan of the Corrigan Group will have to answer remains: Who truly has their hands in the cookie jar?"

Victor banged his fist on his desk. "A goddamn whistleblower! Is my company at a point where there need to be whistleblowers?"

Dixon's only response was to have none. Likely the best response. The receptionist, who had entered the office when she heard Victor, scurried back out to avoid his wrath.

That the guilty parties' names hadn't been released to Maia was Isla's gift to the Corrigans, though she wasn't sure why she'd withheld what she had. She had no allegiance to them. Yet she found herself protecting them as well. She was a hypocrite, becoming more like the kind of people she detested. Isla had squirreled herself into a corner of the huge corner office with a magnificent view of downtown Charlottesville to keep out of sight and out of mind.

The report ended, and the office descended into stifling silence as Dixon tapped furiously on the laptop he had set up on the small round glass table. Victor sat in his chair, seething. His jaw clenched. Isla expected him to explode but was proven wrong, when instead Victor's voice came out eerily calm. "How did his wife get this information? I thought you, Myles, and I, who I tasked to investigate it, were the only ones privy to it."

Dixon multitasked, his fingers still flying. "That's what we're going to find out. Everyone is already en route to discuss."

"And Bennett and Danny?"

Dixon replied, "On their way."

"This is their goddamn mess. How many more times do I have to clean up their bullshit before they stop fucking up?"

Isla hadn't expected the wave of disappointment she felt upon hearing Victor's admission. She had hoped he hadn't known it was them. And it certainly didn't sound like the first time he'd shielded them from any accountability.

Isla ventured to speak from her little corner of the office, her urge to call Victor out greater than her desire to remain unnoticed during a situation they definitely wouldn't want her witnessing. "Sounds like

Danny and Bennett are to blame," she said softly. "Will you clear Leonard's name by naming them?"

The third voice in the room took Victor by surprise. Dixon was equally surprised, as he paused his computer work to gawk at her, neither of them seeming aware that they were not alone in the wake of a crisis.

"Isla. Right, the shadowing." Victor cleared his throat, seeming to remember the reason why she was there. "We'll have to reschedule. Some matters, as you've clearly heard, have come up. I trust you won't repeat anything outside this office and you'll keep it out of that article of yours."

He made her article sound like a high school project, and she supposed she shouldn't be offended by the dismissal. The article was the last on her list of priorities.

"Of course," she said. "But I remember when all this blew up back then. The guy's wife was devastated. Shouldn't the people responsible be held accountable?"

Victor exhaled sharply, rubbing his temple. "I'm not sure what business it is of yours."

"I guess it isn't," she admitted. She decided a little bit of honesty might go further than getting defensive and insulted by Victor's cold shoulder. "But as I got to know you and your work ethic better, I figured you would be fair and do right by the injured parties, even if at the expense of your son."

If looks could kill, Isla might have died on the spot, but she held her ground, meeting Victor's withering glare.

He said, "I planned to handle them in my own way. The company's image is always first. Its protection is number one."

"At the cost of an innocent life?"

"Not so innocent!" Victor bellowed, a fist hitting the top of his desk.

"What Mr. Corrigan means," Dixon interjected, shooting Isla a look of caution and awe at her nerve, "is that Matthew Leonard was indeed involved in this. He was even unfaithful to his wife."

A setup, Isla kept to herself. She wasn't supposed to know that. She was already possibly saying too much. The disappointment she felt tasted bitter and sharp. She'd expected him to be ruthless, but she held out a semblance of hope that he'd hold his son and his son's friend responsible, especially because their actions had resulted in a man's death.

Dixon looked up from his screen. "We have no choice but to act now. Do damage control and launch a public investigation until things die down."

"Then you let Bennett and Danny continue on?" Isla asked. "Throwing money at Mrs. Leonard isn't enough. There should be justice, especially since it sounds like it's not the first time you've covered for Bennett."

Victor deliberately ignored her, maybe even hated her in this moment. She was the good angel on his shoulder, reminding him to make the right decision, holding the mirror up and showing him something ugly that he'd rather not see. She half expected him to throw her out on her ass and revoke all her privileges.

His receptionist burst in, this time with Myles on her heels. Myles took in the scene, his eyes coolly moving from his father to Dixon and finally, with an air of surprise, to Isla. He frowned slightly, as if wondering what she was doing there during this critical time. She merely shrugged and tried to look innocent as she stood, deciding this was a good time to leave.

Victor said, "Have you seen the news?" Myles nodded. "Our competitors will have a field day with this."

"I don't know what happened, Dad, or how the information got out," Myles said. He asked Dixon, "Where are we with this?"

"Damage control. I'm contacting the PR firm in LA that we used."

Isla inched out a little faster at the mention of her employer.

Myles nodded. He slipped his hands in the pants pockets of his suit, no jacket, a vest. Isla decided she definitely liked his style. "Dad? You said you would decide what to do with them. What will it be now that it's out?" Myles was as unreadable as ever, not giving any indication of which way he'd fall.

Victor's head was in his hands as he stared down at his desk.

Bennett and Danny's dirty dealings were out in the open and couldn't be brushed under the rug. Their names might be withheld, but everyone would figure out that they had been suspended, relieved of their duties pending further investigation. Isla knew Victor wouldn't do more than the suspension. He'd wait some time and then allow Bennett to run another one of his many companies. It wasn't total justice, but it was some.

Isla left the office as Bennett and Danny rushed in, the looks on their faces equal parts shock and terror. When Isla passed them, she felt a bittersweet satisfaction. Matthew Leonard had been vindicated, but that he was no longer around made it nothing but a hollow victory.

CHAPTER FIFTY

Isla had been hoodwinked.

"How about you experience another side of Victor Corrigan?" Victor had passed through a message from his executive assistant when Isla made it back to the estate. "A different environment. A fun side." It was supposed to be an apology for the job shadowing gone wrong, though Isla had found her time at the downtown office enlightening and very satisfying.

She should have questioned then what *fun* meant to Victor Corrigan. She thought maybe lunching on cucumber sandwiches at the country club and sitting poolside. Instead, she was trudging through mountains, wearing camo gear and boots, and smelling like Bug Away.

She tried to mask her displeasure, reminding herself that this was for a bigger cause. But every tree branch that smacked her in the face and every errant spiderweb she walked into chipped away at her resolve.

At least she'd remembered to send a quick text to Charli, letting her know she was fine and was on a job for Rey she couldn't talk about. It wasn't answer enough to appease the always-suspicious Charli, who thought everyone was as greedy, suspicious, and scheming as she was. She and Brooke would have gotten along great.

She stumbled over an exposed root, cursing Victor and this damned mountain under her breath. She followed the hunting party deeper into the hunting grounds, deeper into the woods off the Corrigan property. The woods were a burgeoning mix of trees: oak, maple, and poplar mixed with pines and cedars; the rolling hills and valleys that stretched for miles, with the Blue Ridge Mountains serving as backdrop, were breathtaking. At their current high altitude, there was a different feel to traipsing through the dense forest and lush ground cover compared to driving along the tiny roads swirling along these same hills, valleys, and mountains. Walking through the rugged terrain now held a quality she was able to appreciate.

Thick branches filled with lush leaves blotted out much of the clear blue sky, while Isla clumsily tripped along the thick carpet undergrowth in the new boots she hadn't broken in yet and that made her arches hurt. She decided that while their surroundings were beautiful, she preferred the carefully manicured landscapes, sidewalks, and air-conditioning to the literal wilderness as her nerves strained at every mention of signs of recent wildlife movement. Isla decided if she came out of these woods without seeing anything shot, killed, or wanting to eat her, she'd be okay with that.

Isla's discomfort grew with every step as she observed their group, which consisted of Bennett, his friends Danny and Roger—no James, she noted—Victor and Dixon, and Jackson, a last-minute addition who'd managed to pry himself from Brooke's side for the afternoon. There was a smattering of guards, a couple of Corrigan employees, and associates of Victor's she did not know. Isla didn't bother getting to know them all, and they soon forgot she was around. The only person remaining relatively close was the person she thought wanted to be around her the least, Myles. He was a last-minute addition as well. He was originally not going to participate, but when he learned that she'd be tagging along and that Bennett would be there too, Myles's jam-packed schedule suddenly became free, much to Victor's amusement, which he'd conveyed to Isla on their drive there. Isla had learned Victor wasn't above gossip and speculation.

"Keep up, Miss LA," Bennett teased from ahead of her when she paused, again, to catch her breath. "You'll get lost if you don't. This isn't the place you want to do that."

Isla didn't give him the satisfaction of a response. The fact that he and Danny were here after the news break and after Victor had made them step down surprised her. They joked around, like they were cool and had no worries, but they had to be angry and to need to vent that anger on the easiest prey they could find.

Bennett was acting cockier than usual, surrounded by his Neanderthal friends. She was no longer the topic of conversation when he, Roger, and Danny began reminiscing about their high school days, still mindful enough not to be too loud and scare off any game.

"You remember your first ride?" Bennett asked. "The Jeep that you backed into a tree stump that one time, making that dent in the bumper?"

Roger said ruefully, "She was my first love."

"Cops ever find it?" Danny asked, laughing.

"Hell no," Roger replied, sounding wistful. "She was a magnet for the girls too. This is supposed to be safe, small-town Virginia, and look what happens. Someone steals her right from our driveway. Damn, I loved that ride."

Isla fell behind, slipping from the middle of the group to the back, as each step exhausted her. She considered plopping herself on the trunk of an uprooted tree and telling them to pick her up on their way back down, but she wouldn't give Bennett that satisfaction either. Whatever initial interest and intrigue he'd had with her had dissipated, and in their place were contempt and plain annoyance since he'd realized she had wormed her way into his father's good graces and wouldn't be going anywhere anytime soon. Myles, who'd been relatively close by, had disappeared upon hearing someone had spotted a deer, the thrill of the hunt drawing him away.

They moved farther up and into the woods, the terrain growing more uneven and treacherous to Isla's pavement-conditioned feet. Thorny brambles clawed at her jeans, and the thick undergrowth of vines caught her toes, and she stumbled forward, catching herself on a tree, its rough bark scratching her palms. Up ahead, Victor called for them to stop, and the group fanned out to check their surroundings and look for the markings that showed where they were permitted to hunt.

As she battled with a patch of muddied ground for one of her boots and fought the beginnings of panic at feeling enclosed with no way out, Myles materialized beside her. "Don't wander off," he warned softly, his gaze serious.

Isla nodded but felt suffocated by everyone's closeness and being able to see nothing but trees as far as she could tell. She stepped a few paces away to catch her breath, bringing her anxiety down to a manageable level by closing her eyes and imagining what Rey and Nat were doing at the moment. She calculated. They were three hours behind, which meant 9 a.m. their time. Nat was still asleep, and Rey was running security scans or whatever he was supposed to be doing for his clients.

There was a faint rustle, and though she knew better, curiosity got the better of her, and Isla started toward it, debating whether to call out that she'd found something someone could shoot or shoo the thing away to hopeful freedom. She took a step, and her ankle turned horribly when she stepped on a hidden rock or root, and the world tilted before she realized she was falling.

She'd fallen down an incline, and when the shock and pain subsided, she looked around, trying to get her bearings. Nothing looked familiar, and everything looked the same. Woods, trees, leaves, green. She couldn't tell where she'd been or where she should go.

"Hey," she called out, first shakily, but louder the second time. The only response she got back was bubbling water from a nearby creek or stream, and birds. And . . . something else. There was no one around.

Isla's breath came out in hitches as she tried to still her rapidly beating heart. She tried to stand, then cried out when bolts of electric pain radiated from her twisted ankle. She sucked in a long, painful breath to steady herself against a pine tree, trying to listen for sounds of human life. The woods, once alive with crunching leaves and the distant voices of the people she'd trudged up with, had now swallowed all noise, leaving nothing but her ragged breathing, which sounded way too loud and terrified as panic clawed at her chest and she thought her heart would explode through her orange-and-neon-green vest.

"Hello?" she called out again, her voice thin and reedy, sounding like someone else.

She limped forward, grimacing against the pain. Tried retracing her steps as she thought about what had happened. She'd fallen, rolled down an incline that was hidden somewhere in the dense foliage.

A loud crack behind sent her heart to her throat. She spun around, bracing herself to see a bear or bobcat or hopefully a person, but there was nothing—just more trees and bushes and shadows. Even in the bright of day, the woods looked darker and more foreboding, especially when one was alone.

"Get it together, girl," Isla chastised. "Find them, or you won't hear the end of it."

She gritted her teeth with each agonizing step, wishing she had a compass—not that she'd know which way to go. She had nothing of substance except her bottle of water hanging from her wrist and a couple of KIND bars in her jacket pockets. She hadn't planned to actually hunt, so more gear than that wasn't needed . . . until it was.

"Bennett?" she called out, her head on a swivel. "Myles? Anyone?"

Nothing.

Every tree looked the same, and time seemed to stretch endlessly. Confusion and fear scratched at the edges of her. She hadn't fallen far, or long, she thought. So where had everyone gone so quickly? Why couldn't she hear them or they her? The sameness of her surroundings and having no actual path to follow made it impossible to discern the way she'd come. She thought about stuff she'd heard on the news back home. How first responders suggested that hikers in the forests in the California hills and on trails in the canyons should stay where they were and not venture any farther, making it harder for search teams to find them.

Isla was about to do just that. Sit her ass down and go nowhere until someone found her. She'd decided to hell with finding them—she was Miss LA, right? They knew this place better than she did. The rustling started again. Closer this time. It was heavy, deliberate. Not a skittering squirrel, a bird taking flight, or the soft tread of deer. It didn't sound like what a bear would sound like either, not that she'd know. But she imagined bears would sound bigger and would make more sound, even if they were stalking prey. No, this noise sounded much more deliberate.

It stopped when she paused to listen and started back up again when she took a few steps backward. A twig snapped beneath heavy feet, sending Isla's senses into overdrive. Whatever—whoever—it was was after her! Isla's pulse thundered in her ears as blood rushed through and she stumbled forward, using her hands to push away the reaching branches that whapped her in her face and upper body. She ignored the shooting pains in her ankle, though she still limped hard as she pushed through to put space between her and the noise behind her.

Another snap—a branch breaking.

Isla turned sharply, catching fleeting movement out of the corner of her eye. A shadow darting between the trees, not low like an animal would be. Higher. Like a person. Someone was near her, someone who hadn't replied when she'd called for help. Someone who wasn't a friendly, but a foe.

CHAPTER FIFTY-ONE

Fear surged as Isla broke into a hobbled run. The underbrush clawed at her legs, snagging her jeans, pulling at the laces on her boots, untying one. Sharp branches slashed at her arms as she ran with no idea where she was going and only one thought. *Get away.*

A crack sounded through the air, and a piece of tree trunk just ahead of her exploded into sharp splinters. She ducked, covering her head, a yelp coming from her.

Was it Bennett, playing a cruel game, trying to do his mother's bidding and scare Isla off? Or was there someone else she'd inadvertently offended, something she was very good at—another ping whizzed by—and who wanted her gone by any means necessary? Had it come to that, all to keep her from uncovering what had happened to Eden?

The toe of her boot caught on a root and sent her sprawling into a thicket. She landed hard. More pain gripped her, but she scrambled to her feet, hearing crushed leaves and underbrush behind her. They were chasing her now, and getting close.

She refused to give up as a new emotion flooded in. Anger. Could she have wandered into a hunting zone, and someone was mistaking her for game? Or maybe not mistaking her but hunting something else, and she was getting in the way? But couldn't they see the bright vest she was wearing, the kind they were all supposed to wear so others could tell them apart from the wildlife and foliage? What if it was Jackson?

She heard the unmistakable click of a rifle chambering. The sound reverberated through the woods and directly into her ears. She ducked instinctively before the shot rang out, her breath huffing out in shallow gasps. This shot was different from the other two.

She saw more light through the line of trees and ran for it. She burst through the line of trees into a grassy clearing. Her ankle throbbed. She turned in circles, desperate for signs of safety and cover before they shot again. Surely in a clearing she was easier prey. The running feet in the woods behind her sounded closer, like they were going to burst through as well. She'd have to make her stand here. Running would do nothing for her now.

Isla dropped to her knees behind a jutting boulder amid the nearly waist-high grass swaying in the wind. She smashed up against it, trying to make herself small. Her hands groped around the sunburned grass for something she could use to launch at the person when they broke through the line. She grabbed the first thing she came into contact with. A jagged rock, splintered off from the boulder she was using as her cover.

She steadied herself, raising her hand, preparing to brain the bastard as they came up on her. She didn't want to give away where she was. She'd wait until they came to her. She heard them as they broke through the tree line, coming closer. She braced herself, tightened the grip she had on the rock in her hand. She saw the long barrel of the gun first as it appeared just above her, casting its thin, wavering shadow over her and the ground before her. More of the weapon came into view, then a booted foot, a leg, part of the upper torso and head. It was enough. She leaped up.

"You motherfucker!" she yelled. It was primal. Full of rage and insult at being chased and terrified. Her hand snapped back to smash down the rock before the figure had a chance to swing the gun around on her.

"Isla!" the figure said, his face coming into view just as the rock was about to connect with the side of his head.

She breathed out, her arm freezing in midair, inches from his face. "Myles?"

He was lowering his weapon, but she was still frozen in time. His face had paled, his breathing as labored as hers.

"How'd you get out here?" He looked at her fist and the rock in it. "What—what are you doing?"

His startled expression, equal parts relief, anger, and confusion, disengaged her, and she brought her arm down. It fell to her side like deadweight, the rock still wedged firmly in her hand.

"What are you doing?" he asked again as she stepped away from him, so very confused. She looked at him, frowning, trying to differentiate someone she knew, and who was maybe safe, from the person who'd been chasing her.

He asked, "Where have you been?" Slowly, he placed his weapon on the ground, then came back up just as deliberately, trying not to scare her more than she already was.

Isla tried to clear her confusion, to pick reality from imagination and discern if she was safe or still in danger. "Someone . . ." She hyperventilated, her knees going weak. She used her free hand to steady herself, refusing help from Myles when he reached for her rock hand. "Someone was chasing me."

"What?"

"I swear. They—there were shots. In the woods. Got lost and . . . chasing me," she choked out. She finally looked at him. "I thought . . ." Nothing was coming out right. "Where were you?"

And then she buckled, with Myles catching her just in time as more of the group broke through the cluster of trees, heading toward them. He steadied her against the boulder. She was fully hyperventilating now, leaning between her knees to catch her first real, true breath. Myles placed his hand on her back, rubbing ever so softly as she refused to let herself cry. She would focus on breathing.

"You're safe now," he said, though his eyes darted toward the tree line and their group, scanning for signs of the danger she spoke of. "I'm here."

The sounds of the group made Isla flinch. It was the rest of the party, but Isla still didn't want them to see her. Now that she was safe and the confusion was clearing, embarrassment closely chased it and was taking her over. When Bennett saw her. God, when Victor. What Victor hated the most was weakness, and then she'd have lost everything she'd already worked so hard for.

The majority of the group joined them, the rest trickling behind. Bennett, Victor, Dixon, and Jackson reached them first, weapons with them, their faces grim.

Bennett exploded at her, "What the hell, Isla? You left the group and had us looking everywhere."

"She's fine," Myles said tersely, sending his younger brother a warning glare, a reminder of what Bennett should have asked first.

Bennett faltered. "I mean . . . are you?" He looked abashed.

"What happened to you?" Victor asked as he, along with Myles, reached down to help Isla up. Actual worry lined his face as he assessed her appearance. Or perhaps he was calculating just how much this incident was going to cost him. Isla couldn't help thinking the worst.

She held up her hand to wave them off and give herself space. "I'm okay," she managed. She looked up at Bennett. "I didn't wander off," she said pointedly. "I fell down a hill or something and got separated and lost my bearings. I called for help, but I guess everyone had moved on without me."

The men exchanged uneasy glances.

"And someone was chasing me. They chased me all the way out here."

The men grew more uneasy, shifting their feet.

Jackson said, "We heard shots. We thought it was another group out here. Maybe you got turned around and entered the zone, and they mistook you for game or just didn't see you?"

Victor asked, "You think poachers?".

Isla took in her very bright vest, her fire replacing the embarrassment. "Orange stands out against green," she retorted. "You think maybe they're color blind?" It probably wasn't sensitive to say, but at this current moment, Isla didn't give a fuck.

"What's with that?" Bennett asked, pointing to the rock she didn't realize was still in her tight grip. "You were planning to fight bullets with rocks?"

Jackson said, "Cool it, Bennett. For once."

"It wasn't random. They were definitely following me. A shot whizzed right by my head and hit a tree ahead of me."

Dixon had his hand on his hip, completing a revolution as Isla had done when she'd first run out. "I didn't think there were any other groups out here. I checked. And I can't believe they'd be taking shots without confirming it is game they're shooting at. If that was the case here, we'll need to do something about it."

Bennett rolled his eyes and sauntered off to join his friends, where they proceeded to shoot looks at her, clearly talking about how she'd ruined their hunting fun.

Victor said grimly, following Dixon's gaze, "Then let's go check it out."

Half the group followed Isla back in, with Bennett begrudgingly following them after telling his friends to begin their trek to their rally point, where they'd head back down to the forest warden's station and their all-terrain vehicles. Isla steeled herself for reentry into the forest. With a clearer mind, she was able to backtrack to where she'd been. A not-so-keen hunter's eyes could tell where she'd been, thrashing around and marking a clear path.

"Your ankle," Myles commented, his concern evident, when Isla began to walk and he saw how hard she limped, favoring her right leg. He reached to take her arm, offering to have her lean on him.

Again she waved him off, not wanting to seem any more of a damsel in distress than she already appeared. She didn't even want to think about what she looked like after her ordeal. At least she hadn't cried in front of them. That might be reserved for later, when she was alone in the staff housing. And she'd need to make it back to the hotel room, where she kept her map.

She pointed to the tree that had been struck by the bullet, shuddering at how the bullet had dug in, showing the light tan of the tree's inner bark. It had been so close.

Dixon said, "This is definitely not an approved area for hunting. Someone's made a huge mistake."

She wanted to say it was more than a mistake. It was intentional. But it was beyond their realm of comprehension because they hadn't been the prey. It wasn't them who'd been running for their lives. It had been her. And any one of these people could have been on the other side of that rifle.

They started to move away, continuing through as best Isla could recall, but Myles remained, crouched and staring intently at the ground.

Victor noticed first, turning. "Son, let's not lose another person, yeah?" Bennett fidgeted at his words.

Myles stood, his gaze remaining fixed on the ground. "Look at this." He motioned to a set of prints in the mud. "These are hers. I can tell because the left foot digs deeper than the right, since she hurt it and was limping. Plus they're smaller." He looked at her, and she looked back, biting her bottom lip. "But there is another set."

Jackson asked, "Maybe one of ours?"

Myles shook his head. "Can't be," he said firmly. "We didn't come through this way, remember? This set was definitely tracking her. It follows her path directly."

This time Isla couldn't hold back her shudder. She'd known someone was chasing her, terrorizing her. But doubling back and seeing the evidence let the fear creep back in. She only needed to make it a little longer; then she'd be alone.

"And look." Myles gestured to a fainter set of prints nearby, not aligned with hers and whoever was following her. "A third set. Someone else was here. Tracking them."

"What?" Bennett asked seriously, forgetting he had thought this was all bullshit and was pissed at her for messing up their afternoon before he'd caught anything. "What do you mean a third set?"

A chill ran through her. Goose bumps broke out all over her body, and cold sweat dotted her forehead. Instantly she remembered. "The third shot!"

Victor had joined Myles. He looked at Isla, then at Dixon, his concern deepening. "What was that?"

"There were three shots total. The first two were from one gun," she said. "That's how I knew they were following me. Because one shot can be an accident. I called out. They would have heard me yell. But instead they took another shot. But then there was a third shot, and this one sounded different from the other two. Like it came from a different gun."

"Two sets of prints," Victor repeated, his voice low, as if he was simmering at the thought.

"Yeah," Myles said. "One chasing her, and the other . . ." He glanced at Isla, catching her in the snare of his eyes. She did a double take. Gone were the days of his morose and indifferent disdain for her. There was something else he was saying in his glance that she didn't dare puzzle out yet, because if she read him wrong and that wasn't care and concern she was seeing in his eyes, she realized she'd be crushed. She gripped the rock tighter, knowing she would keep it forever.

They headed back to the meeting point, Bennett grumbling that he wanted to leave and the place was giving him the creeps. Isla noted the flicker of unease in his eyes. The way, when he met up with Danny and Roger, they huddled, throwing her furtive looks. Danny gesticulated wildly, then stalked away. Today might have been their warning to stay out of their business and leave, which meant she had to be on the right track.

CHAPTER FIFTY-TWO

The next couple of days were quiet, and Isla was ready to continue on, not letting whoever had tried to scare her in the woods deter her. She was so close to the truth that she could taste it, and she hoped the momentum would keep going. Victor's reception was getting close.

She shoved her hands in the pockets of her jacket as she waited in the empty parking lot of a CVS. The streets at this time of night were spookier than in the day, but that wasn't unusual. What was unusual was her actually agreeing to meet James so they could talk alone and away from prying eyes. She was especially jittery after the hunting party, and her ankle still throbbed. James hadn't been with the party, but what if he had still been there? What if he'd been the one chasing her? So why, again, had she agreed to meet a guy by herself and without telling anyone? She was asking for trouble and probably heading into a trap.

On the phone, James had sounded different. He hadn't sounded like his smug friends or like something was up. He'd sounded horrible, to be honest, worse than he'd sounded when she'd gone to his house.

She sensed she was being watched. The hairs on the back of her neck raised, and goose bumps spread over her arms. She was just about to forget the entire thing when a figure separated itself from the dark shadows of the alley that she stood looking into. She swallowed a scream and clutched the canister of Mace in her jacket pocket, her finger sliding to the trigger.

"Isla." The sudden voice when there had been silence was startling as James became more visible in the beam of a streetlight as he approached. He had his hands out to let her know he meant no harm. "It's me," he said.

"I know," she replied, annoyed at being scared like that. "What's up? You said come, and I came. Are you ready to tell me what happened?"

He looked like he was giving himself a pep talk. He nodded. "I'll do you one better. I'll show you."

That made her nervous. "Where are we going? Can I follow you?"

"It's better if I drive. The road out there can be rough, and I know how to drive it." He pointed at the mud-splattered 4x4 taking up two parking spots. He started walking there, not seeming to care if she followed or not. Isla made a quick and maybe bad decision to follow.

James kept his eyes on the road, which became bumpier as they climbed into what looked like more mountain, woods, and trees. Isla couldn't tell any of them apart, and that probably wasn't a good thing. She had the Find app activated on her phone, so if James had other plans for her, Rey and Nat would know where to start. She just hoped her signal would hold out all the way up here.

"I've been thinking about what you said and what happened to Edie." His eyes darted around like he expected someone to leap from the shadows. "You know Bennett and Danny think you ratted them out to Mr. Corrigan—about the LA situation."

Was he fishing for info? "What makes them think that?"

"Apparently you were leaving his dad's office right before his dad tore them new assholes. He made Bennett and Danny quietly step down from the LA offices, you know. So Bennett's pissed."

"I can imagine," she said. "But pissed enough to try and scare or hurt me at the hunting party?" Isla asked. "That's extreme."

He glanced over at her, then back at the desolate road that disappeared into the forest that closed in around them. Everything felt suffocating.

"Yeah, well, those two can be extreme. You have no idea. And with Mrs. Corrigan and her lawyer always backing him, he thinks he can do whatever he wants. You should stay clear of them."

They kept climbing up and up, and Isla asked him where they were going.

"To the old Abbott farm."

James drove with a white-knuckle grip on the wheel, his nerves palpable in the confined space of the truck. Her heart beat in time with his.

"She wanted money to run away," he said suddenly, his voice strained. "She was going to blackmail us. Said she'd tell everyone about the accident."

"The accident with the four out-of-town family members?" Isla asked.

James didn't answer right away. Instead, he turned onto a dirt path that led deeper into the woods. The towering trees closed in more, the path becoming narrower, the darkness becoming heavier with each passing mile.

"The accident was our fault. When she came back, Edie wanted us to admit what we'd done. She wanted Bennett to give her enough money to leave for good and never come back. At least that's what Bennett told us. Danny was pissed, calling it blackmail. Roger wasn't taking it too seriously because he's a dumbass. Nothing's real—everything's a joke. But that accident, that family. It was all our fault."

"That's not what it said in the paper." The one clipping she'd managed to find. The Corrigans had done a remarkable job killing any press about it.

"Of course not. It had to do with the Corrigans, and Danny's family, and even mine. Our parents ensured that we weren't known to be involved. We were just innocent kids who happened upon a horrible accident and called the cops."

Dread was growing in the pit of Isla's stomach. "But you weren't."

"We weren't innocent. Edie tried to make us tell the truth. That it was a bad prank gone wrong. But Bennett said no way. He guilted her into believing she would ruin the family. He said we'd go to prison. I was terrified, and I went along with them and pressured Edie to keep quiet. After that, she didn't want anything to do with me. And then a little while later she left."

"But then she came back." Isla had to keep the conversation going. They were slowing down now, pulling to a stop. Ahead, the top of some kind of structure peeked up from over the hill.

"This is where we get out," James said.

As they trudged up the hill, Isla was thankful she was wearing the proper shoes, but her ankle was hurting just the same.

James continued, "She wanted to meet at her old stomping ground. We picked her up from a motel."

Isla's memory took over from here. The taillights. The yellow Jeep. Eden telling her that she'd be back.

"Danny and Bennett didn't want to talk about it." James's words came out haltingly. "No use bringing up old shit, they said. But people *died*, Isla. We did that. *Bennett* did that."

Isla's stomach churned. What could she say? How could they have done that? How could Eden? She let out a slow breath.

"They didn't mean for it to happen," he said, almost pleading. "We were supposed to just talk, and Bennett was supposed to meet us. Talk, that's all. But then . . . everything went wrong."

They came upon the old Abbott barn, its weathered exterior looming and ghostly. It was a thing of horror movies. Isla gave James a worried look. She hoped they wouldn't have to go in there. The barn was leaning dangerously, as if it could collapse at any moment.

"It happened in there."

Shit.

Inside, the barn smelled of rot and decay. She followed James to the center, his steps as hesitant as his retelling.

"She was so angry. I'd never seen her this way. But Danny was so damn cocky. He was trying to scare her, you know? Me and Rog, we tried to get in between them. Keep them apart. But Edie kept saying we needed to tell the truth, over and over," he said, his voice barely above a whisper. He gestured wildly as he spoke, reenacting the events of that night. "She was yelling at us, saying she'd go to the police if Bennett didn't get here quick and bring the money. She and Danny struggled, and he pushed her off him. And she fell backward."

He took several steps to a large window with almost all its glass gone. "She fell on the glass. There was so much blood."

Isla wanted to throw up, imagining the last moments, the fear, that Eden had experienced. "Then what?"

"She wasn't dead," James said quickly, as if absolving himself, his voice full of hope. "Bennett got here, and we went out to tell him what happened, but when we came back, she was gone. We searched everywhere. She made it out!"

There was a crash near where they stood and then an explosion as a lantern ignited the dry hay and the fire began to spread all around them.

"James," she said at the moment he seemed to comprehend they were in trouble. He grabbed her arm, pulling her toward the back.

Flames licked high to the second floor, eating hungrily at the dried and rotting wood. Smoke filled the room quickly. Isla's eyes stung, burned. She began coughing, choking. She couldn't see her way out, but James had her arm firmly. He tugged, and she followed.

"Move!" James shouted, pulling Isla toward a ragged hole in the back, the front totally engulfed, the fire roaring wildly, the heat so intense.

James pushed her through the hole, and she turned to help him out. Together, they stumbled away from the barn, coughing and disoriented. They managed to make it back to his truck, and through tears, James pointed. Another set of tires had been there.

"There's no way they're getting away with it this time. I swear." It was the most strongly she'd ever heard him speak. He was determined.

She barely had time to jump in the passenger seat before James reversed, stopped hard—shoving her backward—and made a turn, then raced back down the tiny path they'd come up. The barn groaned ominously as the fire consumed it, licking to the sky. She just managed to put on her seat belt. She looked back and watched as the barn grew smaller and collapsed within itself.

"What if it's her?" James asked frantically, wiping at his still-tearing eyes. "She burned the farm where we hurt her."

"James, that can't be."

The truck careened down the narrow dirt path, James gripping the wheel with shaking hands.

"I can feel it. I can feel her."

He was losing it. She had no way to calm him. She pleaded for him to slow down. Watch out. She didn't want to go over.

Isla glanced through the front window, the two red lights of another truck appearing. "It couldn't be . . ."

James squinted. "That's—that's Danny. The bastard."

Isla's heart leaped into her throat.

"He wants to do this. This time I'm not backing down." James switched off his headlights, and pitch black swallowed them whole.

Isla was growing frantic. It was a dream, a bad dream. They roared behind the other vehicle, hitting all the rocks and branches the other truck kicked up in its wake. "What are you doing? Turn the lights back on!"

Danny's truck turned down another road, disappearing in the darkness. James reached the turn and followed, slowing only slightly to follow suit. Were they on the main road? Isla tried to recall where, on their way up, she had noticed the sharp curve, creeped out then at the thought of having to take such a precarious turn on their way back. Now they had to be charging toward it.

Then, suddenly, opposite them, lights flashed on, high beams blinding.

"James, turn!" Isla shouted.

He didn't listen. The two vehicles were now heading toward each other. James grit his teeth, leaning forward and gripping the wheel tighter.

"I'm sorry," he said. They were getting closer. "It was our fault. All of it. This. This was where it happened."

"What, James?" she pressed, the railing separating them from the drop beyond nothing but a blur touched by moonlight as they whizzed past. "Where what happened?" Maybe if she kept him talking, he'd come back to reality and see what he was doing.

"Where we killed them!" he roared. He was so loud, his words echoed in the truck.

Her hands clamped over her ears to drown out both him and the sound of the vehicle whipping through the wind as James accelerated in this deadly game of chicken.

They roared toward the other vehicle. She begged James to stop, to move over. But he wouldn't, laughing and repeating over and over that there was nothing left. They were just about on the oncoming truck, its horn blaring nonstop. She couldn't watch. She couldn't look away. She couldn't think as she saw Danny's horrified face through the windshield, getting closer, until just as they were about to collide, the other truck swerved at the last minute. Not quick enough for James to avoid smashing into its side.

The other vehicle spun out of control, careening off the road, out of her line of vision, as James lost control from the impact, wrenching the wheel hard to keep them from crashing through the metal barrier and going over the drop. They hit a stone embankment in an amalgamated discordance of clashing metal, squealing tires, and shattering glass. Isla's head smacked into her window as the airbags deployed. She heard, saw, felt nothing more.

CHAPTER FIFTY-THREE

James

Thirteen Years Ago

The old Abbott barn was one of the few places James and Edie could get away from everyone and be together. The way their relationship had evolved had been a slow burn, though he'd liked her from the minute he stepped foot in Bennett's house and saw her there, head in a book. James knew then that she would be the only person he wanted to spend the rest of his life with, and Edie believed she wanted the same.

She wasn't like the other Corrigans. She was sensitive, compassionate, and nice. She never made it seem like she was anything more than a regular awkward girl. James loved that about her. She wasn't like Myles, who was too cool to even be considered human. He was already off in the air force, having made a quick getaway from his overbearing father. She wasn't like Bennett, who toggled between hating Edie with a passion and being overprotective of her.

James only wanted to be with her. But even that, Bennett wouldn't let happen. The moment he suspected James was interested in Edie, he was on James like white on rice, shaming him, trying to get him to fuck other girls, outright demanding they not see each other. All because he knew that Edie was the one their father loved the most. So he made it his goal for her to have the least.

The five of them—James, Edie, Bennett, Danny, and Roger—had gone to the barn to hang out and drink. Bennett, Danny, and Roger were drinking the most, guzzling all the booze they'd found at home and bought from the store, where a fake ID got them all the whiskey and tequila and beer they wanted.

James and Edie sneaked away, climbing up to the loft when it looked like the guys below had finally passed out. Now they could be alone. Quiet, so as not to wake the ones below, but alone.

The two of them finally gave in to the desires they'd kept in check for months. They made love, and it was the most special night of James's life. As they were getting dressed and silently laughing at the hay stuck in their hair, Danny's head popped up through the door in the floor, and he grinned at them lasciviously. Below, Bennett and Roger waited.

Danny sniffed the air and yelled, "Smells like someone's been fucking tonight!" He laughed boisterously. "James, you goddamn dog! I thought Bennett said Edie was hands off for his friends."

Below, Roger, always the clown, whooped and hollered, saying the most asinine things. They were still drunk, even more so if that was possible. The alcohol wafted off them, and they were unsteady on their feet.

"I'm the one who decides who's on or off limits," Edie said, brushing away the last bits of hay.

"You better get your deciding ass on down here so we can go." Danny laughed, climbing back down the rickety stairs.

James and Edie shared a look, knowing Bennett was about to explode, preparing themselves for the inevitable. James knew exactly how it would go down. They'd drop Edie off at home, and then Bennett would get Danny and Roger to beat the shit out of James for daring to be with his sister. All James wanted was to get her home safely. The rest would be what it was going to be.

Bennett watched them hawkishly, his eyes dark and stormy beneath the mess of his curly light-brown hair. His gaze went from Edie to James and back to Edie again, his expression unreadable. The air around him was thick with repressed anger, booze, and all the other demons bottled inside him. Edie stood her ground against him, refusing to make what she and James were to each other something cheap and ugly. She slipped her hand in James's, and for a moment, he relished the feel of her soft hands, remembered the touch of her body beneath his. But he stiffened at the way Bennett looked at their intertwined hands. Gently, James pulled his hand from hers, refusing to face her when she looked at him full of hurt. He couldn't face anyone, ashamed that he was afraid to stand up to Bennett.

Bennett had a bottle of whiskey in his hand and took a deep drink of it. "So this is what you do when Dad's not around. Just wait until I tell him. He'll ship you off to where your fucking mother is slumming in Florida. Get the fuck in the car. I'm taking you home."

James and Edie were the sober ones, and they attempted to get the keys from Roger, but Bennett was insistent on getting behind the wheel, and Roger gave the keys up to him without a whimper. James and Edie said they'd trek down, to which Bennett replied, "This time of night? As far as it is by foot? Over my dead body." He looked at James, his words meaning more than just walking down the hill.

Roger's yellow Jeep raced through the night, slicing through the darkness of the winding two-lane road that cut through the hills. The air was thick with the tension that only comes from too much liquor and the reckless thrill of youth.

Bennett grinned in the driver's seat, his hand drumming against the steering wheel of the Jeep while Edie sat in the passenger seat, her knuckles practically white as she gripped the armrest. In the back, Roger and Danny volleyed between boisterous laughter and nervous yelps when Bennett took curves too wide. James sat rigidly behind Bennett's seat.

"Bennett, slow down," Edie said tersely. Her eyes were glued to the twisting road ahead. "These roads are dangerous."

He glanced at her, his grin widening to a sneer. "Come on, Edie, don't be such a buzzkill. It's just a bit of fun."

James's stomach churned. The alcohol coursing through his veins did little to dull the heaviness in his chest. Bennett was unpredictable, worse than Jekyll and Hyde, and hopped up on wealthy privilege. One moment, he was charming, smooth talking, the center of attention. The next, he was . . . this. Cold. Sadistic.

The others exchanged nervous glances but said nothing. They never said no to Bennett.

"We've had enough fun for one night," Edie said, trying to keep her voice steady. "Let's just get home."

"Nah," Bennett said, focused on the narrow stretch of road illuminated by their beams. "One more game before we get to the house," he said, his tone low and teasing.

"What do you mean a game?" Roger asked from the back, his voice laced with worry, probably about his Jeep. Roger *always* worried about his precious Jeep. It annoyed the hell out of James. James strained to see ahead of them, watching out for any deer or other wildlife that could jump into the road. But it wasn't wildlife he saw. He squinted. Headlights up ahead?

Without warning, Bennett flipped off the headlights, plunging them into total darkness.

"Bennett, what are you doing?" Edie was screaming.

"Holy shit, man! Turn them back on!" Roger said, as panicked as James was feeling. Roger grabbed the headrest in front of him. Danny laughed. He was always unserious until he wasn't.

They sped down the narrow lane swallowed by a dark abyss. Bennett laughed, his foot pressing harder on the gas. The car surged forward, tires whining against the pavement as the road twisted beneath them. The trees that lined the road turned into dark, looming shadows that rushed past in a blur.

"Bennett, stop! This isn't funny!" Edie was frantic, reaching out to grab the knobs around the steering wheel, looking for the light stalk, which wasn't on her side. It was on James's. Bennett batted her hand away with ease, his eyes wild with excitement.

"Relax," he said, his voice calm despite the chaos he'd created. "We're having fun."

In the back, the others fell silent, their breath coming in short, terrified gasps. They all knew better than to challenge Bennett when he was like this, but the fear was palpable. No one wanted to be the one to tell him no.

The car hurtled forward, blind and fast, the road curving dangerously ahead. Then, in the distance, the faint glow of headlights James thought he saw became definite and were getting closer.

"Bennett!" Edie's yell filled the car.

The oncoming car closed in, its high beams bouncing against the tree trunks. His grip tightened on the wheel. In the small rectangle of the rearview mirror, Bennett was a blank canvas and determined. Just as the two vehicles were about to converge, Bennett flicked on the headlights—bright, blinding, cruel.

"No!" James called out, wanting this nightmare to pause. It couldn't be real.

The high beams of light flooded the narrow road with bright illumination just as the minivan in front of them came into full view. From his seat, he could see the driver and passenger throw their hands up in the blinding light. The driver, recovering quickly but not fast enough, grabbed the wheel in his blindness as the vehicles passed each other. The van swerved, banking hard. With a screech of tires and a metallic roar, the minivan veered off the road, crashing through the guardrail and disappearing over the edge.

The silent night exploded in a cacophony of shattering glass and crunching metal.

Bennett slammed on the brakes, smacking into the rail before finally bringing the Jeep to a jarring stop several yards away from the site of the impact. The rest of them were thrown forward, smashing into seat backs and whatever else could stop their momentum. For a second, all was silent before the vehicle filled with heavy, ragged breathing and panic. James's heartbeat thundered in his ears, and his hands were shaking. He didn't want to look behind them.

Edie was the first to unbuckle her seat belt. She flung the door open and stumbled out onto the side of the road. "Oh my God," she repeated over and over, her voice inching higher. "What have you done?"

They stumbled out of the back seats, their faces ghostlike, their breaths ragged. Danny ran a hand through his hair, muttering curses under his breath. Roger bent over at his knees, heaving. James felt like he might be sick, while Edie circled around and around in shock.

But Bennett? He was the last to get out, stepping out slowly and sucking in a deep lungful of air. His face was flushed, giddy, like he'd just finished a ride at an amusement park. He walked around to the front of the car, surveying the damage with a lazy smile.

"Your dad's gonna be pissed about this," he said to Roger matter-of-factly as he assessed the damage from where the front bumper had hit the rail. "I can take care of that for you."

Edie spun on him, her eyes blazing with fear and anger. "You're insane, Bennett! That wasn't a game. You just made that van crash!"

James and the other two huddled close, casting worried looks at Bennett and behind them, where the guardrail was broken and the van had gone down. It took James a moment to realize what had really happened. A vehicle had gone over the ridge, and it was their fault.

Roger finally spoke, his voice shaky. "We need to call the cops. Someone in that van could be dead."

Edie was already heading to the crash site, stopping at the twisted metal, looking down.

"They're not too far down. They may be alive and need help."

"Need help?" Bennett said, his tone chilling. "We need to get our story straight first."

Edie stared at him, horrified. "You did this on purpose playing that stupid game! You caused the crash. You—"

"I didn't know a car was coming up," Bennett said, stepping toward her, his eyes narrowing. "No one comes up this side of the mountain. And we were all drinking. You think any of us make it out of this without jail time? State championship's next week. You can kiss that scholarship goodbye. And your cushy life after graduation? Gone."

James shook his head, his voice trembling. "But we have to do something. The people in there, man!"

Danny said, "Shut the fuck up about the people, okay? It was an accident. Just call it in as an accident."

Edie pulled out her phone. "I'm calling the cops." Bennett stomped over to her, and James rushed to head him off but got there too late. Bennett slapped Edie in the face. And then slapped the phone from her hands.

James edged closer. "Hey!"

"Get it the fuck together. This was a stupid game gone wrong. An accident. They'll say it was bad driving for the road conditions or whatever excuse they give for stuff like this. I don't know, but we're not calling the police until we call our people first."

Edie looked like she was about to be ill. Exactly how James was feeling. "You're disgusting," she said to her brother.

Bennett turned, eyeing each of them until he landed on James. "If anyone says anything other than we were driving, saw them go over, and stopped to see if we could help them, you're dead. Understand? This secret goes to our grave."

Roger and Danny readily agreed. They didn't have the pull like Bennett and Edie. Their dads had business with the Corrigans. They had college and wives and careers to have. Reputations to uphold. No one had to know about this. No one.

"Swear it," Bennett said, his eyes boring into James, making him feel like he was shrinking where he stood.

James nodded, feeling ashamed. His dad's law firm. Edie. Their lives would be ruined.

Edie shook her head emphatically. "No, I won't. We can't."

Bennett leaned in close to her, his voice dropping to a dangerous whisper. "You will, because if you ever mention this again, dear little sis, I'll make sure your life is a living hell. I hope you believe me." Then he flipped, a disarming smile spreading over his face. His voice softened. "It will be all right, okay? They will be all right if you call the ambulance fast enough. You can save them." He picked up the phone and held it out to her.

She recoiled, looked over the ledge at the van, with its wheels still spinning halfway below, and silently took the phone to call 911.

At the same time, Bennett called their father, who came to the scene with Jackson.

What kind of brother—no, human—did that? James asked himself that nearly every day after that night, the guilt eating away at him so that he could barely function. But he was still always too chickenshit to stand up to Bennett and stand up for Edie.

James wanted Edie to never change, like Johnny Cade with Ponyboy in S. E. Hinton's *The Outsiders*—wanted her to stay gold and always remain the sweet, lovable, dreamy Edie she was supposed to be. The princess in the castle that was the Corrigans'. But that night changed him and Edie forever. Neither of them would ever be the same again.

CHAPTER FIFTY-FOUR

Isla

Present Day

Isla woke to the sound of beeping machines, a throbbing head, a sore neck, and Myles looming over her, watching her with concern. He gently held her back when she tried to sit up, disoriented and afraid. The doctors said she was lucky. That the driver's side had taken the brunt of the impact and she'd only suffered minor injuries. She'd be sore for a few days and needed to take it easy but could be released shortly.

Myles tried to distract her when she heard about the driver's side, but her memory came at her in a rush, like the other car barreling at them. Myles finally told her. James hadn't been as lucky. He was unconscious, his condition critical.

"You were lucky," Myles told her, helping her to a seated position. "What were you doing with James? How do you even know him?"

She didn't answer. Brooke and Jackson had her attention as she watched them through the window of her room. They were in the hallway, just outside her door. When they thought no one was watching, Jackson touched Brooke, his finger lightly trailing the back of her arm in an intimate gesture. But Brooke barely acknowledged him. They realized Isla was awake and entered. Brooke wore a smug expression and sauntered to Isla's bedside. Her tone dripped with mockery and fake concern.

"Isla dear, you are either accident-prone or a bad luck charm. First the mishap at the hunt, now this . . ." She tsked. "When did you and James become an item? This is how you normally conduct interviews?"

"Brooke," Myles warned, tensing. Isla coughed a little, signifying it was fine.

Brooke suddenly perked up like she'd been hit with a bright idea. "Now that things have come to this, I think continuing this article of yours is in bad taste. I'm sure my husband will agree. Don't you agree, Jackson? Liabilities and everything?"

Jackson cleared his throat, glancing at Isla and Myles uncomfortably before taking Brooke by the shoulders and whispering something in her ear that ended her victory lap.

"We came to make sure you were okay," Jackson said softly, placing a guiding hand on the small of Brooke's back. "We'll see you both back at the estate and can discuss later."

"What about the other car?" Isla asked when she and Myles were finally alone. "The person who followed us and tried to burn us in the barn?"

Myles hesitated so long she had to repeat herself.

"Danny?" Myles said.

Danny was dead.

CHAPTER FIFTY-FIVE

Things were suddenly spiraling out of control in ways Isla hadn't anticipated when the idea to return to Virginia came to mind after Leonard had died. Now, a second person was dead, and another, James, lay in intensive care. Isla blamed herself. If she hadn't returned bent on uncovering the truth about Eden. If she hadn't pressured James into reliving that night or pushed Danny into a corner where he thought stopping them by any means necessary was his only way, he would be alive now. And James wouldn't be in the hospital.

She was in too deep and feeling what little control she'd had was slipping away. But she couldn't stop now, no matter how scared she was that these people were deadly, or how sore her body was because of the crash. Victor pitied her enough to suggest she put the article on hold until she felt better and things calmed down, but she couldn't. Isla was on borrowed time. A sense of urgency grew like a snowball careening down a mountain slope that she could be sent away at any moment, losing all access she had to these people and this place. So only a couple of days after the accident, Isla went against doctors' orders to rest and was back at Jackson's home. This time, uninvited.

Jackson's home was bordered by sculpted hedges that wrapped around the house, providing cover as she went around to the side door, away from the street.

Isla approached the side door with purpose, as though she belonged there. Jackson's nearest neighbor couldn't be seen. And his high hedges helped hide her as well. Jackson was so arrogant, thinking he was much smarter than everyone else—Victor Corrigan included—that he'd also think no one would have the audacity to enter his home without an invitation. Therefore, his security system would be as basic as he was turning out to be.

It must be difficult to work so closely with Brooke and Victor Corrigan. Isla felt bad for him and imagined having a haven to come home to after dealing with other people's lives around the clock was helpful. She was glad he lived away from the estate and in his own little world. He probably needed his own space after having to serve at the Corrigans' leisure all the time. Isla imagined it was the same for Dixon. While Dixon and Jackson basically served Mr. and Mrs. Corrigan as trusted advisers on business and employee decisions, Victor at least respected Dixon, while he acted like Jackson barely existed. Not only was Brooke a nasty piece of work personality-wise, but she was also needy and exhausting. Isla nearly felt sorry for Jackson, but then quickly remembered that she didn't like him at all.

That made it easier to slink along the bushes and trees that obscured his home from onlookers, as she was now doing. She didn't have to worry about being recognized like she might have at the estate.

She tugged the hood of her sweatshirt lower over her head to obscure her face as much as possible, just in case. She made her way to the side door and shrugged off her backpack. She popped in one wired earbud that was attached to her phone, unable to use Bluetooth. She let the other bud hang over her chest so she had one ear listening for anything off.

She recalled Rey's words from his quick history of frequencies and signals and how she was going to block them over the phone the night before. She took out the square frequency jammer. She flipped it on and waited a moment for it to disrupt any Wi-Fi signal Jackson's security system emitted. She slipped it back in her backpack and took it with her as it stayed on.

For good measure, the jammer was supposed to extend another twenty feet in radius around the home. Rey was too scary with all the ways he found to access things he shouldn't. She couldn't decide whether she felt like a spy or a criminal.

"Wish I'd thought to bring the smart glasses," she muttered, working the picks in the lock until she heard it disengage.

"Yeah, well, with the jammer on they wouldn't work like we'd need them to," Rey answered. "That's why we're on wired buds and an old-school cell. If I were there, closer, like when we do usual jobs, I could work in a separate frequency for you to video what you see in there."

She didn't argue. She was too nervous to do much talking at all, because this wasn't like the jobs they took in LA. Those had nothing to do with her. This was different. She entered the home.

Isla moved quickly toward the master bedroom, remembering its location from her previous visit.

"All right, Isla," Rey said through the earbud, his voice a steady presence in her ear as she entered the bedroom, which was a little messier since this time company was not expected. The bed was rumpled, and there was a discarded dress shirt flung over the back of a chair. A bottle of Armani cologne was uncapped on the glossy black dresser. The ceiling-to-floor blinds were pulled to let the natural light fill the room and revealed a set of sliding glass doors leading out to an expansive backyard.

"When you get to the safe, let me know when you're at the keypad. From what you sent me of its make and model," Rey continued, "it seems pretty standard. Look for a panel on it, and slide it to show the keypad."

Isla found the safe, just as she had the first time she was there interviewing Jackson.

She crouched before the safe, which was tucked snugly under the counter of the built-in minibar in his room. She found the panel as instructed and pressed gently. It slid away to reveal an electronic keypad.

"Okay," she said.

"Good. Now type in the sequence I gave you. This is a force override that will disable the lock for five minutes. You only have one chance before it locks down, so be fast and be right."

She let out a quick breath. Her fingers trembled as she punched in the ten numbers. The seconds ticked like an eternity.

"Rey, I don't think—"

The lock beeped. Then came the blessed sound of the heavy door opening with a vacuum-sealed little whoosh. Isla wasted no time swinging open the door, and the soft dome light cast a bluish glow over what was inside the safe. She did a quick scan of the contents. On the top shelf were stacks of cash that reminded her of a bank vault. Why would he ever need that much cash on hand? The stacks of hundreds and fifties, still crisp from whenever he'd gotten them from the bank, reached the top of the inside. She dug in, feeling around the top shelf and behind the rows of money for anything that might be hidden. Safes almost always contained something the owner didn't want others to see.

Finding nothing there, she went to the bottom half, which held a wooden box of expensive name-brand jewelry and an array of folders and documents. She listed everything she saw in a fast whisper while Rey commented on what she should or shouldn't look into.

"You don't have time to get into those documents and files," he reminded her when she said she wanted to read through them. She was about to listen to him when the words "Last Will and Testament" leaped out at her.

"It's his will," she said, curiosity driving her. She pulled the document out so she could see better, against Rey's advice. Her heart triple-timed as she read the next line, the words leaping off the page. "It's not Jackson's will but Victor's, unsigned," she said excitedly. "But get this—it names Bennett as the sole heir to the Corrigan empire and lists him as CEO." *What the hell . . .*

"Don't worry so much about that right now," Rey said. "There's no way he's getting Victor to sign that unless he's got a gun to the man's head. Also, Jackson would have to get past that guy Dixon too. Not gonna happen. Keep going."

There was more there referencing Jackson and Brooke as greater shareholders, but with Rey in her ear urging her to hurry, she couldn't read further like she wanted. Reluctantly, she put the document back, careful to line it up as it was when she'd found it. She resumed her search, feeling around the sides and reaching in all the way to the back. Behind the documents, in the recesses of the safe, was a small rectangular object encased in some kind of plastic.

"Think I got something," she muttered, grunting softly as her fingertips gripped the object and pulled it toward her. "It's a recorder. You think he's recorded someone on here and plans to blackmail them? Maybe it's Victor, and that's what he'll do with the will. This recorder is old school, though, so maybe an old shady business deal?"

"Let's see."

She pulled it out, opened the large ziplock bag, and pulled out a Sony recorder she hadn't seen the likes of for years, not since before the emergence of smartphones and Voice Memos. Isla felt a surge of trepidation and excitement. She didn't know why, but this find felt like it was going to be game changing, and maybe she'd finally get some solid facts to back up what she'd managed to put together so far. She pressed play.

At first, the recording was muffled static, and then a voice—soft but familiar, unsure—filled the room.

"Testing . . . testing . . . one, two. One, two. Hope this shit works."

The phone nearly dropped from Isla's hands. She was going years back in time: ten, nine, eight . . .

Oh God, it was Eden.

Isla thought of the last moment she saw her. *I might be late, so don't wait up.*

Hearing Eden's voice after so long, Isla felt her throat constricting, the pain reminding her where she was.

Rey from the other end: "What's that? Who is that?"

There wasn't enough air to breathe, let alone answer him. She clutched the recorder tightly, barely managing to cut it off.

"Isla, what's wrong?" Rey's voice became frantic. "Are you there? Do I need to call the cops?" Rey's questions came rapid-fire.

"E-E-Eden." On the verge of hyperventilation, she could barely get the words out. "It's Eden."

CHAPTER FIFTY-SIX

She'd thought nothing else would be able to shock her the way she'd been shocked when she learned of Eden's identity. She'd been wrong, because the world as she knew it had just stopped on its axis.

Rey was on it. "You'll take that, okay?" Rey said slowly, as if to a child. "But you need to get with it. You need to get out of there. Listen later, okay? When you're out of there."

Unthinkingly, she put the recorder back in the ziplock and dropped it in her backpack. Time was slipping away too quickly, and there was nothing else she could take that wouldn't be missed immediately. At least this had been in the way back, probably not thought of for a long while. She checked everything once more, ensuring that nothing would leap out to Jackson immediately if he opened his safe.

Just as she was closing the safe and sliding the panel back in place, headlights swept across the room.

"Oh shit, he's back," she said urgently. "I gotta turn the jammer off and the system back on, or else he'll notice it's not armed." She pushed herself to her feet, looking around for a way out. The sliding doors. But as she was about to cross the doorway to get to them, the front door opened, and Jackson was nearing the hallway, in view. She darted to the nearest hiding place—the closet. She went in, closed the wooden slatted door, and squeezed herself behind his full rack of clothes, stilling them just as he walked into his room.

Jackson's footsteps were heavy as he entered. Through the slats of the closet door, Isla watched him as he unbuttoned the cuffs of his sleeves. He paused, a curious expression on his face as he scanned the room. He started on the buttons on his chest, taking a few more steps. He faced the dresser, opening his shirt. Then he spun around quickly, his laser-sharp blue eyes narrowing and sweeping the room, as if he could tell something was off. Shit, had she forgotten something? Had she forgotten and worn a fragrance still lingering in the air that he found unfamiliar—or familiar—and was connecting to her?

Isla held her breath, willing for some sort of divine intervention, because this wouldn't be like some TV show. He had a recording of Eden from God knows when. He was literally capable of anything. She was afraid he could hear the pounding of her heart, and she was brought back to that hunting party, when she was alone, being terrorized in the woods. That same feeling of terror crept up on her again. Why hadn't she hurried and gotten out sooner? Had she disturbed something in the room?

He approached the closet, his movements slow and deliberate, a cat about to pounce on its prey. He stopped on the other side of the door. His body blocked the light, and he moved to open the door. Isla knew this was it for her. The door began to open. She braced for the worst.

Until the front door beeped and Brooke's voice called from the doorway.

"Jackson? Are you in here?"

Jackson froze, then let go of the handle, leaving the door open a sliver. As he turned, his expression was a mix of irritation and surprise. "Where else would I be? My damn car's in the drive," he muttered to himself. "I just left you, Brooke. What are you doing here?" he asked, meeting her at the bedroom's doorway. "And I told you about letting me know when you were going to come over. We need to be careful. Now more than ever with that woman hanging around."

"Don't mention that brat," Brooke said. "She's like a buzzing mosquito with all her endless questions. You know, Bennett says that she came out of Victor's office right before he pulled Bennett and Danny out of the LA office and accused them of being behind that whole ordeal with that man, that Larry man."

"Leonard."

"Whatever. That old buzzard said they set Leroy up. But I bet *she* was the one who told Victor and told the press. With all her snooping around. What if Victor's onto us and hired her secretly to expose how we've been working to solidify Bennett's position to take over? The whole article shit was a ploy. I always thought it was ridiculous the way she just waltzed into our home and suddenly became Diane Sawyer."

Jackson laughed. "Now the poor girl is a secret agent? Have some wine, Brooke. You need it."

Isla's hands clenched as they talked about her, but she was too scared to be pissed about it.

"You sure you're not just jealous of her? She's pretty. Sexy. Young. All the men are putty in her hands," Jackson teased.

Isla adjusted her position, her legs cramping and her heart slowing down. She watched them through the slats; they were still lingering in the doorway.

Brooke playfully hit him on the chest. "Don't joke around. You're lucky I've kept you around all this time."

"What's that supposed to mean? Kept me around?" There was an edge to him now. Isla itched to get out of there.

Brooke repeated, "Kept you around, just like before I married the man. You're on my team. You're here when I need you, and you like being right where you are, nothing more, nothing less."

"That's all I am to you? Like a servant?"

Brooke pouted. "You know what I mean. You've had my back from the very beginning. Don't be like that. Let's just get that damn bitch out of my house."

Jackson hesitated a beat before slipping his arms around her waist, drawing her to him. "She's a child," he said. "You have nothing to worry about."

"She's probably a gold digger. I just can't tell which she's going for: Myles, with no personality, or—God forbid—Bennett." She giggled as Jackson buried his face in her neck. "She's a problem we need to take care of."

Jackson groaned, pulling away. "What? I thought you were here for something else." He tugged at her top, revealing a lacy black bra and an ample chest underneath.

Brooke pouted. "Jackson."

"I will handle her."

Isla's stomach twisted. In her ear, Rey whistled low, hearing it as well. There was no time to think about how she was going to be handled. She was still in his closet, and if he found her there . . . she didn't want to imagine what *handle* meant.

Brooke asked, "It's done, then, finalized? Victor's revised will?"

"It's done," Jackson said, his voice clipped as he pushed past her, the sizzle between them dying down since she wanted to talk business rather than getting down to business.

"And he'll get it all? And we will get more shares?" Isla heard as Brooke followed him, their voices ringing clear.

"Of course. He's my goddamn son, isn't he?"

Isla clamped her hand over her mouth. Bennett was Jackson's son. How the hell had Brooke pulled this off for thirty years? What if Bennett had come out looking more like his true father than Victor? Would Brooke have claimed it was from the white side of her family, being biracial herself? And Jackson—was money important enough for him to have spent so long working for the man who was raising his son? And on top of it, they were conspiring to change Victor's current will to an heir who wasn't his biological child.

"If I push too hard, he'll be suspicious. You know your husband. If you hadn't coddled Bennett so much, he'd be better at handling issues on his own and wouldn't require me to step in to clean up his messes. Maybe he'd even screw up less."

"Don't worry," Brooke said. "We've waited this long. We just need to bide our time a little bit longer to pave the way for Bennett. He's going to name him his successor anyway. Myles doesn't want it."

"There's no guarantee Victor will. As for Myles, don't easily believe he's really as passive as he's making himself out to be. Just don't get too comfortable. I've waited my entire life for this, Brooke. I've sat by for thirty years because you said it would pay out in the end." His frustration was reaching a boiling point.

"And it will," she said coyly. Isla heard them kiss. "Let me start paying you back now, hmm?"

Isla heard a zipper and other sounds she'd rather have not. Where were they, and could she get out without alerting them?

"What do I do?" she whispered.

"Give them a sec," Rey replied.

When it sounded like they were totally engrossed, Isla opened the door inch by inch, thankful that it didn't squeak loudly enough for them to notice, not that those two would. She eased out of the closet, her movements as silent as possible, hitching the backpack up on her back. She crept to the door and checked to see if they were in her line of vision. She couldn't see them, only hear them. She rushed past the doorway to the other side of the room, the sliding glass door just within her reach. She fumbled with the tiny latch. The tiny click as it unlocked sounded like a foghorn.

She only opened the door as much as her body could squeeze through, then closed it softly behind her. She moved as fast as she could, begging her sore body to not give out just yet. She pushed her way through his wall of hedges to come across on the other side.

She didn't breathe normally until she made it back to the car she'd borrowed to get there, which was parked blocks away. She couldn't move just yet. Her hands trembled, her mind unable to comprehend what she'd never imagined. That Jackson was Bennett's father or that he'd have a recording of Eden that no one ever knew about locked away in a safe.

CHAPTER FIFTY-SEVEN

"That's some bullshit," Rey said over the phone when Isla cut the recording off. She couldn't agree with him more.

"How could they?" Nat whispered. "That's so savage. And who's the person that found her? What happened next?"

Isla said nothing, the sickening click at the end of Eden's recording replaying in her mind. She could think of nothing else. As much as she wanted to believe Eden had made it out of those woods, chances were she had not.

After several moments of silence, Nat ventured, "What will you do, Isla?"

Isla slipped the recorder back in the bag that had held it for the past ten years.

Rey said, "Take it to the cops, of course! Shit. This is murder. Cold-blooded killers. The recording proves Jackson is the last person to have seen Eden before she disappeared."

Nat said, "The recording proves he found the recorder, not that he did anything to her."

"You need to get him before he gets you when he realizes the recorder is missing and comes after you."

All these years of guilt. All the not knowing. Victor's hope that Eden was still out there living her best life, rebelling against him, punishing him.

One day, Isla, I'm going to bring my girl home.

"I can't take it to the cops yet," Isla said. If she handed it over now, they might never find Eden's body.

"But there is no telling if you can get Jackson or whoever to say where she is," Rey rationalized. "This is beyond you now. It's cold-blooded murder. Call the detective."

Nat agreed. "Right, all Jackson has to say is that he found the recorder, and he'll admit to taking the car to protect Bennett and his friends."

Isla said, "That's why I have to wait until the reception, when their guard is down. It's the right setting where they can't take cover or escape. I think whoever knows where she is will make a move to tie up loose ends once I play the recording, and it could mean making sure the truth about her disappearance never comes out. I just need to make sure I'm there to see it."

Isla ended the call and stayed in her room, thinking of all her options. She looked at the notes she'd taken during the interviews she'd conducted. She could write the article, not that anyone was pressuring her after the incidents that had happened to her these few weeks. She couldn't concentrate on a fake article. She couldn't do much else either. She was on edge, feeling more anxious as the clock ticked. She could just go to Detective Bowen and be done with it. But she couldn't bear to put Eden's recording in anyone else's hands before she had a chance to face the Corrigans and see which among them was the one. With the reception only two days away, Isla was on borrowed time.

Eventually, Jackson would realize the recording was gone and would assume that the person who had taken it had seen the revised will. Jackson's patience, his having waited thirty years to steal Victor's company, was remarkable. Isla was so consumed by preparing for the perfect moment to expose the three of them, Jackson, Brooke, and Bennett, that she didn't notice much else until there was a knock at her room back at the estate.

"Brooke's asked you to join them at the house. They're having drinks in the sitting room," Mae announced when Isla opened her room door. Mae did a double take. "You look horrible. Is it because of the accident? A relapse?"

"Did she say why?" Isla asked, touching her tousled hair, ashamed to be seen this way. "I'd rather pass. I don't feel well."

"She insists," Mae said firmly, like she didn't want to be the enforcer. "There's a guest she wants you to meet who she feels will be a great addition to the article you're writing on Mr. Corrigan."

"Guest?" Isla repeated. "Who?"

Mae shrugged. "I just relay the messages. Come at five."

CHAPTER FIFTY-EIGHT

When Isla arrived at the main house, she was led to one of the sitting rooms beneath a glittering crystal chandelier. She acknowledged everyone as they filtered in. Myles sent her a questioning look to ask if she knew what was going on. She shook her head that she didn't.

Victor was in an uncharacteristically good mood, even looking forward to the upcoming reception. Isla tried shaking off her growing unease at the unknown and her irritation at being summoned. Bennett acted as if she didn't exist but looked lackluster. Jackson was already there, forgoing his stick of gum for the scotch Dixon offered him. He and Isla made eye contact, and Isla thought she saw something in his gaze. Anticipation.

Brooke entered, unusually cheerful and more done up than usual. Her smile stretched widely, her laugh boisterous and loud over nothing funny. Jackson checked his watch.

"What's this all about?" Victor asked, accepting his drink and choosing one of the armchairs. He crossed one leg over the other. "You've gathered us together like in a whodunit."

Brooke's laughter carried throughout the room. To Isla, it sounded threatening. Inside her pocket, Isla's phone buzzed. She ignored it, making casual conversation with the others and observing the way

Jackson kept checking his watch as he sipped his scotch while Brooke glanced expectantly at the door as if waiting for someone.

Mae stepped into the room a few minutes later, her expression unreadable.

"Mrs. Corrigan, the guest you were expecting has arrived," she said stiffly. "Should I show her in?"

Brooke nodded. Her eyes sparkled as she headed toward Mae, eager to receive whoever was there. Isla's heart leaped when she heard *she*, and for a brief moment she had a glimmer of hope. Eden.

Except it wasn't Eden, Isla realized when Charli Galveston sidestepped Mae, not waiting to be announced. She went straight for Brooke, and the two women hugged like they were long-lost friends. Isla was too busy contending with her surge of confusion and disappointment that the person wasn't Eden returned that she couldn't feel what she should have, dread and fear. Dressed in a body-hugging dress that accentuated all her curves, Charli looked every bit the wild showgirl she had been when Isla had first met her in Atlanta. Her shrewd eyes bounced from person to person. She took a deep inhale of the room, the people, and the wealth surrounding her. Her smile grew. She had hit pay dirt.

"My God! That thing in the floor in your foyer," Charli gushed, referring to the same mosaic that Isla had been in awe of. "I've never seen something like that before. How much did it cost? Wait, is that rude of me to ask?" Her smile grew and her body language said more as she took in every man in the room. Even bland-looking Dixon wasn't spared a hungry look. All Charli saw was dollar signs.

All Isla saw was the axe swinging at her neck.

It was all over for her.

Charli wasted no time sliding into the empty chair beside Isla, her presence overpowering the room, her perfume even more powerful. "Well, isn't this cozy?" she purred, her eyes darting around the room, finally settling on Isla. "Brooke, can you get one of your maids to make me a vodka tonic? Maybe the one who showed me in?"

Mae glared at her before pointedly walking out.

Charli said, "Can she do that? Isn't the help supposed to do whatever they're asked to do?"

"Don't worry about her," Brooke said sweetly, happily making Charli's drink herself and handing it to her. Isla concentrated on the patterns on the Persian rug in front of her.

"My God, Isla, you've certainly done well for yourself." Charli leaned in close. Her whisper was more a bullhorn, and her breath smelled like peppermint and vodka. "What a great setup. You could have at least changed your name. Haven't you learned anything? Same initials, different name. Running the Con 101."

Isla gave her nothing. She'd let this play out, since her gig was up. It was only a matter of time, and her time had run out.

She thought about Myles, who gawked at Charli, questions surrounding his head like a crown. Victor was confounded, expecting his wife to explain the audacious newcomer. The statuesque Pam Grier look-alike was not the typical guest to grace their home.

"Brooke," Victor said, "what kind of joke is this?"

The only other person not surprised by Charli's appearance was Jackson, as he sat coolly and expectantly.

"Cat got your tongue, sweetheart?" Charli teased, knowing she had Isla's number. She was a fox in the henhouse. "Why didn't you tell me where you were going, huh?" Charli continued, even though Isla wasn't replying to her. She wasn't even looking Charli's way, fixated on the rug. Isla knew the rest of what Charli wanted to say. That Isla should have told her where she was going so Charli could get a cut. "Your hostess, Mrs. Corrigan—"

"Oh please, call me Brooke. We're like that now."

"Brooke was nice enough to invite me all the way from LA. She thought I might like to see the lovely young woman she's been hosting so graciously, especially after some of the accidents you've had. Sweetheart, you didn't tell me this when you said you were going on a job and dropped off the face of the earth."

That was where Isla had made her mistake. In her eagerness to get here, she had only given Charli vague information, when in the past she'd told her when and how long she'd be gone, fueling Charli's curiosity and determination even more. Brooke approached them, and Isla tore her eyes from the rug to face her. The smile on Brooke's face was the first genuine smile Brooke had shown since Isla's arrival. She was happy, relishing Isla's takedown immensely. She would stretch this torture out as long as she could. And Isla would let her, because Brooke had her now. And after tonight, Isla wouldn't have access to Victor again if Brooke had her way, but Isla hadn't planned for this. The take was not with her. The setup was not on her terms. She had to remain silent.

Brooke tutted, "I just didn't feel right, a young lady like yourself here all alone with people you barely know. You never talk about your family. You've been totally entrenched in our lives instead."

Isla understood Brooke's purposeful wording encased in fake concern.

"I know it's been for the article on Victor, but, Isla, you have a whole life in LA that you gave up for this. And quite a colorful past too. Isn't it fascinating how small the world is, Victor?" Brooke said, like a viper about to strike.

Victor said, "What's this about, Brooke? Who is this and why is she here?" He set his drink down.

Brooke's smile slipped, embarrassment reddening her face. But she only had to look down at Isla and Charli and was rejuvenated. "Just wait, dear."

As she turned back to Isla, Charli said, "Why don't you tell them all about LA? And about Daytona. Or should I? We can do it together."

Isla finally said, "Charli, let's step out to talk."

"Oh no," Brooke jumped in. "There are no secrets among family, right? Isn't that why you're here? To sniff out everyone's secrets and blackmail us to keep those secrets?"

"Oh, I think I understand." Charli's voice hardened. "You came here only saying you were going on a job. Even your friends wouldn't spill, no matter how much I tried. So when I get a call, saying a Mrs. Corrigan of Corrigan Enterprises—"

"Group," Bennett said eagerly, when his initial shock subsided. "The Corrigan Group."

"If you say so," Charli said to him. Her eyes traveled the length of him, resting in places it shouldn't have in front of his parents. He squirmed beneath her examination. "You, by the way, are a gorgeous piece of work. God, the things I could do to you." She growled, fanning herself.

Bennett crossed his legs and turned away, the first time Isla had ever seen him uncomfortable.

"No wonder you've been off the grid. You landed yourself a big catch here. Moved up like the Jeffersons. Before your time, but your parents know what I mean," Charli said to Myles and Bennett.

"Enough!" Victor finally boomed, silencing the room. "Someone better explain what the hell is going on and who is this—this woman is."

"Charli." Charli waggled her fingers at him. "Charli Galveston, like the city. But not where I'm from."

Brooke said, "Victor, I know this will be a shock. Believe me, I was as shocked as you will be. But after Isla got hurt, I did some digging, because what if something happened to her? Who'd be her next of kin? But it turned out Isla isn't who she says she is. Or not entirely who she says she is. Do I have that about right, Charli?"

"That you do," Charli said. "I took her in when she was just a kid, gave her a roof over her head, showed her the ropes, and how does she repay me? By skipping town with no word or thanks. See, I met Isla when she was sixteen in Georgia. We were taking the same train to Los Angeles. I took her in while she went to school and got a job at the retirement home I run. She ended up starting a business with a couple of friends to dig up the dirty secrets of celebrities. Think *TMZ* but more low key. But Isla is from Daytona. That's where she said she was coming from when I met her."

Isla shook her head. All the time she'd spent, just when she was about to figure it all out—all undone just like that.

The air crackled with electricity, and she felt everyone's eyes on her.

"Is this true?" Victor demanded, his voice low and dangerous. "You're from Daytona?"

Words wouldn't come to Isla. The walls were closing in, and every pair of eyes was on her.

Charli tutted. "Indeed! I might do a little something-something on the side, but I checked her name before getting her the new ID. Isla Thomas, born and raised in Daytona. You can't get much more than that because Isla was in group homes, so you know, juvenile records are sealed. This daughter of yours, Edie? Well, Isla, isn't that your best friend from Daytona that you mentioned? See, on our way to LA, Isla told me the saddest story of how she was put in the system because her dad died and her mama was in the wind. Then she met this girl named Eden Galloway. Apparently, the girl's mom died, and the two of them decided to skip out to LA together, only they got separated on the way. Real sad story, huh? Should be on Lifetime or the Hallmark Channel or something. I felt for this poor girl and took her under my wing. Treated her like my own. So imagine my surprise when I learn that her Eden Galloway is your Edie Corrigan and that Isla hasn't told any of you of her connection to your girl, and that Isla is writing some article. I hate to think she's running a con," Charli said regretfully. "That's not how she was raised."

"You didn't raise me," Isla shot back. She stood abruptly, the chair nearly toppling back from the force. The room was suffocating, and there were so many thoughts going through her, so many things she wanted to say but couldn't. How dare Charli make it look like Isla was here to steal from Eden's family. Charli was the con, not her.

Everyone's eyes were on her, all their hostility, confusion, betrayal, and satisfaction directed at her. She didn't dare look at Myles. Or, worse, at Victor. She didn't want to see how they looked at her.

"If only you'd kept me in the loop. I'd have covered for you when Brooke called," Charli said and took another deep sip of her drink. "You make a mean vodka tonic, Brooke."

"Isla?" Myles said. She still wouldn't look at him.

"This explains everything," Bennett said, laughing. "She was a con artist from the start. I said she was. I knew something was up with her."

"Is this true?" Victor's voice rumbled, demanding her attention. "Isla?"

She forced herself to meet his eyes. She saw an ocean of emotion coursing through him. He heaved from his restraint. He had been lied to.

"It is true I knew Eden, but I was not here to con you," she started.

"I trusted you," Victor said, his voice shaking. "I welcomed you into my home, and you've been lying to us this whole time? Thank God Holl isn't here to hear this. This was all an act?" One of the most shrewd businessmen in the whole country, taken in by a young woman. When he spoke again, his voice was low and his anger simmering. Isla heard something else there too. A hurt he tried to mask beneath anger and threat, but he couldn't hide from her. "You should get your things and leave. Immediately. Before I call the authorities."

"But, Victor," Brooke complained. "We can't let her go like this. She needs to be arrested!"

Victor said, "What she needs is to get out of my house."

Isla barely remembered leaving the sitting room, her ears ringing with Charli's accusations, Brooke's triumphant smirk, and Bennett's laugh. He laughed her right out of the room. She didn't take the golf cart. She walked the entire way. For the second time, she had been expelled from the Corrigan home in shame. But this time it was no frame-up.

By the time she made it back to her room, her legs felt like lead.

Her phone buzzed again, and this time she checked it. A series of messages from Nat, saying that Charli was gone.

Isla laughed bitterly. Too late.

She was in the middle of stuffing her belongings into her bags when there was a knock at the door. It was probably security, sent to escort her out. Or what if it was Charli, come to stick the knife in more? Or maybe it was Mae or Lawrence, disappointed and hating her for lying to their face. When she opened the door, Myles was on the other side, his expression a mixture of anger and hurt, a younger image of his father.

They stood watching each other for what seemed like an eternity. Neither wanted to start first or face their truth, but she owed him that.

"I'm leaving as fast as I can. I'm nearly packed," Isla informed him, keeping her face blank and voice flat.

"That's good," Myles said, his fists balled at his sides. "You need to make it quick. I will escort you out instead of security so the rest of the staff doesn't see."

Isla was thankful Myles offered her that courtesy. She wanted to ask him why he was doing this when he didn't have to. She decided that there were some things better left unsaid.

CHAPTER FIFTY-NINE

She passed the staff as they lingered around the building, hoping for more fireworks or more gossip to spill. She passed Lawrence, who nodded his support. Isla wanted out before Charli saw her.

Myles drove her home. Home. She didn't have a home anymore. She couldn't go back to the retirement home under Charli's authority or live in the same house. The relationship they had had been that of roommates from the day she got there. It was understood. Yes, Charli had helped her with a job and a fake ID that aged her two years so that she could work without an issue and begin college courses. Charli had never called child services in Florida to take her away, not that they would have by then.

"Make sure she doesn't stay at the estate," Isla said during their long ride, when the silence was too much to bear. "Check your jewelry and fine silverware."

Myles asked, "Did you really come here to con us?" He kept his eyes firmly on the road. It was as if he couldn't stand to spare her a look. She imagined what they could have been if they'd had a little more time. And when she did reveal the truth as she knew it, when she eventually did flush out Eden's true killer, would that make a difference for them?

"Absolutely not. I mean, I did come here to get in with your family. I did omit where I was from and that I knew your sister. I never mentioned that I was there her last day, when she disappeared. But that's why I came back. To find out what happened after I saw her get in the Jeep, because I owed it to her." She couldn't bring herself to say what she thought. She'd let the recording do it for her because she was too chicken to say that she thought his sister was dead.

Myles laughed in disbelief. "You owed her? Don't you think you're a decade late? You could have told him something, anything, that would have helped him. Even if she was to say it to his face again that she never wanted to see him again, at least that would have been something. You were the last person who saw her."

"But I wasn't the last person who saw her. That's why I did all this."

She explained how she'd seen them in LA, how she'd worked as an investigator, for lack of a better word, with two of her friends. She said that was what had brought her here and that she'd had to see which of them might have done something to Eden, because Eden had been determined to move to LA and be an actress.

"You thought one of us could have hurt her?" Myles asked incredulously.

Isla shrugged. "Is that such a stretch? One of you framed her for sending her sister into anaphylactic shock. And framed me for the same thing with your dad. Money, power, and the keys to the Corrigan castle are a huge incentive to knock out the competition."

They made it to town, and he asked, "Where am I taking you?" The way he sounded, like he'd been told there was no Santa Claus, made her feel like complete shit because, in a sense, that's exactly what she was doing. She was about to tell him there was no Edie Corrigan anymore.

"To the Red Roof Inn." She noted the raised brows of surprise at her choice of stay, but if she was going to do things right, she would show him everything and hope he'd let her finish.

In the room she had shared with Eden, she let Myles in. She showed him the interior of her closet, hidden by the clothes she'd left, and the wall of Corrigans that she had pieced together with photos, articles, and notes about them all. It hadn't been updated in weeks.

"This is why I'm here," she said, her voice trembling. "Eden was my friend. She disappeared, and someone you know did it. I didn't come here to hurt anyone—I came here for the truth."

Myles stared at the wall, his expression unreadable. "And what do you plan to do with this truth? Take down my entire family? Expose every secret we've ever tried to bury?"

Isla met his gaze, her own eyes filled with determination. "If that's what it takes to get justice for Eden, then yes. Don't you think it's time to be held accountable for some wrongs your family has done? Don't you want someone to pay for killing Eden?"

"How do you know she's dead? How can you be so sure?" His eyes reddened.

She stared at the wall in the closet. Quietly, Isla pulled out the recorder holding the message she'd already heard twice. Once alone and the other when she'd played the recording for Nat and Rey. She'd relive the hell of Eden's last moments once again.

~

"I will kill him," Myles seethed when the recording ended. His hands balled into fists. "I will fucking kill him. I can't. I can't." He paced the room. Isla didn't know whether to comfort him or let him be. He wanted to break things. He wanted to cry, and he was. He wanted to rip Bennett's head off. She took a chance, putting her arms around him from behind, holding him close while he released his guilt and his grief for his sister, for the pain she'd suffered.

"You have to play this for my father. The cops. They have to know what happened."

"What if your dad buries this like he did that accident when they were kids? And what about Matthew Leonard? Will your dad cover that up for Bennett like he did that accident?" She paused, remembering what Jackson had said back at his house. Myles and Bennett weren't brothers. But it wasn't her place to disclose that. Not now. "If you knew about your brother and Danny, then why is your brother not in jail? Why's he still running your father's LA branch? What will make your father different this time around?"

The look Myles gave her was incredulous, as if she'd lost her damn mind. "We're talking about his daughter, Isla. That's what's different."

"The same daughter who her stepmother framed by tricking her into giving her little sister almond cookies, which he believed, thus forcing her to leave. Same daughter who was struggling after that accident when they were kids and everyone covered for them because money and power erase all guilt?"

Except Danny was dead and James would be ruined for life, his guilt haunting him and the injuries he'd sustained in the accident a constant reminder.

"If you'll let me finish what I need to do . . ." Isla said. "Just give me some time. Please. Everything will come out at the reception. I think the other person who knows what happened to Eden will show themselves, and we'll have the final piece of the puzzle."

"But who did she run into?"

"I don't know. Jackson had the recording and has been hiding it."

"But it doesn't mean he did anything. We never hear the voice of the person she ran into, so it might not be Jackson. He could have just found the recorder and hid it to use it later. Don't forget the letter my father received from Edie after you two supposedly came here."

"We'd already left Daytona by the time that letter was sent to your father. I saw the date on the envelope. So who sent it, and why? To make your dad not look for her. To make him think she rejected him and the family. When I play the recording for everyone, I think it'll force that person out into the open. Jackson will know I stole it from his safe. He'll either call me a thief, pissed I took his insurance, or he—or whomever—will try to tie up loose ends. We need to lay a trap for them to expose themselves. If she is truly dead, I think they'll try to move the body, because no body, no case—"

"This isn't some movie, Isla, it's my real life. And you're no detective."

She'd expected him to say that, not missing a beat. "And with the recording, your father and the police will definitely launch a full investigation and conduct a full-scale search of the entire property. Your dad will turn the world upside down to find her."

Myles sighed, running a hand over his head, knowing she was right and there was no changing her mind. "You're playing a dangerous game, Isla. I don't know if I can let you do this. But if what you're saying is true . . ."

"Then it's a game worth playing," she said. "My dad didn't get justice. I can't let it be the same for Eden, however this plays out."

Myles finally conceded despite his doubt about her plan and his anger at her lies.

Isla would take it without complaint. It was the first time in a long time that Isla had felt a glimmer of hope. At least Myles was giving her the benefit of the doubt. It was more than she could ask for.

"What do you need me to do?" he asked resignedly.

It was all she could do to keep from wrapping him in a bear hug. A weight was lifted from her.

"What do you think about playing double agent?"

CHAPTER SIXTY

The only silver lining from being exposed was that Myles seemed to believe her and had agreed to help her flush out the guilty. So much had happened since she'd arrived at the Corrigans' doorstep, and especially since Charli, that Isla had forgotten one last lead. She couldn't hide out the next couple of days at the Red Roof or her studio apartment as the time ticked by until she could expose Bennett and confront Victor. She scrolled through the photos in her phone until she got to the picture of the invoice for Jackson's storage unit that she'd taken during her noninterview with Jackson. No time like the present.

In the rental car she had to get after being kicked off the estate and having her privileges rescinded, Isla turned off 33 West and carefully maneuvered through Ruckersville, Virginia, along the empty streets toward the storage facility, squinting to make sure she made the right turns while listening to her GPS app calling out directions to her. She got excited when the facility came into view, looming in the darkness. She could already see the rows of brown metal units stretching beyond her line of vision.

As she was about to get out, her phone rang. She considered ignoring it and dealing with whatever issue had now popped up later. But when she glanced down and saw who was calling, she answered, preparing herself for the worst. The first sounds that came through the phone's speaker were ragged sobs.

"Is it true?" Holland asked without any greetings. She sounded bad, and Isla felt worse, because she already knew why Holland was calling. "Is it true you were lying this whole time? You knew my sister Edie and never told us."

Isla sighed, resigned to her well-deserved fate. She owed Holland this. She closed her car door. "Who told you?"

"Who do you think?" Holland yelled. "My mother couldn't wait to call me and tell me the friend I brought home had been using me the entire time."

Just like in the parlor, when the Corrigans looked at her, expecting excuses or an explanation, Isla had none to give Holland without giving away everything.

She let out a breath to regulate the way her heart ached as Holland cried on the other end, a fierce fencing collegian reduced to tears because of Isla's betrayal.

"I'm sorry, Holland." Out of all of them Holland was owed this the most.

"So it really is true? When we met at the shopping center, and you coming to my house with my keys? It was all a setup?"

From the moment Isla had pointed out Holland's flat and let her phone slip through to its demise, but there was no need to add fuel to the fire.

"Yeah, I knew who you were from the beginning, and it's why we met," Isla said. She rushed on, her true purpose for sitting in an unfamiliar town temporarily forgotten. "But our becoming friends, how I was with you, was sincere. Our friendship is real."

Holland hiccupped. "Was it about our money? Is that what you're after?"

"No."

"Then what?" There was silence in the background on Holland's end, and Isla wondered where she was, if she was in a safe space, but she didn't dare ask.

"I can't say right now."

"Why?"

Isla remained patient. "I can't say that either."

Holland laughed dryly. "You're lying. You can say, but you choose not to. You know, I thought that maybe you would eventually be like my sister Edie. I thought you were so much like her and that maybe I'd finally have a sister again, someone I could talk to, since everyone in my family only thinks about themselves. But I guess I'm just an idiot."

Isla's throat constricted. Her eyes burned with tears that threatened to come. She was every bit the asshole that Holland thought she was. She was not a good person, and Holland was too good, just like Eden. But Isla couldn't let herself fall into her emotions. If she did that, everything would fall apart, and she was already hanging on by a thread.

"I have to go," Isla said flatly, her voice not betraying her feelings.

"That's it? That's all you have to say to me, you fucking liar?" The curse sounded all wrong coming from Holland. Like the word was unfamiliar to her.

Isla nodded, though Holland couldn't see her. She swallowed the lump in her throat, telling herself to hang on a little bit longer. This was what Rey and Nat had warned her about. Being in too deep and becoming emotionally involved with the people she was supposed to expose.

"When it's time, I'll tell you everything. You'll be at your dad's reception, right?"

Holland blew her nose. "What do you care?" she said pitifully.

"I care." It was all Isla could offer as consolation. "Take care of yourself, Holland."

She hung up before Holland had a chance to say anything more, and refocused, with only one thing on her mind. Getting into Jackson's unit.

The place was nondescript and old school, a more run-down place than she'd imagined a meticulous person like Jackson would utilize. The main office was dark, which was perfect. And the fact that this place was so old was perfect too. It meant no fancy security cameras or keypad entry systems, just the thick padlocks, and that no one would be paying attention if nothing looked broken into. Isla used all of those assurances to boost her courage as she glanced at the photo of Jackson's invoice and compared that number with the ones above each corrugated metal door. This wasn't like when she had Rey and Nat nearby, working a job with her. She was entirely on her own.

Gravel crunched beneath her boots as she finally stopped in front of H48 at the end of the last row of units in the farthest, darkest area of the grounds. Of course it was. It was one of the largest units, and she wondered what was so big that Jackson needed so much room all the way over here. Surely not old furniture. The units were secured with combination padlocks; this one had a four-digit lock setup. No problem. She'd cracked these before, YouTube videos saving the day as usual. She fished out a tension wrench, put the tiny MAGLITE in her mouth with its beam spotlighting the lock, and began working.

It was relatively warm even this late at night, and humid. Or maybe it was her anxiety and her intense concentration as she worked the lock, using the wrench to add tension to the hook shackle as she started from the bottom row and rotated backward through each number, listening for the distinctive deep tick of the correct number. The first was always the most difficult, in her opinion. The shackle downshifted, disengaging the first inner lock. She repeated the process three more times. Click, click, click. Each time, the shackle shifted with each disengaged portion. At the top roll, the shackle popped open. Her body relaxed with relief. She switched from the mini MAG to the regular one, pulled the latch, and braced herself as she lifted the door.

A thick cloud of dust and stale air hit her full force, making her cough and her eyes water. She waited for the dust to clear and shined the bright light inside. The unit was massive, empty apart from the single object, draped under a heavy cover, sitting in the middle of the room.

Maybe it was old furniture after all, all clumped together. Maybe a vehicle?

Okay. If Jackson was a car collector, again, why would he keep a car in some obsolete facility an hour from town? And why would the unit look like no one had been here for years? There was a thick layer of dust on the built-in shelves, and cobwebs. She didn't want to think of the spiders that had made those webs. Ignorance, in this case, was her bliss.

Dust motes swirled in the strong beam of light as she approached the covered shape. She gripped a portion and pulled, revealing a Jeep underneath.

She yanked the rest, and this time was unaffected by the plume of dust that had collected on the top of the car cover typically used for all weather. She took an involuntary step back as her mind worked to register what she was seeing.

It was the unmistakable yellow that sparked a memory from the recesses of her mind. The Jeep with aftermarket additions for continuous hours of off-roading.

The motel. The Jeep pulling up. The dome light illuminating the figures inside. Eden hesitating before climbing in. Eden looking back at Isla, who was watching from the second-floor walkway, confused and scared. Eden with the imperceptible shake of her head to say Keep quiet.

The vehicle that had taken Eden away.

Roger's Jeep, the one everyone had thought stolen, was here.

There were too many realizations assailing her at once. They made her double over with nausea as the magnitude of what had happened to Eden and who was involved grew. That it was people she knew and trusted made it all worse. There was a reason Danny had wanted to stop her and James, and now she knew. There was a reason why Jackson had hid Roger's Jeep all this time. Because it linked Bennett to Eden the night she went missing, and Jackson couldn't afford for Bennett to be connected to her disappearance. Not when he planned to take over the Corrigan Group.

Isla barely had the presence of mind to get back in the game. She fumbled for her phone and snapped a picture of the license plate and the VIN in the bottom corner of the windshield. She didn't need it to tell her what she already knew, but if things went sideways, this could be proof, placing Roger and one of the others in the vehicle that Isla had watched Eden get into. She replaced the car cover the way she had found it. She couldn't do anything about the disturbed dust should Jackson finally come to check out his little secret. She backed out of the unit, sucking in huge gulps of fresh air, and collected the bag she'd left just outside.

Back in the car, she gripped the wheel, heart still hammering. She had to be smart. Had to be careful.

She thought back to Roger joking around with Danny and Bennett the day they went hunting, talking about his lost first love.

"You remember your first ride?" Bennett asked. "The Jeep that you backed into the tree stump that one time, making that dent in the bumper?"

"Cops ever find it?" Danny asked, laughing.

"Hell no," Roger replied, sounding wistful.

None of them knew what had happened to Roger's Jeep. They had no clue.

But Jackson did.

CHAPTER SIXTY-ONE

The night of the reception, after Victor had received his award, the Corrigan estate illuminated the night beneath a canopy of lights. Everyone was there in celebration of Victor's Man of the Year award. The guests mingled, raising glasses of champagne in his honor.

For Isla, the reception would be the final night of her ten-year journey, and she supposed the opulent setting was fitting and also ironic. She was about to reveal something so ugly against the backdrop of glamour and beauty. The last thing she could do for Eden before she finally, really and truly moved on with her life. She hadn't had contact with any of the Corrigans, and they hadn't reached out. Not even Holland, who Isla knew must have returned home for her father's special evening. Isla didn't want to think about all the lies Brooke must have filled her with.

Their whole sordid mess would come out tonight. Isla was sure of it. She had ignored Charli's calls, heard from Nat and Rey that she'd returned bragging about a windfall of money she'd just come into and that Isla was fired from the retirement home courtesy of her. Isla would miss taking care of Miss Lydia, but she'd see her again, as a guest.

Myles sent an invitation to the reception via courier so she could get past the gates. Isla prepared by going to one of the department stores and buying herself a black gown, elegant but likely modest compared to the shimmering couture that would surround her as she made her way to the Corrigans' theater room. There Myles would lead his family in for the big show. And then the finale would occur. All while their guests were plied with champagne and food fit for the gods.

For the first time since Isla had stepped foot on Corrigan property, the main gates to the estate were open and freely letting the long train of cars in. White-gloved valets in impeccable uniforms guided sleek luxury cars into perfectly aligned rows. Guests draped in gowns and tuxedos that definitely put Isla's off-the-hanger dress to shame floated toward the club's entrance. She stuck to the periphery, clutching her invitation and the cloak that covered her backpack like lifelines. She hoped no one would see her until it was time.

The estate could have been ripped straight from the pages of a fairy tale. Brooke had really outdone herself this time in more ways than one. Gleaming chandeliers reflected off polished marble floors. A string quartet played a lilting waltz from a corner alcove while the jazz band meant for later waited for their turn, when they'd really turn the party up.

Waitstaff glided through the room with trays of champagne flutes and delicate hors d'oeuvres, their movements so synchronized it was like they were choreographed. Victor probably hated it. As he had said, this was all for Brooke anyway. Still, it was a celebration. But Isla wasn't there for that. She was there for one purpose: to make Victor see the truth and the light.

Lawrence got Isla access through the back maintenance entrance, and she was relieved when she ran into Mae, who, after a long look and Isla's promise that she meant no harm, turned her back and continued commanding her troop of staff and hired servers with quick military precision.

Isla passed the doorway to the grand ballroom, where Brooke Corrigan stood at the room's center, her golden gown shimmering like molten metal. She greeted guests with air-kisses and a regal smile, every motion exuding dominance. Isla hesitated in the doorway, captivated by the stunning beauty. It was a shame that Brooke's inside didn't reflect her exterior.

Isla squared her shoulders and headed the opposite way from the mass of guests. To the theater.

She had everything queued when the door opened and Victor walked in, followed by Myles, asking what this was about. She imagined the guests were feeling really good from the champagne at this point because the party sounded a little more raucous, which was good, because it meant their small group wouldn't be missed for her big reveal if everything went according to plan.

Victor's face contorted with fury when he saw her. He shot a grave look at Myles for his defiance at bringing her back, then turned to Isla to vent his wrath.

"What are you doing here, Isla? Weren't you sent back home to LA or Daytona, wherever it is you come from?" Victor said, taking a few more steps in.

Behind him everyone else filed in, confused by Isla's sudden appearance, wondering why Myles had brought them there. She ignored Brooke's glare and Bennett's sneer and the awful joke he cracked as she addressed the only person who mattered.

"What is she doing here? Call security," Brooke said. When no one moved fast enough, she turned to do just that, but Myles barred the door.

Isla began, "Mr. Corrigan, I know I'm the last person you want to hear from, let alone see, and I understand. I betrayed your and your family's trust immensely, and for that I do apologize. But it was the only way. Please sit."

Bennett said, "I thought we kicked her ass out. We need better people running security."

Bennett was irrelevant, and Isla ignored him. There was only one audience member in the room who mattered. "I didn't think you'd want me to broadcast this to all your guests, Mr. Corrigan. I wanted to give you that much respect."

"Respect?" Victor's sharp eyes narrowed as he followed Holland, taking a seat after her. "You come into my home under false pretenses, and you talk about respect? I knew there was more to you than you were letting on. So now we get to it."

Holland watched, wide eyed and confused, then looked to each person, helpless and lost. Isla couldn't bring herself to look at her anymore, the only one of them who'd trusted Isla sincerely. Out of everyone here, it was Holland Isla worried about the most. It was Holland who was Isla's one regret.

"Is the article finished, Isla?" Holland asked, hope in her voice.

"I'm here to give you the truth," she said, her voice strengthening. Brooke and Bennett sat in the next row, Jackson in the last, observing as always as he watched the scene unfold. His calm was ethereal, and it was the only thing about him that impressed her. His ability to bide his time was out of this world. Dixon also sat in the last row, and Myles leaned against the wall.

Isla took her place at the front. She'd set out to expose the truth from the beginning. She'd never expected to care how the truth would destroy even the good parts of this family. Like Holland, and Myles, and even Victor.

Victor asked, "What truth?"

Brooke seemed not to know what to do, whether she wanted to sit or walk out or attack Isla. She said, "Jackson, call the police. This is stalking."

"Shut up, Mother," Holland snapped, and Brooke fell silent, shocked by her daughter's sudden backbone.

Isla replied, "Yes, Victor, I knew your daughter in Daytona. I knew her mom Elise too. I was there when Elise passed and when she told Eden to come back to you." She continued despite Victor's pained expression when he heard Elise's name. Before she could show them their truths, she'd first admit her own.

"I did plot to get into your family because I was in town with Edie. We came because she said she had something to take care of with the Corrigans. The night she disappeared, she told me to wait for her before she left in a yellow Jeep with a dent on its bumper. She said she had unfinished business with the Corrigans. I thought she had a grudge against you for firing her mom and that she blamed you for her mom getting sick and dying. I only found out who Eden was—that she was a Corrigan herself—the first night I stayed here. I only came back to find out what you all did to my friend."

"What *we* did?" Victor's voice came out strangled.

Bennett sneered, "Is this some kind of blackmail? Did she send you here to do her dirty work for her?"

Isla merely stared at him, his nerve beyond her imagination, until Bennett focused his attention elsewhere, guilt and fear written all over his face.

Isla pulled out the recorder, watching Jackson's movements. He barely flinched, self-assured, or playing at it, as he slipped a pack of gum from his pocket and put a stick in his mouth. His eyes slid to Isla, daring her to make the next move.

"I never wanted your money," she said to Bennett. "I owed Eden, and I never wanted anything more from the Corrigans but the truth."

She pressed play, letting the truth be told by the person who knew best.

Eden's voice came through, clear and haunting as it filled the room.

"Testing . . . testing . . . one, two. One, two. Hope this shit works."

CHAPTER SIXTY-TWO

Eden

Ten Years Ago

I grip the handle of the passenger door so tightly my knuckles ache, because Roger is a horrible driver. It's why he has that dent in his back fender from the tree stump he hit in reverse back in high school. The Jeep jolts as it turns off the paved road, the tires crunching gravel and fallen leaves. Roger is driving, his face hard as stone, and Danny is fiddling with the radio like it's the most important thing in the world. James sits in the back seat, silent, staring out the window, sneaking glances at me like he can't believe I'm here. I can't believe it either. My chest tightens as we go deeper down the familiar path I used to travel toward the old Abbott barn. I hope Isla doesn't get too freaked out after seeing me get in with the guys. Maybe I shouldn't have kept who I was and why I was really here from her. I'll explain it all when I get back to our room.

The barn is exactly as I remember it from two years ago: crumbling beams, broken slats of wood letting moonlight streak through the gaping holes in the roof, the musty smell of rotting hay. It's a ghost of its former self, just like me. No, scratch that. I am no longer a ghost. I was a ghost two years ago, flittering in and out of the estate and grounds like some lost soul. I lost my soul that night. Tonight I intend to regain it. I've planned this ever since my mother's funeral. Ever since she told me to stop living in fear, stop living like I didn't belong.

"You belong more than any of them," she said. "I wish I had known that then. But I'm telling you that now. Use what you know to your advantage. Be who you are."

When we finally stop is when I turn on the recorder.

We file inside in a line, Danny then me, followed by Roger, with James bringing up the rear. James is jittery. He's never been one for the hard stuff, because that's what I think these guys are aiming to do. Be hard. Be tough. Scare me into submission. Little do they know that I'll get the last word, and we'll pay for what we did to that family.

Danny circles the span of the first floor. It's wide, like a square, and surrounded by stalls for the horses the Abbotts used to raise decades ago. When I found this place, it was already run down, and I imagined happier times. They kept the upstairs loft for hay and the main floor of sawdust shavings and areas for supplies, feed, tack, and the washrack. Remnants of all those things are stark reminders of what once was when times were good for the Abbotts, before they died off or migrated north or wherever the remainder of their family ended up when their underground moonshine operation went bust.

The staircase leading to the loft where stacks of hay were housed looks perilous and like a skeletal structure of its former self, filled with scraggly holes where steps used to be. The wide, nearly wall-length widows are all broken, tall, sharp shards of glass jutting out at all angles, no doubt victims of target practice from the occasional passersby who happened upon this deserted structure. Or maybe it was these guys, because no one knows this place still exists except us. But times have changed. It has been two years since I saw it last.

Danny chooses a stall, leans against one of the rusted stall doors, and takes up a menacing stance, hands in pockets so his big gun-barrel muscles are on display, one foot kicked behind him and propped against the beam. He wants to look like he's running the show when what he's really doing is waiting for his leader.

My sneakers crunch on the dirty floor, which is littered with hay and glass, pebbles, branches, and leaves. The barn in varying stages of decay. The wind gives off a low howl as it moves from the door we entered to the back door, which is slightly cracked, glimmers of moonlight shining through.

I swallow down my fear because I refuse to back down or let my fear show. "Then do the right thing. Convince Bennett to give me the money I asked for, and I only want to hear you all say it for once. Admit what we did so we're all clear and no one is buying the bullshit we made up. Bennett was the one driving that night. He was the one who flipped off—"

Danny grabs my arm, his grip bruising. "Shut the fuck up," he snarls.

"No, you don't get to make the rules. You lied about that night. We got a family killed. Say it, Danny. Say it was our fault."

He squeezes, and I swallow down a whimper. "I'm not saying shit. You aren't fucking this up for me, Edie. I have a good thing going now. Bennett and I have plans, and we're gonna be partners. He's gonna find a place for me in the company when he gets in the right spot, and I'm not letting you take that away from me."

"Danny," James says gently, moving closer. He places a hand on Danny's free arm. He looks at me, and all the warmth from years of wanting but never acting are bubbling up behind his eyes. If only he had had the courage back then to tell me what he wanted, but instead he let Bennett come between us. Always Bennett first. James hadn't been able to tell Bennett that he and I would find our own way home after the barn, to stand up to my brother and declare his feelings for me even though his buddy Danny had already tried staking his claim and been shut down over and over. James was always too weak then. Just like he's being now.

Danny snatches his arm away. "Get off."

Roger stammers, "Man, we don't need to get all heated. Let's just be cool, all right? Edie, we're just surprised is all. This isn't like you. This is more—" He stops himself.

"Like Bennett? I've learned from my big brother. Maybe it's in our genes. You know, something you're too Neanderthal to comprehend? It's probably why Bennett still keeps your ass around," I say, letting out a dry laugh. I refuse to rub my arm in front of them, though it hurts.

Since he's got me by the other, I slip my free hand in my pocket, palming the can of Mace I bought along with a few other things at RadioShack earlier today. The pad of my thumb feels around for the tiny safety latch, and I push it to the side. The heat rolling off Danny is intense and suffocating, taking up all the space. We face off.

In all the time I've known him, Danny has always been big talk and no bite, strutting around like he's going to do something.

"It's in our genes," Danny mocks, sneering. "Maybe you need to learn when to stop talking." His face is inches from mine, and his breath reeks of alcohol, weed, and stale cigarettes. Bad combination. "Be meek little Edie again."

"Danny, cut it out." James steps forward as if to pull us apart. "You're hurting her."

James has replaced Danny's focus and growing anger at me with himself, something that fills me with a flame of warmth. It reminds me of back then, when James and I kept low profiles, letting the other three fight over who would be top dog, the strongest, the funniest, the smartest, the alpha.

It was always Bennett, though. Bennett is the alpha while Danny is a distant second, always wanting to impress, always wanting to prove himself with the stupid schemes and bullying and excessiveness that makes him the least likable. If it wasn't for his intimidating demeanor, his big burly linebacker self, Bennett would have dropped him long ago, I think. And if it wasn't for that night that binds us together tightly in this soul-eating web dangling over Bennett's head like a swinging noose,

Bennett would have gotten rid of all of them. Me, he thought he had, but I've come back to finish what was started, to hold us all to account even though they think what I want is money. Schemes as debasing as blackmail and power plays are the only things that Bennett and his goon squad understand. Accountability. Remorse. Restitution. Truth. Words never included in their vocabulary and in their world of overindulgence, entitlement, and privilege. A world I hope to free myself of for good.

But now I've come back to do what I was too weak to back then. Right a wrong as best as I can. I will free us all, even if some of us don't want to be freed.

That second of distraction is all I need. I break free of Danny's grip and slap him. It is a sharp crack, a flat-palm-against-flesh crack that reverberates throughout these weathered walls. It is a declaration that Danny can't intimidate me anymore. Not like he used to do before with the teasing and shaming when we were kids, all to impress the unimpressible Bennett Corrigan.

The slap shocks even me. It is the first physical manifestation of my innermost rage. The first I've ever let my repressed anger unleash and spew forth, like a dragon. But I don't let the shock hold me back for long. I hit him again for good measure. And again, the years of bottled-up resentment and fear and appeasement so he won't get angry rises up like a leviathan until everything stops because Roger is holding me back and James grips Danny's bulging arms. Danny's eyes redden. He can barely hold back his rage.

"You'll never be his equal, I hope you know." I want to keep pushing. "He's just stringing you along like he's been doing these past couple of years, and he'll keep doing it until you stop him. He'll keep promising and promising you shit, but you'll never get it." The words spew forth, and I can't stop. "You'll just be his bitch for the rest of your pitiful life. Just like your daddy was for mine, simpering and sniveling, hoping for scraps that Bennett may or may not feel magnanimous enough to bestow upon your dumbass head."

Danny shakes James off, and I'm surprised James was able to hold him back as long as he did. James, a truly gifted pianist who should have gone far if it wasn't for Bennett's poison and the secret we share, pleads with me to stop, just stop.

"If you don't shut the fuck up," Danny warns, taking a step toward me.

James steps in time with him. "Rog, call Bennett. Tell him to get his ass over here now to stop this."

"Yeah, tell him to get his ass over here," I mimic, eyes moving from Danny to James to a way out should I need it, but Danny is too close. Much too close. Reaching-and-grabbing distance.

Roger takes one hand away to get his phone and call my brother. Bennett connects on the other side. "What?"

Roger tells him what, and we all can hear Bennett losing his cool, saying to tell that fucking idiot Danny to back the fuck up. He's going to be right there. He's going over the hill now. It is an eight-minute walk or so up here from the bottom of the hill. But with as hot as Bennett is, it'll be three. He'll be sprinting to get here.

"Wait the fuck until I get there."

Danny tries to speak, but Bennett disconnects mid-speech. Danny stares at the cell, dumbfounded and open mouthed. He doesn't know whether he's hurt or angry.

"You're not even important enough for him to stay on the line."

Danny decides angry.

Danny steps forward, his heavy boots thudding against the dirt. "What's your angle here, Edie? Blackmailing Bennett? Running your mouth about something we *all* agreed to bury? You think you're better than us because you skipped town and played ghost?"

We're nearly there. And we have to get there before Bennett comes because when he does, everything will be shut down. "What did we bury, Danny?"

James shifts uncomfortably, his voice low. "Eden, come on. You don't need to do this. We'll figure something out—"

"Shut up, James!" Danny snaps. He rears on me, tone full of disdain and hate. "It doesn't matter what we did, and she really doesn't care about figuring any damn thing out." He goes off and says it all. Bennett. The prank. The accident. The deaths. The story we made up.

"Is that what you wanted to hear? All you know is how to blow in and out of town and blow shit up. Beggin' for money like you aren't a fucking Corrigan. You don't know how good you got it." He steps closer.

"Danny," Roger warns, moving forward to join Danny or stop him. "I don't know."

At the same time James says, "Hey! That's not right, bro."

But Danny doesn't stop. "Just like your fucking mother. I heard that's why she was kicked out on her ass and sent to Daytona to slum it with the common folk. Because she's nothing but a money-hungry whor—"

He doesn't get to finish. Because he is now sputtering and rubbing his eyes and spinning in circles, crying in pain from the squirt of Mace I unleashed on him. Roger and James, and even I, myself, become collateral damage. The snap in me when he invoked my dead mother's name was instant, volcanic. I can't even say when the Mace came out.

"Don't you dare mention my mother's name. Ever!"

"Danny, no!" James and Roger say together through tear-streaked eyes.

Mine are blurry too, but not enough that I can't see Danny recovering quicker than the other two. He charges and runs into me with more force than I expect. It's like he's back in high school, trying to sack the quarterback before he throws the ball to his teammate to run for a touchdown. I am that quarterback. Danny's shoulder connects with my chest. His impact makes me stumble several steps back, my heel catches on a loose board behind me, and gravity takes over. I am going back, back, back—right into one of the broken window frames.

The jagged pieces of glass bite into my side with a sickening squelch, and my backward momentum is suddenly stopped.

It is not just me that stops. Everything stops. Even the barn, which has been creaking and groaning as the faint wind rustles through the broken slats and rotting wood, goes silent. My shock blocks the pain. All I can do is look down at this alien thing that is not of my body but is now embedded in me. There is a tiny crack as the glass separates itself from its bottom half, and a trickle of warmth begins to move down my side and hip. Red spreads across my sweatshirt. I gaze at it. Alien. Not me. But yes, me. I look at the three guys. Each of them registering different versions of shock.

James doesn't understand what he's seeing, eyes full of complete shock.

Danny is still in his linebacker stance, hands splayed and white as a sheet. Our eyes connect, and it is the first time that even I feel sorry for him. His mouth moves, but no sound comes out.

Roger breaks the silence. "Oh my God. Oh my God!" He looks like he's going to be ill. His already-pale face becomes paler in the dark.

Danny whispers haltingly, "I didn't mean—I was only trying to—I didn't mean to."

Words I haven't heard in two years.

I slide to the ground, my knees giving. The movement jars the glass in me, and the pain radiates outward and nearly knocks me out.

James is jolted into action. He rushes to kneel next to me, his hands hovering over my body like he is casting some sort of magic spell to telepathically pull the glass out. Roger moves toward me. Stops. Pivots. Moves there. Stops. Pivots. Comes back. Stops, too afraid to get closer to me.

James yells, "We need to get help." He goes to touch the glass like he's about to pull it out.

I flinch away from his hands, guarding the glass with a block of my hand. What if it is the only thing keeping me from bleeding out? There isn't much blood. Not yet. But there will be. And then there will be no more me.

Danny is still in shock. His hand is at his mouth, and all he can do is stare at what he's done.

"Ay, yo! Where the hell is everybody?"

"Bennett," Danny whimpers, fresh tears of uncertainty and fear forming. It's one thing for Danny to trash-talk me when Bennett does and throw his weight around. It's another thing entirely to have hurt me. There is no way of knowing how Bennett will take this and who will feel his wrath.

The three of them run for the door, leaving me alone, to cut Bennett off before he walks in and sees me. I have only a moment to decide. We are on a precipice. The wild card is Bennett. What will the story be? There is already an admission, which is all I wanted. For one of them to say in his own words what happened so that when I tell my father, there can be no question. The money was never a factor. I didn't want Bennett's money, wherever he got it from. I only wanted them to admit what we did.

Bennett can blame my getting hurt on them. He can spin the story to say they acted on their own. But they will say he told them to bring me here. There are too many variables, and they all point to me. I am the piece that needs to be removed. And if Bennett is anything, a survivalist is number one. He has too much to lose. I know too much about him.

If I stay, Bennett may finish what Danny started.

I move, but the pain rips through me, and a gasp tries to escape. I suck it in. I can't be heard. Distancing myself is the only way to ensure I have a chance. My hand brushes against the glass and recoils, then moves to clutch it to keep it from shifting or coming out. I need to get to the road.

With the decision made, I grimace against the way thc glass teases that it's still there, probably causing more damage. But I'm more afraid of removing it and bleeding out. I hold it firmer, determined not to let it move more than it is, and I get up. I can hear the guys arguing out front. The four of them are talking at once, so how they can understand the others, I have no idea. Danny is desperately trying to soften the blow, explaining his story from the beginning. Somehow his linebacker move morphs into a defensive maneuver from my Mace and as he tried to deflect my attacks on him. James and Roger interject, James saying we need to hurry. Bennett is asking, "Hurry and do what?" Because no one has cut to the chase yet. He's demanding to know what's happened.

"Where. The fuck. Is Edie?"

I am stumbling toward the back door and squeezing through the ragged gaping hole in the corner of one of the back stalls that easily crumbled away after years of abuse by Mother Nature. I'm in such a rush to get away quickly that as I move through the hole, my bracelet, the one that matches my mother's locket chain, catches on splintered wood and breaks off. I hesitate, about to stop and grab it, but they'll be after me at any moment, and I won't be able to outrun them. Not in this condition.

I walk as stiffly as I can so as not to slice my insides in half, because I have watched too much *Grey's Anatomy*, and they always leave in the impaling object until the ER doctor can miraculously pull it out and save the patient. Or not. I use the shadows to my advantage, the routes in these woods coming back to me as if I never left. I avoid the gully over there, which has grown wider. I stumble over broken branches and bite back against the sharp pangs of pain. I close my eyes and reopen them when the blurriness hits to clear my vision and trudge on.

The muggy night sticks to me, and my breath is shallow. There isn't enough air, especially when I hear Bennett scream.

"Where the hell is she?"

Then Danny yells back, "She was here a second ago."

"Oh my God, she's gonna tell. We are fucked!" Roger exclaims.

James says, "Just find her, okay? She's in a bad way, and we can't leave her like this."

Only James cares, I think. If things had been different. If I hadn't been a Corrigan and he some regular guy who was smart enough to get noticed by Bennett and be in his orbit, James and I might have had a chance. James was too sensitive for this lot. And so was I. And he was too weak to fight them for what he knew was right. Such was the case back then. Such is the case now. And so I begin to run.

My pace quickens. They are going to look for me, and I'm not moving fast enough. I zig and zag so that maybe they'll move parallel and won't pick up my tracks. Luckily the dark hides any blood trail I might leave behind.

All I can think is that no one knows I'm here. No one knows I came back except them and Isla. But Isla doesn't even know who I really am. And what if Bennett finds out about her? What would he have done to a girl who no one would miss? I can't think about that. I don't even want to think about the animals that may be out here, smelling me.

My steps are uneven. The world tilts, and the blood flows freer, my body automatically ejecting this foreign object. The branches scrape my skin, the underbrush tries to catch me, and sticky brambles hang on my clothes and somehow get inside my pant leg, pricking my ankles. I am a human pincushion.

But the tree line begins to thin, and I see a break in it. It is something unfamiliar, a narrow and overgrown road. One that surely has been closed off. A single vehicle has rolled up on it slowly, the brake lights the only things on. It's not the guys. They are somewhere behind me. It is help.

I hitch toward it, grunting as I go, my legs barely holding me up, warning me they only have a little gas left in the tank. My vision blurs again. Out. In. Halfway. It'll have to do.

"Help," I croak, my voice barely above a whisper. It is raw from inhaling the capsaicin from the Mace. "Hey!" I can't be too loud. They'll hear me and come running. The world tilts sideways, but I manage to make it go back right.

Once I've seen help just ahead, my body betrays me, and my legs give way, pitching me forward. The person leaps forward and catches me in their arms, holding me up as if I weigh nothing. I am fading fast, as if coming down from an extreme high, the adrenaline and survival instinct seeping out of me like the blood from my wound.

"Please," I say. "Have to get away. I'm a—" Am I really going to do it? Invoke the name I've shunned for two years because now it will save me? "A Corrigan," I finish with much effort. It's getting harder to breathe. "My father will pay anything. Vic—Victor Corrigan."

Bennett calls my name in the wind. "Edie, please. Come back."

He actually sounds concerned. For me. For himself. Who knows. I nearly say something. But I've been tricked by his faux concern before. Never again.

The figure looks at me, and recognition hits us both. Relief floods me because I don't have to do it alone anymore. There is help. There is no more Bennett and his friends. "Hospital," I say. "Please."

Surprise crosses their face as they take me in, assessing the condition of my body.

We both look to the woods when my name is again called. And then a second time. A third. And a fourth. The figure recognizes the owner of that voice. And those of the other three that follow.

We refocus on each other.

Their face blurs again as their hands roam my pockets. Luck is with them like it isn't with me, and they find the recorder that has been running the whole time. The one that's recorded Danny admitting the truth about the accident they lied about.

The figure never answers me.

Instead of helping me up and guiding me to the car, the figure slides their hands down my side.

"Don't!" I say, trying to stop their hands with mine. There is no hospital around. This will kill me.

They hesitate, but only for a moment, because the surprise and what I thought was concern shift to resignation. And then determination finally takes over, and any consideration for me is wiped into a blank, unreadable mask.

The hovering figure sighs like the weight of the world rests on their shoulders. Many unspoken answers hang in that sound, making everything perfectly clear, making everything final.

My desperate call for help is replaced by the only horrid sound I can make when the figure grabs ahold of the glass shard and—

CHAPTER SIXTY-THREE

Isla

Present Day

The recorder continued with nothing but static filling the air until it shut off, leaving Eden's last words hanging in the air. No matter how many times Isla heard them, each time was a deeper twist of the knife. She imagined horrible images of what Eden had gone through, of how her best friend had suffered.

Outside the doors, Victor's reception went on without its guest of honor while the room descended into chaos.

"What kind of joke is this?" Victor began, searching one face and then another for answers no one wanted to give. "What is that?"

"It's bullshit is what it is," Bennett barked. "I'm going to kick your ass out personally." He charged at Isla, but Myles was quicker.

Myles growled, shoving Bennett back. "Back up."

"Get off," Bennett yelled, launching a wild punch at Myles. Myles parried it easily and delivered his own. Bennett reeled back from the blow.

"Bennett!" Brooke cried, lunging for her son as Dixon pulled Myles off him.

"Myles," Dixon said forcefully. It was the first time he'd acted without Victor giving a command. She saw a flash of his holstered gun under his tux jacket.

Brooke helped Bennett to his feet and tried to stanch the blood running down his face. He snatched his head away.

"What the hell was that for?" Bennett growled at Myles. "Don't tell me you believe this concocted shit." His mouth said one thing, but his eyes said another. He was terrified. This was something he could not hide.

Myles growled. "I can't believe you could do this. Edie was our sister. Our *sister*, man!"

Brooke stood between them, shielding her son. Bennett shrugged his mother off, declaring everything was a setup.

"Don't believe it, Dad," Bennett implored a thunderstruck Victor. "It's a lie. It's fake."

Brooke hushed him, knowing when to back off. "Quiet," Brooke said urgently. "You're bleeding. Just wait."

The other day, Brooke had practically danced when she'd toppled Isla in front of everyone with Charli. She was singing a different tune now. She looked downright terrified, Isla thought with satisfaction.

Isla expected them to leave. She kept silent as Jackson slipped out too. To regroup. To tie up their loose ends—and Isla would be there to catch them.

Victor paid Bennett and Brooke no attention. He was fixated on the recorder in Isla's hand. He repeated his question, a tremor in his voice.

"It's Eden," Isla replied. "A recording she made the last day she was seen."

"What do you mean it's Eden?" Victor said, flustered. "What's the meaning of all that?"

As quickly as she could, Isla told them what she knew of that day.

"Edie was here? She came to see me?" Victor asked, stricken.

"This is the real reason why I came here and deceived you. I came here for the truth about what happened to Eden. I had to know if you or anyone else had anything to do with her disappearance."

"You think I had something to do with Edie being gone? You thought *I* could hurt her?" His anguish cut through Isla. She'd wounded him, and it was only going to get worse.

"That's ridiculous," Dixon snapped. Another first Isla was seeing from him. "All you had to do was tell us the truth from the start."

Isla laughed bitterly. "I doubt even you believe what you just said. I'm a nobody to you all."

Victor looked as if years had been taken from him. The vibrant business magnate who commanded any room now looked older than his sixty-nine years as the reality of what had happened to Eden hit him. He had no more hope or fantasy to hide behind.

Isla had waited for this big reveal till she could put them all in one room unaware and see who reacted and how. She'd chanced everything on finding Eden tonight, but time was of the essence, and if they took any more, they might miss their opportunity to end a decade of uncertainty.

She made eye contact with Myles.

She'd rather have been anywhere else, but she had to finish what she'd started. She owed them all that much.

Victor roared, regaining some of his former self. "Bennett, explain this goddamn recording now!" He twisted in his seat, but Bennett wasn't there. Neither were Brooke and Jackson. "Where the hell did they go?"

Isla pulled out her phone and turned on the tracking app. "I can show you."

CHAPTER SIXTY-FOUR

Bennett

Present Day

The woods felt more ominous than they'd ever been in his whole life. Bennett had a bad feeling. A very bad one.

He parked. Brooke shifted in the passenger seat, peering through the windshield, her fingers playing with the hem of her dress. Bennett tapped a restless rhythm on the steering wheel, his nose still throbbing from Myles's sucker punch. That would be the last time Myles ever laid a hand on him. He was glad to be out of that room and away from the goddamn recording of Edie that Isla had played. *How?* He needed time to think of a recourse. Instead, here he was, summoned like some errand boy by Jackson, of all people. Bennett hated it most when someone told him what to do.

He exhaled sharply. "We need to be talking to Dad, not playing hide-and-seek in the woods with your goddamn lover."

Brooke stiffened. "I don't know what you're talking about. Jackson works for us and the Foundation. Nothing more."

Her response was too asinine to answer, and Bennett didn't have the time or patience for her games now. He pressed his fingers to his temple, anger clawing up his throat. "How the hell does she have that?" he muttered. Had Isla been there with them?

He gestured to the darkness outside. "Why are we here instead of with Dad? There's no telling what she's saying to him after all that other shit."

"You know Jackson," she interrupted, forcing a brittle laugh. "He takes care of things for us. It's always been that way. He'll definitely come up with a fix for this and that woman." She spat out the last word.

That was Brooke's problem. She'd become too reliant on Jackson. She'd become complacent and blurred the lines of employer and employee, giving Jackson all the power. Now they had to suffer his ego.

"What was that recording Isla played, Bennett?" his mother asked cautiously. "Why is your voice on it?"

Bennett let out a primal yell, striking at the steering wheel with his fist, startling her. She called his name, the fear in her voice bringing him to his senses.

He put his hands back on the steering wheel and tightened his grip because there was nothing else to take his anger out on. Jackson used to ask. Now he acted like he was in charge. Like he was more than just the help.

A sharp rap at the window made them both jump. Jackson stood on the other side, a flashlight in one hand and two shovels in the other. Gone was the tuxedo from earlier. Now he was in dark gear, looking like he was about to go hunting—or worse. Bennett's bravery betrayed him just a little.

Bennett rolled the window down. "What the hell, man?"

Brooke's voice was tight. "Why'd you have us meet out here?"

Jackson took a step back, and Bennett saw a large black bag on the ground, which Jackson grabbed as he said, "Out. We don't have much time."

Bennett bristled, resisting the urge to slam the door into Jackson's gut, but complied. Jackson was already moving, vanishing into the trees. Brooke winced as her heels sank into the uneven ground. She whimpered about her $1,000 heels as she clung to Bennett, stumbling every few steps, each yank fueling his rage as they struggled to keep up. First Isla, now this motherfucker.

They reached a clearing tangled with overgrown bushes. Jackson stood there, staring at the ground beyond him as if it held some terrible secret.

"Jackson," Brooke started, her voice uneasy. "We don't have time for this. The guests. Victor. We need to do something about Isla and that recording she clearly manufactured."

Bennett swallowed hard. He wished the recording had been manufactured. He wished that night had never happened. It was the one time he'd ever regretted anything he'd done, because despite all the things his father would forgive him for, hurting Edie was a dealbreaker.

Jackson ignored her, turning abruptly, holding one of the shovels out to Bennett.

"The first thing he'll do is have the whole property searched," he began, his eyes boring into Bennett's. He looked terrifying in the dark. "We can't have them finding anything."

Bennett looked down at the shovel like it was a foreign object. "Find what?"

Jackson's stare was cold. "There's no case without a body. And as far as anyone knows, she could be alive. Though we both now know that's not true."

Brooke inhaled sharply, taking a step and then stopping, unsure of what she wanted to do. "Body? Jackson, what are you saying? What happened at the old Abbott farm? Who's alive?"

Bennett's pulse pounded. "Edie was alive. She left on her own. We all heard it on that tape."

Jackson's expression didn't change. "Didn't your mother say it was manufactured?" When Bennett didn't answer, he continued. "Did you really think Edie's been out there roaming the globe all this time, sipping cocktails on some tropical beach, shunning her daddy? She was impaled on glass that damaged vital organs. You really think she just walked away from that?"

Bennett's eyes went wide. "How would you know that she . . ." he blustered, realization hitting him.

Jackson nodded knowingly. "That's right. Follow me over there." He pointed again to that section of clearing ahead. "To dig her up."

"Dig—dig her up?" Bennett shuddered, seeing Jackson in a new light. He'd always known Jackson fixed messes, but this . . . this was insane.

"Me, insane?" Jackson asked. Bennett hadn't realized he'd spoken his thoughts aloud. He didn't like the look in Jackson's eyes. "Interesting."

Brooke grabbed Jackson's arm, trying to reason with him. She was the only voice of reason in these godforsaken woods. "Jackson, stop this. Let's go back. Let's talk somewhere out of these woods. Victor is probably wondering where we've gone."

Jackson pried her fingers from him. "This is your mess too. You made him this way. False bravado and weak inside."

Bennett willed his hands to stop shaking. "You're insane."

"No," Jackson murmured, his voice low and dangerous. "What I am is tired. Tired of cleaning up after you two when you let your emotions get the better of you and you mess up. It's about time this family started acting like the unit we are."

Brooke gasped. She gave Bennett a panicked look and Jackson a pleading one. "Jackson, don't—"

"Don't what? Tell him?" Jackson turned to Bennett, eyes gleaming with something almost like amusement and contempt. "Why do you think you've been fighting so hard to get Victor to make you his successor, and once he's made you that we'll get rid of him? Because you are mine."

Bennett felt like the ground beneath him had disappeared and he was falling into an abyss. "What are you saying?"

Brooke went silent. She took a step back, her hands trembling. She looked around as if something or someone could help her, but there was nothing. Bennett went from one to the other and saw the answer on his mother's face.

"No." Bennett shook his head. "No way. Mom, tell me he's lying. Tell me he's crazy." But she couldn't bring herself to do it, and her silence validated every feeling he'd had growing up. This must have been why he'd always been jealous of Edie and felt like he could never live up to Myles. Because deep down he'd known he was different. Everything he'd thought he knew about himself was a lie.

Jackson said, "Now he's getting it. From the moment you convinced me to go along with letting another man marry my woman and raise my child as his own, the thought of eventually taking all Victor has has been what's kept me around, taking your and his shit. Don't act so surprised. It's beneath you."

She stammered, incredulously, "I didn't. You want to kill Victor? And, and Edie . . . Edie is there?" Brooke was barely able to get her words out, the truth unfathomable.

"Bingo." Jackson was smug.

Bennett retched. "Oh my God."

Jackson popped in a stick of gum. "This is your reality, son. Victor isn't your father. And if he ever finds out, you'll both be out on your asses. There's no way he's keeping you when you played the oldest trick in the book on him, Brooke." He looked at her pityingly. "That's why we need to make sure no one can ever find her."

Brooke was desperate, caught between the man she relied on and the child she loved more than anything. "Listen to me. Victor loves you. He would never disown you. You are his son in every way that counts."

Jackson scoffed. "Maybe if he hadn't just heard you were involved in Edie's disappearance. But now? The moment he finds out the truth, he will end you, all of us."

"Shut up!" Bennett yelled. Bennett's breath came sharp and ragged, on the cusp of a panic attack. "Both of you, just shut the hell up. Let me think."

"There's no more time. They will start looking. We need to move the evidence and get our stories straight." Jackson stepped closer, and Bennett backed away in a sort of dance. When they were side by side, in a standoff, their likeness couldn't be denied. "First Edie. Then Victor."

Jackson gave Bennett a lasting look before picking up the shovel Bennett had rejected and shoving it hard against Bennett's chest. The force knocked Bennett back a couple of steps, and he realized Jackson wouldn't let them leave. Gingerly he took the shovel from this new man he'd never seen.

Bennett's stomach twisted. "But I didn't—I wasn't even there!" His legs locked; he was unable to step toward Edie's grave.

Jackson snapped, "But you set everything in motion." His patience was gone. "You sicced your friends on her. You didn't take her to the family or tell Victor when he returned from his trip the next day. It was lucky I overheard your call to your friends and followed you because you were acting odd and heard you tell your friends where to take her. What were you going to do about her at the Abbott farm, hmm? I spared you that."

Jackson waited for an admission that Bennett was too ashamed to make.

"Right. I cleaned it up for you. I made sure you and your idiot friends never had to face the consequences. Like with that accident when you were kids. Like with Edie. But now? Now you both need to do your part. We are in this together. Now move."

CHAPTER SIXTY-FIVE

Isla

Present Day

Before Bennett could take another step, a new voice cut through the night. "Not the family reunion you expected."

They whipped around as a flashlight flicked on, and Isla emerged from the shadows and the cover of the trees.

Jackson's incredulity flickered to calculation. His eyes narrowed as he searched the woods from which she'd emerged. "How did you find us?"

"Tracking devices," she said, waving her glowing cell phone. Thanks to Myles, who'd planted them after she'd given them to him the night he took her to the Red Roof.

Jackson snatched the shovel from Bennett's trembling hands and took a deliberate step toward Isla. His intention was perfectly clear, and danger radiated from him.

"I heard it gets easier after the first time," Isla said. "Is it true?"

"If you weren't so stupid, following us alone, I'd be impressed with your courage," Jackson said, raising the shovel. "Thought you were smarter than that."

A sharp crack of twigs and the crunch of dry leaves and underbrush stopped him mid-step.

Figures emerged from the shadows—first a mass, then distinct shapes splintering off as they stepped into the moonlight. Flashlights flicked on, one by one. Myles. Victor. Dixon. Even Lawrence bringing up the rear. They were still in their tuxes, unlike Jackson, who had dressed to get dirty.

Jackson retreated, moving closer to Brooke and Bennett, who had been like deer caught in headlights from the moment Isla had made herself known. Their faces as blank as their minds. But not Jackson's, Isla thought. His mind was churning. He was always two steps ahead and could slip in and out undetected, as he'd done for years. She hoped that for once he wasn't ahead of her and that her gamble would pay off.

"What did you do?" Victor's voice blasted through the night as he stepped through the clearing, closing the distance.

Jackson quietly dropped his hands to his sides, the tip of the shovel sinking into the dirt.

Myles said, "The police are not far behind. If we hadn't gone ahead like Isla said, what were you going to do, Jackson? Bennett?"

"Is it all true?" Victor's voice held hope; what he'd walked in on because Isla had asked him back at the house to let her show him was too unfathomable. Isla knew his feelings because she felt the same.

Jackson's calm was eerie. "You already heard it all, Victor. Why rehash?"

"All these years?" Victor asked, focusing on his wife and son. "You've been lying all these years and colluding with him under my nose. In my home. Bennett isn't . . ." His voice broke, the enormity of their betrayal choking him, and he looked away.

"It's not what you think, Victor." Brooke's voice trembled from where she and Bennett huddled together. "We've been deceived just like you. This is all a misunderstanding."

Bennett pulled at his mother's hand, silencing her before she could make things any worse.

"No! She was alive. She was alive, and you just let her die, and you left her all alone." His gaze swept them; he was desperate for answers that weren't coming fast enough.

"Bennett wasn't even around when Eden was with the boys. You heard how he looked for her. He definitely—definitely didn't," Brooke affirmed. "He definitely did not kill Edie."

"Don't get it confused," Isla said. "Bennett *definitely* set all of this in motion. He is not without guilt. He just didn't actually kill her. Neither did Danny, Roger, or James."

"Then who killed my daughter?" The question was an entreaty to end Victor's suffering.

Jackson cursed, spurts of anger rising to the surface. "I guess you weren't paying attention. No one killed Edie."

Dixon spoke up. "But you did make her disappear." He made a disgusted sound.

"All alone," Victor murmured. "She's been alone all this time."

"Bennett." Jackson took a step toward Bennett, imploring him.

"Bennett nothing," Bennett spat, clutching his mother. "You didn't keep the recording and the truck to protect me. They were collateral to control me with when I took over the company. You would have used them against me if you needed to. My so-called father."

Jackson said, "I am still your father." It was the only time his voice cracked from emotion.

"In DNA only," Bennett muttered, turning away, resigning himself to his fate.

Jackson stood there watching Bennett and Brooke, the family he'd had for only moments before they were taken away. He whipped around and faced the rest of them. Glowering at Isla.

Isla continued, "You buried her. Forged a letter and used her bracelet, knowing Victor would honor whatever wish Eden had. What kind of person does that?"

Jackson said callously, "A smart one. I did what I had to do for my son. Edie was just an unlucky girl, and if anyone killed her, it would be you," he added, sneering at Victor.

Victor moved before anyone could react.

Before anyone knew what was happening, Victor tackled Dixon and ripped the gun from Dixon's holster. Dixon barely had time to react before Victor pulled the trigger.

Jackson dropped hard to one knee, gasping. His hand went to his left shoulder. He clutched it, dark liquid oozing between his fingers as he pitched forward. Brooke screamed and scrambled back, she and Bennett tripping over each other in panic. The gun hit the dirt, forgotten.

Myles and Lawrence grabbed Victor as Dixon recovered and then assisted. It took the three of them to restrain him as he struggled to free himself and get to Jackson again. Isla spun around and saw dots of lights getting closer as reinforcements double-timed, having heard the gunshot.

"Over here!" she yelled.

She looked back at the group, at the tiny clearing they were in, the shovels, the black bag meant for Edie. Oh God. Oh God! She covered her mouth to stifle a scream.

"All alone," Victor sobbed, on the ground, covered in dirt. "You left her alone. All alone."

Sirens echoed in the distance. Victor suddenly sprang back to life with a new purpose. He looked around desperately. "We have to get her out of there. We need to find her. Now."

They looked to ask Jackson, but in the commotion he'd been forgotten, and he'd slipped away.

"They'll find him," Myles said as the reinforcements burst through. He refocused on Bennett, reaching down to grab a fistful of bloodstained shirt. "Where was he going to dig?"

Bennett dropped his head, the fight leaving him. His hand lifted, trembling, and pointed.

Victor followed the gesture. When his gaze landed on the mound of rocks that marked the spot, his breath hitched, and he half ran, half crawled to it, his voice roaring into the night. "No one step in that area!" His hands shook as he grabbed Lawrence. "Get whatever you need. Shovels. A machine. People. I'll pay for it all. Just—" His voice broke. "Just get my girl out. Get her out now!"

CHAPTER SIXTY-SIX

Within the hour, workers and equipment were amassing under Lawrence's orders. He knew every inch of the property like the back of his hand, and he helped with the coordination. Dixon attempted to get Victor to leave while workers assembled to begin the delicate job of exhuming Eden's remains under the direction of the local medical examiner, who happened to be one of the attendees at the reception, along with the rest of Virginia's elites. Victor refused. He would stay until Eden was found, with Myles at his side. And Isla planned to be there with him.

There wasn't far for Jackson to go. Which left Brooke and Bennett. Bennett had nothing to say. He was a shell of the usually flamboyant and boisterous jerk he usually was. His mother had plenty to say, and she wanted everyone to hear it.

Brooke cried, "I didn't know what Jackson was up to, Victor. I swear I didn't!"

"You knew enough," Victor said, his voice so full of grief it clawed at Isla. There was no more pretending. No more maybes to hide behind. There was the cold, hard, hateful fact that Eden was truly gone. She was down there. Not in Bora Bora or the Maldives. She hadn't thrown her family away, or Isla. She had gone. She had been taken. And it shouldn't have been, except for greed and power.

Victor said, "Get them out of my sight. Get them out of my house."

Bennett and his mother were led away, their pleas to Victor trailing after them. Eventually, only Isla and Victor remained by the grave, standing vigil while the crew worked diligently. Both of those who loved her the most, broken to know what she had gone through and that they hadn't been there to help.

CHAPTER SIXTY-SEVEN

The moment one of the workers called out they'd found something was surreal. Isla's heart plummeted to her stomach. This was the moment she'd waited ten years for and the moment she'd also dreaded. The many overhead lights were so bright, they chased away the cool of night and made it look like it was daylight.

A silent hush went over the crowd as the people on top helped the workers in the hole climb out without disturbing anything inside. They stepped back, keeping a respectful distance. Seeing that they'd stopped, Victor rushed to the edge, Isla by his side, with Myles and Dixon returning. Sometime during the digging Holland had appeared, her clothes changed from the reception. She'd looked horrible, having gotten the news about everything that had transpired at the site, of her mother and Bennett being detained by the police and about Jackson and the search for him. She didn't approach the hole, standing back to watch anxiously.

Victor took halting steps toward the edge. He took a breath. And then another, steadying himself. If he felt anything similar to what Isla was feeling as they got closer and closer, each step forward harder to take, Victor was praying the hole was empty, that the dream he'd had for the past ten years of his daughter living her life happily as she wanted it was true.

He leaned forward, inhaling particles of dirt, and looked in.

Even in the dark, the glint of gold and the locket attached to it shone brilliantly like a beacon. It was as if it hadn't spent the last ten years beneath the dirt. He crumpled to the ground, but Isla's feet were rooted, the image of the tattered clothing and brittle remains of Victor's cherished daughter and Isla's best friend searing themselves in her mind.

"That's her mother's necklace," he sobbed. He couldn't look away. He didn't deserve to see anything but what had become of Eden. "Elise, what have I done to our girl?"

"Eden started wearing it when her mom died," Isla explained as verification that the body in the hole was indeed Eden Corrigan. Isla was unable to see well through the tears falling. She barely got her words out. "Eden was wearing the locket chain and her own bracelet with the key together when I saw her last, getting into Roger's Jeep."

Victor was inconsolable, suddenly screaming, "Get my daughter out of there! Get her out. She can't be there. She can't have been there in the cold all this time. How could they have done this to her? How could they have done this to my little girl?"

The realization was too much for Victor, and he clutched his chest, teetering precariously over the edge. Myles got to him in time, grabbing his father before he could fall. Isla got there next. Then Dixon. The three of them holding the strongest man they'd ever known in his weakest moment.

CHAPTER SIXTY-EIGHT

The last thing Isla had expected was to be back in the Corrigan house, trying once again to sleep as she had the first night she'd been there. It was déjà vu, and Isla hated it. Sleep eluded her. Again, the large size of the room, the darkness, and feeling very small in this very big space were too much for her to settle down. And there was all that had transpired tonight, and the gnawing feeling that not everything was done. Not everyone was safe.

Worse than the large oaks outside the window once again casting long, clawed shadows across the room was the deep-set unease from earlier that lingered in the back of her mind. She kicked at the white plush five-star-hotel-level duvet as she flipped onto her back and stared at the ceiling. Her mind was one of those old movie reels with the two spinning wheels of recorded tape, replaying the night's chaos in her mind: Jackson's fury at the recording, his lies and murderousness laid bare; Bennett's smugness and the callousness with which he'd treated his sister and lied about what he knew of what had happened to her all this time, despite knowing her absence was eating away at their father; Brooke's venom, maliciousness, and manipulation and the way she still, even in the end, tried to play victim, acting like everything Jackson had done had been on his own and not because she'd made him think he'd ever have a chance to be in Victor's position.

But most of all, seeing Eden in that grave. Seeing how the chain glimmered like a beacon in the dark, letting everyone know that she was there, had been there all this time, and no one knew. Out of everything they'd discovered that night, knowing what Eden had endured—betrayals on every level, even by Isla, who'd left her behind when she should have spoken up and fought for someone to listen to her—was the hardest to swallow. Isla didn't know how she could live with the guilt, which was exponentially worse than it had been these past years, when imagination and willful ignorance had allowed her to pretend that maybe, just maybe, Eden was okay. Very much like Victor.

Isla couldn't begin to imagine how he was feeling. She hated how he'd had to find out. In front of his family like that, hearing his daughter at the worst moments of her life. But it had been the only way to open his eyes. The only way for Victor to confront the rotten truth about the family he held in such high regard. It had been the only way for him to see clearly how he had caused it all by pitting child against child, wife against lover, company against family. His willful ignorance had been the linchpin to the downfall of the Corrigans as he, and the world, knew them. If he let the world know. That would be his true test. Owning up to his mistakes and the mistakes of his family and letting the chips fall where they may.

They'd all come to the field, their lies exposed, their guilt and need for survival driving Brooke, Bennett, and especially Jackson to the extreme, to their attempt to rid the world of Eden's body for good. What a fucked-up family they were. But the thing that ate at Isla the most was that Jackson had escaped. Even after being shot, in the commotion of the field being flooded with police and security guards and staff, and with their immediate response to see if Eden was really buried there, Jackson had once again used that opportunity to disappear.

Isla didn't believe Jackson would let this be his end. He'd played the long game. He'd done all this simpering behind Brooke and kowtowing to Victor to get his son in the perfect alignment for succession as Victor's heir. There was no way Jackson, who'd done so much they did know and likely much more they didn't, would give up on Bennett or on taking the company from the man he hated the most. The hatred he had in his eyes every time he thought no one was looking was burned into her memory. She shuddered. If anyone ever looked at her like that, she would . . . wait. Brooke had looked at her like that, so scratch that.

Isla tossed and turned. She considered sneaking to Myles's room, wondering if that would make her look pitiful in that she didn't want to be alone. But his room was all the way on the other side of the mansion, and she couldn't bring herself to.

Isla dressed in jeans and the UCLA sweatshirt she'd had with her when she arrived, not knowing where the night's events would take her. She was about to walk out when she stubbed her toe hard on something on the floor. The rock from the hunting party. It had fallen out of the backpack she'd carried with her when she'd arrived at the house earlier, and now the backpack had been kicked over and the rock spilled out to inflict bodily harm on her. Toe stubs in the dark—the worst kind.

After breathing through the pain, she shoved her feet in her sneakers. She picked up the rock and weighed it in her hand, and though it had attacked her, the chunk of granite and stone brought a sense of relief she couldn't explain. It had somehow become her safety blanket. She shoved it in the front pocket of her sweatshirt, not caring that it made the sweatshirt hang low from its weight.

Absent all the chaos of earlier that night, the serenity and quiet in the darkened mansion made Isla instantly feel better. She shoved her hands inside the front of her sweatshirt, holding the rock between her hands as she walked toward the back stairs, heading to the first level.

"Wonder what he'd say if I just showed up," she mused, her steps slowing as she rounded a corner and considered banking left to the hall Myles stayed in when he was sleeping at the house as he was that night, like she was. The wall sconces were turned low, enhancing the ambience that the mansion was down for the night. After all it was past 2 a.m.

"Yeah." She grinned to herself, wild thoughts swirling in her head. It had been that kind of night. "I'm gonna do that." Her lips curled up at the thought. But first, she couldn't show up with this thing. She contemplated jogging back to her room to leave the rock—didn't want to scare the man, after all; she had other things in mind—but that meant extra time, so scratch that. She was about to pull the rock out and place it, temporarily, on a table she knew had to be worth several grand. If Brooke had been here to see, she'd have burst a blood vessel at the thought of Isla possibly scratching one of her overpriced tables.

She heard the faint sounds of heavy, hurried footsteps on carpet and a door opening. She stilled. The house stilled with her. A dead silence before a massive storm. The familiar dread that had kept her awake in bed came back in a rush as she strained her ears to hear where in this massive building the noise had come from.

Another noise—a muffled thump and another sound. Her body tingled, on alert. It was coming from the direction of Victor's study. She reached for her phone because something was wrong. But she found two things wrong. One, her phone was back in her room. She'd left the phone but taken a rock. Dumb move. Second, what if she was overreacting—extra jumpy after that whole scene in the woods and at the grave? Victor probably decided to work late as he usually did in his study. Maybe he was feeling sentimental and looking once again at that wooden box where he'd kept his most precious treasure. Yes, that was understandable, and it made sense after what he'd learned tonight.

Or . . . and now her mind raced with something else . . . not racy thoughts of a naked Myles, the irritating hunk Corrigan, but terror-filled ones. Thoughts that there was one thread that still dangled menacingly.

She moved cautiously, the thick carpet muffling her steps as she hurried in the direction of Victor's study. Her heart lurched as she noticed dark droplets marking her path, guiding her to the sliver of light spilling from the study. She dropped to a knee, pressing a finger into one of the droplets. She was both disgusted and curious at the same time and positive she was about to regret her life choices. In the dim light, she stared at the wet smear on her fingers, rubbing them. She looked closer. Not water.

But blood.

CHAPTER SIXTY-NINE

She snatched her hand back as if she'd touched something hot and the sensation of burning had just hit. Every sense in her was telling her to get up and get help. Call out. She opened her mouth, preparing to scream. It was the sudden pressure of something hard pressed into the back of her head that silenced the scream in her throat.

"Ah, ah, ah. Not a good idea," the voice behind her said, low and urgent. The presence of a solid body radiating heat too close to her, having materialized from nowhere, made her lose her footing. A hand grabbed her tightly by the elbow and yanked her up and flush with his body.

"You just don't know how to stay out of shit, do you?" Jackson breathed into her ear. "You've got to be the nosiest bitch I have ever met."

She swallowed hard, her mind going blank as he shifted the pointy pressure from the back of her head to in front of her, showing her the black GLOCK he held. He made his point silently, shutting her up.

"Since you decided to crash our party of two, you can serve as both witness and motivation. Not a word. Go."

He squeezed where he held her upper arm, his fingers digging deeply into her muscle. Isla gasped from the pain. He pushed her forward, keeping close to her, toward the cracked door.

"Dixon? Myles? Is that you?" Victor called from inside. "Get in here. You asked to meet, didn't you?"

Jackson nudged the door open with his toe, opening it wide enough for them to shuffle in, Isla first with him right behind, holding her by the arm, with the muzzle right to her head. That was what Victor saw, his mouth dropping open in shock and horror as his eyes jumped from Isla to Jackson.

Jackson kicked the door closed behind them. He repositioned himself behind her so she couldn't get out of his grasp easily.

"Sorry I lied, boss. That would be me who dialed in that emergency meet to you."

Victor thundered, "What the hell—" He sucked in air as Jackson pressed the gun harder against Isla at the volume, a warning to Victor.

Victor lowered his voice to a loud whisper. "Let her go. She has nothing to do with this."

"She has *everything* to do with this," Jackson retorted. "She is the reason for all this. And if you don't sit the fuck down, old man, I will kill her right in front of you. And you'll be next before anyone gets here." He waggled the muzzle in the air. "Crazy the things you can buy. Thank God for capitalism, the NRA, and the freedom to buy whatever the fuck you want, even if it's only used to kill people. Who needs a silencer but people intending to kill others without being caught, am I right?" He chuckled.

"Asshole," Isla breathed, wiggling to get out of his tight grasp. She whimpered when he hit her with the butt of the gun, not hard enough to make her pass out but enough to let her know not to test him.

Victor put his hands up to appease the both of them. "Okay, okay. You're the lead here," he said.

Jackson growled, "Don't play me like we're in the boardroom, old man."

"What do you want?"

Jackson scoffed. "What do you think? For you to sign over everything to Bennett. Name him as the next CEO taking over the company." Jackson pushed Isla into a chair and repositioned himself between her and Victor, aiming the gun at Victor when Isla was too scared to move. She was obsolete. Victor was his intended mark.

Victor said from behind his desk, "Threatening me isn't going to make me sign anything over to Bennett. You'd need to kill me anyway for his succession to be put in play if I was stupid enough to sign. And who's going to believe I did that willingly?"

Isla's hands dampened—the opposite of Victor's cool, unruffled demeanor. She was barely hanging on. Once Jackson was done with Victor, she would be next.

"No one will believe it."

Jackson laughed. "Just like no one thought Eden was dead until you uncovered her bones? I had you believing she was alive all these years from one little letter and a couple of little international transactions. You don't think I can make people believe you killed yourself and"—he looked at Isla—"her in a fit of grief over your daughter and rage that she knew something had happened and lied all this time? Absolutely I can. And without even being around. Bennett will know what to do when he sees what your will says."

Jackson was sweating bullets. He winced as he pulled a stack of papers from inside his coat and tossed them on the desk. His wound. Isla had forgotten that Victor had wounded him. She'd forgotten that the blood trail on the floor belonged to him. Having a gun to your head made you forget things quick.

He motioned with the weapon for Victor to pick up the papers.

Calmly, Victor sat in his high-backed chair, always cool, ever defiant. "You're crazy."

"It doesn't have to end like this," Isla said, trying to keep Jackson calm to buy them some time. He had the gun on Victor. He'd shoot without hesitation. He had nothing more to lose.

"Shut up," he seethed without looking at her. "If it wasn't for you . . ." He didn't finish, and Isla didn't want him to.

Jackson's face was smeared with blood and dirt, his clothes torn and dirty with bits of leaves and grass. And though the clothes were dark, Isla could see large dark stains around his shoulder. Blood from where Victor had shot him. Jackson held his gun, the barrel trembling slightly from his anger but aimed directly at the chest of Victor, who remained seated at his desk, appearing composed despite the gravity of the situation. Jackson's eyes flashed like those of a rabid animal. He would do anything. He no longer cared. Except for one thing.

"You're going to sign it all over, you arrogant son of a bitch," Jackson snarled. "The company, the estate—everything. You've stolen enough from me. Made me live my life like one of your lapdogs. It's my son who'll inherit all you built for all the pain and suffering I had to endure from your bullshit. You'll die with that knowledge."

"You think you deserve any of it?" Victor's voice was calm, cutting. "You're a parasite, Jackson. You've always been."

Isla shook her head furiously at Victor, silently begging him to stop. But there was no imploring Victor of anything. He matched Jackson's hatred, unyielding, like he was ready to take down the man who'd killed his daughter. Victor was pushing Jackson so he would make a mistake. Maybe Victor was buying some time for help to arrive, though Isla couldn't help wondering why he didn't have some silent alarm button to call forth a whole army. Or maybe that was her wishful thinking. Whatever the case, Isla didn't need him pissing Jackson off further for him to shoot them both.

Jackson's face twisted with rage. He stepped closer, the gun steadying. "Shut up! You had everything handed to you by your father—your wealth, your family, your power. I had to scrape and claw for every inch of ground I gained. And now you're trying to take that away from me too?"

"I took everything?" Victor was incredulous, losing his cool at Jackson's audacity. His tone rose an octave from outrage, his hands balling into fists from his pent-up fury, but his usual ironclad restraint was slipping. Something needed to be done. There wasn't much time before one of these men lost his last thread of tolerance and snapped.

Victor's gaze blazed like lava. "Are you mad, man? You've been cheating with my wife since before I married her. You passed your kid off as mine, and I never knew. You came up with some scheme with her to steal my company from under me using your kid while making me think you were loyal. That she was loyal. And you say I took everything from you? You never had what I wanted in the first goddamn place."

No, no, no, Isla chanted silently, wincing every time Victor spoke, antagonizing Jackson when he should have been calming him. The two men had seemingly forgotten she was in the room with them.

"You lost the moment you betrayed me. And your son? If he's weak and inadequate, it's because he has your blood in him. I raised him like my son. I loved him, tried to make him strong. I would have and have given him the world, and it was still never enough. But you, you killed, lied, and cheated. You say it was for Bennett. But, Jackson, it was only for you. Bennett was never going to be CEO. Understand? Not even if any of your crimes panned out. I understood what type of man he'd be long ago and was giving him chances to succeed. Yet he failed at every chance. He is your son, after all."

"Say that again," Jackson growled, his voice breaking with fury.

Why'd Victor's study have to be so far that no one would hear anything unless they came this way? It was by design, and probably ideal, to ensure privacy when Victor was doing business, but now Isla thought it was the worst idea ever. Anything could happen—was happening—and no one would know until it was too late. Why the hell hadn't Victor put cameras in this damn house? Oh yeah, privacy. Fuck the damn privacy—they were about to be killed.

The tension in the room was reaching a boiling point. She looked around for something, anything, that could be used. She moved her leg, and the weight inside her pocket moved as well, alerting her. The weight . . . her hunting rock. Slowly, she slipped her hand inside her pocket.

Jackson's laugh came out hollow, manic. "Do you have any idea what I've sacrificed? Decades of work, planning, manipulation—and for what? For you to just tear it all apart at your whim?"

"You can still walk away from this." Isla spoke up, palming the rock in her hand, slipping forward to the edge of the chair slowly. Her mind raced. She needed to stall him, to give someone—anyone—time to intervene. "If you do this, you'll never get away with it," she said, her voice steady despite how dry her mouth was. "You'll destroy any chances Bennett may have. You don't want to do that, right? Because under all this, you do care about him. He's your son."

"Isla," Victor warned with a quick headshake. But they needed Jackson off guard and confused. They couldn't have him concentrating on just one of them. And Victor pushing Jackson to the breaking point would be a mistake neither of them could afford.

Jackson concentrated his attention on her. "I should have dealt with you earlier and permanently. You wouldn't get the hint . . . not at the hunt, or when Bennett's idiot friend followed you to the barn. Not even when we brought that fucking leech of a woman to expose you. You waltzed right in and set decades of planning on fire. You, a cheap con with an act Victor the Great bought hook, line, and sinker. Put that in your fucking article," he said with a sneer. He took a step back, swinging the weapon in her direction. "Bennett doesn't need chances," Jackson snarled. "He needs power. And I'll make damn sure he gets it, one way or another. So sign the goddamn papers, or I will shoot her dead right now. Right the fuck now!"

"What do I care about her, huh?" Victor asked suddenly, flipping the script.

Ice ran through Isla's veins. *What?*

"What the fuck are you doing?" Jackson asked, his sweat-slicked face crumpling into confusion and wariness.

Victor glanced over at her. His eyes went over her as if she were just another piece of furniture. There was no care there. He was cold. He was angry. At her.

Victor shrugged. "Like you said. She's a con artist and a liar. She let me go years without telling me something might have happened to Eden. She let Eden come here and got her killed. You think I care about what happens to her? She deserves it. Maybe you're right. Maybe if she'd never come here, I could have continued my life of blissful ignorance, believing Edie was still alive out there and just mad at me. My family would be as it was. Bennett would still be a Corrigan, and you wouldn't be wanted right now. So go ahead. It's what she deserves. For Edie."

What the hell? "Mr. Corrigan, wait! I—" Isla stammered in disbelief. If looks could kill, she'd be dead from that and then dead from the coming gunshot.

Jackson grinned, grabbing her by the hood of her sweatshirt and snatching her up. "All right then," he said, calling Victor's bluff.

She tried balancing herself so she wouldn't stumble and fall. She clamped her mouth shut so she wouldn't cry out as the gun's muzzle pointed at her chest. Her right hand gripped the rock harder as it slowly slid out of the pocket and kept it at her side. One shot. She only had one and needed to make this count.

Jackson growled, "We'll make a deal."

Victor looked from Isla to Jackson and to the stack of papers dotted with blood. He nodded, making his executive decision. "A deal. Because you really got me between a rock and a hard place."

A rock. That was when Isla knew and made her own executive decision, raising her hunting-nightmare souvenir, which would now actually serve its purpose. She swung upward with all her force, mashing the sharp edge of the rock into where the spreading dark blood on his shirt was seeping through, an especially wet patch. The gun went off, its shot going wild. Jackson stumbled backward, grunting in surprise and pain. He was still gripping her hood, and she swung again, not sure where the rock connected, maybe the edge of his jaw. He stumbled back into a floor lamp and fell with it as it crashed down, with Isla on top of him. Victor was next to them in a blur, pinning Jackson's hand, wresting the gun from his loosened grip. Jackson took his free hand and thrashed wildly, landing a blow that hit Isla square in the face.

She saw stars, and her body followed them, half sliding off him while he kicked at Victor, who had been trying to separate him and

Isla. Jackson kicked his feet, sweeping Victor off his and onto the floor. The gun skipped over the rug like a rock on the surface of water, away from them, and both men struggled to reach it first. Isla swam in pain, her lip wet from the blood trickling from it. Something caught her eye in the corner, and she crawled to it.

A loud crash sounded, and the door burst open, Lawrence and Myles charging in like two linebackers. Holland crowded the door behind them, yelling and jumping frantically for help as she took in the scene. In a blur of movement, Lawrence tackled Jackson. Myles dove for the weapon as well just as Jackson threw a vicious punch at Lawrence, catching him across the jaw.

The men grappled, crashing into the furniture. Isla scrambled to her feet and grabbed the handle of Holland's saber from behind a nearby table where she'd left it after one of her visits—the joys of living with a new adult who thought the world was her closet. Jackson gained the upper hand, shoving Lawrence onto the ground and reaching for the gun that was nearly in his grasp. His fingers pulled it toward him as he kept Myles at bay. Then he howled as Isla ran the saber through the palm of his hand.

"You killed my best friend," she seethed. She wanted this monster to hurt as much as he'd hurt others for too long. This wasn't enough. She kicked him. "You fucking bastard."

She pushed the weapon down farther into his flesh as he screamed, bucking from the pain. All she could see was Eden driving away and then Edie in that pit, the gold of her necklace glinting against her remains. Isla would have kept pushing her weight down, forcing his arm to bend back toward his body until the blade pierced his chest. But large hands appeared, covering over hers, and, with gentle force, pried her fingers away, pulling her from that madness, off the dark path she had walked, and into a warm, solid embrace that smelled of sandalwood and safety.

It was finally done.

EPILOGUE

As the dawn broke and the last of the police—including Detective Bowen—and the paramedics and all the others cleared out, they left a weird calm in their wake. Isla stood on the balcony, watching the sun rise. Myles joined her, his hand brushing hers.

"You were amazing tonight," he said softly.

It was the exact opposite of what she felt. The thought of how Eden had died made everything worse. Maybe Victor had had it right, wanting to believe Eden was somewhere sunny. "What about Bennett?"

"He might not be a Corrigan by blood, but he's still my dad's son. At least for now. I don't know if Bennett will see jail time. For what? And Brooke? They have Holland. My dad will divorce Brooke and likely cut her and Bennett out of our lives with a settlement."

Isla didn't comment, not trusting the bitterness she felt that those two wouldn't really pay for the hell they had put Eden and her mother through.

Myles continued. "But I think this is it for my dad. He'll probably step down after all this. He's lost so much. I mean, we all have. But he'd been living on a hope he'd made real for ten years," Myles said. Looking meaningfully at Isla, he added, "Maybe now *we* can have a real chance to get to know each other on a fresh, entirely truthful note."

Isla looked at him, suddenly unbelievably tired. All the adrenaline had left, and exhaustion had set in. "Are you really talking about you and me at a time like this?"

"If there's anything I learned tonight, it was to waste no more time."

As devastated as she felt, Isla understood. She didn't want to waste any more time either. "That might be nice," she said. "I'd like that a lot."

When Myles left and she finally had a moment alone, Isla sat with her friend at Eden's new grave near the solarium, which had been cleared of Brooke's things and was now filled with hope and love like it was meant to be. This was now Eden's special place, in memory of her, with a plaque to memorialize her: **THE GARDEN OF EDEN**. Just as her mother would have wanted. She didn't have to run anymore, feel guilt for wrongs she'd committed, or be angry. She could just be.

When Isla had first told Rey and Nat her plan to find the truth, they hadn't understood why she owed Eden anything after ten years. She hadn't had an answer for them then. But as she sat with Eden now, catching up on the ten years they'd missed, the answer came to her. It was because with Eden, Isla had been able to do what she hadn't for her father. For Eden, she had been able to find the truth. She had been able to find justice. She had been able to find closure, and most of all, both Eden and Isla had been able to find peace.

"Found you, Eden," Isla said. "You'll never be alone again."

ACKNOWLEDGMENTS

Thank you to my lovely genius of an editor, Megha Parekh. You let me grow and stretch, and your continuous support, positive reinforcement, and trust in me when I doubt myself keeps me going. Melissa Edwards, my agent, you are a true force, and you always have my back. Jennifer Richards, you are so very sweet, have become one of my people, and have been the best publicist.

My ever-patient developmental editor, Charlotte Herscher, does the Lord's work and seems to magically know the story I want to tell, how I want to tell it, and is able to pull the best story from me that hopefully captivates the readers. To the amazing Thomas & Mercer editorial team, Gracie, Liz, and Jessica. You always treat me like family whenever we see each other, and you don't know how much I appreciate it.

To the copyeditors, Annie S. and Mark G., your laser eyes and spot-on suggestions whipped this book into shape.

And then, to my mom, Evelyn, who cracks me up, and my entire family in the States who refill my well when it's depleted and I am full of doubt. Lastly, to my family in Ghana, who always think of and support me from afar.

ABOUT THE AUTHOR

Photo © 2021 Rodney Williams, Creative Images Photography

Yasmin Angoe is the author of *Her Name Is Knight* and a first-generation Ghanaian American currently residing in South Carolina with her family. She has served in education for nearly twenty years and works as a developmental editor. Yasmin received the 2020 Eleanor Taylor Bland Crime Fiction Writers of Color Award, was a Goodreads 2024 People's Choice nominee for Mystery & Thriller, and was a finalist for the Library of Virginia's People's Choice Award for Fiction. She's a member of several organizations like Crime Writers of Color, Sisters in Crime, and International Thriller Writers.

To learn more about the author and her work, visit her website (https://yasminangoe.com) or follow her on X (@yasawriter) and Instagram (@author_yasminangoe).